BAD BLOOD

A blur of red filled Creek's vision, knocking him to the ground. Acid pain tore through his shoulder. Fangs hit bone, tore flesh, snapped sinew. Blood gushed over his body, soaking his clothes. Then heat. And light. And the keening wail of a creature in pain.

Creek opened his eyes, forcing himself to his feet. His arm hung limp. The Castus staggered backward, his body a flickering wick of fire. He clawed at his maw and belly where the flames concentrated. His arm shot out, his hooked finger pointing. 'Kubai Mata,' he snarled.

'Damn straight,' Creek answered. He took a step toward his halm. Maybe he could finish this demon off after all. His hand stretched toward his weapon. The earth tilted, throwing him to the ground again. His vision tunneled down to nothing, and the press of asphalt faded as his body went numb.

By Kristen Painter

House of Comarré
Blood Rights
Flesh and Blood
Bad Blood

BAD BLOOD

House of Comarré: Book 3

KRISTEN PAINTER

orbit

www.orbitbooks.net

ORBIT

First published in Great Britain in 2011 by Orbit

Copyright © 2011 by Kristen Painter

The moral right of the author has been asserted.

Excerpt from *Tempest Rising* by Nicole Peeler
Copyright © 2009 by Nicole Peeler

A CIP catalogue record for this book
is available from the British Library.

ISBN 978-1-84149-971-0

Typeset in Times by M Rules
Printed and bound by CPI Group (UK) Ltd, Croydon, CR0 4YY

Papers used by Orbit are from well-managed forests
and other responsible sources.

MIX
Paper from
responsible sources
FSC® C104740

Orbit
An imprint of
Little, Brown Book Group
100 Victoria Embankment
London EC4Y 0DY

An Hachette UK Company
www.hachette.co.uk

www.orbitbooks.net

For my parents:
thanks for not sending me to
Outward Bound like you threatened
so many times. I hope I make you proud.

In these untried days, the power of belief and the lack
thereof shall give rise to new evils, new challenges,
new gifts. None will be immune.

—SCYLLIS, FAE PHILOSOPHER, CYPHER CLAN

Chapter One

Paradise City, New Florida 2067

As the car pulled alongside the gates to Chrysabelle's estate, Mal stared through the metal bars at the stucco-and-glass fortress she lived in. Eight days she'd refused to see him. *With good reason.* His patience with the situation was worn paper-thin. Not just because of the waiting to find out if the Aurelian had given her a way to remove his curse – and knowing what a monster he was, why would the Aurelian do that? No, that wasn't it, although that question was a constant presence in his head, alongside the voices that constantly mocked and tormented him. His lack of patience came from not knowing how Chrysabelle was recovering from the physical damage that had been done to her. That was the worst of it. That part gnawed at him with gut-deep pain.

Doc, the leopard varcolai who'd become the closest thing he had to a friend, threw the old sedan into park, tossed his arm over the bench seat, and twisted to look at Mal in the back. 'You sure you don't want me and Fi to talk to her? I'm sure she'd let us in.' Fi, the first of Mal's voices to manifest as a ghost, turned to look at Mal, too.

'No. If I have to knock on her door all night, she's going to see me this time.' *That's it. Force your way in. Drain her dry like you know you want to.* Mal ignored the voices and held tightly to the little calm he had left. Since Chrysabelle had regained consciousness, she'd refused to see him or Creek. Mal could understand her not wanting to see the Kubai Mata, but Mal's blood had healed her. *Ruined her.* He'd gotten her out of Corvinestri and back to her own home. That had to count for something, even if Creek had helped.

Doc shrugged. 'Suit yourself, bro. Fi and I will swing by after the movie to see if you need a ride home.'

'No need.'

'It's going to rain.'

'Don't care.' If things went right, he'd be inside anyway. *They won't go right. Not for you.*

'Stubborn as always.' Fi smiled. 'Don't forget the cookies I made. She's gotta let you in with those. Double chocolate chip!'

Mal nodded. It was a little scary how domestic Fi had become since she and Doc had coupled up in a serious way. Or maybe she was just happy not to be stuck in the nightmare loop of reliving her death night after night. He grabbed the plate Fi offered and got out of the car. He waited until they pulled away, then jumped the wall surrounding Chrysabelle's estate and walked to the front door.

Velimai, Chrysabelle's inherited assistant and deadly wysper fae, opened it before he could knock. At the sight of her, the voices ramped up into an irritating whine. Chrysabelle's ever-present scent didn't help matters either. Velimai shook her head no, anticipating his question.

'At least tell me how she is.'

Velimai started to sign something Mal wouldn't understand, when a soft voice broke the silence. 'Let him in.' Chrysabelle. At last. Just the sound of her voice relaxed him and helped him fight the chaos in his head.

Velimai looked to one side, then signed a few words and nodded. She held a finger up, making Mal wait. Footsteps receded. At last the wysper fae opened the door and moved out of the way.

She led him down a hall and into a library – a part of the house he'd never been in before. He gave her the plate of cookies and went in. The room was the first he'd seen that had any color besides white or ivory. The pale blue was subdued, but in a house so serene, it might as well have been red. He inhaled. Fresh paint. Interesting. Maybe Chrysabelle was finally coming to terms with living here.

Chrysabelle stood at the far end, facing the wall of windows that seemed to dominate the back of the first floor. Her beautiful sunlight-colored hair was unbraided, another rare sight. The ever-present glow around her, something all comarré had but visible only to vampires, seemed darker somehow. More alluring. *More biteable.*

The window coverings were pulled back, and beyond the grounds and pool, the bay shimmered in an endless black mass that reflected the stormy night sky. Only a reading lamp illuminated the space, but she'd still angled herself in such a way that the small portion of her face visible in the glass was distorted and hard to see, even with vampire eyes.

'Rain again.' Great. Start with the weather. That was safe. And boring. *Like you.* What he wanted to do was crush her in his arms and tell her how damn glad he was that she was still alive. *Or just crush her.* Then ask her what the Aurelian had said. 'Good for the new sod you had put in.' Sod meant to cover the pressure sensors installed as part of a new beefed-up security system. He knew only because he'd watched the workers leaving after dusk, not because she'd told him. Had Creek been behind that? If so, good for him. The upgrade was long past due.

'Mmm-hmm.' She shifted slightly, revealing a slim white cane held against her side. Her knuckles were pale from gripping it.

He wanted to reach for her. Help her. But he refrained, sensing it wouldn't be welcome. *Nor are you.* 'You should sit.'

'You should stop telling me what to do.'

The voices cheered. He dropped his head, studying the pattern of the wool rug covering the dark wood floors. Anger he could deal with. He'd been the target of her ire more than once. *For good reason.* 'Not much chance of that.'

She shook her head. 'You've seen me. Are you satisfied? Is there anything else you require from me?'

Yes, but she'd yet to look at him directly, and something told him asking her about the Aurelian now wasn't going to get him an answer anyway. He took a seat in one of the ivory silk club chairs. It was the exact opposite of what he felt like doing, which was charging to her side and holding her against him. Maybe it would confuse her as much as she was confusing him. 'How about you explain what's going on?'

'I don't need to explain myself to you or anyone else.'

This approach wasn't working. He got up and walked to her, stopping a couple yards away. Like her glow, her scent had changed as well. It was deeper and sharper, but just as seductive. The perfume wrapped around him, teasing him with the promise of blood. Blood he could taste by memory. Blood the voices howled for. 'I know you're angry. What I don't get is why.'

She barked out a short laugh and, at last, faced him. 'Are you kidding? Velimai told me what you and Creek did to me.' She grabbed the back of the nearest chair as she approached. Using the chair for support, she stabbed her cane into his chest. 'You put your blood into me.'

'I saved your life.' This attitude from her, this sharp tongue and verbal biting, wasn't something he was entirely used to, but he understood she had a right to be angry after what Rennata did to her. He just hadn't expected it to be aimed at him. *Get used to it.*

'You had no right to defile me that way. It wasn't your place.'

'Defile? Is that what I did to you?' He knocked the cane away. 'You would have died.'

'I doubt that. The comarré ability to heal is more than sufficient.'

He wanted to grab her by the shoulders and shake some sense into her. *Do it. Bite her. Drain her.* 'Your signum had been stripped off your back in two bloody filets. By *Rennata*. You were bleeding out faster than any of us knew how to deal with. And then there's that whole thing where *you're not comarré anymore.*'

Her clear, blue gaze pierced him. 'Not with your blood in me.' She pulled herself up a little taller. 'I may be disavowed, but I am as much comarré as you are vampire. If you've ruined things for me, I will kill you myself.'

'Ruined what things? Is this some fever madness?' Maybe he should call Velimai, get Chrysabelle back to bed.

'I have to go back to the Aurelian.'

'Yes on the fever, then. Why would you go back to her? She's the reason you almost died.'

'No.' She walked around him and took a seat on the edge of a chaise, resting the cane beneath the folds of her flowing white robe. 'You and Creek are. Following me to the Aurelian was what got me disavowed. Now I have to find a way back to her to ask who my brother is.'

'Following you was an accident. You know that. And we'll find your brother together. Creek isn't without skills. Dominic might know someone to talk to as well. The man's better connected than anyone I know. You can't go back to her. It's too dangerous.' *Not as dangerous as you.*

'There you go again, telling me what to do.' She shook her head and looked away but not before the reading lamp caught the glitter of angry tears in her eyes. 'I hate this life. Always on guard, always waiting for the next attack. It's no way to live. I'm done with it. Done waiting for Tatiana to show up again. I'm taking control and doing things my way, and you can't stop me.'

'Chrysabelle, please—'

'Shut up, Mal. Every time you patronize me, I just want to stick something sharp through you.'

Smart girl. 'I wasn't patronizing you.' He backed up a step, her demeanor more serious than he'd seen before. 'There's not a sword hidden in that cane, is there?'

'Maybe. Maybe not.'

'I'll put money on maybe.'

The shadow of a smile danced across her face, quickly replaced by stern determination again.

It was enough of an opening for him. He knelt at her feet. The position grated against every fiber of his being but seemed the perfect way to show his sincerity. It also put him in striking range. If she chose to lash out with a hidden blade, she could do him real harm. Even kill him. 'I am sorry that putting my blood into your body has upset you so much. My intention was to save your life, not further complicate it. You must know that.' *An apology. Someone's in love.*

'I do,' she said with a heavy sigh. She lifted her hand like she might touch him, then dropped it back to her lap. 'I appreciate that you and Creek saved my life, but I wish you'd found another way. What happened to me happened because you two interfered, plain and simple. And now, once again, I am left to deal with the consequences of your actions. You don't think. You just do. Both of you.'

At least she was mad at Creek, too. 'I don't blame you for being upset, but as far as saving your life ... there was no other way that we could see. So you know, I would have done anything to make sure you lived that night.'

She stared intently into his eyes. Almost challenging him. 'Why is my life so important to you?'

The true answer that came into his head made him dizzy. He couldn't say what he felt. Wouldn't give it words like the voices in his head. She'd threatened to kill him once already. She didn't need ammunition. 'For the same reasons you wouldn't let me remain mortal and age to death. We're ... friends.' What a strange way to describe what they were. 'More than friends. There was no way I was going to watch you die knowing I could have prevented it.'

She narrowed her eyes, assessing him. 'Dominic's mortality potion made you soft.'

Yes, the voices chimed. *No,* he wanted to say. *Knowing you has given me a heart again.* It was a weakness, but one he was willing to bear. *Fool. Fool in love.* 'Then he's the one to blame for giving it to me in the first place.'

She stared at him as if she were seeing him for the first time. 'I refuse to be scared anymore.'

'You shouldn't have to be.' He hated that she was. *Then stay away from her.*

'I need to find my brother. He's the only family I have.'

'I know.' An impossible task, the way he saw it.

'I need the Aurelian for that.'

She was too determined for him to keep her from doing it. 'If you think you're going without me—'

'After what happened last time, you shouldn't even ask.'

'So what's your plan?' He almost didn't want to know.

She held up one finger. 'First, to see the Aurelian.'

'How are you going to get there without the signum on your back?'

'Dominic has a signumist. I've already sent him a message that I'm coming to talk to him tonight. I don't know if the man's any good, but I'm hoping he can put the correct sequence of signum into my skin again.'

Mal's jaw dropped open and he sank back onto his heels. 'Bloody hell. You're in no shape to undergo something like that. Are you crazy?'

'Crazy mad, and I'm in fine shape.' Her hands tightened into fists, and a tarnished spark lit her eyes. 'Once I get to the Aurelian, I'll obtain the information I need, then slip out of the Primoris Domus undetected and find Tatiana.'

The name of his ex-wife and the woman who'd put him under his curse was like salt on an open wound. 'Why would you want to find Tatiana?'

'Why else?' She held up a second finger. 'To kill her.'

Mal ground his back teeth together. 'I'm going with you—'

'I already said—'

He pushed to his feet and held up his hands. 'Try to stop me and I'll prevent you from going at all. You'd insist the same of me. You know you would.'

Chrysabelle was silent for an uncomfortably long time. 'Fine.' She stared up at him expectantly. 'I'm surprised you haven't asked about the Aurelian's answer.'

'I'm biding my time.'

'Because you think I'm not going to tell you?'

'The possibility had occurred to me.'

She eased back into the chaise, her chest rising slowly with a lengthy inhale. She let the air out again before she spoke. 'She had a way to remove your curse, but' – a second sigh and she shook her head – 'it's almost not an answer at all.'

Tremors of possibility ran through him. 'What? Tell me.' He'd do *anything*, anything at all to break free of the hellish weight pressing him into darkness. *Even kill your pretty little blood whore?* His jaw tightened, his anger at the voices almost unbearable. He forced the emotion off his face as her head came up.

Her eyes focused on him and yet looked emptier than he'd ever seen them. An unnatural coldness settled in his belly as she began to speak. 'You must right a number of wrongs equal to the names on your skin. One for every life you've taken.'

He reached for something to steady himself. Finding nothing, he collapsed into the chaise beside her. 'It's impossible,' he whispered. A hurricane of laughter shook his bones. Even the voices knew what a Herculean task that was. 'I am never going to be free.'

'Mal, stop.' She grabbed his hands, her touch white-hot on his freezing skin.

He looked down. Beneath her pale fingers, blood seeped from his tightly clenched fists. He opened them. Deep gouges marked his palms. They healed as he watched, but the blood that dripped onto the carpet was there to stay. Like his curse.

'You vow not to prevent me from getting to the Aurelian and to Tatiana, and I will do everything I can to help you with this.'

Focusing on her was the best thing he could do right now. 'I have a better plan. You go alone to see the Aurelian then come back through the portal and give yourself time to heal properly. Then, when you're ready, we go together to Corvinestri and take care of Tatiana.' If Chrysabelle meant to kill his ex-wife, there was no way he wasn't going to help. The voices cried out. He knew they believed Tatiana to be the cure to his curse. He knew better. 'You know how dangerous she is. This isn't something you should do alone. Not to mention I have enough of my own reasons to want her dead.'

She was quiet for a few moments, probably thinking. 'Agreed. But we will also find a way to remove your curse.'

He closed his hands again, looking away from her. 'No. We won't. Because there isn't one.' He stood and walked to the door. 'Let's go see Dominic about this signumist.'

Chapter Two

Dolores Linley Diaz-White, Lola to her friends and family, pinched the bridge of her nose and inhaled the well-conditioned air of her city hall office. The report open on her desk was one of a hundred, maybe two, that had come in since the beginning of the week. Every day brought new ones, but they were all basically the same. Strange, unexplainable creatures had begun showing up in her city. The kind of creatures people called *vampires* and *shape-shifters* and *bogeymen*.

She glanced up as something swooped past her window. Something that looked very much like one of the gargoyles carved into the corners of the building. But she wouldn't think that, because acknowledging that such a thing was even possible meant the things in her reports were possible, too. Instead, she shifted her gaze to the panel of wall monitors positioned across from her desk, the left side currently showing live feeds from Jacksonville, Tallahassee, Orlando, and Pensacola, the right showing feeds from various cities through the Southern Union. These creatures weren't special to Paradise City. They were in every city in New Florida. All of the Southern Union, actually. New Orleans seemed oddly quiet, but then it had been that way since the rebuild after 2054's Hurricane Edmund. As the mayor of a city that often took the brunt of such storms, she paid attention to those kinds of things.

She closed the report and added it to the stack of those waiting to be reviewed. Another hour of reading them wasn't going to make the problem go away.

A knock on the door startled her. She checked the time. Almost nine. Was Valerie, her secretary, still here? Couldn't be, Lola had sent her home two hours ago. Must be John Havoc, her bodyguard. But why? The man was as silent as a ghost. Followed orders like a born soldier and had already saved her life twice. In the last few weeks, he'd become more distant than usual and had taken to wearing sunglasses night and day. There was something else about him, too. Something that fell into the same category as the reports and the gargoyles. Something she kept pushing from her mind every time it reared its ugly head. But what she thought didn't matter. He did his job. He could dye his hair blue if he wanted. His position was secure. 'Come in.'

The door opened, and John stepped in, his shades securely in place. Behind him, a uniformed police officer entered. The officer cast a wary gaze at John, who waited for her nod of approval.

'Thank you, John.'

He grunted softly and left, back to his post.

'Sorry to disturb you at this hour, Madam Mayor, but the chief said you'd probably still be here.'

'No problem, Officer ... '

He removed his hat. 'Rodriguez, ma'am.'

'*Hola*, Officer Rodriguez. What can I do for you at this hour?'

He glanced quickly at the floor, then back to her. He was

young, probably hadn't been on the job long. Whatever he had to tell her, it wasn't good news. Regardless, she could take it. She hadn't been mayor this long without some rough patches.

'We believe we've found your daughter.'

St Petersburg, Russia, 2067

Times like this, the need to kill coated her mouth like the remnants of a lover's kiss.

Tatiana tapped her head against the high-backed wooden bench. One hundred ninety-two hours wasted. Eight bloody days they'd made her wait. She hadn't even had a chance to deal with the two runaway comarrés. Madame Rennata would replace them gratis or Tatiana would find a way to make her pay.

Which reminded Tatiana that she could have returned to New Florida and done away with that other comarré whore by now, but no, she'd been trapped in St Petersburg at the whim of Lord Grigor and under the watchful eyes of the rest of the House of Rasputin. Because of the powers this house possessed, she'd been forced to leave Octavian behind in Corvinestri. He was just a vampling, far too young and inexperienced to guard his mind against the likes of Grigor and his ilk. She couldn't have Grigor tapping into Octavian's thoughts and gathering information to use against her. Like Zafir's death. Or that of his brother, Nasir.

She glanced down at her leather-clad hands and flexed the metal prosthesis that filled the right glove. Zafir's alchemical masterpiece. Also his undoing.

She snorted softly. Part of her wished Grigor knew exactly what she'd done to those who opposed her. It would serve the mind-reading prat well to fear her.

A creaking sound brought her head up as one of the tall double doors across from her opened. Svetla, Grigor's right hand and the Elder of the House of Rasputin, slipped out. Her midnight-blue silk gown swished around her wiry form, her frigid blondness too comarrélike for Tatiana's taste, but then she'd disliked the woman since the first time they'd met. Svetla was hard to read. Her simplicity seemed too practiced to be real. She'd only just attained Elder status after Tatiana was awarded it. Before Tatiana, there had been no female Elders. Curious how Svetla's predecessor, a noble who'd come to be a thorn in Grigor's side, had mysteriously decided he'd had enough and walked into the Siberian sunlight. Regardless of her connection to Grigor, Svetla best remember whose hard work had paved the road to Elder. Tatiana had no time for weak imitators.

Svetla's porcelain façade cracked enough to allow a narrow smile. 'You may come in now.'

Returning a false smile, Tatiana forced down her anger at being made to wait. She steeled the mental barrier already in place and strode through the massive mahogany doors and into the chamber beyond. The council had long been called to order, and now the lords sat around Grigor's table like fat Romans, a few with their Elders positioned behind them. Zephrim, Dominus of the House of St Germain, smoked a cigar. Carafes of blood and vodka littered the table. She kept her lip from curling. How anyone could drink the two mixed was beyond her.

Grigor lifted his glass, half full of the rosy-pink concoction. 'Svetla, shut the doors.' He tilted the glass slightly toward the seat beside him. 'Then come sit.'

No chairs were available beside the one Grigor had reserved for his chew toy. Tatiana remained standing as Svetla did what she was told.

Once the other woman was seated, Grigor spoke to Tatiana. 'Tell us what happened.'

'Lord Ivan is dead.' Tatiana reached into the pocket of her varcolai leather coat, curled her gloved fingers around the broken bits, and tossed what was left of him across the table. The shards of stone skipped over the wood; the largest – a bit of eye and forehead – came to rest in front of Syler, Dominus of the House of Bathory.

She'd once considered him a tentative ally. Now with Ivan gone, she wasn't so sure. The security of that connection had to be determined.

The other Dominus looked on with curiosity. Timotheius, Dominus of the House of Paole, gasped, always the dramatic. 'How did this happen?'

'Yes, I would love to hear that explanation. I'm sure you expect us to believe you had nothing to do with this?' Zephrim asked. He ruled the House of St Germain fast and loose, letting just about anything go unchecked as long as it was in the name of alchemy.

'I didn't. Not in the slightest.' Tatiana's rage curled around her with comforting warmth. Behind secure mental barriers, she imagined turning her metal hand into a sword and skewering Lord Zephrim in the manner Vlad Tepes most often favored – through the groin and out the throat. The thought caused an inappropriate smile to crease her lips. She covered it quickly by drawing a hand across her mouth before speaking. 'The comarré whore is now in league with a powerful coven of witches. Lord Ivan and I went after her. She and her compatriots ambushed us. The anathema, Malkolm Bourreau, was with her.' Several of the lords glanced at one another. 'Not only is he alive and well, but he has also become her lover.'

'Poppycock. He's been ashes for years. The report is in the council archives.' Zephrim refilled his goblet with blood.

'I can prove it.' She glanced at Grigor. Perfect. His family power of mind reading was just what she needed to corroborate her story. She opened her thoughts to him as she spoke, careful to show him only the parts of her memories that held Malkolm hoisting Ivan into the witch's circle and Ivan being turned to stone. The part where she'd smashed his statue into rubble she kept hidden. 'There. I've shown my thoughts to Lord Grigor.'

The other lords turned to him. Grigor pursed his mouth. 'I never knew Bourreau myself. I cannot be sure this is the one of whom she speaks.' He stroked his narrow beard. 'It does seem another vampire was responsible for Ivan's death in conjunction with the witches.'

She smiled sweetly. 'Thank you. I assure you, the vampire you saw was indeed Bourreau.' Blighty old ratbag.

'What is it that you desire, Tatiana? Your petition stated you had a request to make,' Syler asked. Something about his expression gave her hope. Perhaps the alliance still stood.

She paused, as though needing a moment to gather her thoughts. 'This crime against the House of Tepes was perpetrated by the rabble that calls the Southern Union home. Anathema, witches, varcolai, remnants, and fae.' She threw up her hands in disgust. 'New Florida is a ghetto of othernatural undesirables, and while it's well and good that they should be contained in such a single, vile location, Lord Ivan's death must be avenged, the anathema Bourreau must be put down once and for all, and the comarré whore must at last be brought to justice.' She paced a bit for dramatic effect, stopping to give the appearance of an idea suddenly coming to her. 'I am sure I could take care of these things. I know New Florida. I have connections in place. I just need the right resources to make my attempt successful.'

'What kind of resources?' Syler asked.

She fixed her face into the most neutral expression she could muster. 'Unlimited access to Nothos, to family funds, the ability to command an army of fringe—'

Timotheius interrupted. 'The kind of resources a Dominus has.'

'What? Well, yes, I guess they are rather similar—'

'You want the council to appoint you the new Dominus of Tepes in Ivan's place. Is that it?' Hints of silver played in Syler's eyes, a mark of emotion. Whether from anger or elation remained unclear.

She held out her upturned palms, a recognized sign of submission among the nobility, knowing she must tread carefully so as not to upset the plans she'd been crafting for so many years. Slowly, she spun the words out. 'Lord Ivan's passing makes this necessary transition uncomfortable, I understand. It pains me to move forward with such haste, but Dominus is a position I am well suited for and a title I would be honored to wear.' She dropped her hands back to her sides. 'I would take every necessary precaution to prevent Lord Ivan's death from throwing the House of Tepes into disarray. Without reservation, I know that is what Lord Ivan would want.'

Lord Zephrim jumped to his feet. 'This is outrageous.' He glared at the other lords. 'She's been Elder little more than a month and now she wants to ascend to Dominus? Forget that she's a woman. She has no place asking such a thing.'

Lord Syler set his glass down. 'If something happened to Grigor, would you balk at setting Svetla in his place?'

Lord Grigor nodded in approval. 'It is the natural order of our system, Zephrim.'

'The natural order?' Lord Zephrim bridged his fingers on the tabletop and leaned in toward Grigor. 'No one achieves Dominus without the say of the ancient ones. *That* is the natural order of our system. Unless you wish to go against them as well?'

Lord Grigor sat back, the nerves around his right eye twitching. 'I would never go against the ancient ones. I live to serve them. For you to suggest otherwise, in my home, at my table . . . ' He shook his head slowly. 'Do not press my hospitality, comrade.'

Lord Zephrim took his seat. 'I am only saying things must be done properly.' He turned to look at Tatiana. 'Unless you have something to say about that?'

This time her smile was genuine. After all, the Castus Sanguis had chosen her as their instrument to break the covenant between humans and othernaturals, and their leader, Samael, had given her some of his power. She had nothing to fear. 'No, please, the ancient ones must be consulted. And, of course, I am willing to abide by whatever they decide. May the ancient ones be served.'

The others recited the words in unison. 'May the ancient ones be served.'

Lord Timotheius nodded toward Grigor. 'As we have gathered in your house, it is your right to call upon them.'

Yes, Tatiana thought, *because the rest of you are like frightened little rabbits running from the hawk.* And well they should be. The Castus did as they pleased. Even if that meant turning on their children.

Lord Grigor whispered something to Svetla. She nodded,

then got up and left. The other lords took notice and sent their Elders out also. Cowards. If the Castus wanted a sacrifice, a few walls would not prevent them from taking what they desired.

She moved one of the vacated chairs to the foot of the table opposite Grigor and sat, folding her hands in her lap as one might when awaiting the arrival of a friend for tea. Grigor ignored her. Fool.

He pushed back his chair, the felted feet making little sound on the cold marble tiles, and stood. His fur-trimmed robe fell open, revealing a charming pair of mother-of-pearl daggers on his belt. She would appropriate those as spoils of war when the time came. 'It is my honor to call the ancient ones.'

Tatiana smiled at his bravado and settled back to await Samael. She'd not seen him in some time. Her smile faded, and she closed her eyes to send a silent plea that he was not displeased with her efforts.

When she reopened them, Grigor's arms were outstretched, his palms up. An almost-imperceptible quiver shook his body. 'Castus Sanguis, hear your children, come to us and grace us with thy presence.'

The lords around her stiffened. Seconds ticked by. She inhaled, seeking the scents of brimstone and rotting flesh. Nothing but blood and the reek of ancient vampires. Grigor dropped his arms.

'Perhaps call one by name,' Lord Syler offered.

'Yes.' Lord Zephrim nodded.

Lord Grigor frowned. Tatiana bent her head to hide her pleasure. Calling one of the Castus by name would be no one's first choice. He shook his hands and stretched out his arms again. 'Hear us, ancient ones, the purest of blood, the Castus Sanguis, those who made us. We bid you come into our midst.' He stepped back. Did he expect a bolt of lightning?

Once again, moments slipped away and nothing happened. Tatiana's nerve rose. This could be a test. For her. If she called Samael by name and he came, the lords would have no other option but to accept her as the powerful force she was. They would *have* to make her Dominus. The power of possibility shivered over her skin.

She stood, shoving her chair back. The lords whipped around to look at her. She bowed her head slightly, reveling in playing the eternal ingénue. Let them think her incapable. So much sweeter would her victory be when she removed each one of these buffoons and built a council that suited her reign. 'I will call him, if you wish.'

Lord Timotheius barked a laugh. 'You know not what you do.'

She tilted her head, widening her eyes the way an innocent might. 'Should I be afraid of our fathers?'

'She wants to call them, let her.' Lord Zephrim waved a hand through the air while the other hand dug something free from beneath his robe. He then swallowed whatever he had procured. No doubt a potion of his own making. Something to protect himself. How desperate did he imagine things would become? 'The consequences are hers.'

She lifted her head all the way. 'And I accept them.'

'If you fail, they affect us all.' Lord Syler's eyes told her she best know what she was doing.

'I will not fail.' She could not. She would not.

Lord Grigor sat. 'You are a fool.'

'No,' Lord Zephrim countered, turning to the others. 'She toys with us. We should not allow this.'

He was afraid of the power she might gain. His fear rolled off him in waves. She decided to push him a little further, to test how far he would go. 'I do not undertake such a thing lightly. If – when – I succeed, you will know I am capable of the position of Dominus. Do you not think such a test fair?'

Lord Zephrim hesitated. 'And if you fail?'

'Then I will await the council's decision until such time when one of the ancients can be summoned.'

'And you will abide by our rules for such a decision?'

'Of course.'

He sat back. 'Proceed.'

Victory sang in her blood. She opened her arms, palms skyward, and closed her eyes. Her moment was at hand. 'Oh great and powerful Samael, your humble child calls upon you.'

She tensed, every cell and sinew on hold until the greatest of the ancients showed himself. She braced for the rumble of thunder, the putrid scent, the . . .

She opened her eyes. The lords stared back at her through the still empty room.

She swallowed. 'Samael, come to us.'

Nothing.

'Samael,' she whispered, fear creeping through her gut.

The room was as still as a mausoleum.

She slammed her fists onto the table, splintering wood beneath the metal one. 'Samael!' she bellowed. A bottle of vodka shattered with the force of her voice.

Lord Zephrim picked a shard of glass off his robe. 'Tatiana, Elder of the House of Tepes, you are hereby remanded to Corvinestri to await the decision of this council. You may not leave the city until such decision is made.'

'Samhain is in three days. I need to be back in New Florida

by then.' She couldn't afford to miss the chance to catch the comarré during all that chaos.

'The final merging of the mortal and othernatural worlds will present some interesting opportunities wherever one is.' He lifted one shoulder. 'If New Florida holds more interest than our decision, I urge you to go. There are others who would gladly accept the mantle of Dominus.' The corners of his mouth tipped upward ever so faintly. 'You are dismissed.'

Chapter Three

New Florida

'Settle yourself, demon. There's no getting out of there, so quit trying.' Aliza sighed, shoving a loose dread out of her face. Securing an all-powerful demon in a pentagram was a grand feat, the kind of thing that took noble vampire blood, earth from the Potter's Field, salt from Lot's wife . . . the rarest ingredients she'd ever gathered. But having that demon secured in that pentagram when it was located in your living room was a real pain in the keister. Really made it hard to watch her stories with all that noise and smoke.

Samael raged against the invisible barrier keeping him prisoner. 'Let me out, witch. I am being summoned.'

She took a slug of cold beer and hit pause on the TV, stopping Dr. Lassiter just as he was about to revive the woman he was in love with from a coma. Poor man had no idea she was actually his long-lost sister. Damn, this was gonna be good. She glanced over at the unholy creature. 'You've already been summoned. To here. One more word out of you and I'm going to put the lid on that aquarium.'

She and Evie had figured it was best to keep him indoors after they called him the first time outside on the porch picnic table. Too wide open out there. No need to let the rest of the coven know what she was up to. Besides, a good breeze and half the pentagram would be gone and then what would they have? No demon, that's what. And without that demon, there was no way they were going to get that ring the vampires were after. Trouble was, the demon was getting antsy.

Inside an old hexagon aquarium Evie had once bred Chewie's feeder goldfish in, they'd remade the calling pentagram. Evie had glued the lines of salt and earth down onto a piece of cardboard, just to be sure there was no breaking it. Then they'd lit the candle, written the name in blood, and brought the demon back to them. It was better this way, with the pentagram safe inside the glass. Popping the lid on and throwing an afghan over the whole contraption was easy enough if they needed to hide him. So far, they hadn't had to.

Right now, he spiraled out of the twenty-five-gallon container like a tornado, all smoke and hooves and hard red eyes. Mean-looking thing. But you couldn't expect a demon to be soft and cuddly. Not the granddaddy of the whole entire race anyway. She rubbed a pale hand over her brow.

'Look, I know you're in charge of other things, but we need that ring. You locate that for us and we'll set you free.' Like hell. They'd track down the ring, then as soon as they had it, they'd contain the demon permanently. She wasn't a fool. The instant they let him go, he'd take back the ring and strip the meat from their bones.

He scowled and bared his teeth. 'I told you, I can't locate it. It's being protected. Hidden.'

'Well, you just keep trying, then.' She hit the PLAY button and went back to *Mercy Hospital*.

The demon wailed in anger.

She turned up the volume. Out here in the Glades, the closest neighbors were members of her coven, and they knew better than to complain about noises they heard coming from her house. There was good reason they lived out here – privacy. Who were they going to complain to anyway? She was the one in charge, the one with the most power. Power the rest of them didn't even know about. Like the power she'd built this coven on, which is how she'd come to be its leader. Wasn't like the lot of them had half the skills she did in any case.

Evie came round the corner from the kitchen. 'Ma, it's loud as blazes in here.'

Aliza hit the PAUSE button again as she pointed the remote at the demon. 'That thing's acting up again.'

Evie's shoulder jerked forward of its own accord. Ever since being released from her stone prison a week ago, she'd been twitching more and more. Aliza had tried to ignore it, hoping it would just go away, but it was happening more frequently now. Too bad Dr. Lassiter wasn't real. He'd know how to fix it. 'We should give him something to do.'

'Release me,' the demon growled.

Evie ignored the creature. 'Let's send him out to check on the shifter and the ghost.'

'I don't have a use for them yet. I need that ring.'

Evie rolled her eyes and flopped down on the worn sofa. 'You said this thing was going to make us rich.' She stuck her finger through a threadbare spot. 'When does that start?' She dropped her head back and stared at the ceiling, sighing loudly.

'Patience, child. These things take—'

'Patience?' Evie's head came up, her eyes glinting with raw emotion. Her right arm convulsed like it had been hit with a live wire. 'I had enough of being patient trapped in that stone tomb. I'm done with it. I'm tired of waiting.' She jumped off the couch and paced to the other side of the room. 'I want something to happen now.'

Aliza nodded, hoping to calm her daughter down. Evie had been gone for so long, having her back, alive and safe, made every day a gift. 'What do you want to do?'

She stopped her pacing to study the demon. 'We should send him out to do some little thing.' She took a few steps toward him. 'Make sure it goes right.'

The demon snarled. 'You think I am capable of failing?'

'You haven't gotten us the ring.'

He grimaced and spun like a dervish, coming to a stop a moment later. 'Ask me for what *can* be obtained and I shall bring it to you.'

Evie rested her fingers on her chin for a moment. 'I want a house. Bigger than this one. Everything in it new and beautiful.'

His ugly face contorted. Aliza realized he was smiling. 'Where would you like this house? Europe? The Caribbean? An island of your very own?'

Evie pointed out the window. 'Here. Next door.'

Aliza's heart swelled. Nothing like having your pride and joy close.

The demon snorted. 'Humans.'

'That's not all.' Evie lifted her chin. 'Inside the house, I want something special waiting for me. A man.'

Shock coursed through Aliza's blood. 'Evie child.'

She turned. 'Don't look so freaked out, Ma. I'm not a kid anymore. Being trapped in stone was like prison. I have needs. And I want to take care of them.'

The demon chortled. 'Tall? Dark? Dumb? At least make it sporting.'

'I want the blue-eyed half-breed.'

'Half-breed what? Fae? Varcolai?'

'Seminole. The Mohawked one who came here with the comarré and the vampires.' Evie snatched a crystal orb from the nearest bookshelf and conjured a picture of the man, holding it out to the demon. 'And I want him under some sort of spell so he can't refuse me.'

He leaned as far as he could, studying the image, then snorted. 'Spells are your language, witchling, not mine. If you can't control him, that's of no concern to me.'

'Witchling?' Evie moved to within inches of the aquarium's edge. Her knuckles paled from squeezing the crystal sphere. 'I know enough to contain you, demon, and enough to destroy you as well.'

His red eyes glowed. 'You amuse me with your threats.'

'Build me the house, hell spawn.' Her shoulder jerked. She crossed her arms. 'Then bring me the man.'

He shrugged. 'As you wish.' And disappeared.

Doc shot up out of the bed, his heart racing, his body strung in the halfway state between man and beast. The sheets lay in damp shreds around him, the casualty of a varcolai's night terror.

'You okay?'

He looked up, still trying to bring his breathing back to

normal. A fully corporeal Fi sat on the dresser across from the bed. Her legs were curled beneath her, her eyes as round and worried as when she'd been stuck in the time loop, forced to repeat the night of her murder.

Murder. The word pulled a shudder through his body. He ignored the sudden urge to check his hands for blood. To wipe the imagined wetness of it from his muzzle. 'Fine,' he whispered through a split upper lip and teeth too long for a human mouth.

'Is that why your claws are out and your eyes are all yellow?'

He concentrated for a moment, and the signs of his true leopard self melted into full-on human. 'Just a bad dream. Sorry for chasing you out of bed.'

She shrugged. 'Once you've been dead a few times, the self-preservation instinct kicks in automatically.' Her eyes narrowed to slits as her mouth thinned. 'You've been having bad dreams a lot lately. Ever since you went through the smoke.'

He'd realized that a few days ago but hadn't wanted to say it out loud. Walking through the witch's spelled smoke might have given him the ability to shift into leopard form again, but he'd known there would be a price to pay. Anything that involved the witches did. 'Naw, that smoke was cool. That movie we saw tonight really freaked me out.'

Her brows rose incredulously. 'I'm a ghost, you're a shape-shifter, you live with a cursed vampire, and a zombie movie freaked you out. Honey, I love you, but that's a bold-faced lie. What gives?'

He dropped his head into his hands, rubbing the stubble of his shaved scalp. 'I can't stop thinking about Preacher. About that baby. That's all.'

'Babies scare you, huh? Good to know.' She laughed, but it was soft and gentle and didn't feel aimed at him so much as intended to soothe. Fi was good like that.

'No, it's just . . . I don't want to talk about it, okay?' A vampire child couldn't bring anything good into this world. He stripped off the ruined top sheet and patted the space beside him. He needed the distraction of Fi's affections to blank out the nightmare threatening the edges of his consciousness. 'Come back to bed, sweetness.'

She scooted off the dresser but didn't come any closer. Damn, she meant business. 'Suit yourself, but you really need to tell Mal about what you saw. You know Preacher's got hard feelings for him. Mal deserves to know about anything new going on in that crazy daywalker's life.'

'I will. Promise. First good chance I get.' Which hadn't happened yet, and with the way Mal's moods went, might not happen for another year or so. Truth was, Doc didn't think Mal knowing Preacher had fathered a kid was such a good idea. No one knowing was a better idea. Hell, Doc was sorry *he* knew.

'I'm serious.' Her eyes strayed from his face down his bare chest and lower. She flipped a length of chestnut hair over one shoulder as the tip of her tongue wet her lips. She reached the end of the bed. 'You're not playing fair.'

He stretched, showing off the muscles in his arms and chest. He ached for her. For the unconditional way she gave herself to him. It was the greatest luxury in his life. One he'd kill to protect. 'I never play fair. That's part of my charm.'

She crossed her arms and shook her head. 'Charm isn't going to protect you if Mal finds out you're keeping a secret like this. You need to tell him.'

'I will. Soon.'

'Promise?'

Doc crossed his fingers behind his hip, hating himself for doing it. 'Cross my heart and hope to die.'

Fi frowned. 'Don't say that. That's the last thing either of us wants to come true.'

He held his hands out to her. 'C'mon, baby. Nothing's gonna happen to me. I'm a big bad leopard again. C'mere and let me show you.' He growled softly from deep in his chest. Silently he wished away the words he'd spoken. *Hope to die.* Why had he even put that thought out into the universe?

'Speaking of big bad leopards, are you going to go back to Sinjin now? See if he'll reinstate you into the pride?'

'No. Never. He threw me out when I needed the pride's help and support the most. That man is dead to me.' He patted the bed again and gave her the most wicked look he could manage, then stroked a finger down the side of his goatee. 'Now come here, woman, or I'll come get you myself and I really don't think you want that.'

She shrieked, then laughed as she jumped into bed beside him. 'You have the devil in you.'

Happily distracted, he pulled her beneath him and sank into her warmth, nipping her throat lightly. 'And now, so do you.'

'You the one who found her?' The officer handed Creek his license back and gave him a hard once-over. 'You're a ways off the reservation, aren't you?'

He really needed to get his mother's address off his license. 'Yes, I found her.' Creek ignored the officer's second question as he blew out a slow breath and tried to erase the mental image of the girl dying in his arms and how at first glance, he'd thought she was Chrysabelle. How that had sucked the breath out of him. Charged him with a rage he hadn't felt since he'd pulled his father off his sister.

But the girl he'd found wasn't Chrysabelle. She wasn't even a real comarré. And the puncture wounds on her neck were meant to look like the work of a vampire, but he had his doubts. A vampire wouldn't have had any reason to carve the girl up like that. Or leave that much blood behind.

'I understand they already have your DNA and prints.'

It was no secret he had a record. 'Yes.' He wiped his hands down his jeans again, but they were stained with blood. Her blood.

The officer pulled out an e-tablet and stylus. 'Tell me what happened – start from the beginning.'

'I was on my way home, and when I passed this alley, I heard her moaning.' Actually, he'd been tracking a fringe vamp that had been going after street people. The smell of blood had drawn the fringe into the alley.

'On your way home? Your license says you live on tribe land.' The officer's eyes narrowed.

'I used to. That's my mother's place. I live down near Pineda.'

'We'll need to verify that. And you need to get your license updated.'

'Will do.' Better tell Argent, his Kubai Mata sector chief, the cops were going to be calling. Good thing the KM had a system in place for that kind of stuff, but then what didn't the KM have covered? They hadn't stayed a secret society for so many years by being unprepared.

'What happened after you heard her moaning?'

He'd staked the fringe and cleaned up the ashes as quickly as he could. 'I saw her lying there. Looked like she'd been run through a shredder. I was surprised she was still alive.' He shifted, blew out a breath. 'I yelled for help, but no one came.'

He hadn't yelled for help because he knew there was none. Plus the smell of blood had already drawn new fringe. 'I held her. She died in my arms.' At that point, the fringe had been curious, but not a threat since the girl was no longer a viable meal.

'And that's how you got her blood all over you?'

'Yes.' They'd searched him for weapons. Since Argent had yet to show with his replacement crossbow, all they'd found on him was a titanium stake and his halm, which they'd thought was just a length of pipe. Most people in Little Havana carried a lot more than that.

'Then what?'

'I went into that bodega and they called nine-one-one. The rest you know.'

'You touch or move anything else around the scene? We gonna find your prints on anything you want to tell us about now?'

'No, I know better than that.' Maybe a street person had seen the gold and stripped her flesh trying to harvest it.

'What were you doing in this part of town?'

There was no *good* reason to be in Little Havana unless you lived here. Clearly the cop was trying to trip him up. 'I told you, passing through on my way home.' Half a dozen new fringe lingered in the gathering crowd like circling sharks. They came and went, sniffing around, figuring out the blood wasn't from a live source and disappearing again.

'Do you know the victim? Ever seen her around here before?' Red and blue LED police lights illuminated the sheet now covering her.

'Never seen her before.' But he knew what she was. The brunette roots of the platinum hair and simple signum, what was left of them, anyway, pegged her as one of Dominic's fake comarré. One of many things the officer probably had no clue about. Another was that the vampires in the crowd had now doubled in number. Things were getting ugly in this city. He'd seen more othernaturals openly mingling with humans than ever before. Any day now, humans were going to stop pretending they weren't seeing things and figure out the world around them had become a very different place. The night of Halloween would be the end of the innocence if it didn't happen before that.

Another officer ushered a vaguely familiar woman under the crime scene tape and through the milling forensics team. A man, clearly her bodyguard, judging by the loosely concealed piece, dark suit with matching shades, and general protection vibe, accompanied her. Wolf-shifter by the looks of him. Creek inhaled. Too many othernaturals in the crowd to make a positive ID.

The officer escorted her to the body and pulled the sheet back enough to uncover the dead girl's face. The woman went pale beneath her sleek, brunette bob and heavily lined eyes. Her mouth opened in shock, then she snapped it closed, swallowed as she regained her composure, and nodded. Pain bracketed her eyes. She said something normal human ears wouldn't have heard from this distance. 'That's her.'

Creek tipped his head toward the woman. 'Who is that?'

The officer looked up from moving his stylus across his e-tablet screen. 'The mayor. Delores Diaz-White. Don't you watch TV?'

'Don't own one.' Ugly didn't begin to describe what was about to go down in this city. Creek cursed softly.

'You can say that again.' The officer's head went back down to focus on his notes. 'Don't leave town. Chances are a hundred percent we're going to need you again for questioning.'

Creek jerked his head in response, but his eyes were on the mayor. She spoke to the officer who'd led her to the body, her gun-toting muscle scanning the crowd like he expected trouble. Creek had planned to head out again on patrol, but stopping by Seven to let Dominic know about his comarré might not be a bad idea. Maybe the anathema could give him a heads-up on who might have had a beef with the girl. An angry customer, maybe, or a heavy-handed boyfriend.

The mayor's bodyguard stopped his constant scanning and faced Creek. Because of the man's dark shades, Creek couldn't tell if the shifter was looking at him, the cop, or someone in the crowd behind them.

The shifter turned, leaned toward the mayor, and whispered something too soft for Creek to catch. She nodded. Her next words to the cop at her side were easy enough to make out. 'I'd like to speak to the man who found her.'

Creek followed the officer over. Sorrow filled the mayor's large brown eyes, but he could imagine that when she smiled, she was beautiful. 'Madam Mayor, I'm Thomas Creek.'

She reached to shake his hand, then stopped when he showed her the bloodstains covering them. Her gaze skipped back to the covered form of her daughter about ten feet away. 'I understand you found her. Did she say anything before she . . . ?'

'No, ma'am. She was too far gone.' The pain on her face made him ache for her. He could imagine what it would have felt like to lose his sister, Una, if he hadn't stopped his father in time. 'I'm very sorry for your loss.'

Her mouth twitched, too heavy to smile. 'I'm sure you know Julia and I were estranged.'

The papers had made certain everyone knew during the last election, but the mayor had survived for another term. 'I'm sure the PCPD will do everything they can to find out who did this.'

Fresh tears filled the mayor's eyes. She looked at the officers swirling around them, blinked, and nodded. 'I'm sure they'll do their best. They keep asking me about the gold marks on her. I don't know why she would tattoo herself that way.'

Creek hesitated. The covenant had been broken for over a month. The mayor must have some idea of the chaos erupting in the city, the strange creatures walking among the human citizens. There was no ignoring the news reports. Or the fact that the gargoyles on city hall had taken to evening flights. She *had* to know.

'What do you know?' The bodyguard's stern voice snapped him back to the moment.

Creek looked around. 'I would be willing to talk to you, but not here.'

The mayor's brow unfurrowed. 'Tomorrow, then, first thing. My office. Eight a.m.'

Creek nodded. 'I'll be there.'

He started to slip away, but the bodyguard blocked his path. 'You don't show and I'll hunt you down, understand?' He smiled, showing larger-than-human teeth. 'I'm very good at hunting.'

Creek squared his shoulders and wished he could see through the guy's shades. 'Most wolves are.'

The bodyguard's jaw went slack. Without a backward glance, Creek disappeared into the crowd and away from the scene. Normally, his ratty jeans and hoodie made a great disguise for blending in, but not with bloodstains covering them. Maybe he'd grab a shower, then take another crack at seeing Chrysabelle. She had to let him in sometime, right?

A block away and the little hairs on the back of his neck went up. A heavy sense of foreboding pressed down on him, along with the stench of brimstone and putrid flesh. His first thought was Nothos. Since bringing Chrysabelle back from Corvinestri he'd run into two, probably left behind by Tatiana's hasty departure. With the blood scent he was leaving, they could probably track him with their eyes closed.

He kept his senses open as he maintained his pace. No sound of footsteps. The weight increased and the KM brands on his back began to itch. If this was Nothos, it was a new breed.

Water pooled in his mouth as nausea threatened to bring his dinner up. He took the next right, ducked into an alley, and crouched behind a Dumpster. A second later, his halm was out and fully extended, ready to take down whatever stalked him.

Seconds flowed into minutes and nothing happened. The pressure and smell stayed constant. His stalker must be at the mouth of the alley, waiting for him to make the first move.

Quietly, he grabbed a discarded beer bottle and pitched it toward the back of the alley. Something shot past, a ripple of heat over asphalt on a summer day.

He lunged, plunging the halm through the center of the thing, only to be thrown back against the wall. A rib cracked, but he held onto his weapon. The shimmer of movement turned toward him and solidified into a creature that Creek had only ever seen before in drawings. Castus Sanguis. The ancient ones.

Callous red eyes, hands with scythe claws, and skin that oozed foul fluid. The Castus was everything he'd been described as, but seeing him in person was infinitely worse.

Fear, something that not even the Nothos made him feel, stuck its cold hand into Creek's chest and squeezed. The brightest KM minds had yet to come up with a way to destroy the Castus. They were reportedly undefeatable.

The demon's hooves scraped the ground as he charged. Creek feinted, rolling beneath the outstretched arms and stabbing his halm through the demon's side as he came up. The creature howled, seemingly more out of anger than pain.

'You dare strike me, mortal?' The demon struck out again, and again Creek escaped the blow within a hairsbreadth.

He didn't bother answering. Instead he took aim and let the halm fly straight toward the heart of the beast.

The demon swatted the titanium quarterstaff away. It clattered to the ground far beyond Creek's reach. Behind him, the alley went a few more feet, then ended in a tall building without windows or fire escapes. He was trapped in a concrete canyon.

With a blood-freezing laugh, the demon stalked forward. 'Too bad the witchling wants you alive. Maybe just a taste . . . '

A blur of red filled Creek's vision, knocking him to the ground. Acid pain tore through his shoulder. Fangs hit bone, tore flesh, snapped sinew. Blood gushed over his body, soaking his clothes. Then heat. And light. And the keening wail of a creature in pain.

Creek opened his eyes, forcing himself to his feet. His arm hung limp. The Castus staggered backward, his body a flickering wick of fire. He clawed at his maw and belly where the flames concentrated. His arm shot out, his hooked finger pointing. 'Kubai Mata,' he snarled.

'Damn straight,' Creek answered. He took a step toward his halm. Maybe he could finish this demon off after all. His hand stretched toward his weapon. The earth tilted, throwing him to the ground again. His vision tunneled down to nothing, and the press of asphalt faded as his body went numb.

Chapter Four

The wait to get into Seven was ridiculous. Despite Mal's presence, every vampire in the crowd around Chrysabelle had scoped her out at least twice. Even if she hadn't seen the shifting eyes and flaring nostrils, she would have known something was up by the silver glazing Mal's gaze. The attention was no surprise. The perfume of her blood was unmatched by Dominic's fakes. Most fringe had probably never smelled anything like her before.

Someone brushed her from behind. Mal growled as she turned to see who it was. A fringe vamp raised his hands in surrender and scurried off. After the news she'd given Mal, his fuse must be very short indeed.

She couldn't think about that now. Or how just seeing him had made her want to forgive what he'd done. Her body was weak, her emotions weaker. She must be strong. Must focus on what she needed to accomplish.

Like seeing Dominic and getting his blessing to use his signumist's services. A bolder fringe bumped into her, his hands finding her arm and waist. Mal snarled like a rabid dog, snapping his jaw as all traces of humanity disappeared from his face. The guilty fringe disappeared into the crowd, and a moat of personal space opened around them, but more heads turned to ogle the genuine comarré and rare noble vampire. Mal shifted back to his human face, but that did nothing to quell the staring.

She sighed. She preferred the private entrance to Seven, but the ground between her and Dominic was unsure after what had happened at the witches' house. He might not want to see her at all. She'd threatened him with the same thing herself, but he hadn't carried through his plan of killing Doc and had agreed things were even after Mal had given his blood to the witches in exchange for them returning Dominic's. Things should be square between them, but with a vampire like Dominic . . . who knew? It was probably a good thing Mal was with her.

The line surged a few steps forward. Speaking of the hulking, broody, rarely pleasant anathema vampire currently glued to her side, part of her was happy Mal had inserted himself back into her life. The same part that was grateful to still be alive. But the rest of her wasn't so sure. Yes, she was alive, but at what cost? She had vampire blood in her veins now. Every time she remembered that, a wave of shock washed through her. Vampire blood. In a comarré. Although Mal was technically right about the latter. She wasn't *truly* comarré anymore.

Thanks to him.

And so went the circle of thinking. Which was why it was time to stop thinking and start acting. Her fingers drummed the handle of the cane at her side. A cane she didn't exactly *need* but one that served its purpose. She wasn't ready to let anyone know just how healed she was. The wounds on her back should have kept her bedridden for weeks. But two days after Mal's infusion, she'd managed a painful half hour in the gym. Not the hardest training she'd had, but training nonetheless.

All that remained were the vicious scars streaking down her back like lightning strikes from shoulder blades to tailbone. And the pain. But pain she could deal with so long as she didn't overdo it and ended the day with a good hot soak. The scars worried her. She prayed to the holy mother they wouldn't prevent the signumist from replacing the signum taken from her. If Dominic's signumist was for real and not just a glorified tattooist.

The crowd moved forward, at last depositing them at the head of the line. The wolf-shifter at the door eyed them both but unclicked the rope from its stanchion anyway. He held his other hand out. 'Fifty each.'

Mal's lip curled. 'What? Like hell—'

'Here.' Chrysabelle slipped the plastic bills into the varcolai's palm before grabbing Mal's elbow and pushing him forward.

He glanced over his shoulder. 'Dominic's got a lot of nerve charging that kind of cover.'

'You're not even supposed to be here. That means you don't get to complain.' She leaned heavily on the cane and exhaled like she was more winded than she actually was. It refocused him nicely.

'And you should be home in bed.'

The response that filled her mouth brought such heat to her skin she looked away in case the evidence showed on her face. Since being disavowed, she'd become wickedly aware that her precious chastity no longer held much currency. Maybe it was the cursed blood coursing through her system, maybe it was the fever brought on by the healing, but her dreams these last eight days had been filled with heated visions of Mal and Creek in situations she'd never before entertained.

Another reason not to think.

Mal held the red and gold dragon double doors open for her. Music poured over them as they entered the main room of Seven. Seemed the cover charge wasn't the only thing that had changed. She caught the attention of the first server that went by. 'Excuse me, I need—'

'You need something, you talk to Katsumi or Jacqueline.' The young man, a fae-varcolai remnant by the looks of him, was clearly perturbed she'd stopped him. 'You comarré don't run this place, you know. I have paying customers to take care of.'

He took a step toward the bar he'd been headed for. Mal clamped a hand on his arm, stopping him cold. The server lifted his head to stare at the vampire towering over him. 'Can I help you, sir?'

'Yes.' The silver glow in Mal's eyes marked him as noble, something the server had probably never seen before except on Dominic. And now, of course, Katsumi. The appropriate fear registered in the server's eyes. 'You can start by never talking to her in that tone of voice again. She's not one of Dominic's fake comarré – she's the real thing and she deserves your respect, understand?'

He swallowed. 'Yes, sir. My deepest apologies.'

The show was touching but unnecessary. 'Mal, it's fine. Really.'

But he didn't let go of the server. 'Tell Dominic Chrysabelle is here to see him.'

'Yes, sir.' The server glanced down at Mal's hand. Mal moved it and the server dashed off.

Chrysabelle folded her arms. 'I love when you're all sweetness and light.'

'Kid's a punk.' He spoke without looking at her, his head swiveling to take in the crowd. 'I don't see Katsumi.'

'Good. Which reminds me, has Ronan ever shown up? Or is it pretty much assumed he bought it in the swamp?'

'Not sure, but you shouldn't assume anything when it comes to Ronan.'

'Or any vampire for that matter,' she muttered.

'I heard that.'

The server returned, practically jogging. 'Dominic's in his office. He says for you to come up.'

'Thank you.' Chrysabelle smiled as pleasantly as she could.

The server stayed put. 'Anything else, sir?'

Mal shook his head. 'You're dismissed.'

The server took off as Chrysabelle shot Mal a look. 'You're dismissed?' She rolled her eyes. 'C'mon, let's go see Dominic.'

At his office door, she knocked twice before he called for them to enter. Was that a sign he wasn't happy to see her? She went in, Mal behind her, and relaxed slightly to see Dominic on the phone. He held up a finger, then motioned for them to sit.

He continued on for a moment in Italian. '*Sì, sì. Buono.*' He nodded a few times, shook his hand at the heavens, then finally, '*Devo andare. Ciao, Luciano.*' And hung up. '*Scusi*, but I had to take care of that.' He came out from behind the desk to take Chrysabelle's hand between his. He leaned in and kissed her on both cheeks. 'It is good to see you, *cara mia*. I know of your troubles. My heart aches for you. This woman, Rennata ...' He scowled. 'If you wish, I can have her dealt with.'

'As much as I appreciate the offer, no thank you.' Apparently she'd worried for nothing.

'You are feeling better now, though, eh?'

'I'm doing well enough.'

His gaze traveled to the cane at her side. 'And this? What is this?'

'I still have a little pain.' Not a lie, except for the little part. Sometimes she could feel the knives cutting her skin as fresh as the moment it had happened. The phantom echoes of those blades woke her at night.

'Malkolm, I trust you are well also?'

'I'm fine.' Mal paused, like he was unsure why Dominic was being so cordial. She wondered that herself. 'The club is busy. Business must be good.'

Dominic sat on the front edge of his caramel-swirled marble desktop. 'It's very good, actually. So good I'm bringing my nephew Luciano in. Many times removed, of course, but the blood is there. And with Ronan gone . . . ' He shrugged.

Chrysabelle leaned forward. 'Is Katsumi no longer here?'

'She's here. There's just so much to take care of. The comarré business alone takes most of her time.'

'That's partly why I'm here.' Chrysabelle took a breath. 'I would like to speak to your signumist.'

Dominic tilted his head. 'May I ask why?'

Her thumb rubbed the cane's pearl handle. 'I need some new signum.'

He smiled gently. 'New signum? *Cara mia*, you have no room.'

'I do. On my back.' The signumist would tell him anyway. 'I need to replace the signum that was stripped from me.'

The smile vanished as he stood up. 'What? Why? I know

what it is to undergo such a thing. Your mother took the last of her signum the first year of our affair. The pain was more than I thought a human could bear.'

'Dominic, I know very well what the pain is like.' She opened her arms, twisting her hands to flash a few of the numerous signum she still bore. 'I need to get back to the Aurelian.'

'What for?'

'I have unfinished business with her.'

He snorted, throwing a hand in the air. 'You are just like your mother. *Ostinato*.'

'Sometimes stubborn is good. Will you let me talk to him?'

His mouth leveled into a thin, hard line. 'No. It is not for the best.'

'Tell him,' Mal urged her.

She responded with a look she hoped said no.

'Tell me what?' Dominic asked.

She exhaled. 'Maris had a son. My brother. I need to see the Aurelian to find out everything I can about him. So I can locate him.'

Dominic's mouth slowly parted. 'Another child?' He shook his head. 'I still don't like it, but I will think on it.' He checked his watch. 'There is something I need of you as well.'

Which might explain why he'd been so nice. 'What might that be?'

After a quick glance at Mal, he continued. 'I have two comarré here. A comarré and a comar, actually. They cannot stay here.'

'Why not? You've got plenty of space. Where do the rest of your comarré stay?'

'Except for a few special cases, they live in their own homes.

But these are not *my* comarré. They are Primoris Domus comarré.'

She sat back, surprise flooding her. 'How on earth did you get hold of them?'

'They came to me. Escaped from Tatiana.' He lifted his shoulders. 'They saw one of mine in the street and followed her here. Begged asylum. What was I to do? Throw them out to the Nothos? Let the fringe devour them?' He walked around to his chair and sat. 'I am not an unkind man, Chrysabelle. Despite what you may think of me.'

'I don't think that.' She did, however, think he was prone to unreasonable decisions, hasty judgments, and bouts of temper. 'Still, I don't understand why they can't stay here. I'm sure they'd be willing to exchange blood for room and board, that sort of thing.'

'Perhaps, but I have yet to broach that subject with them. They are . . . a bit timid around me. And I cannot keep them here because I cannot protect them the way you can. Your house is warded, and no vampire can enter without an invite.'

Mal shook his head. 'Tatiana doesn't need any more reason to come after Chrysabelle. It's a bad idea.'

The tiniest bit of silver sparked in Dominic's eyes. 'I would never put Chrysabelle in harm's way. I will assign guards to the house.'

She stared at the carved, gilded legs of his desk. She had no desire to add to her household, especially not two comarré who would remind her every day of her past and what had been stripped from her, but neither did she wish to get on Dominic's bad side. She sighed slowly. 'I'm still recovering, you know.'

He clutched at his long-dead heart. '*Bella*, I would do

nothing I thought might hinder you returning to full health. They will be quiet as mice.'

'They can move in on three conditions. One, I want to meet with the signumist tonight. Two, I want you or Mortalis to move them in – no one else comes onto the property. And three, I don't want to see them. Not right now. Make sure they know that. My hospitality is not to be mistaken for an invitation to be friends.'

'Perhaps you are more stubborn than your mother.' He nodded, fingers steepled against his chin. 'Agreed. It will be done.' He pressed a button on a small silver device resting on his desktop. 'I'll have Mortalis take you to the signumist. That doesn't mean I support what you're doing.'

'Understood. Thank you.'

A few moments later, Mortalis entered. 'Chrysabelle, good to see you up and about. Mal.' He nodded in greeting before addressing Dominic. 'You need me?'

'Take Chrysabelle to Atticus.'

His brows lifted a centimeter or two, but it was his only reaction. He turned to her, gesturing toward the door. 'Follow me.'

The throbbing woke Creek. It radiated from his shoulder into the rest of his body like a raging infection, cutting through the fog of medication in his blood.

'You're awake. Good.'

He opened his eyes but knew who'd spoken just by the scent of wolf filling his nose. He blinked as the green-walled room and the man standing over him came into focus. 'Shouldn't you be guarding the mayor?'

'That's being taken care of. Right now, you're her first priority. Anything you know about what happened to her daughter matters most.' LED panels on the ceiling framed the varcolai in bright white light. He leaned closer, still wearing the dark shades. 'How are you not dead? Your wounds would have killed most mortals.'

Creek ignored the question. Judging from the black sky visible through the blinds, it was either a few hours later or the next night. 'How did I end up in the hospital?'

He pushed to a sitting position, testing the muscles in his ruined shoulder. Fresh pain cramped his body, and his bones felt on the verge of shattering. Nothos poison was a Swedish massage compared to the bite of the Castus Sanguis. Not that he really knew. Like all KM, he'd been sealed against Nothos venom.

A second later, a headrush nearly laid him down again. He rubbed the back of his head to buy some time. How much blood had he lost? Speaking of lost ... he scanned the room as the dizziness abated. No sign of his halm. Argent wasn't going to be happy about a second lost weapon in less than two weeks, but then, his sector chief was rarely happy about anything.

'I secured the mayor in her vehicle, then followed you. By the time I found you in the alley, you were a bloody, pulpy mess. I figured you'd be out more than just a few hours.'

So it wasn't the next night. 'You should have seen the other guy.'

The joke was lost on the varcolai. 'I didn't. What was it?'

'Don't worry about it.' Creek pulled the tape off the IV in his hand and slid the needle out. Time to go before he had to explain to a doctor why his blood was a few degrees off normal and his body regenerated at a non-human rate.

The varcolai's beefy paw came down on his wrist. 'I don't think you're showing the proper appreciation. If not for me, you'd have bled out in that alley.'

'Not a chance.' Creek squinted and stared into the shifter's dark shades. If eyes were the windows to the soul, this guy's soul must really need hiding. 'I would have been fine. Been through worse.' Like getting staked to the floor with his own crossbow bolts. The memory caused a new twinge of pain through his shoulder.

The shifter's hand lifted. 'I get it. Self-proclaimed superhero, huh?' He snorted. 'You think what's happening in Paradise City is some kind of phase the city's going through? You have no idea what's happening, buddy. None.'

'Look . . . ' Creek hesitated. 'You have a name?'

'Havoc.'

Beautiful. Must have picked that one out himself. 'Look, Havoc, you're the one who has no idea what's happening.' He swung his legs out of the bed. 'Where are my clothes?'

'Trashed. You want out of here, I'm your best bet.' The shifter smiled, an altogether unpleasant expression. 'Actually, I'm your only bet.'

'I said I'd talk to the mayor and I will, but first I need to go home and get things together.' Like alerting Chrysabelle someone had just taken out a fake comarré. The possibility existed that the killer had been after the original, not a copy. Creek stood. The draft from the AC sent a chill into the open back of the hospital gown. They couldn't have left his boxers on? This was going to be a fun day.

'You're going now.'

'Already agreed to eight a.m. tomorrow. I'll be there.'

Havoc shook his head. 'Can't take the chance you'll go vigilante on me again and get yourself killed.' He gestured toward the door. 'Time is now. Don't make this any harder than it needs to be.'

Harder? Damn shifter had no idea who he was talking to. Creek really wasn't in the mood for this, but luckily for Havoc Creek wasn't in any shape to brawl with a guy who outweighed and outreached him. 'Does the mayor ever ask why you need the night off when there's a full moon?'

Havoc leaned forward, the smell of wet dog wafting off him at close range. 'I'm sure that wouldn't interest her nearly as much as the words branded on your back.' He jerked his thumb toward the wheelchair in the corner of the room. 'Get in. I've got a car waiting.'

Chapter Five

Mal hated being this far down into the bowels of Seven. It was like being in the ruins where Tatiana had imprisoned him. Where his curse had first manifested. *Where you should still be.* Gave him that hopeless, buried feeling. Like he wanted to claw through the concrete and— At last, Mortalis slowed. The twists and turns they'd taken had led them through thick metal doors and simple concrete corridors with no signs of the opulence visible in the general living quarters occupied by Dominic and his staff and those reserved for guests. Only the glow of the phosphorescent ceiling lit the way. If Dominic kept the signumist down here, chances were good the man was being held against his will.

'We're here,' Mortalis said, turning to Chrysabelle. The curve of his horns cast sharp shadows on his cheeks. 'You'll be coming in alone?'

'No,' Mal answered. 'I'll be with her.' This signumist could see Chrysabelle as a chance to exact his anger at Dominic, especially with her still weak and recovering. If he knew Chrysabelle wasn't alone in this venture, he might not act out.

Chrysabelle's mouth bent downward and both hands gripped the cane's handle. 'If you come in, you have to behave. No comments about what a stupid idea you think this is or how the guy better be careful or you'll kill him or any of that.'

'Done.' But the man better watch himself or death would be a merciful dream compared to what Mal would do to him. *Yesss*, the voices hissed. *Blood blood blood.*

Mortalis pressed his hand to a panel of concrete. A blue-green glow emerged on the wall, outlining the shape of a door. He stuck a finger into the middle of the space and began to draw. The light followed his finger and runes appeared in the air.

'Those are signum,' Chrysabelle whispered. 'This is comarré magic.'

Mal nodded. 'Like the portals at Tatiana's.'

'Yes,' Mortalis answered. The last rune drawn, he pressed the door once again. This time it opened. He walked through. 'Quickly.'

Chrysabelle went next, Mal behind her. When he was through, the door slid shut again. '*Just* like the portals at Tatiana's.' He looked at Mortalis. 'Are we stuck here for a certain length of time, or can this door be opened at will?'

'At will. Follow me.'

Here, carpet lined the corridor's floor, and the walls were dry-walled and painted. A minimal number of antiqued sconces lit the way. Less like a prison cell but still not close to the same richness Dominic and his staff enjoyed.

At the hall's end, a simple paneled wood door awaited them. Mortalis pressed a small button by the doorjamb. Muted chimes sounded from within. Chrysabelle leaned against the wall, the cane in front of her. Mal wondered if the walk had tired her. Her pulse hadn't increased, so if she was in pain, she hid it well.

Several moments later a man answered. He wore the familiar white tunic and loose pants Mal had come to know as the comarré uniform, but he bore no signum that Mal could see. The man stared past them into the corridor beyond. 'Mortalis. Good evening. Forgive me, I must have forgotten I had work tonight. No matter. I can prepare quickly.' He smiled softly, his gaze shifting across them. 'What is the name of the comarré to be marked?'

Chrysabelle glanced at Mal, then back at Atticus. Her pulse had kicked up the moment Atticus had opened the door. Mal doubted it was pain. Something akin to fear played in her eyes. No doubt memories of the past signum she'd endured. And here she was, ready to take on more. That she could face something that scared her so deeply amazed him. Her brother best appreciate what she was doing to find him. Mal reached out for her, not entirely sure what comfort he could offer, but she shook her head slightly. He retracted his hand without touching her. Just as well. Comfort had never been his strong suit. *More like killing.*

'Good evening, Atticus. No work tonight, not exactly. But I do have a comarré with me.'

Atticus tipped his head a little and flared his nostrils. 'And a vampire. This is . . . unusual. All is well?'

'All is well. May we come in?'

'Of course.' Atticus stepped aside.

Darkness and shadow cloaked the apartment's interior. Atticus went ahead of them. 'Let me turn on some lights. I don't normally use them. Seems wasteful.' He smiled again. If he was being held against his will, he seemed happy enough about it. 'Lights, please,' he commanded.

Instantly, soft illumination removed the darkness. Minimal

but expensive furnishings filled the space. Several closed doors led off the main room. Atticus walked a distinct path to take a seat on the rounded-edge sectional. He held his hands out, displaying intricate signum on his wrists. That was a good sign, Mal guessed. *Like you'd know.* 'Please, sit.'

Chrysabelle passed Mortalis to sit beside Atticus. Her chest rose and fell, matching the pace of her heartbeat as she tucked the cane against her side. 'You're a real signumist.'

Atticus turned toward her. 'Yes.' He leaned in toward her an inch or so. 'And judging by the perfume of gold that surrounds you, you're a real comarré. Haven't been around one of you in a long while.'

Mal crossed his arms. What kind of games was this guy playing? 'You can take one look at her and figure out she's real.'

Atticus faced Mal. 'I suppose *you* can.'

'Mal.' Chrysabelle's voice held a warning.

Atticus lifted his hand, displaying a sun-shaped signum on his wrist similar to the one Chrysabelle bore on the nape of her neck. 'It's all right. The noble one does not know our ways. He does not realize I am blind.'

'Blind?' Mal uncrossed his arms and lurched forward. 'You're going to let a blind man engrave your skin with molten gold? How can you think for a minute this man knows what he's doing?'

Chrysabelle pushed to her feet, blocking his path. She grabbed his arm with her free hand, the strength of her grip bordering on painful. The fear had vanished from her eyes and her voice was low and stern. 'Mal, all the signumists are blind. It's a requirement. To keep the purity of the comarré intact.' She softened her voice and her hold on him. 'They work on every part of our bodies. It's the comarré way.'

Images of an almost naked Chrysabelle swarmed his brain, of the delicate swirls and patterns that covered every inch of her. Heat rose in his body, matching the whine in his head. He shook her hand off him. Mal wanted her touch, but not this way. Not when she thought he needed to be restrained lest he do something foolish. He relaxed, let the tension out of his body in a noticeable way for her sake, then lowered his voice. 'You're telling me there are enough blind people interested in the job of signumist that it just happens to work out that way?'

'No, it's—'

Atticus laughed, a low, nonthreatening sound. 'No, friend. Just like you, I wasn't born into my current state.' He blinked but his eyes remained focused on nothing. 'I gave up my sight voluntarily.'

That, Mal thought, was where the similarities between them ended.

Tatiana settled into the handsome leather chair in Ivan's old office, one room in the massive estate she would very soon become the rightful owner of. A few preliminaries and it was done. She knew it in her gut.

Octavian stood at the bar, pouring them each a glass of Ivan's best red. He stoppered the decanter and brought a glass to her. 'Are you sure it's wise to set these things in place before the council has made it official?' He set her glass down, then took his own and retired to the chair adjacent to her desk.

She sipped the red before answering. Ivan's taste was impeccable. She'd give the old pile of rubble that. 'The council's decision is merely a formality. The ancient ones will tell them to make me Dominus and they will obey. Lining up a loyal noble to take over the position of Elder just makes good sense. Especially because it allows whomever I choose to prove themselves.' She offered him a rare smile. 'You'll see.'

He returned her smile and lifted his glass to her. 'As always, I learn so much from you.'

'In bed as well as out.'

He dipped his head at her words, making her laugh with her own wickedness. Turning Octavian was one of the best decisions she'd ever made. He was young, but a quick learner and capable of anticipating her needs, just as he'd done when he'd been the head of her household staff. Yet another position that needed filling. 'Any ideas as to who might be ready to take over your old position?'

He swallowed his wine. 'Yes. Kosmina. She was part of Ivan's household staff and would be perfect. She's a good worker. One of the best.'

'You trust her? Think the rest of my staff will work well with her?'

'Implicitly. Yes, absolutely. Kosmina is iron-fisted.'

'I like her already. Make it so, then. One less thing to do.'

'I'll talk to her today.'

'When is my meeting with Madame Rennata?'

'Tomorrow.' He grimaced. 'At eight a.m.'

'Damn that woman. *Her* comarrés run and I'm the one who has to breach daylight to rectify the situation. Someone needs to put her in her place.'

A knock rang out against the door.

'Come,' Tatiana called.

One of the staff opened the door. 'My lady, the noble couple whose company you requested has arrived.'

'Send them in.'

With a short bow, the servant left. He returned a few moments later to usher the vampire couple into the office. She stood and walked around the desk to greet them. She didn't know the couple that well, but the male, Laurent, was the next eldest after her and therefore by rights next in line to be Elder. 'Welcome. Please sit.'

Daciana, his wife, curtsied with her palms upright, a move that instantly won her some favor. Marriage among the nobility wasn't unheard of, but that didn't mean Tatiana saw any good reason for it. Perhaps these two had simply clung to the old ways. If that was true, they should be very respectful and easily malleable.

Laurent held the chair for his wife, then sat beside her. 'Very kind of you to invite us, Lady Tatiana. I know how busy you must be with your pending promotion.'

'Not so busy to attend to my house.' She glanced at Octavian. 'Perhaps our guests would like wine.'

He looked horrified for a moment, obviously unhappy he'd yet to make the offer himself. 'Of course, let me take care of that.' He leaped to his feet and set about pouring two more glasses.

Tatiana decided to test her guests. 'Octavian is newly turned.' His previous position as head of her staff was well known. How Laurent and Daciana received him would tell much.

Daciana accepted a glass of wine from Octavian as Laurent spoke. 'How marvelous for you, Octavian. To have Tatiana as your sire is quite an honor.'

Daciana set her glass down without drinking and looked at her husband. 'We should throw a party for him.' She smiled and turned back to Tatiana. 'Wouldn't that be wonderful? There hasn't been a debut party in years. I'm going to do it.' Her smile faltered, her gaze flicking from Laurent to Tatiana, seeking approval. 'That is, if you haven't already planned something.'

Tatiana smiled. 'I think it would be rather appropriate for the House of Tepes's newly appointed Elder to host a debut party for my first turned.'

Daciana's eyes lit up like silver sparklers. The woman was far too emotional in Tatiana's estimation, but if she could scatter, she'd be perfect. 'Are you saying . . . ' She squeezed Laurent's arm.

Laurent bowed his head but failed to hide the pride on his face. When he lifted his eyes to Tatiana's, he had regained his composure. 'I am honored.'

She leaned back in her chair and shrugged. 'It is your right. You are eldest in the house.'

'Even so, I know exceptions have been made.' He straightened. 'I understand that I will not truly be Elder until the council proclaims you Dominus, but I will strive to fulfill that position to the best of my abilities regardless.'

Tatiana held back a grimace. Gah. The pair of them were like eager little puppies. 'Wonderful. It just so happens that there is a matter I need attended to.'

'Of course.' Laurent nodded, already agreeing to Tatiana's request. Excellent. Well-trained puppies made the best lapdogs. 'Whatever I can do, just name it.'

Tatiana swirled the wine in her glass before sipping it. She savored the dark tannic red as it eddied past her fangs and tongue. At last she swallowed. 'Are you capable of the job of Elder? Of the ruthlessness sometimes necessary? Can you dispatch justice when need be?'

Laurent puffed out his chest, his eyes going half silver. 'I am Tepes born. I am completely capable.'

'Good.' Tatiana set her glass down. 'Can both of you scatter?'

'Of course,' Laurent answered before Daciana could say anything.

Tatiana leaned forward. 'What do you scatter into, Daciana?'

'Wasps, my lady.'

The plan was complete, then. Tatiana sat back. 'I need you to go to New Florida and retrieve something for me.'

'I would be honored,' Laurent said.

'As would I,' Daciana added softly.

'Wonderful.' Except that Daciana was a little too meek for Tatiana's liking. It was what it was. With that morsel of information tucked away, she set out her plan, knowing full well that before this pair set foot on Southern Union soil, Tatiana was going to get to know Laurent's bride a great deal better.

So much better, no one would be able to tell them apart.

Chapter Six

'Mayor.' Creek got off the couch to stand as Mayor Diaz-White entered the living room of her home. The tan suit she'd worn at the crime scene was gone, replaced by jeans and a tank top with a loose V-neck sweater over it. Her pretty face was scrubbed clean, her eyes red-rimmed from crying, but her expression seemed calm. As calm as could be, given the circumstances.

She extended her hand. 'Thank you for coming.' She exchanged a look with Havoc, who stood near the exit. 'I understand it wasn't your choice.'

'I intended to meet with you tomorrow morning as we'd discussed, but your goon decided otherwise. I don't like being strong-armed.'

'I understand and I apologize. It's not Mr Havoc's fault. After we spoke, I realized I couldn't wait until morning to have things explained. It's not in my nature to be so impatient, but this is my daughter. My city. So I sent him after you.' She sat on the couch across from him, a marble and bronze coffee table separating them. 'I know you're upset, but I also know his arrival saved your life.'

Creek tilted his head toward the wolf shifter. 'Can we talk in private?'

'Of course. John, thank you for your work tonight. I'll see you in the morning.'

Havoc grunted. 'You want to be alone with this guy?' He shook his head. 'If it's all the same to you, I'll wait in the front room and escort him out when you're through.'

'If you wish.' One hand strayed behind her back to tug at her sweater. 'But I'll be fine.'

Was she carrying? It wouldn't surprise Creek if the mayor of this screwed-up city kept a gun or five. He sat back down. His clothes, borrowed from Havoc – jeans, a T-shirt, and a pair of flip-flops – fit okay, but since getting out of the pen, wearing anything he hadn't personally bought grated on him. 'He didn't save my life. I was hurt, but I would have been fine.'

Her sculpted brows arched as her gaze scanned his upper body. 'Havoc said your shoulder was torn open. Some kind of animal attack.' Her hands clenched, then relaxed. 'I've been receiving reports of some sightings in the city lately. Large cats. A wolf or two. Even ... well, it's ridiculous, but some-one saw an enormous flying lizard-bird thing a few weeks ago.'

Argent needed to be more careful. 'Most likely it was a dragon. Just like the strange bats you've been seeing around city hall aren't bats. They're the gargoyles on the building come to life, but I suspect you already know that.'

She laughed until she noticed he hadn't joined her. The smile vanished. 'It's not possible.'

That was enough for now. No point rattling the hive past the point of recovery. 'What would you like to know about your daughter?'

'Why did she have those gold tattoos all over her? Do you know?'

'Yes.' But where to begin? 'They are an ancient way of purifying the blood.'

The mayor's face screwed up. 'Purifying the blood? Like some kind of ritual? Do you think whoever killed her did that to her?'

'No, she chose to have those marks placed on her body. They're called *signum*.'

'Why would she do that?' She tucked her legs beneath her. 'As a teen, Julia thought tattoos were ugly.' Her gaze snagged on his well-inked forearms before shifting back to his face.

He leaned into the couch, spreading his arms over the back so she could get a better look at his *ugly* tats. The move sent a ripple of pain through his still-healing shoulder. 'Comarré do what they do because they have chosen to serve a particular master.' Telling this woman her daughter had decided to become a blood whore pimped out by the local vampire kingpin wasn't going to be easy. Well, the telling might be easy, but her reaction wasn't going to be.

'This involves a cult, doesn't it? *Dios mio*, what did she get herself into?' The mayor crossed herself and whispered a few prayerful words in Spanish.

Creek tipped his head back and sighed. This was not the right place to start. There was too much she needed to know first for any of this to make sense. He edged forward on the seat and leaned his arms on his knees. 'It's not a cult, but there are some other things I need to explain first.'

'Like what?'

'You said you've been getting reports about animal sightings. Anything else?'

She hesitated, her mouth hardening. 'Yes. Many other things. Things that should not – do not – exist.'

'They do exist. And you need to accept that.'

She stared at him, her jaw working like she was going to scream or cry. 'I don't think you have a clear idea of the kind of reports I'm getting.'

'Vampires. People who shift into animal forms. Creatures with horns. Unnaturally colored skin.' Gold tattoos. Branded skin.

She shook her head. 'Those things aren't real. No intelligent person would ever believe that.'

'They will. Halloween is three days away. The potential exists for greater chaos to erupt. It's part of the reason I'm here. To protect mankind.'

The doubt and fear on her face gave way to anger. She slit her eyes at him. 'I don't appreciate being made a fool of.'

He straightened. 'I'm telling you the truth.'

She untucked her legs. 'John,' she called. 'Please escort Mr Creek out.'

Creek stood and yanked his T-shirt off over his head. 'Look at my wounds. Do you think most humans heal this fast?'

Havoc ran into the room, but the mayor's gaze was on Creek's shoulder. 'I don't know how hurt you were to begin with.' She looked away. 'You need to go.'

'And you need to face what's happening in this city.' He held a hand out to keep Havoc at bay.

She stood. 'You told me you could explain what my daughter had done to herself. You haven't done that. What you have done is waste my time.'

'Your daughter became a kind of counterfeit comarré. Comarré, the real ones, are an elite source of blood for *vampires*.'

'I don't want this to be real.' The mayor shook her head. 'It's a nightmare.'

'That's enough,' Havoc warned.

Creek glared at him. 'Don't tell me what to say, shifter.'

'Shut your mouth, *tribe*, or I'm going to make you hurt.' Havoc approached, arms reaching.

Creek backed up, buying time. 'Mayor, I can introduce you to a real comarré and a real vampire. They can help explain. Prove what I'm saying and what you're seeing is true.'

'No, I'm done with this. These lies.' She covered her face with her hands.

'Not lies. Truth. Watch.' Creek charged Havoc, ducked the man's punch, and came up behind him, snaring him in a headlock. He yanked off the shifter's sunglasses. Havoc growled and the mayor's mouth dropped open.

She held out a shaking finger. 'His eyes ... '

'He's varcolai. An animal shifter. Wolf, in case you hadn't guessed.' He released the snarling Havoc, pushing him away at the same time.

'*Dios mio.*' She sank back onto the couch, going slightly green. 'John, is that true?'

Havoc snatched his shades and shoved them back onto his face. 'Yes, Madam Mayor. I'll get my things and go.' He pointed at Creek. 'You, I'll be waiting for outside.'

'No, John, wait.' She stopped him. 'I've known something was different about you lately.' She inhaled. 'I don't know what to think.' Her gaze drifted from Havoc to Creek and back again. 'You've been an exemplary employee. Your ... situation doesn't change that, does it?'

'No, ma'am.'

She nodded, looking dazed. 'You wouldn't hurt me?'

'I would take a bullet for you.'

'You've proven that, haven't you?' She glanced at her hands. 'You stay. Nothing changes. Nothing between us anyway.'

'Appreciate that.' Havoc didn't sound like he fully believed what she said, and Creek didn't blame him. How could the mayor not look at him differently now?

'You.' She tipped her head at Creek. 'You get this comarré woman and this vampire here by tomorrow night at the latest. If you're trying to pull something, you can consider yourself the main suspect in my daughter's murder.' She stood up, brushing herself off. 'With your record, I can put you in a holding cell so fast it'll make your head spin. Am I clear?'

'Crystal.' No way in hell was he going back in and losing his position with the KM. That would mean losing Una's tuition money. Not happening. 'Getting the comarré here is not a problem.' Except Chrysabelle had refused to see him every time he'd been to her house. 'Not a problem at all.'

After calming Mal down, Chrysabelle was about to return to Atticus's side when Mortalis spoke. 'If things are settled here, I have duties I should attend to. Atticus, if you need me, you know how to reach me. I assume you two can find your way out when you're ready to go?'

They both nodded. As soon as Mortalis was gone, Chrysabelle returned to Atticus's side. 'Are you being kept here against your will? We can get you out if—'

Atticus laughed, patting her hand. 'I am here freely and quite happy.'

She shook her head. 'How is that possible? I didn't think signumists were allowed to leave the houses they worked for.'

His smile disappeared. 'They aren't. But now is not the time for my story. Tell me what brings you here.'

She launched into the explanation of what had happened at the Primoris Domus the last time she'd been there and everything that had led up to her signum being stripped. 'What I need is for those signum to be restored so I can make one last trip to the Aurelian, get the information that will help me find my brother, and I'll never bother anyone at that house again.' She hoped her voice conveyed the sincerity of her heart.

'No signumist working for any comarré house would put those marks back on your skin. It would be an unforgiveable action.'

Her heart dropped. Of course he would say that. He was a real signumist. She hadn't counted on that, assuming Dominic's man would be some self-trained hack doing his best.

'Fortunately for you,' Atticus continued, 'I am past caring about unforgiveable actions. If you desire these signum to be replaced, it would be my honor to do the skin work. It has been many, many years since I have stitched gold into one such as you.' He shook his head slowly. 'These mortals Dominic brings me. They are so weak. So unprepared for what must be endured.'

She exhaled. 'Thank you, Atticus. You can't know what this means to me. When can we do this?'

His hand reached out, seeking something. It landed on the cane at her side. 'When this is no longer necessary and you have properly prepared your body and mind.'

'The cane is just a ruse. I don't need it.'

'What?' A muscle in Mal's forehead twitched. 'Why would you pretend to be more injured than you are?'

She met his eyes only briefly. 'I have my reasons.' She

returned her attention to Atticus. 'I can prepare myself in a day. Maybe less.'

'Is there scarring?'

She nodded then remembered he couldn't see her. 'Yes,' she said softly.

He raised his hands, splaying his fingers. 'I need to examine it.'

Without looking at Mal, she stood, pulled her hair over her shoulder, then slipped her tunic off. Mal had seen her in her bra before, but she hadn't planned on it happening again. Not like this anyway. Clutching her tunic to her chest, she turned her back to Atticus. Mal's gaze might as well have been a ton of red-hot coals the way it burned her skin. She held her head a little higher, refusing to be ashamed of the damage Rennata had left on her body. To Mal's credit, he said nothing save an almost inaudible curse, but she knew if she met his eyes, they'd be dead silver. He couldn't be pleased about what he was seeing, knowing he'd been the cause.

Atticus stood behind her. She gasped as his cool fingertips found her back, tracing their way to her spine. His hands were thickly calloused like every signumist she'd known. The heat of their trade turned their skin leathery. She knew when he'd begun to outline the scars because the sensation blurred into something more like pressure than true feeling. Perhaps the loss of feeling would make the new signum easier to bear.

'Hmm.' Atticus followed the wrinkled marks down the sides of her spine. 'I'll have to sand these scars first. They won't take signum.'

'Sand them?'

'Smooth them out. Not a pleasant process, I'm afraid, but necessary.'

Her resolve wavered. She lifted her chin a little higher. 'It will be fine.'

His hands left her and he sat. 'Tomorrow, then, this same time. It will take me a little time to prepare the gold once you arrive, then we will begin. You will recover at home or here?'

'At home.' She tugged her tunic down. Getting home afterward was going to be unpleasant, but she couldn't ask Dominic to use one of his suites. Things were tenuous enough. 'Can't you prepare the gold before I arrive?'

'Ah, yes, of course. I didn't realize you had it with you.'

'I don't.' This was not good. 'I thought you'd have gold, actually. I can get some – that's not an issue. I just wasn't prepared.'

'I have gold,' Atticus assured her. 'But what I use is common gold. The mortals I engrave are not true comarré. You know that. They never will be.' He shrugged. 'Sacred gold would be wasted on them. But for your purposes, I assumed you'd want sacred gold as has been used for all your other signum.'

'I do. I guess. Is there a way to purify the gold you have?'

'Unfortunately, I do not have that capability. And without the proper gold, the signum won't have the power to open the portals or access the Aurelian.'

She sighed and shook her head. 'Where am I going to find sacred gold?'

Mal cleared his throat. 'What about the ring?'

'What—' She looked up and the lack of expression on his face caught her attention. Only the pain in his eyes let her know he was still thinking about what he'd seen. She dropped her gaze to her hands. 'Yes, I suppose that would do.' The ring of sorrows would certainly qualify as sacred gold. But that gold had its own power, and she had Mal's blood in her veins now. Both made everything she was about to do much more risky.

Would the ring's power manifest when laid into her skin? Would it react to the vampire blood she carried? That much power could kill her.

Or worse.

Chapter Seven

'You failed, demon.' Aliza stared down the slightly crispy monster once again contained within Evie's old aquarium. 'A simple task and you failed.'

'Yeah,' Evie added, her left eyelid flitting up and down. 'The house you made me is great, but I really wanted the guy.'

'The half-breed is Kubai Mata,' the demon snarled. 'You tricked me.'

Aliza laughed. 'We tricked you? That's rich.'

'What's a kubay mada?' Evie asked.

The demon bared his teeth at the words, then crouched down and began to flick his forked tongue over his oozing wounds.

'Tell us, demon,' Aliza said. 'What is it?'

But the creature just hissed a string of curses and went back to tending its wounds.

She raised her hand to smack the side of the aquarium, then thought better of it. The pentagram that held him might be glued down, but the aquarium wasn't in the best shape. No point tempting fate and getting themselves killed, because there was no chance the demon would leave them alive if he got loose.

'Damn thing smells like road kill,' Aliza muttered. 'Makes my whole house stink. Evie, light some of those candles.'

'Will do, Ma. Then I'm going to my place. I'm worn out.' She popped the lids off a few jar candles and lit them with a simple fire spell, one of the first Aliza had taught her. 'There you go. I'll see you tomorrow. We can send him out again then.'

'Sure thing. Night, Evie girl.' Aliza waited until the scrape of Evie's kayak leaving the dock reached her ears. She picked up a spray bottle of holy water she kept handy since bringing the demon into the house and gave the creature a squirt.

It yowled and shot upright, foaming at the mouth and cursing in a language she didn't understand. 'Do that again and I will flay your skin from your bones.'

Aliza leaned as close as she dared to the foul thing. 'You can't find the ring, you can't get the man my daughter wants . . . maybe I should just turn you into ash and call it a day.'

'Perhaps the Kubai Mata will find you and kill you first.'

'You're just making crap up now. Guess that means you don't know what the kubay thing is either. Dumbest demon I ever summoned.'

'The Kubai Mata is a great evil,' he spat. 'Greater than anything you can imagine. Meant to destroy my kind. My children.' Fire danced in his eyes. He growled loudly, pounding his fists against the magic barrier that held him.

'Then you better hurry up and do what you're told so you can get free.' She squirted him again for good measure. With the sound of howling filling her living room, she went into the bedroom and closed the door. Through another door in her closet, she entered a small secret space not even Evie knew about.

Clearing the altar, she lit an oil lamp burner and laid out some new supplies – hawthorn, sulfur powder, the finely ground bones of a money cat. She added each to her mortar and pestle, then a few drops of her own blood and a pinch of earth. After muddling, she tipped the mortar's contents into a silver bowl and placed it on the burner.

The flame blackened the metal and smoke rose in a thin trickle out of the dish. A shiver of anticipation brought goose-bumps out on her skin. She smiled at her own cleverness. 'Let me see through his eyes,' she whispered.

The smoke fanned out until it became an undulating screen. Images flickered in the smoke, the edges blurred and ragged. She reached out, smoothing the smoke with her hands. The images began to clear.

Dropping her hands, she sat back and watched what her power had wrought. A girl came into view, one Aliza had never seen before. Must be the ghosty one. Aliza frowned. Ghosts were pretty useless when it came to getting them under your control. Damn things did whatever they wanted.

Now, the one watching the ghost girl, Doc, the varcolai who'd brought Evie the drugs that had turned her to stone, he was going to come in handy. Aliza laughed, a dark sound that pleased her to the core of her witchy, black-magic soul.

Tucked against Doc's side, Fi lay still and dreaming, the sheen of perspiration gleaming on her chest. She shimmered in and out of her ghost form, something she couldn't control during sleep. The next time she went corporeal, he brushed a strand of soft brown hair off her cheek. She didn't wake or shift, so he risked a kiss to her pale forehead.

Unlike his woman, sleep eluded him. Even after making love. Fine with him. He didn't want to relive that damn dream again, but he couldn't just lie here either, thinking about what it all might mean.

He crept out of their room and eased the door shut behind him, praying the whirring fan covered the door's telltale squeak. He'd meant to oil that about three hundred days ago. Waiting several seconds, he listened, but there was no sound from Fi.

Only a few hours until dawn. The solars were depleted this late, leaving the narrow passages on the old abandoned freighter completely dark. He made his way by memory, catching a shadow here and there where a solar had a hint of power left in it.

The last door took him onto the ship's main deck. The smell of salt water, oily refuse, and fish greeted him. The smell of home since Mal had found him and nursed him back to health. He stretched, the ache in his body matching the ache in his soul. He *needed* to run. Every night since he'd regained his ability to shift into his natural, animal form of a leopard, the urge to run had pressed on him like a junkie's craving for a hit.

He chalked it up to the years he'd spent with no other outlet than the form of a house cat. Who wouldn't want to run after that?

In a fluid move, he leaped across the deck, shifting in midair and landing on all fours in his natural state. The world opened up to him, the scents and colors and sounds intensifying, automatically categorized and processed by his animal brain. Which one to follow? Which one to ignore? He flipped off his human half and let his leopard side take over.

The evening breeze brought the subtlest hint of something new and unnamable. His ears twitched forward, his whiskers quivered, and every muscle in his body flexed in anticipation.

The hunt was afoot.

He followed the scent for miles, dashing over broken streets and through abandoned lots, past burned out cars and down littered alleyways, mindful of nothing but the chase. The force of it was almost physical, pushing him forward as if something else drove him.

Halfway down a new street, his human memories kicked in and reminded him he'd been here not long ago. The familiar smell of blood slowed him down. He went a few more blocks, keeping to the darkest parts of the sidewalk. Few people were out at this time, but self-preservation was a strong instinct.

A spire rose against the bleak downtown skyline, outlined by the faint nudge of dawn just as it had been in his night terror.

Fear clawed at him. He should go, get back to Fi. His brain decided otherwise, shifting him into human form to break the desire to run. He hadn't intended to, but seeing this through might be the only way to ditch the bad dreams. He stalked forward, found a way into the dilapidated church, and crept quietly through the sanctuary. In the mask of shadows, he listened and found what he was looking for. A heartbeat.

Using it as a beacon, he continued through the maze of rooms until he came to the one he'd peeked in on before. The door was open, a single hand-cranked light giving the room a soft glow.

Preacher sat in a rocker, a baby cradled in his arms, silent tears wetting his face. He rocked slowly, singing a lullaby. Or a hymn.

Doc couldn't take his eyes off the sight. He felt glued to the spot, even though his instincts told him enough was enough.

A breath of wind sighed past Doc, enough to carry his scent. Preacher's eyes opened. He tensed, nostrils flaring. 'Who's there?' he called out, shielding the child with his arms.

The words broke Doc's concentration and he backed up, searching for a way out that wouldn't put him in Preacher's direct sight line. There was none. He sank into the shadows. He'd have to run for it. A few sounds came from the room Preacher was in – the rocking chair squeaked, the child shifted and yawned, fabric brushed over fabric, metal hissed as it was removed from leather. Preacher was preparing to fight.

'I know there's a shifter out there,' Preacher said. 'If you're the one who killed Julia, so help me God, I'll turn your hide into a rug.'

Footsteps approached. Doc darted back out to the sanctuary. Was Julia the comarré Doc had seen here before? The girl who was one of Dominic's comarré. The same girl he'd been dreaming about. Dammit. Was that who Preacher had had the baby with? Doc ducked behind a pew as Preacher skidded into the open. A knife sank into the wood above him.

'Come out, shifter. Face your end like a man. I'll kill you fast and painless and you can go to hell where you belong.'

'I don't know anything about Julia,' Doc answered, trying to buy time. From his spot in a low crouch on the floor, he kept track of Preacher's position while inching backward under the pews and toward the door. If he could just get outside, he could shift and put enough distance between them to be safe.

'Doesn't matter. You've seen the child. You have to die.'

'I don't care about the kid.' Although he knew a lot of people would. A half-vampire child, especially one whose vampire father could daywalk – the black market potential for the child's blood alone was astronomical. An urge rose up in him to see the child again.

Preacher edged down one side. 'Your words mean nothing.'

Doc pushed out from underneath the pews and crawled to the

main aisle, opposite where Preacher stood. The double doors he'd come in were closed. A car drove by, lights shining through what remained of one stained-glass window. It was about the only one that wasn't boarded up. Hopefully he could shift and jump through it before Preacher recognized him. Doc didn't need him showing up at the freighter with his threats and crazy talk.

Doc took a deep breath and leaped, shifting in midair as he had on the freighter. He ducked his broad head to protect his soft nose. Glass shattered, most of it glancing off his sleek furred body. A sharp stinging in his flank made him yowl. He hit the sidewalk and his rear leg went out from under him. Preacher's blade had found its target.

He twisted to yank the dagger out with his teeth, then, limping, set off as fast as he could. If the coming dawn was enough to keep the trail of blood he was leaving from attracting fringe vampires, he just might make it home.

Chapter Eight

Mal paced outside of the signumist's apartments while Chrysabelle made her final arrangements and said good-bye. The hall disappeared in a haze of anger and screaming voices until all that remained were two jagged white lines. His hands fisted, his body tensed like piano wire.

Those scars on her back were his fault. *Yes*. His. Not Creek's. *No*. She'd gone to the Aurelian to get an answer for him, not the Kubai Mata. *You almost got her killed. Monster.* Rage boiled up in Mal. For once the voices were right. Barely quelling a howl, he punched the wall. Concrete crumbled, lines cracking out from the impact. He pulled his fist away, mindless to the pain, mindless to the crunch of broken bones as he flexed his fingers. The voices laughed. Mindless to everything except the hard, ridged flesh streaking alongside Chrysabelle's spine.

Because of his arrogance, she'd paid. His blood may have saved her life, but it had done nothing to preserve the perfection of her body, nothing to save her from all that pain. He punched the wall a second time, leaving blood on the concrete.

She was right to hate him. He hated himself. *Who doesn't hate you?*

The exterior door whooshed open and Chrysabelle emerged. It slid shut and became part of the wall again. She pointed her prop cane toward the crumbling hole across from him. 'What happened?'

'Nothing.' *Liar liar liar.*

'Oh good. I was afraid it was something else for me to deal with. Happy to hear everything's fine. Should probably tell Dominic his walls are leaking blood.' She twisted away and headed down the corridor, her cane lightly tapping the floor.

Son of a priest. He went after her. 'Sorry isn't good enough for what I did to you, but I *am* sorry. If there is anything I can do to make it up to you—'

She stopped. 'There isn't.' Her gaze dropped to a spot between them. 'Except for helping me get through these next few days.' Her head lifted and she met his eyes again. 'Without drama, without threats, without making me wish I'd said no.'

'I can do that.' *No, you can't.* In theory. He'd been who he was for five centuries. *Five hundred years of killing and terrorizing.* Changing now wasn't exactly as easy as putting on a different T-shirt. But if it meant being at her side and being able to protect her, he'd find a way. Even if it killed him. *If only.*

'Can you?'

'Yes.' *Liar liar liar.*

'All right, then. I just need to speak to Mortalis and then we can go.' She started walking again.

He matched her stride. 'Anything I can help with?'

'No.' She kept silent a few moments. 'It doesn't matter now, so you might as well know. He's been keeping the ring safe for me.'

Mal just nodded.

'No comment?' she asked.

'No.'

Her brows lifted, but her mouth thinned with obvious disbelief. 'How quickly the leopard changes its spots.'

He slanted his eyes at her. 'The spots might change, but the teeth are still as sharp.' *Show her.*

'So noted.'

Little more passed between them until they emerged on the main floor of Seven. They found Mortalis in Greed dealing with a gambling dispute. They waited until he was finished, then she motioned him over. 'I need what you're holding for me.'

He glanced at Mal, then back at her. 'I'll get it as soon as I can. Hopefully by tomorrow night.'

'Fine. Do you want me to meet you back here?'

'No. Too dangerous. I'll come to your house.'

She nodded. 'I'll be there. Thank you.'

'You're welcome.' His gaze went back to Mal. 'Sun's coming up. Need a car?'

'It's taken care of,' Chrysabelle replied before he could answer. 'I'll see you tomorrow.'

Taken care of? Mal kept his mouth shut with great effort, despite the voices' pestering.

'Good night, then.'

As Mortalis went back to work, they made a quick exit. The driver Chrysabelle had hired, a varcolai named Jerem, had the car idling one street over. He jumped out and opened her door before she could reach for the handle.

When the door shut, Mal spoke. 'I appreciate the ride home,

but I could have let Mortalis take care of it. You should be home, resting.'

She tapped her cane. 'This is just for show, remember? And I'm not giving you a ride home. Not to your home anyway.'

'You're not?' He sat back. 'Where *am* I going, then?'

'My house.' She sank deeper into her seat and stared out the window like she'd said something about the weather or how pretty the sky was or wasn't it nice to see Mortalis again.

Her house. Maybe she's going to try to kill you at last. Was this one of those times he should shut up and let things happen, or should he ask? *Ask.* Damn, this new-leaf business was hard work.

Minutes ticked by before she said anything. 'No questions? My, my, you are giving this your all, aren't you?' She looked at him, a wicked smile bending her lush mouth. 'How are you not hyperventilating?'

'I've never hyperventilated. I don't even breathe, for crying out loud.' Hades on a cracker, he wanted to kiss her in the worst way. Literally. With fang. *Bite her. Drain her. Kill her.*

'You know what I mean.'

He shrugged and took his own turn looking through the helioglazed windows. The best games had two players. 'I'm doing what you asked. Is that a problem?'

'No.'

They rode the rest of the way to her house in silence, Mal dying to know what was going on in her head because he knew what was going on in his. Torturous thoughts about why she might be taking him to her house. Most of which started with them undressing each other and ended with him kissing the scars he'd caused before spending the day memorizing every silky, golden inch of her, making her writhe with pleasure and pant his name. He tried to exhale the heat building in his body.

That couldn't be the reason she was taking him home.

Could it?

Chrysabelle's enjoyment of Mal's discomfort turned to real concern as they pulled through the gates of her estate. He leaned forward with a hard gasp.

She laid a hand on his back before she realized that she'd touched him. She pulled her hand away. 'What's wrong?'

'Dominic moves fast. Your new guests are moved in.' Glints of silver danced in his eyes as he straightened. 'The scent of comarré blood is thick as smoke. I wasn't prepared for it.'

Indeed, the lights in the guesthouse were on. 'Fast is right. He must have really wanted rid of them.' She shook her head, sighing. 'I truly don't need the company right now.'

'You should have taken me home.'

'I didn't mean you.' But when she looked back at him, she understood. His eyes were still silver-tinged, his fangs jutting past his lip. He needed blood. 'I know what you want. We'll take care of it.'

'I'm fine.'

'*I'm* fine. *You're* a bad liar. I'm perfectly capable of providing you with blood.'

'I don't need—'

'Remember how you were going to leave the arguing and the drama behind?'

Hardening his mouth into a narrow line, he crossed his arms and leaned back.

She slid closer. 'I know you're dying to say something.' Maybe as much as she was dying to be in his arms. No matter what had passed between them, no matter that he made her mad enough to punch a few walls herself, something about him felt like a safe place to her.

He nodded toward the house. 'Creek's here.'

'Nice change of subject. I saw his motorcycle parked by the gate when we drove through.'

Creek's lean, shadowy form sat on the base of the fountain in the center of the circular drive. Even in silhouette, there was a lethal energy to the Kubai Mata. It was one of the things he shared with Mal. Like the way both men made her body tighten in anticipation. Of what, she refused to acknowledge. She smoothed the edge of her tunic. Anything not to look at either of them for a moment.

Jerem parked the car on the curve closest to the front of the house and came around to open her door. She glanced over her shoulder at Mal before she got out. 'Relax. You're the only one spending the night.' So far, anyway.

She turned away before his shocked expression caused her to laugh. If Mal wanted to be with her, he would do so under her terms.

Creek walked toward her, his face twisted in a mix of concern, upset, and longing. His hands flexed like he wanted to touch her. 'You look pretty good for someone who didn't have the strength to take visitors for the last eight days.'

She leaned on her cane. 'I had my reasons for not seeing you.' But the anger she'd worked up toward him was fading fast, just like it had with Mal. It was hard to blame them when they so clearly wanted what was best for her. Not that she'd asked them to take on that concern.

He jerked his chin toward something behind her. 'But not Mal?'

'No, me too.' Mal walked up to stand beside her. 'She's mad at both of us.'

Creek nodded, his big, fight-scarred hands clenched so that the words *hold* and *fast* tattooed across his knuckles stood out. 'I figured that. Would've been nice to have the chance to apologize, though.'

'Is that what you're here for now?' she asked. He wasn't getting off so easy, no matter how much she was cooling down about the whole thing.

'Yes. But that's not all.'

'Come in, then,' she said. 'We'll discuss it inside.' Creek might as well find out now what was going on. It would save Mal the trouble of filling him in later. Velimai opened the door before Chrysabelle got two feet on the landing.

Are they both coming in? she signed.

'Yes.' Trying to keep them out at this point was a waste of energy, something Chrysabelle was losing quickly. Twinges of pain danced along her spine, small torments of what would come later. Maybe the excursion to Seven had been more than she was ready for. It was her first trip out of the house since the incident.

Velimai's fingers kept going. *You look tired. I can send them home.*

No, Chrysabelle signed back, keeping the conversation private. *I'm well enough to do what needs to be done. I need some sugar, something to get my energy up.*

Velimai nodded and glided off to the kitchen. Chrysabelle made her way into the living room and eased onto one of the leather chairs so neither Creek nor Mal would try to sit by her. A little distance would help hide her weakness. The last thing she wanted was Mal and Creek freaking out and adopting some ridiculous protective stance. They did that well enough without her giving them an excuse. She gestured with the cane at the couches as the two men entered the room. 'Sit.'

Mal narrowed his eyes, giving Creek a look. 'Be warned. She's gotten bossy. Bossier.'

Creek snorted, his icy-blue eyes sparkling. 'I like bossy women.' Was he that happy she'd let him in? Or just happy to see her again?

'Not enough to listen to them,' Chrysabelle shot back, earning a half smile from Mal.

Creek settled onto one of the sofas. 'Point taken.'

She waited until Mal took the other sofa. The juicer whirred to life in the kitchen. 'What's on your mind, Creek?'

'Besides how good it is to see you healed up?' He leaned forward, elbows on his knees. 'Where to start?' He stared past her, his mouth tight. 'One of Dominic's comarré was murdered tonight.'

Mal shifted forward. 'How do you know?'

'I found the body.' Creek shook his head as if the image were stuck in his brain. 'Real mess. Whoever did it stripped the gold out of her skin. Or tried to. Blood everywhere. Place was crawling with fringe.'

Chrysabelle forgot her aching back. 'Holy mother.'

Velimai came in carrying a glass of pineapple juice. Her eyes held a thousand questions as she handed the juice to Chrysabelle.

'One of Dominic's comarré was killed,' Chrysabelle filled her in. 'Stay if you want.' She tipped her head to the empty end of the sofa Creek occupied. Velimai sat, tucking her feet underneath her slim form. Chrysabelle took a long swallow of the juice.

Creek continued. 'Not just any comarré either. The girl was the mayor's daughter.'

Mal cursed softly. 'If Dominic knew who that girl was and let her work for him anyway, he's a fool. Does he know about the murder yet?'

'If he doesn't, he will soon,' Creek answered. 'There were more fringe and othernaturals around the crime scene than humans.'

Mal turned and shot Creek a look, but Chrysabelle caught it. She knew what he was thinking, so she said it out loud. 'You think it was Tatiana? You think she's sending me a message? Letting me know she's here?'

Both men looked at her. Creek spoke first. 'This wasn't just a case of a vampire who drank too much. She was shredded. Someone meant to make an example of her.' He leaned back. 'We can't rule out Tatiana at this point.'

She drained the last of the juice, then stood and walked toward the back wall of glass doors. The lit pool glowed, but beyond that only the narrowest hint of dawn broke the blackness. When Tatiana had burned the *Heliotrope*, the dock had gone up in flames, too, taking out the dock's security lights. 'Creek, a while back you told me Algernon was some sort of KM double agent. Does the KM have anyone in Corvinestri now who can tell us if Tatiana's there or if she's already come back here?'

She watched his reflection in the glass. 'I can find out. No promises. They don't always give me that kind of information, and when they do, I'm definitely not supposed to be sharing it.'

'Understood.'

He hesitated, like he had more to say.

She faced them again. 'What?'

He glanced at her, then at Mal, then back to her. 'The mayor has threatened to charge me with her daughter's death.'

'What?' Chrysabelle's brow furrowed. 'That's ridiculous. Doesn't she see what's going on in the city? You're the last person who should be on her suspect list.'

Creek tipped his head to one side and lifted his brows. 'I agree, but as I was covered in the girl's blood from holding her while she died, they see it differently.'

Mal stood and paced a few steps. 'The mayor better wake up and realize the things going on in this city aren't just going to magically resolve themselves.'

'I explained to her about the covenant and, well . . . I tried to explain. Even outed her bodyguard as a varcolai.'

Mal snorted. 'Bet he didn't take too kindly to that.'

'No, he didn't.' Creek sighed. 'I don't know if she's ignorant by choice or if she's just having a hard time facing reality or what.'

'Come Samhain, she won't have a choice,' Chrysabelle said.

'Yeah, I know,' Creek answered. 'Anyway, I offered to introduce her to some genuine othernaturals.'

Chrysabelle went back to her seat beside Velimai. The sky was almost purple now. 'You want me to talk to Mortalis? Maybe we could get his girlfriend, Nyssa—'

'No.' Creek shook his head slowly. 'I told her I'd bring you and Mal. She wants to meet a real comarré. Try to understand what her daughter was doing. I figured Mal would be the icing on the cake.'

Velimai laughed, a wheezy sound like wind through a screen.

Mal froze. 'You want me to teach the mayor Vampire 101? Why not just paint a target on my back?' He cut his hands through the air. 'No bloody way.'

'When?' Chrysabelle asked.

'Tomorrow night.'

'I can't. I already have plans.' Mortalis would be bringing her the ring. The mayor could wait.

Mal made an unhappy noise. 'She's going to see Dominic's signumist.'

Creek frowned. 'What for?'

She gave Mal a look. Why couldn't he keep his mouth shut? 'So much for not causing any more drama.'

He shrugged. 'I'm not causing drama. You're the one who's going to get your signum put back in.'

Velimai squealed, one of the few verbalizations she had that didn't cause death in vampires. Her fingers began moving rapid-fire.

'What the hell?' Creek's whole body jerked back. 'Why the hell would you do that?'

Mal answered, looking smug. 'She plans on going back to the Aurelian.'

'I can speak for myself, thank you.' She rolled her eyes before walking back toward her chair. 'Velimai, it's all right. Calm down. I can't read when you sign that fast anyway.' She stopped and sat between Velimai and Creek. 'I need more information about my brother so I can find him. All she told me was that I would know him by his signum. Like that's any help. All comarré have the same two basic sets of signum, just in different patterns and variations according to the signumist's style. The last five sets are different for women and men.'

Creek still looked dumbfounded. 'I understand wanting to find your brother, but there's got to be another way. After what they did to you, how could you want to go back there?'

Velimai nodded.

Chrysabelle patted the wysper's leg, careful not to make skin contact. 'If I can open another portal and you two can protect it from being closed, I can come back that way without ever stepping foot in the Primoris Domus. I'll be perfectly safe.'

'Yeah,' Creek said. 'Because the Aurelian is such a warm, fluffy bunny of a woman.'

Mal threw up his hands. 'My point exactly. Not to mention the pain of enduring those signum when she's not even properly healed.'

Fed up with being talked about instead of talked to, Chrysabelle stood. 'What I'm going to do is not open for discussion. I don't care if you agree or not. I'm doing it. You're either with me or you're not, and if you're not, you'd better stay out of my way or, as the holy mother is my witness, I will remove you myself with whatever means necessary.'

Creek and Mal went mercifully silent. Neither of them made eye contact with her for a few moments. Finally Mal looked up.

'I'm with you. You know that. I don't agree, but I'm not going to stand in your way. I'll do whatever needs doing.'

Creek nodded, his gaze meeting hers again. 'What he said. Although there's one little thing that might need taking care of first.'

She put her hands on her hips. 'And that is?'

'After I found the comarré's body this evening, but before I went to speak to the mayor, I got into a little fight.' He rubbed at his shoulder. 'I've never seen one before in real life, but I'm pretty sure it was one of the ancient ones.'

'Castus?' she whispered, not daring to say the whole name out loud.

'Yes.'

She slumped back down onto the couch. 'I guess we'd better go see the mayor after all.'

Chapter Nine

Standing in the middle of an all-too-familiar hangar, Tatiana stretched. Being cooped up with Laurent on the plane was almost as bad as being back in New Florida. 'Wretched place,' she muttered, trying to find the energy to get through the next few days, because she wasn't going to last much longer than that. Wearing Daciana's skin wasn't as draining as wearing that of a varcolai or a remnant, but it still required a heavy usage of power. Combined with the creeping fog of daysleep, she was ready to pass out, but a few moments away from Daciana's husband was worth fighting off the tiredness for.

'What was that, love?' Laurent asked as he strode down the jet stairs. He stopped beside her, looking far too pleased with how things were going. Apparently, and despite his age, he'd never dreamed he'd make Elder, due to the politics afoot in the House of Tepes. A topic she'd listened to ad nauseam on the plane ride over.

'Nothing.' At the last moment, she remembered to smile pleasantly.

Laurent smiled back, sympathy in his daysleep-weary eyes.

'My poor pet. Traveling doesn't agree with you, does it? Not to worry.' Struggling with a yawn, he held up the dossier Tatiana had given him. Any spare moment he wasn't chatting her up, he was reading through it. 'I have Tatiana's instructions and directions to the safe house. As soon as the sun goes down, I'll commandeer a vehicle and we'll be on our way. We'll get settled in, then head out to the comarré's home. Until then, let's get back in the plane and bunk down. I'm knackered. Not sure how you're upright.'

Because I'm not Daciana, you twit. How she wished she were home with Octavian. Or Octavian was here with her, but someone had to keep an eye on Daciana, make sure she stayed contained in the suite of rooms they'd prepared. 'Yes, of course, we should sleep. I was just so excited to see New Florida.'

He put his arm around her. 'I'm going to do a bang-up job of this mission. Make Tatiana proud. Make it impossible for her not to appoint me Elder.'

Her skin itched where he touched her. She managed to hold on to the sickly sweet countenance Daciana seemed to favor. Bloody good chance the prissy miss wasn't smiling now. 'I guess we'd better sleep, then, hadn't we? So we're fresh for the mission.' *And so you'll stop touching me.*

He kissed her temple. 'Back in you go, then.'

She swallowed the urge to gag. 'Yes. See you at twilight.' She scooted past him, hoping to make it to the bed before there was any more touching.

He swatted her backside as she left. 'Twilight it is, my pet. Then I'll do what I've come to do and we'll be on our way home to get what we deserve.'

'Indeed.' Tatiana laughed softly. He might get what he deserved a lot sooner if he touched her like that one more time.

If only she could kill him and go back to being herself, but she couldn't take the chance the council might find out she'd left Corvinestri. If things went according to plan, she'd nab Chrysabelle, get the ring once and for all, and be back before anyone was the wiser.

Then she'd kill him. And his simpering wife.

Doc woke up to a shriek and the sound of flies buzzing. 'What? What? I'm up.' Pain radiated from his left hamstring. He pushed up onto his hands, the freighter's deck gritty beneath him.

'You're hurt. What are you doing out here anyway? What happened?' Fi hovered over him, literally.

Fortunately he'd collapsed in a shaded part of the deck. Unfortunately, the wound Preacher had given him hadn't completely healed and was oozing pus and a slight stench. Which was drawing the flies. 'Damn, that's nasty.' He reached for a metal stanchion and pulled himself up. 'What time is it?'

'Almost nine. Stop stalling and answer my questions.' Fi punched his arm lightly. 'What happened? Who did this to you?'

'Preacher.' Doc twisted to look at his injury. 'And apparently he puts some kind of poison on his blades.'

Fi looked at his leg. 'Is that why you didn't heal?'

He nodded. 'And why I passed out before I got inside. I don't even remember getting here. I think it's mostly out of my system, but I better clean that thing.'

'Why did you go see Preacher? Last I knew you were asleep next to me. When did you leave?'

'After we . . . you know. You were asleep and I couldn't. Kept thinking about that nightmare and how real it felt. I couldn't shake the urge to check things out for myself.'

Fi crossed her arms. 'You are telling Mal about this immediately.'

He nodded again. When she was right, she was right. 'Yeah, I agree. Things are weird.'

She reached for him. 'You can explain weird while we get you inside and start cleaning that leg.'

He put his arm around her shoulders and, limping a little, let her lead him into the freighter. 'In my dream last night, I killed the comarré I saw at Preacher's. When I went there last night, Preacher threatened me, said if I was the one who killed Julia, he'd turn my hide into a rug.'

They followed the main corridor to the galley. Fi pulled a chair out for him and he sat on the edge. 'I think Julia must be the comarré he had the baby with, but how can she be dead? I dreamed it, but I didn't do it.' At least he didn't think he had.

Fi cranked the tap and filled a bowl with steaming water. Solar made sure they never had a lack of that. 'Of course you didn't kill her. Just because you kill someone in a dream doesn't mean it really happens. If she's dead, someone else did it.' She threw a few clean towels over her shoulder, hooked a finger through the ancient med kit, then hoisted the bowl of water with both hands and carried it all to the table. 'You need to lose those jeans.'

He raised a brow.

'So I can clean that cut. Save the cute for later.'

'I'm making a mental note of that.' He stood and dropped trou.

'Good. Now bend over the table.'

'I love when you talk dirty to me.' He did as she asked, resting his forearms on the old Formica top.

'Stop changing the subject.' She dipped a towel into the water, then wrung it out. 'What else was weird?'

He inhaled as she laid the hot towel against his wound. It was a good distraction from the question. 'Holy crap, that's hot.'

'Needs to be to get the poison out. Now, what was weird?'

Like a dog with a bone. He shook his head, unwilling to mention how he'd felt coerced while he was there. Like an unseen force had wanted him to look at the child. It was just natural varcolai curiosity, that was all. 'Seeing Preacher with a baby isn't weird enough?'

She removed the towel, rinsed it, and started wiping at the cut. 'Yeah, but it's not new weird. You've known about that for over a week. What else?'

He gritted his teeth against the pain and twisted to watch her work. 'Nothing. Are you almost done?'

She flicked his thigh with her finger. 'You're a bad liar. We're going to see Mal after I wrap this.' She applied a layer of ointment, then fished out a roll of gauze.

'I'm not waking him out of daysleep.'

'I will. I don't care if he gets mad at me. He needs to know what's going on.' She secured the gauze with tape and looked up at him. 'Done. Pants. Let's go.'

He hitched his jeans up and zipped them, giving her a wink. 'You woke up on the pushy side of the bed this morning.'

'Pushy?' She stood and gave him an appraising look. 'You left after we made love last night. You're lucky I didn't wake up stabby.' She pointed at the bowl of water and first-aid kit. 'You can clean this up after we talk to Mal.'

He surrendered, hands up. 'Will do. Let's go see the old man. But first . . . ' He grabbed her and kissed her hard, letting her go a long minute later. 'Thanks for fixing me up.'

'Bothersome creature,' she whispered, her cheeks flushing. Squirming out of his arms, she grabbed his hand and tugged him down the hall toward Mal's room. The solars were bright this time of day, but the passage dimmed as they approached Mal's. Here a section of solars had been removed to keep the light to a minimum when he slept.

Doc stopped a few feet from his door. He tipped his head and kept his voice down. 'Go ahead. You wake him.'

'Coward,' she teased, reaching her fisted hand toward the door. She knocked softly. 'Mal? Can we talk—'

The door swung open. The room was empty.

Chapter Ten

Ting, ting, ting.

The soft chiming opened Chrysabelle's eyes, erasing the remnants of the dream lingering in her subconscious. Velimai stood near the bed, ringing a small crystal bell. Chrysabelle yawned and sat up, pushing the hair off her neck. 'What is it?'

Velimai set the bell down on the nightstand and signed, *Mortalis is here. He won't come in.*

Suddenly more awake, Chrysabelle's heart rate kicked up a notch. Mortalis was early. And about to hand her the ring that had started all this trouble.

The ring that was going to change her life once again.

She nodded. 'Let me get dressed and I'll be right down. Mal and Creek still sleeping?' Because of the late hour last night, she'd let both men stay. *Not* because she needed the protection with a Castus in town and not because Mal's presence would assure the guest comarré stayed in their own quarters. Those were just perks.

Velimai shook her head. *Doorbell woke them both. Breakfast?*

'That would be great. I'm sure Creek's hungry after his fight last night. And I can always eat. Mal . . . ' Mal's need for blood hung in the air like a bad smell. 'I guess I can't send Mal to the guesthouse for his breakfast, can I? Wouldn't be very hospitable of me.'

They should contribute something, Velimai signed, a wicked glint in her soft gray eyes.

'Vel, you're a bad influence. Is there any blood in the fridge?'

Yes, but it's old.

'It'll have to do. I could use the strength the exchange would give me, but I am not kissing Mal right now.' Although she'd planned to last night. Just like she'd planned to let him stay anyway before Creek had shown up.

You tell him that. He doesn't like me. Velimai, whose tolerance of Mal had only grown marginally in the last few weeks, frowned, took the bell, and left.

'Really? Sure it's not the other way around?' Chrysabelle called after her. Kissing Mal while his heart beat with the power of her blood would give her a share of his power, the same exchange that normally happened through a bite. But her emotions, both good and bad, were too close to the surface this morning for such intimate contact.

Shaking her head, she slipped out of bed and stretched slowly. The ache in her back had become a permanent thing. Leaning forward, she took a few deep breaths to push it away. At last she rose and shed her silk nightgown for a white tunic and pants and white leather slippers. A quick brush of her teeth and hair and she was ready. Heading downstairs, she twisted her hair back with a band and inhaled the happy scents of coffee and breakfast wafting up from Velimai's kitchen. In the living room, Creek sat on the edge of one leather sofa while Mal hung

in the most shadowed corner near the foyer. Both men looked
as rested as she felt, which wasn't very. 'Morning.'

'Morning,' Creek said.

Mal lifted his chin toward the door. 'You expecting company?'

'It's Mortalis.'

'Then I'm going back to sleep.' Mal disappeared down the
hall to the windowless interior room he'd racked out in. Built as
a hurricane shelter, it did great double duty protecting the UV-
intolerant, although Maris was probably rolling in her grave that
there was a vampire in her house. Chrysabelle couldn't help but
hope her mother would have thought differently if she'd had a
chance to know Mal.

Creek stood, shifting uncomfortably. 'I'll help Velimai. Give
you some privacy.'

It wasn't necessary, but she appreciated it. 'Thanks. I'll just
be a sec.'

She opened the door and stared out at the empty front porch.
'Mortalis?'

'Here,' he answered, the sound of his voice closer than she'd
expected.

She stared harder, finally picking out the faint outline of the
fae. Shadeux fae couldn't be seen in the sun. 'Will you be visible if you get out of daylight?'

'A little more.'

'Then come in, please.' She moved out of the way.

'Don't you have company?'

'Yes, but they know what's going on.'

'Fine.' He crossed the threshold into the foyer and took on a
slightly more tangible form. 'Look, I don't have good news.'
The barbs on his forearms flexed in and out, like they were
breathing. He was clearly agitated.

'About the ring?'

He looked off to one side for a moment. 'Yes. I don't have it.'

'What? Why? I need that ring. I gave it to you for safekeeping.' Warning bells clanged in her head.

'I know. And it's still safe, but . . . ' He sighed and grabbed hold of one horn, rubbing the hard surface as if he were trying to remove a spot of dirt. He dropped his hand and made eye contact. 'I gave the ring to one of the elektos, a fae council member. They have the ability to cross into the fae plane much more easily than the rest of us. Keeping the ring there means no one can detect it – Castus, vampire, or otherwise.'

'And?' Her patience was thinning.

'And now he won't give it back until he speaks to you in person.'

'What?' Her teeth clenched, her body tensed, and a new spike of pain drove into her back. 'I *need* that ring.'

'I know, I know.' He exhaled and rubbed at his horn again. 'If I had known this would happen, I would have tried to cross into the plane myself, but—'

'Mortalis, I want that ring and I want it now.' She could see why Mal punched walls. 'You tell this elektos that ring is *my* property. If I don't get it back, I will hunt him down and kill him.'

Mortalis swallowed. 'You have every right to be angry.'

'Angry? You're lucky I don't have a blade on me now.'

'Hey,' he snapped. 'I didn't mean for this to happen. I was doing you a favor, remember?'

She cradled her forehead in her fingers. 'Why does he want to speak to me?'

'I don't know.'

'Good. Great.' The pain echoed in other parts of her body

now. 'Let me get armed and we'll go. I want to get this over with as quickly as possible.'

'That's the other part of it. The elektos reside in the haven city of New Orleans.'

She paused for a second. 'And he's not coming here, is he?'

Mortalis's jaw tensed. 'No, he's not.'

She was definitely going to punch something. Maybe the fae in front of her. 'Can't fae transport through glass or something like that?'

'Silver-backed mirrors, yes.'

'So take me that way.'

'I can't. Only fae can travel that way.'

'I have a driver. How long of a trip are we talking?'

'By car?' He winced. 'Thirteen, maybe fourteen hours.'

'Unacceptable. Get Dominic's plane.'

'I can't just take his plane.'

She poked her finger into the chest of one of the world's deadliest creatures. 'You can and you will.'

'I can't and I won't. You want his plane, you ask him.' His expression hardened.

'You two planning on going somewhere?' Creek materialized out of the kitchen to lean against the wall. She knew he expected her to talk to the mayor.

'I was just about to ask that same question.' Mal's voice sounded from the gloomy recesses of the hall behind them. He'd lobbied for them to talk to Dominic first about the dead comarré.

Looked like one of them would get their wish early. Chrysabelle forced herself to unclench her fists and maintain a civil tone. 'Yes. We're going to see Dominic—'

Mortalis glanced toward the wall of windows at the far end

of the living room. 'Now? You're going to wake him from daysleep to ask him for a favor?'

She tipped her head back and stared at the ceiling, taking a deep, cleansing breath before she brought it back down again and looked at Creek. 'We're going to see the mayor.' She turned to Mal. 'Then we're going back to see Dominic.' And finally Mortalis again. 'Then we're getting on a plane and going to New Orleans.'

Mal growled softly. 'Vampires aren't allowed in New Orleans.'

Mortalis nodded. 'Not since the late 1920s.'

'I know,' Mal said. 'I found that out the hard way when I first came to the States.' His mouth settled into a hard line. 'They won't let me in.'

'We'll get you in,' Chrysabelle said. She turned to Mortalis. 'He's coming. And so is Creek. Your fae friend wants to see me, he sees me on my terms. Otherwise, I'll have Creek tell his boss where the missing ring of sorrows is and let the KM deal with it themselves.'

Would it have hurt Mother Nature to make the day cloudy? Aliza squashed her ball cap down over her dreads a little harder. Damn sunlight was hell on albino eyes, and her cheapie sunglasses weren't cutting it. She ducked into a doorway, content to rest a minute in the shadows while she got her bearings according to what she'd seen through the varcolai's eyes. Things looked different in the daylight.

How hard could it be to find the old church? She stared down the street, looking for something familiar, but the slummy buildings and dirty stucco blended into each other block after block.

She started down the street again, skirting a pair of old men squatting on a stoop. Two steps past them and she stopped. 'You know of an old abandoned Catholic church around here?'

'*Si, si,*' one said, smoking a fat cigar. He pointed down the street. 'Is not far, maybe four, five blocks more.'

The other one smiled, revealing yellow teeth. 'You going to pray, *mami*?' He grabbed his crotch. 'You can kneel right here if you'd like.' Both men started laughing.

She pulled down her sunglasses, showing them her nearly colorless gray eyes. 'You're the one who should pray, *amigo*.'

'*Ai! Fantasma,*' the man cried, crossing himself.

The other one spat at her, then threw his hand up, making the sign of horns. '*Fuera!* Go away!'

Laughing, she shoved her sunglasses back into place and took off. Sometimes being albino had its uses. Two blocks down and the church's steeple came into view. She kept walking until the building was just across the street. From there, she took her time, studying the dilapidated structure for a way in that wouldn't make too much noise or arouse too much suspicion.

Not that she cared about the vampire inside. He'd be knocked out with daysleep. It was like a coma, almost impossible to wake them from, and it left them massively sluggish. She would grab the kid and be out of there before the vamp knew what had happened. And if he did wake ... she slid her hand into the messenger bag strung across her body and wrapped her fingers around the wooden stake in the bottom. The bag was empty otherwise. Just enough room for a baby.

She chose a side door shielded by a small porch and tried the knob. Locked. She placed her fingers against the keyhole and shot a small burst of freeing magic into it. Tumblers clicked. She tried it again. This time it turned.

Smiling to herself, she quickly checked the street in both

directions. Assured she wasn't being watched, she opened the door and slipped inside.

She took off her sunglasses as she entered the sanctuary. Incense hung in the air and light streamed through the broken and boarded stained glass, picking up heavy swarms of dust motes and speckling the remaining pews with colored splotches. Everything held a thick layer of grime except for a spot on the kneeling bench in front of the altar and on the altar itself. The bench was shiny with use, and across the way, votive candles flickered in a tiered holder, casting small shadows on the dingy plaster walls. She didn't get how a vampire could live here, but the idea that he might actually worship in this space was weirder still. Her brows lifted and she shook her head. All that mattered was that he'd fathered a child. A half-vampire child.

Her smile returned at the prospect of controlling such a being. Of having it at her beck and call. Of testing the power of its blood.

She listened for the sound of a baby but heard nothing. Maybe the vampire halfling was lost in daysleep like its father. Wouldn't that be grand? Easy to get away with and simple to care for.

Down a hall and through a set of double swinging doors, she started checking rooms. In the last one, she found what she was looking for.

In what reminded her of a nativity scene manger, a pale, pinkish infant slept on an old quilt. Its eyes were closed, dark lashes fringed against its fat cheeks. Tiny fingers curled into fists, one of which rested near its rosebud mouth.

For a brief second, Aliza recalled Evie in her crib, the smell of her peach-fuzz head, the softness of her skin, her dovelike cooing ... but Evie was human. This child was not. Not fully.

Stretched out on a military cot across from the makeshift crib was the halfling's father. The vampire she'd come to kill. He, too, lay with eyes closed, but that was where the similarities ended. His shaved head, camo pants, and khaki-green T-shirt pegged him as the one she'd seen through the shifter's eyes. Ugly cuss.

She reached into her bag, got a good grip on the stake, and inched closer. The baby shifted, making a soft mewling sound. She froze, glancing back at the tiny creature.

A cold hand clamped around her throat while a second snaked around her body and tightened on her wrist, squeezing until her bones ground together. Gasping from the pain, she dropped the stake. It clattered to the floor. The infant's eyes fluttered open.

'You think you can waltz in here and steal my child? You're wrong. Dead wrong.' He shook her, rattling the beads and bones tied into her dreads.

'Take your hands off me, bloodsucker.' She wriggled to get free, but it was no use. He was wickedly strong. Magic was her only hope.

He reeked of blood and formula, two scents Aliza had never smelled together before. 'Did you kill my Julia? Is that why you're here? To kill me and take our child?'

'I don't know what you're talking about.' She remembered he'd mentioned Julia to Doc, too. Must be the halfling's mother. How was this monster not deep in daysleep?

He growled in rage. 'The stench of blood magic and demons covers you, witch. You must be cleansed.'

'Cleanse this, you freak.' She jerked her head back into his nose. The sound of breaking bone rewarded her, but his grip didn't loosen. She worked her fingers around in his direction, bent her head out of the way, and shot a blast of fire at him.

He ducked, taking them both down to the floor. The fire hit the ceiling, spreading along the dropped tin panels and dying out. The baby yowled. The vampire spun Aliza around, pinning her hands with his palms to prevent her from trying the fire trick again and laying his shins over hers. Blood leaked from his broken nose, splattering her face and mouth. She tried to buck him off, but he weighed a freaking ton.

His fangs dropped. 'Who are you working for?'

'Get the hell off me.' She called fire again, this time letting it build in her palms. He'd feel the heat soon enough. 'I ain't telling you anything.'

He snarled, baring his teeth some more. 'Then your time has come to an end.'

Dread wormed into her belly. The fire dancing on her palms died out as she tried a different tact. 'I got a daughter, too, you know. You want to leave another child motherless?'

He leaned down a little more, dripping more blood onto her skin and into her mouth. 'In your case, I would be doing her a favor.'

She spit his blood back at him. 'You son of a—'

The vampire struck, nailing his fangs into her throat. She cried out as much from shock as from the white-hot pain. Her bones went brittle with fear. Death danced in her dwindling field of vision like stars, and as he sucked the life from her body, all she could see in the growing darkness was Evie's face, the only sound she heard the wailing of the child she'd come to steal.

Chapter Eleven

By the time Doc stopped Mal's old sedan by the gate at Chrysabelle's estate, it was after noon. He and Fi had stopped for burgers on the way and eaten in the car. She sat beside him finishing the last of the fries. He spoke toward the intercom. 'Hey, it's Doc. Is Mal with you?'

'Yes, he's here,' Chrysabelle's voice responded through the speaker. 'I'll buzz you through.' A second later the gates swung open.

Fi pointed a fry toward the massive fountain that stood in the center of the circular drive. Parked near it was Creek's V-Rod. 'Chrysabelle got a motorcycle.'

'No, that belongs to Creek, the Kubai Mata I told you about.'

She stuffed the fry into her mouth. 'Is he cute?'

He cocked an eyebrow. 'He's an ex-con with a lotta prison ink and a Mohawk. That sound cute to you? And why do you care?'

She swallowed. 'Just wondering. You think he spent the night or just got here? I mean, if Mal spent the night, then ... just wondering.'

Doc looked over at her. 'You're nosy, you know that?'

'I'm curious.' She raised her brows, smirking. 'Like a cat. There's no crime in that.'

He threw the car into park. 'C'mon, crazy girl. Let's go see Mal and get this over with.'

She grabbed his arm. 'Look. There's people in there.' She nodded toward the guesthouse.

He peered through the palms that screened the smaller house from the main one. The blinds were up, offering a good view into the living room. Two comarré, real comarré, not Dominic's fakes, sat in plain sight. The female paced back and forth while the male watched her from the couch, frowning. 'I'm sure Chrysabelle knows they're there. If she doesn't, she's got bigger problems than we can help her with.'

He grabbed Fi's hand and gave it a playful tug. 'Let's go, busybody.'

As they approached the front door, Chrysabelle opened it. Doc hadn't seen her since she'd been injured. Which was right around the same time he'd regained his ability to shift into his leopard form. 'Hey, you look good.' It wasn't a total lie. She looked tired, but considering that she'd almost died, like, nine days ago, she looked great.

Her smile was thin. 'Thanks. You too.' Her smile grew a little bigger. 'And Fi. Nice to see you both under better circumstances.'

Fi gave a little wave. He nodded. 'That's for damn straight.' He frowned as the scent of blood reached his nose. 'Everything okay? I smell blood.'

'Velimai just poured Mal a glass. Come in.' She led them through the foyer and into the living room. Mal and Creek were already there. Mal sat sipping a glass of dark red liquid, wearing the same clothes he'd had on when they'd dropped him off the day before and looking like he could use a few hours of daysleep. Fi elbowed Doc in an I-told-you-so kind of way. Subtlety was not her strong suit.

'What's up?' He nodded at Mal and gave the Kubai Mata a look. He still didn't trust the man. Not the way he sniffed around Chrysabelle like she was a T-bone and he was a hungry stray.

Mal nodded back. 'All kinds of things. What brings you here?'

'He's got big news.' Fi strolled through the room and climbed into the chair near the back wall of sliding glass doors.

'Fi.' Doc raised his brows. He could do without the help.

She shrugged and picked up a fashion magazine from the nearby table, tapping the cover to animate the model on the front. Fi and clothes. They were her drug.

Mal swallowed and rested his glass on his leg. 'What is it? I don't know how much more news we can deal with right now.'

Chrysabelle took a seat on the couch near Mal. 'He's right. If this isn't important, it's going to have to wait.'

Exhaling hard, Doc shoved his hands in his pockets. 'It's pretty big. Unless you don't consider a vampire child news.'

Silence deafened the room. Mal broke it first. 'There's no such thing.'

'Yeah, there is. Saw it with my own eyes.' He glanced at Fi. She lowered the magazine to give him a reassuring smile. 'It's Preacher's kid. His and one of Dominic's comarré. I think her name's Julia. She might be—'

'Dead,' Creek finished. 'She is.'

Doc squinted at the man. 'How you know that?'

'I found her. She died in my arms. Badly attacked.'

The man had a way of getting involved in all kinds of things he didn't belong involved in. 'When?'

'Last night. Are you sure she's the mother of this child?'

Doc shrugged. 'Pretty sure. Preacher asked me if I was the one who killed *his* Julia. I saw him with a comarré earlier, so I have to assume that's her.'

'You were at Preacher's?' Mal's index finger tapped the glass of blood.

Doc sat on the far arm of Creek's sofa and nodded.

'When?' Mal's tone was less question, more demand.

'Last night.'

'That's when you first saw this vampire child?'

'No. Before then.' Might as well come clean. 'The night Fi and I used the spell Aliza gave me.'

'Wait.' Chrysabelle tipped her head. 'What do you mean *you* and Fi used it? That was for Fi alone, to get her out of that death loop.'

Doc sighed a curse and closed his eyes. Any second now the lectures would start.

'It was my idea,' Fi said. 'I made him go through the smoke.'

Doc opened his eyes, wondering if the gratitude he felt showed on his face. Still, he wasn't going to let Fi take the fall for his actions. 'It was my decision.'

Mal growled. 'It was a stupid decision. You have no idea what kind of dark magic that old witch could have worked on you.'

Doc shrugged like he didn't care. Like he wasn't already thinking Aliza had gotten ahold of him through his dreams. 'What's done is done. Can't change it now.'

'So . . . your curse?' Chrysabelle looked from him to Fi and back again. 'Are you better? Can you shift?'

'Sure can.' He rubbed a hand over his scalp, dreading the next part. 'Been having nightmares, though. That's how I ended up at Preacher's last night. Had to see for myself that what I dreamed wasn't real. But now I know it was.' He moved off the sofa arm onto the cushion, then raised his head to stare directly at Creek. 'You said she was badly attacked, but it was more than that, wasn't it? She was torn up, wasn't she? Shredded.'

'The comarré?' Creek nodded. 'Yes. Like someone tried to strip the gold from her skin. Almost did it, too.'

'Exactly the way I saw it.' Doc dropped his head into his hands. The nightmare replayed itself like news footage.

'You didn't do it, Doc.' Chrysabelle scooted forward. 'You can't hurt people in a dream.'

Creek shifted. 'He should come with us to the mayor's. She's going to want to hear this.'

Doc narrowed his eyes. 'What's the mayor got to do with this?'

Creek stared at him for a long second. 'The dead comarré was her daughter.'

'That's just flippin' great.' Doc muttered a curse that got him a raised brow from Chrysabelle. 'You going to tell her about her grandchild?'

Creek, Mal, and Chrysabelle looked at each other. Chrysabelle spoke first. 'I don't think we should. Not yet anyway. That's a lot of information to process in one lump.'

Mal nodded.

'Agreed,' Creek said before turning back to Doc. 'And just because that's not enough to deal with, there's an ancient one in town.'

Doc leaned back. 'An ancient one?'

'A Castus.' Chrysabelle's eyes held a dark light. 'Like what we were up against at Tatiana's in Corvinestri.'

Doc swore again. 'This day just gets better, doesn't it? What else? Tatiana here yet? Ronan suddenly come back from the dead?'

Mal shook his head. 'Creek's going to work on finding out about Tatiana, but Ronan's not even worth talking about. No vampire could come back after what that gator must have done to him.'

'Also ... ' Chrysabelle raised her hands. 'Mal, Creek, Mortalis, and I are going to see Dominic tonight after we talk to the mayor. We plan on borrowing his plane because I have to go to New Orleans to see the fae elektos about getting the ring back.'

Mal's face darkened, his eyes glinting with silvery displeasure. 'She's getting her signum put back on so she can see the Aurelian one last time.'

Doc wasn't in any position to tell someone what was safe and what wasn't, so he just nodded. Nor did he need to know how the elektos had come by the ring in the first place. 'NOLA isn't a very friendly place for vampires. Hasn't been for years. They know you're coming?' he asked Mal.

'No, but we'll work it out.' He downed the rest of the blood in his glass and set it on the side table.

Chrysabelle nodded. 'Mortalis will be with us, too. The thing is, I'd like you to stay here while we're gone. You and Fi both. With the two new comarré on the property—'

'What's up with that?' Fi interjected.

'Favor to Dominic,' Chrysabelle answered before continuing. 'It would just be nice if you could be here, provide an extra set of eyes.' She exhaled slowly. 'And I think, considering the circumstances, the visiting comarré should stay in the house, too. Regardless of the new security measure I've had installed, it's too dangerous with a Castus on the loose. I may not want them here, but neither do I want them dead.'

'Sure,' Doc said. 'Be happy to.' And in truth he was. Time away from the freighter and the nightmares he'd been having there would be a good thing. Maybe sleeping in a new bed would give him the first peaceful sleep he'd had since walking through Aliza's smoke. And maybe it wouldn't. But Mephisto Island was a long ways from the abandoned shipyard and rusted-out freighter he'd called home for the last few years.

Change could be a good thing.

'You go through weapons like a child goes through sweets,' Argent said, dropping the new halm and crossbow Creek had requested on the workbench he used as a kitchen table. The halm rolled to a stop beside Creek's motorcycle helmet.

Not exactly that fast, Creek thought, but held his tongue. You didn't argue with the sector chief. Not a sector chief who was also a dragon varcolai. He picked up the weapons, tested their weight. They seemed identical to the ones he'd lost. 'It's all in the line of duty.' He turned as Argent did, unwilling to let the dragon-shifter get out of his peripheral range.

'Try not to lose this, too.' Argent tossed something his way.

Creek dropped the halm and caught the sleek black rectangle just in time. It was no bigger than his palm, but weighty enough to be more than just the slab of glass it seemed to be. 'What is it?'

'Tap the front.'

Creek did. It lit up. 'I thought phones were a security issue?' Not to mention crazy expensive since the supplies of rare earth were so tightly controlled.

'This one is completely secure. And for KM use only.' The sector chief stopped and blinked the inner membrane over his unnerving green eyes. 'All the numbers you need are programmed in.'

'How very full service.' Creek tucked the device into his front pocket. Now the KM could find him wherever he was. Hell. Nothing like being monitored 24-7. He'd had enough of that in prison.

Argent rested against one of the steel support poles holding up the sleeping loft. 'This thing that attacked you. You're sure the creature was one of the ancient ones?'

'Positive.' He picked the weapons back up and slid them into place on his chest holster, comforted by their presence against his body. 'What else would light up like that from biting me?'

Argent lifted a brow. 'Any vampire. The brands you wear ensure that level of protection.'

Creek stilled the urge to comment on a level of protection that required being bitten to kick in. But then considering those brands had been burned into his skin in the first place ... He took a few steps back to lean against the sink. He'd kill for a beer, but he needed a clear head for tonight. 'This wasn't a vampire. I've been bitten before; there was never this much fire or this much pain. Trust me.' Not that the KM really trusted its grunts. Not from what he'd seen so far. He was just a tiny cog in what he suspected was a very large machine.

Argent eyed Creek's V-Rod just like he always did. The lure of chrome was too much for him. Dragons might have a high heat tolerance, but they had a serious weakness for shine, which was why Creek kept the thing polished as best he could. Any distraction with Argent was a welcome one. The varcolai took a few steps toward the bike. 'Where are you with getting the ring back?'

Lying by omission was still lying, but it didn't exactly feel like oath-breaking either. 'I'm progressing. I know it's not in the comarré's possession, but I'm working on finding out who has it.' A little truth, a little half-truth. And now a change of subject. 'Something new has come up. One of Seven's manufactured comarré was murdered. Turned out to be the mayor's daughter. Mayor thinks I know something since I'm the one who found the body, but I've offered to educate her a little on what's happening in exchange for removing me from the investigation's focus.'

Argent's gaze stayed fixed on the machine. 'The KM supersedes the mayor's power. You don't need to do anything for her.'

'If I'm to live and work in this city, I do.' He checked his watch. He had to do it soon, too. He'd promised to be back at Chrysabelle's by dusk. That gave him thirty minutes to get out of here and to her house. 'Getting on her bad side will only make my job harder. If she feels indebted to me, I can use that down the road.'

Argent shrugged as he strolled slowly around the motorcycle. He trailed a finger over the handlebars. 'Suit yourself. But we need that ring back. Samhain is tomorrow night.'

'What do you think could happen?'

Argent stilled and looked at him. 'That ring has the power to raise and command an army of undead souls. With the covenant broken, the wrong person gets hold of that ring and even the KM may not be able to save the world from the hell that's unleashed.'

Damn. 'Thanks for the info.' Creek studied the varcolai, thankful Argent couldn't read his mind. If he, Mal, and Chrysabelle couldn't get things taken care of in New Orleans and be back before tomorrow night, the KM wasn't going to be happy. Hell, they weren't happy with him now. Wait until they found out he'd voluntarily let Chrysabelle have the ring and that she planned on melting it down and embedding it into her skin.

Could the ring's power transfer into her? Did she even know what the ring's power was? Not that it mattered. Chrysabelle wasn't exactly the world-domination type. Which reminded him of a woman who was. 'I could use a little intel.'

'On?' The sector chief's nostrils flared like he was trying to smell the chrome.

'Tatiana. I know we had a source in Corvinestri. Did we get a replacement after Algernon's death? Because I need to know Tatiana's status from them.' He moved away from the sink and grabbed his jacket from the hook by the stairs, hoping Argent would take the hint.

Argent's head whipped back around. 'KM deep-ops are above your pay grade.'

Creek held his hands up, his leather jacket swinging from his fingers. 'I'm not asking who the source is. I don't want to know. I just want to use them to make my job a little easier. That is what they're there for, isn't it?'

'Yes.' If Argent had feathers, they would have smoothed. 'You suspect she's here, then.'

'Don't know.' He slid the coat on, then scooped his helmet off the workbench. 'Since the Castus is, that could mean she is, too. Or the Castus has found another way of getting the ring. Maybe she's screwed up one too many times. Maybe they're no longer using her.'

Argent half shifted, a sure sign that this conversation was near its end. Wing tips jutted from behind his back, his forked tongue flicking out to lick his lips. 'I'll see what I can find out.

Regardless, you follow your leads, get that ring back. If it's used tomorrow night, the world will never be the same place again.'

Creek snorted before he could catch himself. 'It's not now. And it certainly won't be after tomorrow night.'

Argent shifted completely, his eyes hooding with a darkness that seemed both threatening and worried. 'What it is and what it could be are as different as heaven and hell, because hell is exactly what this world will turn into if that ring gets slipped onto the right finger.'

Chapter Twelve

'Ma?' Evie called as she entered the house. She let the screen door slam behind her to announce her presence further. 'Ma, you here?' Not that Evie expected an answer. The airboat normally parked beneath the house was gone, and she'd been phoning the house for hours without an answer. Evie's left eye fluttered involuntarily for a second, then calmed. Damn spasms were getting worse. 'Ma, where the heck are you?' Wasn't like the old woman to go into town without asking if Evie needed anything. Or even to be gone without anyone knowing where she was. She was the coven leader. She had to be available.

'Anyone home?' she asked the empty space. A coffee cup and breakfast dishes sat in the sink. She passed the kitchen and went into the living room. TV was off. The demon was at rest in his aquarium, which meant only a boiling mass of black-red smoke was visible. Her mother's bag, usually on the side table next to her recliner, was gone. What could be keeping her in town this long? It would be dark in an hour.

Evie flicked one long, clear-polished nail against the

aquarium to wake the demon up. Since being unfrozen from her stone prison, the twitching made it impossible to give herself a decent manicure with colored polish.

The smoke shifted and the demon roused enough to form a face within the smoke, nothing else. Daylight wasn't its best time. 'What do you want, human?'

'Find the ring yet?'

He sneered. 'No.'

'Where's my mother?'

A flicker of a smile. 'Gone.'

'I know that. Where?'

'Not my problem.' He closed his eyes.

She picked up the spray bottle of holy water and gave him a spritz. Flames shot up from the aquarium as if she'd just doused hot charcoal with butane. She squinted at the heat.

The demon burst up through the fire. 'Human, you try me.'

'Where is my mother?'

'I told you I do not know.'

'Use your power. You're connected to her. To both of us. I know you are – our blood is mixed with the vampire's we used to draw you. Find her.'

Nostrils flaring, he lowered his head. His eyes went almost completely black for a few seconds before returning to their usual red. 'She's not on this plane.'

'What the hell is that supposed to mean?' She planted her hands on her hips. 'Speak English.'

Wisps of smoke curled from his forehead. 'I cannot sense her.'

Evie threw her hands up. 'Just like you can't sense the ring. I'm not sure what good you are, demon.' She leaned toward him, her right shoulder suddenly hitching up. She hugged her arm to her body, trying to hold it still. 'I can't wait to destroy you.'

He smiled, reminding Evie of the body they'd found floating in one of the marshes. Time in the sun had tightened the skin into a very similar look. 'I eagerly await your attempt.'

'You think I can't do it? You have no idea, demon.' The years she'd spent in her stone prison had not been wasted. She'd cast and recast spells in her head until she dreamed them better than she'd done them in real life. What else was there?

It was how she had a feeling where her mother might be. Or at least how she'd gotten there. She gave the demon an exaggerated grin as she walked away. 'You just sit tight. I've got some work to do.'

Her mother had a secret room, one Evie had never known about until her stone statue had been positioned in front of the glass windows overlooking the glades. Amazing how those windows worked as mirrors at night. How the angle of the mirror on the living room wall reflected her mother's room and the door into her closet. Made no sense why her mother would spend hours in that closet. Not at first anyway.

Evie opened the closet door. The scent of smoke lingered, the last reassurance of what she already knew. It wasn't uncommon for a witch to have a private altar. Evie'd had one in her old bedroom, just a simple wooden box she kept tucked under the bed. Nothing like the one she had now in the new house the demon had built for her.

She felt behind the clothes, along the wall, her movements releasing the fragrance of patchouli clinging to her mother's things. Evie's hand sank into a strange dimple on the wall. She pressed it and the click of a latch being released caused her to nod. A shiver ran down her spine.

She pushed the clothes back, gripped the protruding edge, and opened the door. The smell of burned eggs and earth greeted her. She felt for a switch, found it, and flipped it.

Atop a small altar were the trimmings of the spell her mother had worked to fix the ghost girl's troubles. The one she'd inlaid with a trap for the varcolai she'd known would pass through the smoke as well. More than that, Evie could tell by the arrangement of things and the freshly burned wick on the oil lamp that her mother had opened the trap and used it. Her disappearance meant the trap had worked. She was out hunting down whatever she'd discovered through the varcolai's eyes. If she was gone this long, she'd found something good.

Evie kneeled on the pillow before the altar and set about opening the trap again. She threaded a new wick through the oil lamp and lit it, then picked up the mortar and pestle, giving it a good sniff. It seemed her mother had been so sure about her secret room that she'd left all the ingredients sitting out. There was no need to sift through her mother's supplies for the hawthorn, sulfur powder, and ground bones of a money cat Evie smelled in the mortar, because they all still sat on the altar. Another nearby container held silver filings, but those wouldn't be necessary to open the portal, since it was tied into the original spell. Although . . . she picked up the vial of silver filings. Her mother had them laid out but, based on the leftovers in the bowl, hadn't used them. Silver would strengthen the spell, make it possible to control the subject's movement and actions, but it would also make the spell heavy-handed. The subject would feel the control.

She weighed the vial in her hand, her fingers twitching. Screw whether or not the varcolai knew what was happening. She needed to find her mother.

A heavy pinch of silver went into the bowl, then she tipped a little of each of the first three in as well. That done, she pricked her finger with the blade beside the pestle and squeezed in a few drops of her own blood. Last went in the pinch of earth necessary to ground the magic. She crushed the contents together with the pestle, then tipped them into a flame-blackened silver bowl and placed it on the burner.

The flame licked the metal, heating the mess until a curl of dirty smoke spiraled out of the dish. She smiled. 'Like mother like daughter.' Didn't hurt that this was the last spell her mother had taught her before the fateful night.

She bent closer, watching the smoke spread out like a curtain. 'Show me what the one joined to this spell sees.' Hopefully she'd find out where her mother had gone. The demon's words that her mother was no longer on this plane rang in Evie's ears as shapes and movement wavered on the surface of the smoke. Pushing the meaning of those words away, she smoothed the smoke until the images became clearer.

She would find her mother. She glanced back in the direction of the demon. If anything had happened to Ma, anything at all, Evie would bring hellfire down upon the person responsible.

At the sound of Laurent walking toward the dining room, Tatiana bent over the dossier he'd left splayed out on the table, fixing her face as though she were intently studying the detailed notes. She had every intention of getting through the next few hours as quickly as possible. Giving Laurent no reason to question his wife's knowledge of Tatiana's information would go a long way in that direction.

'Evening, my pet.' He kissed the top of her head. 'No need to wear yourself out memorizing all this information.' He scooped the papers away from her and into the leather portfolio. 'I know the dossier inside and out. I should have no trouble apprehending the comarré at her home this evening, then we'll return to Corvinestri tonight. Tatiana will be pleased, don't you think?'

'Very.' Tatiana smiled, and for once it wasn't forced.

He tucked the portfolio under his arm. 'Not sure why she couldn't accomplish this herself the first time she was here. Doesn't say much about her as a leader.'

Her smile vanished. 'Do you think it's wise to speak of her so boldly?'

He laughed. 'What? You think this house has ears?' He shrugged. 'I don't worry about such things and neither should you. She's a dangerous woman, yes, but one who relies more on muscle than brains.'

Tatiana knew her eyes must be silvering but didn't care. She shivered with the force of repressed anger, playing it off as fear. 'You risk what I wouldn't.'

He chucked a knuckle under her chin with more force than seem warranted for such a gesture. 'That's why I'm the man and you're the woman.' He glanced around. 'You have the satchel of supplies she sent?'

How did Daciana stomach this buffoon? 'Yes.' Tatiana touched the small pouch tucked into her interior jacket pocket.

'Then let's go. This place wears on me. It has no character, no sense of history. I'll be happy to leave it behind and return to Corvinestri to claim my new position.'

That makes two of us, Tatiana thought. But if she could help it, only one of them would be returning. And it would not be Laurent.

Chapter Thirteen

Just from watching the subtle play between Mal and Chrysabelle in the car, Creek knew she'd made her choice and it wasn't him. He was okay with that. Not happy. But okay. The more he got to know Mal, the more Creek understood the vampire wasn't the monster he believed himself to be. He clearly cared for Chrysabelle and would do anything to protect her. Creek could respect that. Didn't mean he wasn't going to watch out for her, too.

The guards at the mayor's gate had let them pass but not the car, so now the car was parked on the street and the three of them strolled toward the front door of the mayor's house. Havoc stood on the porch waiting for them. From the expression the shifter wore, it was clear he hadn't expected Creek to actually show up with a vampire and a comarré.

'Havoc.' Creek nodded, knowing his smug look wouldn't help the already-icy relations between them, but proving people wrong felt damn good. Not as good as walking out of the Florida State Pen, but close.

'Creek.' He lifted his chin, indicating Mal and Chrysabelle. 'I take it these are the guests you promised the mayor?'

'That's right.' Like Havoc didn't already know that. What varcolai couldn't identify a vampire? And Chrysabelle, hell, anyone who saw those signum would know she was something special.

'Gotta be frisked.'

Chrysabelle shook her head. 'Touch me and you'll sing soprano, wolfie.'

Creek and Mal looked at each other simultaneously. The new Chrysabelle was a real kick in the pants. Creek stepped up to defuse the situation as best he could. 'She's got blades on her, nothing else. Same for the vampire. I've got my halm and crossbow. None of us will use the weapons. Especially not them.' He nodded at Mal and Chrysabelle. 'They're here to help me.'

'Doesn't matter. They don't get in to see the mayor carrying anything sharper than a button.' He put one hand on his hip, sliding his leather jacket back enough to reveal the piece holstered on his side.

Mal snorted.

Creek's brows pulled together. 'You really think that's going to stop a vampire or a comarré?' Or a KM for that matter, but no point in giving away more than necessary.

Havoc's face registered no emotion. 'The bullets are hollow-tipped silver, quenched in holy water. So hot I can't load them without gloves.' Creek glanced at Chrysabelle. Her sacre were also hot, made to do lasting damage to the undead. 'They may not stop the vampire, but they sure will tickle. The comarré I'm not concerned with.'

Mal laughed. 'Then you clearly haven't met one before.' He turned to Creek. 'Look, we showed up. Did our part. I'm ready to go—'

The door behind Havoc opened a few inches, spilling light

and the mayor's familiar flowery-limey scent into the evening air. 'Is there a problem, John?'

Without taking his eyes off them, he leaned back. 'Ma'am, Creek's back with the alleged vampire and comarré, but they're armed and refuse to give up their weapons.'

'Armed with what?'

'Blades only.'

After a brief pause, she spoke again. 'Let them in, but you stay with them. Now. I'm tired of waiting and not knowing.'

'Madam Mayor,' Creek said. 'The vampire needs to be invited inside.'

Realization lit Havoc's eyes. He tipped his head toward the mayor again. 'I don't think that's such a great idea, ma'am. Perhaps you could meet them in your office at city hall.'

Before she could answer, Chrysabelle spoke up. 'We meet now or not at all. I have other business to take care of this evening.'

A small snort of disbelief answered them, followed by, 'Fine. You are all invited in. John, keep a close watch.'

He jerked his head in a quick acknowledgment. 'Yes, ma'am.' The door shut. 'You heard her. But one move I don't like and I'll ask after I shoot. Got it?'

Chrysabelle stood at Creek's side. 'Yes, we get it. Let's go. Filling the mayor in on what goes bump in the night isn't my evening's top priority. I want this over with as much as you do.'

Creek walked to the door and opened it. 'You heard the lady.'

Havoc kept Chrysabelle at his side as he guided them through the house and into the living room Creek had been in the night before. The mayor sat facing them, a tablet PC balanced on her knees. Creek caught the dull gleam of nickel-plated metal tucked behind the pillow under her elbow. A gun. Probably the same one he'd suspected her of having earlier.

The mayor waved her hand over the PC, darkening the screen, then set it beside her chair and looked at him expectantly. 'These are the people you told me about.'

'Yes.' Creek held his palm toward Chrysabelle. 'Chrysabelle Lapointe. She is a comarré. One of the originals, not a . . .' He searched for the right word, one that wouldn't offend the mayor.

'Not a counterfeit like your daughter,' Chrysabelle supplied. 'I am very sorry to hear about her death. My sympathies.'

But the sincerity sounded thin in her words. Creek understood Chrysabelle had a lot on her mind, but the mayor might not get that.

The mayor's mouth bent a little and she nodded. 'Thank you.' Her reply was as falsely genuine as Chrysabelle's. At least both women were on the same page. 'Lapointe. Any relation to Maris Lapointe? Her cosmetics company makes its headquarters here.'

'She was my mother. I am the figurehead CEO of Lapointe Cosmetics now.'

The mayor tipped her head slightly to the side. '*Was* your mother?'

'She died about a month ago.'

'I'm sorry to hear that. Your mother was a very generous woman.'

Chrysabelle's body stiffened. 'You knew her?'

'I had the pleasure of meeting her a few times at various fund-raisers.'

Chrysabelle nodded and seemed to retreat within herself. Memories, maybe. Questions more likely. Creek cleared his throat and pointed at Mal. 'This is Malkolm Bourreau. He's a noble vampire. The nobility are considered a superior class to fringe vampires, which are mostly what live in this city and the rest of the continental U.S. Or what's left of it. The nobility prefer Europe and the Middle East.'

The mayor's gaze narrowed on Mal with laserlike focus. '*Noble* vampire? Seems like an oxymoron to me.'

'Doesn't it, though?' Mal stared back just as hard. 'You should know I'm not nobility anymore. I'm anathema. An outcast.'

'Why is that?' the mayor asked.

Mal waited the space of a breath. 'I killed my sire.'

Something they had in common, Creek thought. 'I'm sure you'd like to hear about the comarré, Madam Mayor.'

Ignoring Creek, the mayor stood, walked around the coffee table that separated them, and stopped in front of Mal. 'I can sense that you're not exactly human, but how do I know it's not some kind of trick? Prove you're a vampire.'

Mal shot Creek a look that spoke volumes. Like *crazy*. And *death wish*.

'Go easy,' Creek muttered, but it was too late.

Mal shifted his human face away, flashing fangs and silver eyes along with the hard angles of his true self. The mayor cursed in Spanish, stumbling backward and crossing herself. Havoc pulled his weapon.

Chrysabelle stepped between Mal and the mayor, throwing a hand up at Havoc. 'You got what you asked for, Madam Mayor. Call off your dog.'

The mayor's mouth closed slowly, her gaze flitting from Chrysabelle to Mal. She nodded, finally glancing at Havoc. Her eyes hardened. 'You think this is a game? You think to scare me? I am not someone you want to make an enemy of.'

Mal's face went back to human. 'I did what you asked. Your reaction is not my problem.'

Chrysabelle flashed a look at him, then went back to the mayor. 'We're here at your bequest, yet you threaten us. You're human, and this world you live in, the one you think is so safe? It isn't. Not anymore.'

'My daughter is dead. I am aware of the world we live in.'

Chrysabelle shook her head and dropped her hands with a sigh. 'If you'll keep an open mind and understand that we're not here to hurt you, I will answer whatever questions you have within reason. I have other matters I must attend to this evening.'

The mayor hesitated, studying the group before her with an expression Creek couldn't fully read. She seemed torn between wanting to know more and tossing them out. Finally, she pointed to the couches. 'Sit.'

Chrysabelle took a spot on the couch nearest the mayor, Mal beside her. Creek sat opposite on the other couch. Havoc stayed standing, arms loose at his sides. The mayor went back to her seat, her fingers disappearing beneath the pillow at her side. 'Chrysabelle – may I call you that?'

'Yes.'

'Thank you. You may call me Lola. Tell me what you think I should know.'

Chrysabelle rubbed a hand over her mouth, her sleeve slipping back enough to reveal the sheaths of her wrist blades. 'There was a covenant in place that kept a level of peace between humans and othernaturals. Humans weren't able to sense the othernaturals that lived among them, and after a while, humans forgot the othernaturals had ever been real. They became fairy tales and nightmares and fantasies. In that way, the othernaturals were protected from being hunted and killed by the mortals whose world they inhabited. It became an unwritten rule among most othernaturals that humans were to be left alone in all aspects. For almost a thousand years, this covenant held fast.'

'But that has changed?'

'Yes. The covenant was broken.'

The mayor uncrossed her legs only to recross them in the opposite direction. 'When?'

'About a month ago.'

'About the time your mother passed?'

Creek ached for Chrysabelle in a way he hadn't expected. This had to be hard for her.

She nodded slowly. 'My mother was comarré like me, only she kept her signum hidden. Her death was . . . instrumental in the breaking of the covenant.'

The mayor's brow wrinkled. 'Was she some kind of keeper of this covenant?'

'No. She was the human sacrifice that broke it.'

'*Ay yi yi*,' the mayor whispered. 'How awful. Your mother was a good woman. She did not deserve such an end.'

'I couldn't agree with you more.' Liquid edged the lower rims of Chrysabelle's eyes, but sparks of anger lit them from within. 'You should also know the vampire who killed her might be here in Paradise City.'

Fear bent the mayor's mouth. 'Why?'

'She wants something I have.'

The mayor's mouth opened and a small, strangled sound came out. She rose from the chair, her hands trembling as they clasped before her. 'My daughter. She looked just like you when she died.'

Chrysabelle glanced at Mal, then Creek before making eye contact with the mayor again and giving the barest of nods. 'I know what you're thinking. Because I've been thinking it, too.'

Doc lounged on the sofa in the living room, a beer in one hand and the remote for Chrysabelle's holovision TV in the other. It was a mighty big change from the freighter, despite the crowd in the house.

Not that any of them were around. The visiting comarré had retreated to their guest suite right after Velimai had introduced them to Doc. Then she and Fi had headed off to the kitchen to whip up some dinner. Fi was picking up the fae's sign language fast. Her laughter and favorite radio station drifted out from the kitchen. She was probably dancing to the music. He turned the volume up on the TV a little. Life hadn't been this easy in forever. If only it could be this way all the time. His gut told him it wouldn't last so he'd best enjoy it while he could.

Maybe later he'd get Fi into the hot tub. With a wicked grin, he channel surfed until he found a football game. Fi came in as he set the remote down.

He smiled. 'What's up, baby? Dinner ready? Smells great.'

'No, not ready yet.' She put her hands on her hips and shook her head at the beer. 'Aren't you supposed to be protecting us?'

'Relax. Chrysabelle's place is wired up like Fort Knox. No one's getting on the grounds, and even if someone did, there's a wysper in that kitchen who could open her mouth and turn them into bloody pulp in a few seconds. And now that I can fully shift, I'm no slouch in the hard-core dangerous department either.' He patted the cushion next to him. 'Sit down and chill, baby girl. Let's enjoy a quiet evening in the kind of luxury we'd normally have to pay for.'

She crossed her arms. Damn. Not going for it one bit. 'The last time Tatiana crossed the woman in the kitchen, Velimai ended up bloody and broken. And do I need to remind you what Tatiana did to me?'

Point taken. 'All right. I'll do a little patrol outside. Maybe send the comar out after dinner to do the same. Cool?'

'Cool.' She smiled as she leaned down to kiss him. 'Love you.' With a wink she scampered back to the kitchen.

'Dinner had better be tight,' he called after her. With a sigh, he set his beer down and headed for the front door, leaving the TV on. The things he did . . .

He shut the door behind him and paused to let his senses work their magic. Everything sounded right, smelled right. Then the compulsion hit him. It wasn't as subtle as the time he'd woken up from the nightmare and felt the urge to run and investigate Preacher and the old church. No, this was like a hand forcing him forward. Like another mind inside his head.

His feet started moving, and he began a tour of the grounds, investigating every small thing. Every nuance of the estate became more interesting. He finished walking the grounds and stared at the house. He should try to get back inside. Maybe it would help. But he'd been inside the church and that hadn't offered any protection.

The compulsion pushed him again, this time to inspect the house. He walked around it. The new security lights did a decent job of dispelling shadows, but the eerie feeling of being watched through his own eyes hung on him like a desperate woman.

The thought brought Aliza's name to the forefront of his thinking. He knew in his gut she was behind this. Ignoring his suspicions wasn't going to make the truth go away. When he'd

passed through the smoke that had set Fi right, he'd somehow
put himself under the witch's control. He'd known that was a
possibility when he did it, but being whole again had been too
strong a temptation.

Now he was paying the price.

He was back at the front door, but his feet wouldn't take him
inside. 'Fi!'

His body turned him around and started moving him around
the side of the house toward the garage entrance. It wanted him
in the car. He yelled for Fi again as he tried to resist by dragging
his feet. 'Fi, get out here, now.' Nothing. Dammit. 'Velimai! Fi!'

The compulsion was screwing with his head, pushing him
back to where he'd felt it the last time. Preacher's. Under no circumstances did he want to step foot in that freak's joint without
backup. Preacher's need to protect his child had turned his crazy
up to eleven.

Doc searched his brain for some way to fight Aliza off, but in
the fog of the spell, the only thing he could think of was to shift.

Like an involuntary shiver, it was upon him and done. In
leopard form, he stood on the cobblestoned sidewalk that led
from Chrysabelle's circular drive and connected the main house
to the guesthouse and secondary garage. Beneath his paw pads,
the stones were warm from the day's heat. All traces of the compulsion were gone. Shifting had kicked it out of his system like
a bad habit. He let the nocturnal sounds roll over him. The low
buzz of insects filled the air more than usual. He inhaled and his
nose wrinkled at a sudden wash of bitterness. There was only
one kind of monster that smelled like that. Vampir—

*Leave the property. Go back to where you last felt the com-
pulsion.*

The need to warn the people in the house weakened until he

couldn't hang on to it. He took a few steps forward, yowling softly in his throat because it was the only opposition he could manage. There was something he needed to do, to tell Fi. *Go.* He trotted toward the gate, which he nudged open with his big head, then slipped out and started down the road, his direction clear.

The gate clanged shut behind him and the last unaltered thought faded from his brain.

Shifting had made the spell stronger.

Chapter Fourteen

Tatiana came back together wasp by wasp as Laurent did the same beside her. They'd left the car parked near a boat ramp in a public park not far from Mephisto Island. If things went as planned, they'd be driving straight to the hangar and be in Corvinestri for breakfast. For now they were on the back edge of the comarré's property, near the waterline. A few charred pilings were all that remained of the dock. She smiled. That destruction was her handiwork. As was this whole brilliant plan.

The front gate wasn't visible from here, but her ears easily picked up the sound of the pedestrian entrance opening and closing. As they'd flown overhead, they'd seen the leopard on the front drive headed toward the gate. A shifter no doubt, here to protect the comarré maybe, but he was leaving. Why, she didn't know, didn't care. The animal was gone, one less thing to worry about.

Laurent brushed himself off, but his head was lifted, his nostrils widening to take in the air. His fangs were out and his mouth open. 'No mistaking there's a comarré nearby with that scent in the air, is there? Hells bells, I miss mine.' He gave his jacket a tug. 'I cannot wait to be home.'

'Nor can I.' She fished in the bag at her hip and extracted two pairs of earplugs. 'Here.' She tossed a pair to Laurent, then wiggled hers into place. The specially designed iron-mesh inserts negated the effects of a wysper's scream. He put his in while studying the landscape.

They couldn't get into the house without an invitation, so the plan was to make enough noise to bring someone outside, then use that someone as a negotiating point to get the comarré. Unless they got lucky and the comarré was the one who came out to investigate. The girl was so stupid there was a good chance she would.

Laurent pointed toward the house, then indicated that Daciana should go to one side to make the distraction while he went to the front to capture whoever came out. Tatiana had planned it that way to feed his ego and protect herself. Her metal hand was proof of the comarré's dangerousness. If he ended up ashed, she'd still have time to scatter and save herself. It was perfect, really.

They headed toward the house together, she with a fat roll of fireworks and he with chloroform, steel cable zip ties, and a body bag for the captured comarré. When the path separated around the pool, they did, too. He had sixty seconds to get into place near the front door before she lit the combustibles near the guesthouse.

Counting off the time, she slipped through the shadows, working her way toward the edge of the property. She started across a small patch of grass. A tiny click sounded when she lifted her foot, a sound so soft she knew human ears would never have picked it up. It hadn't sounded like an insect, but in this hellish jungle of a state, who knew. She ignored it and kept going. She heard it a second time when she reached the guesthouse. It seemed like it had come from the grass. She stomped her foot down and ground it into the grass. Whatever was living in there wasn't anymore.

Tatiana flattened herself against the building, pulling the firecrackers and lighter from her waist bag as she ticked off the last remaining seconds. On three, she flicked the lighter under the fuse. On two, it burst into flame. On one, she tossed it into the yard and ducked behind a windowless part of the guesthouse.

The fireworks went off like gunshots, cracking through the night's silence and reverberating over the water. Another few seconds into the noise and new sounds emerged from the house. The sounds of movement and scuffling, then the noise they'd anticipated. The wysper's scream.

Despite the earplugs, it raked through her like sharpened tines until even her fangs ached. The sound was her cue to run, which was exactly what Laurent would be doing. If he wasn't dead.

She leaped the security wall into the neighboring estate, making her exit from there and speeding back toward the car. Laurent joined her there a few minutes later, a full body bag slung over his bleeding shoulder, the scent of ash thick around him.

'Darling,' she purred. 'Did you get hurt?'

'Damn hot blade, sliced right through my shoulder. Going to be a nasty scar.' He patted the limp, female figure shrouded in plastic. 'Other than that, the evening went rather well. I managed to get a few licks in myself before bagging our prize.'

Sheer delight sucked a gasp from her. Bloody hell. The prat

had done it. She clapped her hands as she imagined Daciana might. 'Let me see her!'

Laurent frowned. 'Don't be foolish, Daciana. You know what comarré look like. Get in the car. I want to go home.'

Lola's skin no longer itched with the desire to flee. No, that feeling had been replaced by vision-blurring anger. She worked to unclench her jaw. 'You think this vampire killed my daughter because she thought Julia was you?'

'No, she knows what I look like.' Chrysabelle leaned back in her seat, her mouth a hard, determined line. This was not a woman Lola wanted to be on the wrong side of. 'I believe Tatiana killed your daughter to show me she was here, to show me what she would do to me when she had the chance.'

The anger turned red-hot. A *vampire*. What good would a gun do against such a monstrous creature? 'My daughter's life was worth more than being someone's calling card. Why is this vampire after you?'

'I agree about your daughter's life.' Chrysabelle bent her head for a moment, sighing, then she lifted her gaze to Lola. 'Tatiana wants something I have. I won't tell you what. To do so would only put you in danger.' Chrysabelle's eyes stayed focused on Lola like a challenge.

Yes, Lola thought. *She hides the information from me for my benefit.* It made her want to spit. Instead, she kept her composure, such as it was, and focused on the problem of such a creature loose in her city. 'I will help you find this Tatiana, then, and kill her. What do you need?'

The comarré shook her head. 'We're not even sure she's in town.'

Lola slapped her hand down on the chair's arm, causing

John's eyes to widen. Of course, he'd seen her upset, but never angry like this. Time he learned the extent of her temper. 'Then who killed my daughter? The police have told me nothing so far.'

John cleared his throat. 'It's only been two days. I'm sure they'll come up with something.'

'They'd better.' She exhaled through her nose, trying to find a molecule of calm. 'It was this vampire, I feel it.' She jutted her chin toward Malkolm. 'You, you're one of her kind. You know this vampire that killed Julia? How do we stop her?'

His eyes narrowed imperceptibly. '*We?* You're human. What do you think you can do?'

'Answer the question, vampire.'

His jaw popped to one side before realigning itself. 'I know her well enough. Stopping her is not going to be easy. She's very powerful. Too powerful.'

Lola stood and walked to the wet bar. She splashed rum into a tumbler and swallowed half of it. It burned down her throat, matching her mood. She turned and leaned against the counter. 'Everyone has a weakness. What is hers?'

The comarré looked at the vampire. Creek watched them with interest. Lola could tell they were all thinking the same thing, but from the looks on their faces, they would not be sharing that thing with her. Chrysabelle tucked some hair behind her ear, her gold marks flashing light.

Had Julia looked like that? She'd not seen her daughter in so long and then to see her lying bloody in the street, torn apart and broken ... Lola drowned the image in the remaining rum. The liquid heat seared away the threatening tears. 'Well? What is it?'

'Power. She wants power.'

More exchanged glances before Chrysabelle answered,

'Which is why she wants the thing she thinks I have. It isn't in my possession at the moment but it will be. Soon. Which is why I can't stay here much longer.'

Lola went back to her seat, but only took the edge, putting herself closer to the comarré. 'I may be human, but I have my own kind of power as mayor. I have people and resources. I will do whatever I can to bring this monster down. You go and get this thing, then, but when you return, you come back here immediately. Your friends can educate me some more while you're gone.'

Malkolm's brows lifted. 'First of all, Creek and I are going with her. Secondly, there seems to be an implied "or else" in that statement.'

She narrowed her eyes and met his gaze without flinching. 'Or else I will turn this city against you. Declare open season on Paradise City's newest plague. Vampires, shape-shifters, whatever else is out there. There will not be a moment's peace. And I will make sure they know you're the reason. *Comprendes*?'

His eyes flashed sliver like they had earlier but his face stayed human. He would have been beautiful if not for what lurked beneath. His upper lip twitched in a partial sneer. 'I understand.'

'Do you?' she challenged him. 'Tell me, then.'

'I understand you think you have some power.' The silver faded a little. 'I also understand you are mistaken, but then, like many humans, you have no real idea of what you're up against until there are fangs in your flesh.'

The words should have frightened her. Instead her pulse surged with an entirely different emotion. One her husband had not aroused in her for many years during their marriage. Was this another of the monster's powers? She swallowed, tasting the sweetness of the rum on her tongue, and lifted her head with an arrogance meant to match his. 'You and Chrysabelle may go, but Creek will stay here. With me. No discussion or I will have him arrested immediately.

'You two will return within twenty-four hours with this *thing* the vampire wants and a plan to take her down or your friend' – she pointed at Creek – 'will be charged with Julia's murder and remanded to the state penitentiary immediately upon arrest. This time, there will be no early parole. I will make sure of that.'

She stood, made quick eye contact with John, then turned and walked away. 'You are dismissed.'

Chapter Fifteen

Fi ran back into Chrysabelle's house, her stomach a queasy mass of knots, her mind a million whirling thoughts coming as fast as her breath. 'Doc? Doc! Where are you?'

Damian, the new comar, ran in behind her. Blood dripped from his sacre, a slice across his ribs and a second on his shoulder. Velimai followed, a nasty bruise on her cheek.

Panic rose in Fi's chest like bile. If not for Chrysabelle's new security system alerting them to someone on the grounds, they might all be dead. Which made it all the more important she find Doc. 'Have you seen Doc? Is he still outside? He went out there to patrol the grounds.'

'I didn't see him. That vampire . . . ' Damian blinked hard and took a step back toward the door. He grimaced in pain. 'Got Saraphina.' He staggered. His sacre dropped out of his hand and clattered to the floor. 'I think there was poison on that bastard's blade.' He went to his knees and his eyes rolled back in his head as he collapsed.

Fi rushed to him, cradling his head. Velimai kneeled beside

Fi. Her fingers started to move, but Fi's brain was in no place to process.

'I don't know what you're saying. Can you take care of him while I go look for Doc?'

Velimai nodded and made motions toward the door like Fi should go.

'Thank you. I'll be back as soon as I can.' She took off for the door, then skidded to a stop. 'If I don't come back or if anything happens to me, I've gone after Doc and I've got a pretty good idea that if he's dea—' She couldn't bring herself to speak the word. 'If he's not here, he went to Preacher's. That'll be my next stop.'

Velimai signed, *Okay*. Then her hands twisted in the sign for luck.

Fi dashed outside. Saraphina's sacre lay on the ground, glowing softly in the security lights. Fi scooped it up. She wasn't entirely sure how to handle a blade like that, but it was better than being totally unarmed. 'Doc?' she said softly, suddenly unsure if she was completely alone. They'd only seen one vampire, but the underground motion sensors had picked up movement in the side yard *and* in the front yard where Damian had taken a hit and Saraphina had been snatched. They shouldn't have gone outside, but with Velimai's scream to protect them . . . Except that hadn't worked for some reason.

Fi hadn't recognized the male vampire, but that didn't mean Tatiana wasn't involved. She stayed close to the house as she made her way around. Doc wasn't anywhere. She set the sword down and shifted to her ghost self, then floated above the roofline until she could see the entire property. No Doc, but Mal's old sedan was still there. That meant if Doc had left, he'd done it on four feet.

Back to the ground and corporeal form. She grabbed the sacre and jumped into the car, laying the blade on the seat next to her. Keys were in the ignition. It had been a long time since she'd driven, but in her current state of mind, she could probably fly a plane if she had to. Doc needed her. She could feel it. The engine jumped to life. She programmed the GPS for Umberto's in Little Havana, the only landmark she could think of there. A minute later, Mephisto Island was disappearing in her rearview mirror.

The drive felt like it took a year and a half, enough time for her to formulate a plan if Doc wasn't at Preacher's. She knew that Mal was with Creek and Chrysabelle and that the three of them planned on going to New Orleans with Mortalis as soon as Dominic gave them permission to use his plane, so her best bet was to hit Seven and see if she could catch them there if Preacher's didn't pan out.

If she missed them, then . . . she didn't know what. Wait for them to get back? While who knew what was going on with Doc? Didn't seem like a very good option. There was always a chance he'd gone back to the freighter. But why would he leave Chrysabelle's without telling Fi where he was going?

Deep down in the recesses of her mind, she knew why. She just didn't want to give credence to the thought because that seemed too much like making it real.

The witch's spell. The smoke they'd both walked through in the belly of the freighter. The one that had made them both whole again. She would have closed her eyes if she hadn't been driving. If the witch had done something to Doc with that spell . . . Fi exhaled a sigh that was almost a sob. It was her fault. She'd convinced Doc to go through the smoke. Whatever was going on, she had to find him.

On the street ahead the neon lights from Umberto's restaurant shone like a carnival ride. Little Havana was mostly dark otherwise, a few dull glimmers from windows where folks were up and still had juice in their solars. If Umberto's could afford to run their electric, business must be good. She drove by slowly to look through the bars on the windows. Place was full.

A block up, she found a parking spot under one of the dim streetlights. She parked and got out, tucking the sacre through the belt in her jeans. In other parts of Paradise City, walking around with a sword hanging off your hip might attract attention, but in Little Havana, people did what they had to do to stay safe.

Putting on her best touch-me-and-die attitude, she strolled to Umberto's and went inside. The customers gave her and her sword a wide berth, and while her Spanish was passable, she didn't understand a lot of the things being said. Still, it was pretty plain they weren't exactly thrilled an *Americana* with a three-foot sword had just interrupted their *ropa vieja*.

She beelined for the bar, finding an open space with no problem. *'Hola.'*

The bartender, a fat man with a thin mustache and a wandering eye, waddled over wiping a glass with a rag of questionable cleanliness. Lovely. He nodded at her. *'Buenas noches. Que te puedo hacer?'*

'Hables ingles?'

'Si. What do you want to drink?'

'Nothing. I need some information.'

He cocked one eyebrow. 'I have paying customers, *señorita.'*

'I just want to know where the old Catholic church is.'

He shrugged. 'And people at the other end of the bar want more *cervezas*. It is a cruel, cruel world.'

Time mattered more than playing games with this butt munch. She dug into the pocket of her jeans, pulled out a twenty, and slid it toward him. 'Where's the church?'

He took the plastic bill and tucked it into his shirt pocket. 'You don't want to go there. *Muy peligroso.*'

She already knew it was dangerous. What she needed to know was its location. Her hand went to the sword's hilt without too much thought. 'Tell me. Now.'

'Or what? You going to cut me, *comebola*?' He laughed and a stream of Spanish slipped past his puffy lips too fast for her to understand.

If only Mal were here. One look at his vampire face and this guy would need fresh pants. *His face.* The image gave her an idea. Mal wasn't the only one with a second nature. She'd never done it before, but she had nothing to lose. The next step was whipping out the sword, and that was a big step. She climbed onto a bar stool, leaned over, and grabbed Fatty by his shirt. When he was inches from her, she called up the darkest part of her ghostly presence. The part she'd used to haunt Mal in the years after he'd killed her. The part she'd hidden away when Doc had come into her life.

The dark emptiness of death spread through her, trying to transform her whole being, but she used her anger to control it and hold it on her face alone.

Fatty dropped the rag he'd been holding. *'Santa Maria.'* He scrabbled at her fingers, trying to pluck them off his shirt. His black eyes reflected her sunken ones, the deep hollows of her cheeks, the torn and ruined flesh of her neck. *'La iglesia—'*

'In English,' she said, the words as gravelly and cold as the darkness within her.

'The church is that way.' He pointed, hand shaking. 'Two blocks down, two blocks right, one left.'

She released him and the ugliness she'd summoned, sliding off the bar stool and back to her feet. '*Muchas gracias,* fat boy.' She sauntered out of the bar, making deliberate eye contact with any customer who looked her way. Few did.

She drove the man's directions as fast as she could, saving the last block to walk. If Preacher was there, if he had Doc, a little surprise could be good. The tiniest bit of light twinkled through the church's few remaining stained-glass panels. She tried the massive double doors, but they didn't budge at the first try and she didn't fight them for fear Preacher would hear her.

On the side she found an open door tucked under a small overhang. Cautiously, her hand on the hilt of the sacre, she crept inside. The twinkle she'd seen coming through the windows came from a stand of votive candles flickering in red glass cups. She hung by the door, letting her eyes adjust while she scanned for Preacher or Doc.

She didn't see or hear either of them, so she ventured into the sanctuary. A worn spot marked the floor before the altar. Like someone kneeled there a lot.

A cold hand grabbed her arm, yanking her fingers off the sacre's hilt. 'Witch! Have you come for your mother?'

Fi jerked away, but Preacher's grip was too strong. Why couldn't vampires make more noise? 'What? No. I—'

'Good, because you won't find her. She's dead.' A little dried blood clung to the corner of his mouth. He must have been out feeding.

'Who? Who's dead?'

'The witch you sent to steal my child.'

'What? You're crazy.' Did he mean Aliza? If she was dead, she couldn't be working a spell on Doc. Fi kicked Preacher in the shin. He didn't move. 'Let go of me, you freak. I'm not here for your kid.'

He squeezed harder. 'Then what are you here for?'

Telling him the situation wasn't going to help, but what else could she do? 'I'm looking for Doc. You know, the varcolai who lives with your best friend, Mal?'

Preacher's mouth hardened into a scowl. 'So he's coming back here, is he? I got home just in time. Thanks for letting me know.' He pulled a camo-painted knife from a sheath on his belt. 'I'll be ready for him this time.'

A squeak from the floorboards drew their attention. Preacher twisted in the direction of the sound, dragging Fi with him.

Doc stood in the doorway on the opposite side of the sanctuary, a wrapped bundle in his arms and a full backpack strapped to his body. He must have helped himself to the kid's supplies, too.

'Put my daughter down!' Preacher yelled as he dropped Fi and lunged for Doc, his knife out.

Doc's eyes were glazed with the look of heavy drugs. Or magic. Fi leaped onto Preacher's back. 'Stop it. Hurt him and you could hurt the baby.'

Preacher slowed enough to grab her arms and flip her over his head. Her back made hard contact with the floor. The air whooshed out of her lungs. She gasped, trying to get it back. Preacher grabbed her up again and put the knife to her throat. 'Put my kid down or your girly gets it.'

Doc stared blankly at Fi for a moment, then down at the bundle in his arms before answering Preacher. 'Don't ...

hurt ... her.' The words came out like the effort was almost more than he could handle. 'Witch,' he managed, his gaze solely on Fi.

So he *was* under a spell. To let him know she understood, she nodded but stopped when the movement caused the knife's edge to dig into her skin. Doc was in no shape to fight off Preacher, and she could defend herself. They could deal with the witch and the baby problems later. And now she knew where he was headed. 'Go,' she mouthed.

Suddenly time seemed to slow down. Doc tossed the baby toward Preacher, who let Fi go to catch the child. As soon as Doc's arms were empty, he turned, pushed through the door behind him, and ran into the night. The bundle of blankets unraveled in the air. Empty.

Preacher howled with anger and ran into the room Doc had come out of. The sound of things breaking followed him as he returned to the sanctuary, his face a black mask of fury. 'He kidnapped my child.' He stalked toward Fi, the knife pointed in her direction. 'I'm going to kill you, then I'm going to track him down and strip the hide from his flesh. You think I can't find my own flesh and blood? No one will keep me from her.'

Crap. This had gone way worse than Fi anticipated. At least she had a way out. She whipped out the sacre. Wasn't like she could take it with her anyway. She glanced behind her. About fifteen feet to the door, but Preacher had a vampire's speed.

Preacher laughed. 'You think that fancy sword is any match for me? I'm a vampire and a Marine. You don't get more dangerous.'

The sacre fell from her hand. Now wasn't the time to school him on just how mistaken he was. 'Look.' She put her hands up as she slowly edged backward, concentrating on maintaining the image he saw. The longer she kept him busy, the more get-away time Doc had. 'We can go after him together. He's under the spell of the witch Aliza. He doesn't know what he's doing.'

'Nice try, but dead witches cast no spells.'

Twelve feet to go. 'What?'

'Aliza's dead. That's what happens to people who touch my child.'

Okay, that was news. 'Well, he's under some kind of magic, then. He'd never steal your child. Someone is making him do this.' Eleven feet. She hoped she'd bought Doc enough time to get away.

'No more talking. Time to die.' Preacher lunged, slicing through her belly with his blade.

But Fi had left her corporeal body behind when she'd dropped the sacre. His blade sliced through the intangible form of her ghost self. With a roar, he tried to grab her, his arms meeting air.

'Time to leave,' Fi corrected him. And with that, she slid through the wall and out into the night.

Chapter Sixteen

Chrysabelle had barely closed her eyes when Dominic's plane touched down in Metairie. He'd given her the plane without any argument, even calling ahead to have it fueled and ready for them when they got to the airport. Apparently, he was willing to keep her happy so long as she was willing to keep those two comarré. Considering she'd had them move into the house while she was gone, it still seemed a slightly unbalanced deal on her end. The only comarré she wanted around her was her brother. Her family.

She tapped her finger on the window, watching the tarmac vanish beneath the halo of the plane's lighting. What would her brother be like? Would she find traces of Maris in his face the way she could in her own? Was his patron kind to him? Or cruel? She wouldn't think that. She closed her eyes and tried to focus on what awaited her in New Orleans. She had little idea, but no matter what, she would get the ring and come home with it. Atticus was on standby, waiting for her the moment she returned. As soon as the ring was melted down and the gold stitched into her skin, Tatiana would have nothing left to hunt for.

That melting would irrevocably disperse the dark power whatever twisted being had laid into the sacred metal. She shuddered at the thought of a being powerful enough to meld the sacred with the profane and prayed the melting would be enough to keep her safe. There was no way the ring could hold its power through that, was there? Because if something that dark was laid into her skin and it reacted with Mal's blood now coursing through her veins … She shuddered. Pain skittered down her spine and she inhaled, the plane's air conditioning icy in her lungs. She closed her eyes and concentrated on a long slow exhale to flush the pain out.

Sometimes it worked, sometimes it didn't. Mostly it didn't.

Movement jostled the seat beside her, sending tiny shards of pain into her back and opening her eyes. 'You okay?'

She nodded at Mal as he settled into the seat. Mortalis must still be sitting near the cockpit. He and Mal had left her alone during the flight so she could sleep and gather her strength. Not that she'd told them that's why she needed to sleep, but Mal had a way of figuring things out, and chances were good he knew she was still in some pain. She should have let him kiss her after she'd given him that last draught of blood at the house, but she wasn't even sure how effective days' old, cold blood was in strengthening him. Still, any power from the transfer would have helped. Her back throbbed. 'Great. You?'

'Fine.' He cocked a brow. 'Any reason I shouldn't be?'

'We are about to enter a city off-limits to vampires.'

'Only recently off-limits.' He settled back while the plane

continued to taxi. 'But New Orleans has always been a tricky city for vampires. Every time I've been here, I've had to watch my step. But once you understand the place, its draw is hard to deny. It's like a beautiful woman.' He looked at her, his eyes slightly hooded and flashing small sparks of silver. 'Difficult, but worth the effort.'

She pursed her lips. 'Are you saying I'm difficult?' She ignored that he'd also called her beautiful.

He sighed and went back to staring straight ahead. 'Yes.'

'When were you here?'

'Been coming here since the city was founded in the early 1800s, but my last trip was in the 1920s, right before the ban went into place. After that I returned to Europe.'

And Tatiana, Chrysabelle thought. 'What makes it tricky?'

'Besides the varcolai and witches, the city is rife with churches and cemeteries. Many of the estates even have their own chapels. That's a lot of enemies and hallowed ground to deal with. Plus there's the heavy fae population – although it wasn't a haven city when I was there. That happened while I was in the ruins.'

'So now that it's officially off-limits to you, how are we going to get you in?'

'I'm your personal escort and bodyguard. They have to let me in.'

Mortalis walked toward them, his jaw tense and his gaze distant. 'No, they don't. And chances are zero they will. Even if I vouch for you.'

Chrysabelle sat up a little. 'But you're willing to vouch for him?'

Mortalis sat across from them, his six-fingered hands folding over his kneecaps. His eyes lost their faraway glaze to penetrate in Mal's direction. 'I don't know what weight it will carry, but yes.' He scratched one horn. 'You need to know that there are some here who care very little for me and my family.'

Chrysabelle tried to hide her surprise. It was the first she'd heard of Mortalis having family. Not that his past was any of her business, but she'd always thought of him as such a solitary being. 'You mean like parents or—'

The plane came to a stop and he stood. 'Gather your things. It's time to get going.'

So much for that conversation. Easing to her feet, she pulled on the long white leather coat she'd found packed away in the depths of her mother's closet. She'd found her mother's silver body armor and a few other comarré things as well.

A light drizzle greeted them as they exited the plane. Mortalis had a car waiting for them, a sleek navy SUV. A driver, a young shadeux fae with budding horns and the requisite six fingers, got out from behind the wheel and popped open a large black umbrella. He met Chrysabelle as she stepped onto the tarmac. 'Ma'am. I'm Amery, your driver. Do you have baggage?'

'No,' Chrysabelle answered. She wasn't staying that long.

Amery pointed toward the sacres in her hand. 'Would you like me to put those in the back?'

She hadn't bothered strapping them on beneath her coat since she was getting into the car anyway and they made sitting uncomfortable for any length of time. She glanced at the fae thinblade at his hip. 'No. They stay with me.'

'Very good. To the car, then.' He walked beside her to the vehicle and opened the rear passenger door, holding the umbrella until she was in.

Mal climbed in from the other side, taking the captain's chair opposite hers as he shut the door. Mortalis settled into the front passenger's seat. Amery dropped the umbrella through the back hatch, closed it, and got back behind the wheel.

He looked at Mortalis expectantly. 'I can't bypass the checkpoint.'

Mortalis stared straight ahead. 'I know. I'm willing to vouch for him.'

'That will just get you banned, too.' The driver glanced briefly back at Mal. 'He could ... go around.'

Mortalis turned his head, finally making eye contact with the driver. 'Hugo know you make those kinds of suggestions?'

Amery paled beneath his smoky gray skin. 'No, sir, I just thought—'

Mortalis held up a hand. 'It's a good one. What about once he's inside?'

Amery shrugged. 'He keeps his head down and his fangs in, he should be okay. The checkpoints are hella tougher than the patrols. The current guardian is pretty slack, and if a patrol does pick him up, a couple of bills will set him loose.'

Mortalis twisted to look at Mal. 'How well do you know the city?'

'Well enough.'

'Good. You'll stay with us until Amery says you can't go any farther, then you hike in and meet us at Jackson Square. It's always crawling with tourists and those damn vampire tours, so you should blend in fine.'

Mal frowned. Chrysabelle didn't blame him. Getting dumped in some random spot would have ticked her off, too. She expected an argument any moment, but Mal just slanted his eyes at her and nodded. 'I don't like it. But I'll do it.'

'So noted.' Mortalis jerked his chin forward. 'Let's go.'

She peeked at Mal. Maybe this was all part of Mal's decision to stop arguing with her. But she was surprised how quickly he'd decided to do this. She leaned over toward him. 'You okay with this?'

'Yes.'

Not like he had a choice. She shifted forward, grabbing the back of Mortalis's seat. 'Can't we try to go through the check-point with Mal in the car?'

Mortalis turned the air conditioning down. 'Amery?'

Amery met her eyes in the rearview mirror. 'We could all get banned.'

'Vampires that big a problem here?'

He shook his head. 'Used to be. Not since New Orleans became a fae haven. We gave up Manhattan in exchange.'

'We?' She laughed without much humor. 'I didn't realize the fae and the vampires had gotten together and divided the States up.'

'Not the States. Just certain cities. Keeps peace.' He looked out the window. 'Or it did.'

'Why is New Orleans such a draw for vampires? The city seems synonymous with them. Or did.'

Mortalis made eye contact with her, one brow raised like he wished she hadn't asked the question. Then he shifted to Mal. 'You've been here before. Why did you come?'

Mal was silent a few long seconds. 'New place to go, I guess.'

'But you've been here more than once. Why come back?'

A rare, puzzled look crossed Mal's face as he thought. 'I don't know. But even now, I feel drawn to the city.' He narrowed his gaze. 'Why is that?' His question held the implication that Mortalis best explain.

Mortalis took a deep breath. 'Not long after New Orleans

was founded, a French witch, Aurelia La Voisin, took a fae lover, who proceeded to break her heart. She cursed the city to get revenge on him. From that time forward, any vampire who set foot within the Orleans Parish was able to daywalk so long as they stayed within those limits. The fae counteracted with a spell that causes the effect to be erased from a vampire's memory the moment he leaves the parish, but the urge to return always remains.' Mortalis paused for a moment. 'You'll be able to see me during daylight hours, too. Because of the fae's distant shared bloodlines with nobility, shadeux are also visible.'

Chrysabelle's jaw went south. 'Are you telling me New Orleans is the *Ville Éternelle Nuit*? That's not real. It's a legend, a myth like—'

'The Kubai Mata,' Mal interjected.

She closed her mouth and rested back in her seat. Mal looked as shocked as she felt. No wonder every vampire she'd ever known had spoken about the *Ville Éternelle Nuit* as if it were Valhalla. Organized search parties had been sent out to find it. Starting in the late 1700s, the ancient books were filled with the mention of the mystical place.

Except it was real. And right in front of them. New Orleans was the City of Everlasting Night.

Doc had just left Fi to die and there was nothing he could do about it. Driven by the other mind inside his, all he could manage was to keep his human form and head toward the destination the compulsion demanded. If he ended up somewhere besides the Glades, he'd be shocked. He pushed hard for more speed. Jostled, the baby in his backpack began to cry.

He rolled his eyes. The vampire halfling was nothing but trouble. Preacher would be after him. As would any nearby fringe who enjoyed the taste of newborn blood and heard the wailing. It was like a siren. He had to get the halfling quiet. He shifted his movement to adopt the most even rhythm he could. Finally the crying faded.

And as long as the compulsion didn't force him to shift into his leopard form, he could manage this small grasp on reality. In his animal state, fighting the compulsion was impossible. In his human state, at least part of his mind was his own, and with that thin sliver he was able to formulate a plan.

He would deliver the little beast to Aliza, or if she was really dead, then he'd find whoever was behind this spell and sever this control they had over him. By any means necessary. Then he could get back to Fi. Mother Bast, if Preacher had hurt her, Doc would hunt the daywalking bastard down and shred him to ash.

Miles disappeared under his feet and the landscape around him shifted to a very familiar one. An hour later, he came to a stop in front of Slim Jim's cabin.

The old man was on his narrow front porch, the glowing end of a cheroot lighting up a patch of his face. An assault rifle rested on his knees, and a long-faced hound curled around his booted feet. 'That you, Doc?'

'Yes, sir.' Doc prayed the baby kept quiet. He liked Slim Jim and didn't want to involve him in any unnecessary trouble. 'How are you tonight?'

'Jess fine.' He pushed up his Florida Gators ball cap to scratch his forehead. 'That pretty little blonde thing come out with you?'

'Chrysabelle? No, sir, she's on other business.'

Slim Jim nodded. 'Quite a looker, that one. You should bring her around again sometime.'

'Will do.' Doc pointed toward the line of airboats out at Slim Jim's dock. Aliza's was parked at the far end. 'How long ago did Aliza come through here?'

'Earlier today. Strange her being gone so long but' – he shrugged – 'I keep outta other people's business. You need a boat?'

'Sure do.'

'Got anything to do with the old witch?'

Doc suppressed a smile. Interesting question for someone who kept out of other people's business. 'I have a delivery for her daughter.' That sounded plausible, especially since he used to deliver Dominic's drugs to her on a regular basis.

Slim Jim's small eyes opened a little wider. 'The stone girl?'

'She's not stone anymore.' The compulsion came on strong again. It wanted him to stop talking and move. He flicked a talon out on one finger and dug it into his thigh. The pain helped fight the urge.

'You don't say. Haven't been out that way myself lately. Most my hunting trips been taking me down toward Deadman's Key and thataway. Snakes down there is something awful.' He grinned, showing off a missing tooth. 'Money in skins is better than ever.' He shifted to scratch the hound's back end. 'And Aliza said she'd take her own deliveries with her when she got back.' He stood, hoisting the gun over one shoulder. His other meaty hand went into the pocket of his overalls, coming back out with a set of keys. He tossed them to Doc. 'Last one on the right. Y'all can pay me when you get back.' He sat down, but the dog got up, gave Doc a hard stare, then woofed twice before lying down again.

Go. Now.

Assuming he would be able to come back. 'Thanks, Slim

Jim. Appreciate it.' Keys in hand, Doc headed for the boats. He climbed aboard, then eased the backpack off and nestled it down between the metal ribs of the boat's hull. He unzipped the pack and checked on the baby. Sleeping. He guessed. He thought about checking for a pulse but wasn't sure a half-vampire child would have one. Satisfied, he got the electric engine going, the carbon fiber blades whirring softly to life, before hopping into the driver's seat.

He glanced back at the cabin. A small light glimmered through the window, and only the dog remained on the porch, staring out at Doc as if watching him.

Doc turned back around and moved the boat forward. Maybe the dog was watching. Maybe the dog wasn't just a dog. Who knew? He had a half-vampire, half-fake-comarré child on board and his mind was being controlled by a witch.

Nothing was what it seemed anymore.

Forward.

'I hear you,' he said to whoever was in his head. *And I'm going to kill you if given the chance.* But that last thought he kept to himself. Or tried to. If Aliza was dead, whichever one of her coven had taken over must be controlling him. Witches had magic, but varcolai had strength and speed and a great need for revenge.

It wasn't going to be a fair fight. Not by any stretch of the imagination.

The Glades whizzed by with all the usual hellish sounds and smells. How anyone could live here was beyond him. Soon, Aliza's house and the houses of her coven appeared on the horizon. A new house sat to the left of hers. He squinted at it. From what he could see, it looked complete. How could anything have been built that fast?

He slowed the boat and the compulsion took over again, stronger than it had before but still not as strong as when he was leopard. Following the commands inside his head, he docked the boat at Aliza's, scooped up the baby in the backpack, and climbed the stairs to the house.

He opened the screen door and went in, past the kitchen and into the living room. It was empty.

Except for a demon, trapped in the base of an aquarium. The thing reared to life when Doc walked in. Recognition filled him with dread. Not just any demon. The Castus he'd seen at Tatiana's. Maybe the one Creek had just tangled with. Bitter fear soured Doc's gut. This was way more than he'd bargained for. The Castus pointed a talon-tipped finger at him. 'What's in the bag, shifter?'

Doc backed up. 'Nothing.'

'I smell new blood.'

Of course he did. 'That's probably because—'

Evie came in from another room. 'Shut up, Doc. You too, demon.' She held a small undulating ball of smoke in one palm. The compulsion. He pushed against it and while it was still there, it was definitely weaker. 'You.' She jerked her chin at Doc, then the thumb of her free hand back toward the room she'd just left. 'Inside. Quietly.' She glanced at the bag on his shoulder.

So she didn't want the demon to know about the kid. Too bad. Doc nodded and dropped the bag off his shoulder. The jostling caused the baby to stir. The demon's gaze riveted to the backpack. Working quickly, Doc got his fingers inside the zippered opening and yanked it down, revealing the child, who immediately started to cry. 'Don't you want to make sure the kid's okay? After all, who knows how much a half-vampire, half-comarré baby can take?'

'A halfling? Give the child to me,' the demon howled, straining against the invisible barriers keeping it in the aquarium.

'No!' Evie lunged for the backpack, dropping the ball of smoke. 'It's mine.'

The compulsion disappeared. Doc gasped at the sensation of it leaving his body but recovered in time to snatch the baby away from her. 'Like hell.'

Evie called up fire, juggling it over one palm. 'Give me the baby.'

Doc lifted the backpack over his head. The kid was wailing like its lungs were police sirens. 'Touch me and I drop the backpack.'

'You wouldn't.'

'Try me.' He wouldn't. Vampire, comarré, or whatever the kid was, it was still the innocent here.

The fire vanished from her hand. 'I'll just recall the compulsion then and make you turn the baby over.'

'Try it and I'll kill you.'

Her shoulder twitched, jumping toward her ear. 'Kill me and the spell that keeps the demon bound will disappear. And if you think he won't kill you for the child, you're a fool.'

The demon was practically drooling at the child. 'She lies!' it howled. 'I will spare you. The varcolai are as much my children as the vampires.'

Evie snorted. 'When my mother gets back, you're in big trouble, demon.'

'I wouldn't count on that. Your mother's dead.'

Evie's face went blank, then morphed into a mask of rage. 'She's not dead.'

Sensing a nerve, Doc pushed, hoping to throw her off balance. 'You don't believe me, ask Preacher, the vampire who fathered this child. He killed Aliza when she tried to abduct the kid. Or didn't she bother telling you she was headed out there?'

With a scream, Evie whipped her hand up and shot a bolt of fire at him. Doc dodged it, almost dropping the child. He slid the bag across the floor and into the safety of the kitchen, then grabbed her around the waist and brought her down. He straddled her, holding her arms down. She twitched like crazy beneath him. 'Get off me!'

'Not until you're tied up.' He looked around for something to secure her with.

The demon hissed. 'Fire!'

Doc glanced back down in time to see both of Evie's palms lit with blue flame, her fingers pointed in his direction. He lurched back and rolled away, grabbing a metal tray off the ottoman and holding it up as a shield.

The fire struck instantly, exploding like fireworks and heating the tray until his skin sizzled. A snarl of pain echoed over the sound of the baby's wailing, the demon's howling, and the crackle of flames. Doc tossed the tray, shaking his burning fingers.

Evie lay where he'd left her, a dark hole scorched in her chest. Small flames and wisps of smoke danced off her clothing. Her open eyes stared lifelessly at the ceiling.

Doc felt for a pulse. Nothing. The aquarium shattered behind him. He jerked around in time to see a red blur streak past. *The baby.* He scrambled to his feet, making the kitchen a split second later. The Castus had the infant in its massive hands. The smell of sulfur was unbearable.

It took one look at Doc and smiled. 'No one else can know about this child. You must die.' He cradled the child in one arm, his other shooting out toward Doc.

Doc tried to move, but the tip of the Castus's razor-sharp nail caught his forearm. A white-hot streak of pain flared with the line of blood.

The Castus reared back again. Suddenly his face contorted and his hard red eyes rolled into his head. 'Not now!' he bellowed. A second later, he disappeared in a flash of smoke and fire.

Chapter Seventeen

'What exactly are we looking for again?' Creek asked Lola. Havoc hung near the opening of the alley, but they stood in almost the exact spot where Creek had found Julia. Police Chief Vernadetto studied something on his e-tablet, notes from her homicide report, or maybe the new homicide report. A second dead comarré had been found, this one on the opposite side of Seven.

Lola's gaze never left the pavement and the circle of light thrown from her flashlight. 'Anything that might have been missed by the police.'

Vernadetto sighed. 'Ma'am, we've been over this ground thoroughly. I assure you we've picked up every bit of evidence.'

She turned on him. 'Then why haven't you found any leads?'

'These things take time. This case is our number-one priority.' His gaze shifted to Creek for a long moment before he answered her. 'Especially now that we have a second victim.'

'You've had two days.' She leaned in, her face hardening in anger. 'I will not have a serial killer terrorizing my city. I want new information on my desk by morning or you're going to have the city auditor breathing down your neck.'

Vernadetto scowled right back. 'I know this is difficult for you, but threats aren't going to make the forensics come through any faster. Now if you'll excuse me, I have work to do.' He walked away from them.

'By morning,' she called after him.

'No wonder her husband left,' Vernadetto muttered as he got into his car, slammed the door, and drove off.

Creek looked at Havoc. The varcolai had to have heard that, although the mayor wouldn't have. Havoc shook his head as if warning Creek not to say anything. Behind the mayor's back, Creek held up his hands to indicate that wasn't something he was considering. Did that dumb shifter think he was some kind of idiot? He turned back to what the mayor was doing, but his mind drifted to Chrysabelle and New Orleans and what might be going on there. If Mal hadn't made it in, she'd have only her skills and Mortalis to keep her safe. That worried him. Not that she wasn't skilled, but—

'Are you paying attention?'

'What?' Creek tried to recall what the mayor had just said.

'I just thought you'd find it interesting.' Lola's flashlight swept the ground methodically. 'That there was "forensic material" beneath her nails.'

'It is interesting. Why hasn't that led to a suspect? DNA recording has been mandatory since what, 2029? Unless whoever that DNA belongs to is older than thirty-eight. Still, that's a clue in itself, right?'

She stopped scanning the alley to face him. 'The forensic material didn't hold any DNA. The detective on the case said it came back as mostly carbon.'

'Carbon?'

Her gaze stayed fixed on his face. 'Ash.'

'Did they find any ash under the nails of the second girl?' He inhaled, testing the air. At the edges of his sensory limits, he picked up two scents. Varcolai and vampire. The first was probably Havoc, although it didn't smell canine.

'They found something but won't confirm until the tests come back. I'm sure it's the same thing.'

Creek held his expression in neutral. 'Wonder what that means?' It meant when the comarré had scratched her attacker, the skin beneath her nails had died and turned to ash. Which meant the attacker had been a vampire. Probably the one who'd left some scent trace behind.

'You know what it means.'

He stared at her without speaking. This was the kind of information that could rouse a witch hunt. Not that he was against tracking down the vamp responsible, but there were a good number of fringe who were just trying to live their lives. The ones who weren't, he took care of.

'You have no response?'

'I'm sure the police will come up with something.'

'Don't vampires turn to ash when they're killed? Or is that just a myth, too?'

He hesitated. Lying wasn't going to make things better. 'No. Not a myth.'

She said something, but a noise at the end of the alley pulled his attention. John was focused in that direction, too. He held a hand up to the mayor, then pointed down the alley. Quietly, he said, 'We've got company.'

Was this the vampire who'd killed Julia returning to the scene? If so, Creek would end this game here and now before

Lola had a chance to declare martial law. 'Stay here,' Creek whispered. He pointed behind a stack of pallets. 'There. Get down.'

Lola moved toward the pallets, and he joined Havoc near the alley opening. The bitter scent he'd smelled earlier increased, confirming what he'd already thought. 'Vampire.'

Havoc nodded, his voice low. 'Three, I think. Maybe more.'

'Youngbloods?' Creek asked, referring to the gang name some of the fringe had lately taken to sporting on the back of leather jackets and tagging on abandoned buildings.

'Probably.'

Creek nodded, freeing his crossbow from its holster. 'You stay with the mayor. I'll see if I can draw them away.'

A dark shape dropped into the alley in front of them.

'Too late,' Havoc answered, whipping out his pistol and charging the vampire, his nails and teeth bared. He fired off a few shots, striking the creature but not bringing it down. One more reason guns were so inefficient when it came to killing bloodsuckers. Smoke rose from the bullet holes, where the hot silver had made its mark. At least Havoc's ammo caused some pain.

A soft thud behind Creek twisted him around. A second vamp. Lola let out a short yelp. Creek snapped his crossbow up and fired off a bolt as the creature turned toward the mayor. It tagged the vampire's shoulder, knocking him to the ground. Creek was on top of him a second later. He yanked out the bolt and drove it straight through the vampire's heart. It went to ash beneath his feet.

'You okay?' he asked Lola.

She sat against the alley wall, her face pale, her eyes round. 'No,' she whispered.

'Stay where you are. We'll have this over in a minute and get you home.' He ran back toward Havoc, who now fought three vampires. A female clung to his back. Creek put a bolt in her first. She was ash before she hit the ground.

Havoc took down another, pinning him to the asphalt. He planted the gun's muzzle against the creature's chest and pulled the trigger. A third pile of ash joined the other two. The last vampire, realizing he was outmanned, ran.

Havoc got up, brushed himself off, and extended a hand to Creek. 'Thanks.'

Creek shook it, surprised. 'You too.'

Havoc tipped his head toward the mayor. 'Guess she'll believe you now, huh?'

Creek shrugged and tried to lighten things up. 'You never know with women. Let's get her back home. She's probably had all the reality she can handle for one night.'

Tatiana woke before Laurent did, but only by force, not because she felt rested. Wearing Daciana's image for so long made her weary to her bones. Too weary to be bothered killing Laurent off. Just staying awake during the car ride to the hangar had been a struggle. She'd dropped into bed almost the minute they'd entered the plane. She didn't even remember takeoff. If only she could be herself, gain her full strength back. But they had a few hours yet before they landed and she could be rid of Laurent and the charade.

She glanced at him, naked and sleeping beside her. In a small way, it was too bad she had to kill him. He might be overbearing with his wife, but he was quick, crafty. And he'd captured the comarré with what seemed like very little effort. She should hate him for that, but he'd made her life so much easier by doing it. Maybe she could explain what she'd done, get him and Daciana to understand the necessity of it. Let them live. They would, after all, be in her service for as long as she was Dominus. If the Castus ever showed up and made that happen.

She rolled her eyes and threw off the covers. If only she could stay herself; but she couldn't let Laurent catch her as Tatiana. Not before she'd had a chance to explain, if that was the route she was going to take.

Reaching for her locket, she remembered that it was back in Corvinestri with the rest of her things. She let out a half sob, so completely and utterly drained, but forced herself to assume Daciana's identity, then dressed and went out to check on the comarré. Laurent should have locked the girl in the coat closet like they'd discussed on the way to the plane.

Had he taken her out of the body bag? Probably. Tatiana hadn't heard any screaming. Not that she would have, considering how deeply she'd slept. She tried the closet door. Locked. She listened. Breath and heart sounds and the scent of comarré blood. She smiled and reached for the key in the overhead compartment. She grabbed the small pistol she'd brought along as well. Comarré were human enough that bullets could still be persuasive.

She unlocked the door and opened it, keeping the gun aimed forward. The full body bag was huddled against one wall. So he hadn't let her out after all. 'Well, well, comarré. You're mine now.' Tatiana reached for the zipper and tugged it down a few inches. 'And once I have the ring, I'm going to take great pleasure in—'

Bright blue terror-stricken eyes stared back at Tatiana. She pulled the zipper down farther. The face was familiar, but not because it belonged to the comarré whore who had taken up with her former husband, Malkolm. It was the comarré she'd purchased for Nasir, the one who had run away from her with her own comar, Damian.

The girl gasped. 'Please, whoever you are, you must get me back to my patron, Nasir, or the vampiress Tatiana. I was forced to run away with her comar, but I didn't want to and—'

'Bloody hell,' Tatiana whispered. She shut the closet door and locked it, then tossed the key and the pistol back into the overhead, wishing she could slam it shut. Bloody, bloody hell. She stomped up to the cockpit and went inside. 'How far are we?'

'Less than three hours,' the pilot answered.

Tatiana stifled another curse. 'Turn around and go back.'

The pilot made a face like she'd lost her mind. 'We can't. Not enough fuel.'

She clenched her fist but somehow managed not to maim the pilot. No wonder Laurent had taken the girl with such ease. She was the wrong damn one. Tatiana forced her body to relax. Killing Laurent now meant no chance of sending him back to Paradise City to rectify his mistake. And since Tatiana was supposed to be Daciana, she couldn't say a single bloody word without giving herself away.

Mal waited until the SUV pulled away. At least the rain had stopped. They'd dropped him in a residential area off of I-10, far enough away from the checkpoints masked as tollbooths so that there was no chance of him being caught. Sun would be up in about an hour. Plenty of time to make it from Jefferson Parish into Orleans Parish. *Or die.* Then he just had to wind his way through the city, down into the French Quarter to Jackson

Square, and find Chrysabelle and Mortalis. *If they haven't ditched you.*

He walked at an easy gait, scanning the working-class neighborhood, but the few people he saw were more interested in the coffee clutched in their hands or getting to work on time. Despite Mal's long black coat and sunglasses, he drew no stares. Still, he kept to the shadows for a few more blocks until, confident there were no fae patrols in the area, he picked up his pace and followed the directions Mortalis had mapped out for crossing the parish border.

Half an hour later, the pale gold blush of dawn – a rare color in his world – edged the horizon. It reminded him of the glow that surrounded Chrysabelle. And how much he was willing to do to keep her in his life. *Bite her, drain her.*

He crossed street after street, angling farther away from the interstate until he came to the canal he'd been anticipating. He just hadn't expected it to be so wide. Looked like a hundred and fifty feet, maybe more. Too far for him to jump and there was no way he was swimming through that brown, murky soup. *Try it. Maybe you'll drown.*

Mortalis had told him to get across the canal before the sun came up or seek shelter. Time was running out. So he started running. He kept between the water's edge and Orpheum Road, which ran parallel to the canal. Traffic was light but picking up.

He'd hoped to be lost in the city streets by now, not out in the open of the residential area. He pushed himself to go faster, but he'd been slack about feeding the last week and the blood he'd had at Chrysabelle's had been old and done little for him. Not that he would have expected her to give him fresh while she was recovering. As a result, he was slower, less powerful, and faster to fatigue. *Easier to kill.*

The road veered off but the neighborhoods remained. He ran under an overpass, the noise of the passing cars drowning out the sounds of the city waking up. The sky brightened with each minute, urging him forward faster and faster. The voices started to howl. At last, a train bridge appeared. He sped forward, using the last of his immediate strength to traverse the tracks.

His feet touched land on the other side just as the sun's brilliant light cast its first rays on his body. He flinched, but no fire burst off his skin. He'd made it.

Tipping his face toward the sky, he took a moment to breathe in the air and smell the earth. The sun made it all different somehow. Except for the brief hours he'd spent under the influence of Dominic's daywalking potion, he hadn't spent time in the sun in almost five hundred years. And now he could do it without the threat of aging. Or dying. *Too bad.*

Cracking the thinnest of smiles, he headed off to find Chrysabelle. Today was going to be a very good day. *A good day to die.*

He found his way to Canal Street and, flipping his collar up, did his best to be invisible. Keeping his head down was harder than he thought. The urge to look at the clear blue October sky was almost as great as the desire to stand still and drink in the daylight. But he kept going, thankful he had a place to be or he might have disappeared down a side street after the tantalizing scent of warm humans. *Blood blood blood . . .* He was hungry. And suddenly very aware of it.

His mind drifted as he walked, back to the last time he'd been here: 1926. Two years before the ban. The memories had been fuzzy, but stepping onto New Orleans soil had lifted the fog.

He'd been a killing machine, sticking to the French Quarter, which then had been a slum, full of easy pickings if you could stomach the sickly sweet aroma of too-ripe bananas being carted in from the nearby port. He remembered the crimson-lipped prostitute he'd lured into the hedges surrounding Jackson Square and there, amid the other working girls earning their pay, he'd drained her and walked away from her corpse like a discarded newspaper. Now he wore her name across his left thigh.

Had he been that much a monster? Yes. *Oh yes.* But not anymore. *Still.* He couldn't imagine doing the same thing today. *Yes, you could.* Chrysabelle was right not to want him to lose the curse that kept him bound. The moment it was gone, he had no doubt he'd return to that life. *Blood blood blood . . .*

He checked traffic and the people around him. The prickling sensation of being watched had crept onto his skin a few blocks back. Seeing no one, he crossed to the other side of Canal and ducked down Chartres Street. He sidestepped a man hosing down the sidewalk, paying little attention to the way the man's heartbeat filled his head or the warm scent of his blood curled into his nostrils. Beyond that, the aromas of chicory coffee and frying beignets mingled with the garbage waiting to be carted away.

Just a few more blocks and Jackson Square would open up before him. He crossed Conti, and a fae stepped into his path. He had short gray horns, silvery skin, and lavender eyes. Smokesinger maybe. Low against his side, he held a blade. From the sour tang, the powdery coating on it was laudanum. 'Far enough, vampire.'

Mal's peripheral vision showed two more fae of the same variety at his back. Son of a priest, he had been followed. His whole being wavered with the slip-switch decision between fight or flight, but with Chrysabelle's reason for being here, neither one made good sense. He didn't want to be the cause of her not getting the ring back, and without being able to make eye contact with all three of the fae, using his power of persuasion wasn't an option. Not that he was even sure it worked on fae, but since it worked on varcolai, trying it out was a chance he'd take at the right opportunity.

He held his hands up casually. 'I'm sure we can work something out.'

Interest crackled over the fae's face. 'Like what?'

Chrysabelle had slipped him a fat roll of bills before they'd parted ways. He loathed giving up her money, even if that's what it was for. 'Cash.'

The fae behind Mal tightened in. 'How much?' one of them asked.

'A thou.' Mal had separated the slick plastic bills into smaller rolls ahead of time.

The fae in front of him snorted. 'We look cheap to you?'

'Each,' Mal added. He could almost hear wheels turning in the heads of the two behind him. What he actually heard over the thrum in his head was their heartbeats kicking up. They wanted the money. Probably needed it if the desperation wafting off them was a clue.

The lead fae waggled his blade. 'You even got that kinda cash on you?' He dropped his gaze to a small hole in Mal's sleeve. 'You don't exactly look flush.'

'I have it. That a deal, then?'

The fae grinned. 'How do you know we won't just roll you and take it all?'

'Because I'm a five-hundred-year-old noble vampire, and the kind of power I could unleash would turn you into stains on the sidewalk quicker than you could take your next breath.'

'That so?' The fae hitched one shoulder like he'd just developed an itch. 'Then why haven't you?'

Weakling. Fight them. Kill them. Drain them. 'Because I don't need trouble. Do you want the money or not?'

'Deal.' The word came from behind him. The lead fae shot a look at his partner.

'I'm going to reach for the money.' Mal slipped a hand into the inside pocket of his coat and snagged the first bundle, then into the back pocket of his jeans for the rest. The bulk of the ten thousand was in his boot. He pulled his hand out and splayed the three rolled bundles like playing cards. 'Here you go.'

The lead fae came closer. Mal inched his hand back a little and slipped some persuasion into his voice. A little test couldn't hurt. 'You have a name? In case I need help getting out of another *situation*?'

The fae's gaze went slightly murky. His mouth opened and stayed that way for a long moment before any sound came out. 'Jester.'

Mal flipped the money into the air and took off, the sounds of scrabbling fading behind him. His head spun, but three grand and a sudden bout of nausea was a small price to pay to find out his power worked on the fae. Something told him that might come in very handy helping Chrysabelle get her ring back.

Fi had scoured Little Havana, gone to the freighter, and talked to the bouncers outside Seven. Doc was nowhere. Now, hours later, she pulled the sedan back through the gates at Chrysabelle's, exhausted and heartsick. She knew Doc must have taken the baby to the witches. Why else would he have said *witch*? It must have been a clue for her. But knowing that and finding him were two different things. She had no idea where the witches lived, and she didn't know anyone who did, besides Dominic, and chances of him helping Doc were none. Maybe Velimai.

The fae might come with her. The idea of going after such a powerful force alone frightened Fi. She'd do it if she had to, but a little company would be a great thing. Times like this, she wished with her whole heart that Doc had made peace with the leader of his pride and gotten himself reinstated. Then she could go to Sinjin and get help. Now, with Mal and Chrysabelle gone, she was practically on her own.

And there was still the matter of the kidnapped comarré, Saraphina, to deal with. The comar, Damian, would want to go after her, wouldn't he? He had no reason to help Doc over one of his gold-marked sisters. Fi parked, turned off the engine, and rested her head against the steering wheel. The early morning sun beat down on her through the windshield. She wanted to cry, but tears weren't going to do anything but make her eyes puffy and her nose red.

She left the car, trudged to the door, and knocked, knowing it would be locked. A click of the tumblers and Velimai answered, looking like she'd had as much sleep as Fi had, which was none. 'How's the comar?'

Velimai signed that he was okay. *Did you find Doc?* she asked.

Fi swallowed to keep from crying. 'No. But I'm about ninety-nine percent sure I know where he went. Just not how to get there. Or what to do when I find him. Or how to get him out of the mess he's in.' She sighed as she came in, shutting the door behind her. 'This whole thing is a nightmare.'

She followed Velimai into the kitchen. The wysper went back to scrambling eggs and frying bacon and potatoes. The smell was like heaven and a little bit of solace for the night Fi had spent, but as much as she loved food, she would have traded it all in a heartbeat to have Doc back. She sniffed away a new surge of emotion as Velimai pointed to the coffeepot.

'Thanks.' Fi was going to need all the awake she could get. She took a mug down and filled it, then grabbed a seat at the table and sipped her coffee, mentally urging it to work faster than usual. 'Any chance you know where Aliza the witch lives?'

The wysper shook her head.

'That's what I thought.'

Fi was halfway through her coffee when Damian came in. 'Morning.' Above his loose white drawstring pants, gauze wrapped his middle, leaving his broad upper body bare except for another bandage on his shoulder and the swirling, jagged signum that covered his skin. She tried not to gape. Dark circles shadowed his blue eyes, but that was nothing compared to the sharp edge of anger sparking through them. Clearly he was ticked off. And had every right to be.

'How are you feeling?' Fi asked, dragging her gaze back to her coffee. 'You passed out right before I left last night.'

'Fine.' The word came out almost a snarl. He took a chair as Velimai placed a massive platter of food in the middle of the already-set table.

'You don't look fine.' Fi took a long swallow of coffee, wondering if she'd pushed the comar too far. Chrysabelle had a temper. Maybe they all did.

He stared at her. 'I'm well enough to do what needs to be done.' He picked up the serving spoon. 'Are you going to eat? Because I am and quickly, but politeness dictates I serve you first.'

Fi held up a hand. 'You go ahead.'

He shoveled food onto his plate and started eating as if someone might snatch it away from him. Fi kept her fingers on her side of the table. 'I take it you plan to go after Saraphina as soon as you finish?'

He stopped eating abruptly, the muscles in his jaw ticking. 'Not a chance. She's the one who put the gash in my shoulder.' He shook his head, a little of the fire dimming in his eyes. 'I never should have made her leave in the first place. She's a lifer.'

'A lifer?'

Another forkful of eggs vanished into his mouth. He swallowed before speaking. 'She likes the life. Loves it, actually.' He shoved a hand through his near-platinum locks. 'I thought if I got her away from it, showed her what freedom was, she'd change her mind. She didn't. I take the blame for not figuring that out sooner.' He scooped up another helping of potatoes. 'I'm sure she's the reason Dominic wanted us out of his hair. She wouldn't leave him alone, begging him to be her patron.' He scowled. 'She doesn't get that we're about more than that.'

New hope filled Fi. 'So maybe you'd help me find Doc?'

Damian frowned. 'He never turned up last night?'

'No. I went after him, well, where I thought he was going and I was right. He was under the spell of a witch – the one who'd put him under a curse before. Anyway, I lost him again because of the spell. I looked everywhere I thought he might be but couldn't find him. My best guess is he's gone to her house, but I don't know where that is and everyone who does is off to New Orleans.'

'Most varcolai have packs, don't they?'

'Doc's feline. They call it a pride. And yes, they do, but in Doc's case, no.' She didn't have it in her to explain that history now.

'What about Dominic, then? He seems pretty connected.'

'He is, but . . . ' Fi bit the inside of her cheek. Doc sure had his enemies, didn't he? 'I don't think he'd help Doc. They have a long past. A bad one. Like Dominic almost killed Doc a few weeks ago.'

Damian tapped his fingers on the table. 'He'd probably give up the witch's location in exchange for the right information.'

Fi held up her hands. 'Like what? I have nothing to tell him.'

'But I do. The vampire who took Saraphina is named Laurent. He's next in line to take over the position of Elder, should Tatiana become Dominus, which is what she wants more than anything. There's a good chance Laurent's working for Tatiana.' He paused for a moment. 'Tatiana could even be the second presence on the property last night. Dominic would want to know that, wouldn't he?'

Fi nodded slowly. 'It's pretty common knowledge Dominic wants Tatiana dead for killing the woman he was in love with.' She pushed away from the table. 'Let's go. I'll drive.'

Chapter Eighteen

Tatiana stomped down the stairs ahead of Laurent, whom she'd left to deal with the comarré. Octavian waited for them with the car inside the dark hangar, away from the blazing afternoon sun. Being back in Corvinestri was like a weight lifted off her shoulders. He came forward to meet her, his brow furrowed, his eyes wide with worry.

'The Elders called for you early this morning.' He kept his voice to a whisper. 'The ancient one finally showed. They want you in St Petersburg by tonight.'

Bloody hell. Of all the bad timing. 'What did you tell them?'

'That yo— that Tatiana had some bad blood and was feeling ill. I blamed it on a servant, said the blood hadn't been properly refrigerated. I told them things hadn't been easy since your comar ran away.' He shrugged. 'I had to buy time. I didn't know when you'd be back. I was ready to come get you myself.'

She frowned. She didn't like the council thinking she was sick, but what else was there? 'Good enough. Let's get Laurent back to the house quickly. Damn fool captured the wrong comarré. But you don't know that, understand?'

Octavian nodded even as he looked over her shoulder. 'Ah, Laurent, there you are. Need help?'

Tatiana turned to see Laurent coming down the jet stairs with the bagged comarré over his shoulder.

'No, I've got it.' He patted the comarré's rump through the bag, causing the girl inside to move. Tatiana shot him the look she expected Daciana would have. He ignored it.

Octavian opened the trunk. Laurent took the hint and dropped the girl inside. She let out a small 'ooof' but otherwise kept quiet. After the girl's outburst in the closet, Tatiana figured she was just happy to be out of New Florida. Tatiana certainly was. But if the girl thought she was going to be welcomed back without some sort of punishment for running, she was sadly mistaken.

Tatiana got into the limo and slid to the seat farthest away from the door. Octavian got in ahead of Laurent and she tapped the seat beside her. He took the spot she indicated, forcing Laurent to sit alone.

'What are you doing on that side, pet? You know I like you to sit beside me.'

'I'm fine where I am.'

He scowled but said nothing. She was completely over the charade. In fact, if she was going to kill them both, she wasn't sure why she was even maintaining it. Laurent and Daciana had one chance to hear her out and come aboard or she would remove them from her service permanently, although she was starting to feel for Daciana a bit. Laurent was a bloody bore. And excessively affectionate. And more than a little controlling. Not that Daciana had seemed to mind when they were in her office. Tatiana forced a thin smile and batted her eyelashes. 'Do you miss me already? We've just been on that wretched plane together for a thousand hours.'

Octavian coughed, blinking hard.

Laurent gave her a very unpleasant smile in return. 'As long as you're comfortable, love.'

'Very. Thank you.' She turned back to the window and dropped the smile. Beside her, Octavian shifted, drawing her attention.

He leaned forward, opened the bar's refrigerator, and extracted a stainless-steel thermos. 'Blood?'

She and Laurent answered yes at the same time. Octavian poured hers first and she greedily drank it down. She could have polished off the whole thermos, but that would raise questions with Laurent. Soon, very soon, she'd be able to sleep and recover the drain on her strength from holding Daciana's image so long.

By the time they reached the house, she'd formulated a plan. Getting in front of the council was important, but heading off to St Petersburg could wait until she'd dealt with Laurent and Daciana. Too many loose ends wore at her nerves, and with her strength so low, she couldn't handle having another thing to worry about.

She went inside with Octavian and Laurent, who had the comarré over his shoulder again. They followed Octavian into the main parlor of her house. She inspected as they went. The new head of staff Octavian had hired seemed to be doing an excellent job of keeping the estate in order.

As soon as they entered the parlor, Tatiana turned to Octavian. 'Could you direct me to a washroom? I'd like to freshen up before we see Tatiana.'

'Of course. I'll show you.' Octavian gestured toward the comarré and Laurent. 'You stay here, keep an eye on the package. I'll send Kosmina in to bring you some brandy.'

'Wonderful. I could use a stiff drink.' Laurent dumped the comarré onto a sofa, then settled into one of the plush armchairs before the empty fireplace.

Tatiana followed Octavian out of the room, and when they were a safe distance away, she let the guise of Daciana finally fall away. She stumbled, catching hold of Octavian and leaning on him.

'Are you all right?' He held on to her, concern silvering his eyes.

'I'm exhausted.' She allowed him to bear her weight for a moment. It felt wonderful and she realized how much she'd actually missed him. 'I've used a tremendous amount of power and had little time to recover.'

Without a second of hesitation, Octavian scooped her into his arms and carried her into the nearby library, where he set her onto a chair. 'Rest. I can make an excuse for you.'

'No, no.' She waved a hand at him but made no move to get up. 'There isn't time. I must do what needs to be done.'

'What first?'

She tipped her head back against the chaise. 'Daciana.'

'I would be happy to kill her for you, if that's what you want.'

'I'm going to talk to her first. Give her the option of joining us.'

Octavian raised a brow. 'You always surprise me.' He bent toward her, bringing his mouth to hers and kissing her softly. 'I've missed you. If it makes me weak to say so, then so be it.'

She smiled against his lips, reaching up to clasp the back of his head. 'I've missed you, too. No one takes care of me like you do.'

He straightened and offered her his arm. 'Let's go see Daciana, shall we? The sooner we get you through this and on the plane to St Petersburg, the sooner you can have some time to sleep and recover.'

She took his arm, letting him pull her up. How had she ever gotten along without him? 'You're right. Let's get this done.'

Daciana was being held in a small apartment in the lower level of the estate. It sat adjacent to the dungeon and, like the dungeon, was silver-lined to soundproof the space. Octavian unlocked the door and stepped aside to let Tatiana through.

Daciana leaped up from the chair where she'd sat reading. 'I demand you let me out of here. Where's my husband? I want to see Laurent this instant. What game are you playing?'

Tatiana took the chair across from her while Octavian stood in front of the door. 'Sit, Daciana. We have much to discuss.'

Heat and stench. Those were the first things that leaked through the chaos in Aliza's mind. She'd expected both from hell, but the heat was bearable and the stench smelled of dirty diapers and rotten fish, not sulfur and brimstone.

The noise in her head was horrible. Loud and jumbled, like she could hear everything. She blinked in the darkness. Shapes and a thin sliver of light formed as her eyes adjusted sharply.

She moved. Plastic crinkled beneath her. She stuck a hand out and hit metal. Hell was a Dumpster. Her fingers went to her neck. The gash that should have been there, left behind by that no-good, scum-sucking vampire, was gone.

She sat up and hit her head on more metal. It jumped from the impact, letting a brilliant flash of sunlight in. She really was in a Dumpster. But at least she wasn't dead. How had she survived the attack? Didn't matter. She had. And now she was going to hunt that bastard down, set him on fire, and take his kid. Lousy bloodsucker.

The very thought of blood made her gut clench in hunger. Dread filled her a split second later. There was only one reason the idea of blood would make her hungry. It was the same reason she could have survived the attack.

Her fingers went to her throat to find a pulse. She shoved her fingers harder against her neck, deeper into the flesh, searching, searching ... but there was no pulse. Just like there was no breath in her lungs, no rise and fall of her chest. Her hands went to her mouth, her fingers running across her teeth. She moaned as she found the razor-sharp tips of brand-new fangs.

She slumped into the pile of trash supporting her. She hadn't survived the attack. She'd been turned. Gagging on the knowledge, she pushed to her feet, shoved the Dumpster's lid open, and hoisted herself over the side. She dropped to the concrete below, fell to her knees, and vomited. The last meal she'd eaten came up and her stomach instantly felt better. Mentally and emotionally, she could have vomited a dozen more times without feeling better.

A vampire. Her. Of all people.

She looked up and blinked hard. The sun bit into her eyes, making them water. *The sun?* How was she not a bonfire right now? Maybe she wasn't a vampire. She hadn't drunk his blood. A little from his bleeding broken nose had dripped into her mouth, but that wasn't enough to turn her, was it? Or maybe being a witch had prevented her from fully turning. Maybe she was something else entirely.

She looked around, trying to place where she was. Still in Little Havana by the looks of it. Smelled like Little Havana. Rice and beans and garbage. The Dumpster was in the back of a restaurant. Made sense he'd used a Dumpster that would get emptied pretty frequently. She brushed herself off and got to her feet. Reopening the Dumpster, she rifled through the trash and found her bag and sunglasses.

Tossing the bag over her shoulder and the sunglasses onto her face, she walked to the end of the alley and looked both ways. A car drove down the street, but the driver paid her no attention.

One good thing about this neighborhood: freaks were either ignored or given a wide berth. With no real sense of direction, she started after the car. A few blocks went by and her body began to ache. Like she was hungry, but the gnawing feeling came from every muscle and every bone.

A stray dog scampered past. She could hear its heartbeat. Could feel it in her body as if it were her own heart beating. And beyond the stink of the street in its fur, she smelled blood.

She followed the animal down a new alley. 'Here, doggy, doggy,' she called, reaching out for it and clicking her tongue.

The dog stopped, scratched at its ear, eyeing her as if trying to determine if she had food to offer.

'C'mon, you mangy mutt,' she singsonged, creeping closer. 'Come and see what Aliza's got for you.'

The dog came toward her, cautiously, tail wagging. Only a few feet separated them.

'That's a boy,' she encouraged.

The dog took one more step and its nose wrinkled. It sneezed and growled, baring its teeth, and started backing away.

She lunged, grabbing it by the scruff of the neck as she threw herself on top of the struggling animal. It kicked and snapped at her, but subduing the creature took almost no work. Her strength had tripled. Maybe quadrupled.

With a guttural cry, Aliza reared her head back, opened her mouth, and tore into the dog's neck. It thrashed and whimpered, but after half a minute, it lay limp. Blood poured into her mouth.

She swallowed and drank, the hot, earthy liquid filling her body with an almost orgasmic surge of energy.

Suddenly the taste of the blood changed into something ashy and bitter. She pulled away and spat out the last mouthful. The dog stayed limp on the oil-slicked pavement. She sat on her knees staring, oddly at peace with what she'd done. The world around her seemed a very different place. Brighter. Louder. Hers for the taking. And she was hungry for more. The dog had barely touched the hunger in her gut.

She pushed to her feet, using her sleeve to wipe the blood from her mouth. So she was a vampire, or some sort of creature that required blood, but what of her witch side? Fire had always been her best element.

Cracking her knuckles and shaking out her hands, she took a deep breath out of habit and centered herself. She extended her fingers toward the animal and called fire.

Flames burst from her hand and devoured the dog as if it were dried leaves. In seconds, nothing remained but smoking bits of bone. She studied what she'd just done, then looked at her fingers. She'd never had that much control or power before. If this was being a vampire, maybe it wasn't so bad.

She laughed at the absurdity of it all. What would Evie say when she heard her mother had joined the dark side? There'd be no stopping them now.

Aliza took off down the street. There was plenty of time to get home. First she had to fix this craving in her belly for more blood. The dog had taken the edge off, but there was still a gaping, hungry hole there and something told her nothing was going to make it go away until she drank something human.

Chapter Nineteen

Creek sipped what had to be the best coffee he'd ever tasted. How many other convicted murderers had sat at the mayor's dining room table and eaten breakfast? Probably the same number as those who'd been paroled by the Kubai Mata and consigned into a life of secret service. One.

He'd rather have been in his own bed last night, but he couldn't blame Lola for not wanting him or Havoc to leave after what she'd seen last night. And speak of the devil . . .

Havoc staggered in, for once not wearing the black sunglasses he was never without. He nodded at Creek on his way to the side table where an expanse of food had been laid out by the mayor's staff. He filled a mug from the coffee urn, then took a seat at the end of the table.

'You don't look like you slept.'

'I didn't.' Havoc stared at the table like he was somewhere else. 'Spent the night setting up some new security measures. The mayor wants at least two more people added to the team.'

'You have names already?' Creek immediately thought of

Doc. The guy had the right look and could obviously throw down when needed.

Havoc sipped his steaming coffee, then shook his head. 'Just one. My brother, Luke.'

Creek got up for more coffee. 'I know a guy. Leopard varcolai. Good man. Goes about six foot six, two forty. Lotta street smarts. Knows his way around the othernatural side of the street better than most.'

'Sounds like a candidate.' Havoc rubbed at his eyes. 'Gimme his info and I'll take it from there.'

'Good morning.' Lola strode in, her makeup doing a fair job of hiding what had surely been a night low on sleep. She was dressed in a tan pantsuit and fitted white button-down. All business, as usual. 'Creek, I'd like you to come to the office with me today so you can continue educating me on what to expect.' She fixed a plate of fruit and scrambled eggs and a large coffee heavy on sugar and cream. 'John, you should take the day off. I can have the police send a few officers to city hall. I need you rested and on your game.'

Creek leaned against the table, expecting Havoc to protest. He didn't. 'I should have the two new security people you asked for in a day or so.'

She sat, bowed her head, crossed herself, then began eating. 'Good.' She glanced up at Creek. 'If you're going to eat, I suggest you do it soon. I want to be at my office in half an hour. The car is waiting to take us.'

Creek leaned his hands on the dining table and bent to her eye level. 'I realize you're used to people asking how high when you say jump, but I've spent two days in borrowed clothes. Haven't set foot in my place in that long. I'm going home to shower and change, and then I'll come to your office when I'm ready.'

She raised her brows but said nothing while she chewed. Finally she swallowed. 'The mayor's office has a bathroom. You can shower there. I'll have appropriate clothes brought in. If you're going to be taking on the role of advisor, I can't have you looking like a convict.' Her gaze went to his Mohawk.

'No,' he said, anticipating the next action item on her list. 'The hair stays. And I never agreed to any kind of advisory role.' No way Argent was going to let him work for anyone but the KM.

She opened her mouth to respond, but a maid came in and said something in a mix of Spanish and English. Creek picked out the name Vernadetto. Lola nodded and answered, '*Si*. Send him in.'

The maid nodded and left, only to return a minute later with the police chief. Vernadetto's cap was tucked beneath his arm. 'Ma'am.' His face was drawn from lack of sleep, and he wore a look that said the man would rather be anywhere than here.

'Chief.' Lola lifted her mug. 'Coffee?'

'No, thank you.' He flipped open his e-tablet. 'Forensics confirmed that the material beneath the second victim's nails matches what was found under your daughter's. We also identified the second girl as Amy Montrose. She worked at the nightclub Seven. The owner of that club, Dominic Scarnato, has been less than forthcoming, but we're working on him.' He shifted nervously. 'Also, the ME found something new in the last round of tests from your daughter's autopsy.'

Lola placed her mug on the table and pushed back in her seat until she sat straight up. 'Yes?'

Vernadetto dragged his fingers through his close-cropped salt-and-pepper hair. 'Perhaps you'd rather discuss this in private.'

Without a glance at Havoc or Creek, she answered, 'No. Go on, please.'

The chief sighed. 'The ME found elevated levels of human chorionic gonadotropin in your daughter's blood.'

'What does that mean in English?'

He made eye contact with her briefly, then broke it to stare at the table. 'A few weeks before your daughter's death, she gave birth.'

With Octavian and the surprisingly willing Daciana at her side, Tatiana, now blissfully in her own skin, strolled back into the salon to confront Laurent. Daysleep tugged at all of them, but things had to be taken care of. After only a few minutes of conversation with Daciana, Tatiana had revised her previous plan and brought Daci, as Tatiana found her new acquaintance liked to be called, into the fold. Daci might prove to be an exceptional asset. Provided she was as trustworthy as she claimed to be. If she wasn't, and the next few minutes went poorly, she would not get a second chance.

Octavian went ahead of them and pushed open the doors. Laurent stood, his face brightening into a well-pleased smile despite his obvious tiredness. 'My lady.' He sketched a short bow, then held his hand out to Daciana. His smile faltered as he took her in. 'Did you change? I don't recall your blouse being blue.'

She shook her head as if saying, *Not now*.

Octavian closed the doors behind them, as Tatiana faced Laurent. 'Be seated. We have much to discuss, and I'm sure you're as eager to sleep as we all are.'

Without waiting, she took a chair. Octavian sat beside her as Daci and Laurent settled into their seats. 'Laurent, Daciana did not accompany you to New Florida. I did.' She paused, waiting to see his response. Daci's gaze was fixed on him as well.

'What? That's impossible. She was with me the whole time.' He frowned, studying his wife for a brief moment before looking back at Tatiana. 'Is this some sort of test? I'm too tired for games.'

'Yes, as a matter of fact, it is a test.' Sitting made her want to lie down, so Tatiana stood and walked to the bar. 'My powers are great. They allow me to mimic anyone I choose. I took on Daciana's appearance and went with you to Paradise City. Daciana remained here.' She poured a glass of wine for herself, then lifted the bottle toward Octavian. She'd rather have blood, but this would have to do for now. 'Would you care for a glass?'

Laurent sputtered to life. 'How can you offer him wine after telling me such a thing? Explain yourself. Why would you do this?' He stood, his gaze flicking from Daci to Tatiana. 'If you harmed my wife in any way ...'

In a nanosecond, Tatiana set the bottle down and flew to face Laurent head-on. 'Do not threaten me, Laurent. You're not in any position to make such statements.' She thrust her metal hand against his chest, putting enough force behind it to push him back into his seat.

He popped up as quickly as he'd gone down. 'Now see here, I did as you asked. I brought back the comarré.' His eyes silvered around the edges, narrowing as they took her in. 'Which is more than you were able to do on your previous trips.'

All traces of humanity left her face as she bared her fangs in a hiss. 'You're a bloody fool, Laurent. A pompous, prattling fool.' She leaned in, hating that she wasn't tall enough to stare down at him. 'You brought back the wrong comarré.'

He deflated a centimeter. 'What? No. I did exactly as—'

'Oh, be quiet, Laurent, will you? Or do you just enjoy the sound of your own voice that bloody much?' Daci snorted softly in disgust. 'You just can't stand taking orders from a woman, can you?'

He whirled to face her. 'How dare you speak to me that way.' His hand cocked back as if to strike her.

Daci flinched. Octavian jumped up, moving with extraordinary speed, and restrained him. 'If you think you're going to hit a woman in my presence, you're dead wrong.'

Laurent snarled. 'Take your hands off me, vampling.'

Daci leaped to Tatiana's side like a frightened doe. 'Please, I just want to be done with this. With him.'

'What are you talking about? Let me go or I'll thrash you within an inch of ashing.' Laurent struggled to get free of Octavian's grasp. 'Now, vampling.'

'Not a chance.' Octavian's face colored with the exertion.

Laurent had years of strength on him, but Octavian was fed and rested. Still, chances weren't good Octavian would be able to hold him much longer. Tatiana gave Daci one last out. 'You're sure?'

Laurent wriggled an arm free. Eyes metallic with fear, the petite blonde put a chair between her and her husband. 'Yes.'

Tatiana stepped in front of Laurent, drawing his attention and his ire. 'Because you've failed me as a potential Elder and have been an abominably wretched husband to Daciana—'

'That's a bloody lie—'

' – your services as both are no longer required. But because of your standing in the House of Tepes, I shall allow you a dignified out. Tomorrow morning, unable to face your failings, you'll walk into the dawn and meet your fiery end.'

'Like hell I will—'

'Now,' Tatiana commanded.

Octavian shoved Laurent forward. At the same time, Tatiana

thrust her prosthetic hand out, turning her fingers into a razor-pointed stake. It found its target in Laurent's chest, piercing his heart. His eyes went wide, his mouth rounded into an O, and then he was ash, floating to the floor. Daci let out a sudden solitary sob. Tatiana returned her hand to its usable state and shook the debris off it. 'At least that's what I'll tell the council when I see them in St Petersburg tomorrow.' She turned to Daci. 'Get some sleep. The plane leaves at dusk and you're going to be on it with me. You're about to become the second female Elder of the House of Tepes.'

Daci blinked, her fingers touching her lower lip. 'I can't believe I'm free.'

Tatiana laughed as she stepped over the ash pile and made her way to the door. 'I wouldn't exactly say you're free, Daci. You've just traded one master for another.' She paused, her hand on the knob, smiling to soften the blow of her words. She knew how Daciana must feel to finally be her own person after so many years. 'Not to worry. I have great faith that you and I are going to get along famously.'

And if they didn't, if Daciana did something to lose Tatiana's trust, well, that was easy enough to take care of, wasn't it?

If not for the slow-moving gate letting her back into Chrysabelle's estate, Fi would have raced up the driveway and screeched to a stop in front of the house. It was exactly what she felt like doing, but the best she could manage was to slam the door when she got out. 'I should have known.'

Damian closed his door more gently. 'Daylight hours aren't the best for speaking to a vampire. You're right – we should have known.' His long legs ate up the ground, putting him in step with her. 'But that wouldn't have stopped you from trying, would it?'

'No,' she grumped. 'At least the cops weren't having any luck either.'

'Doesn't make you feel any better, though, does it? Wish you could have kicked down that door and forced him to see you, don't you?'

'Yes.' She looked at him. 'You're all right for a . . . '

'Comar?'

'Guy.' She hit the doorbell, surprised Velimai hadn't already opened it for them. 'Most of the guys I know aren't big on talking about feelings and stuff like that.'

'Maybe you need to meet more guys.'

'No, I like the one I have just fine.' Fi smiled, unable to help herself. Was Damian coming on to her? It was sweet. Especially since the last time a guy hit on her, she'd been totally alive. Damian knew about her ghosty side – he'd just seen it when she'd had a little freak-out at Seven – and he still wanted to take a chance? Definitely sweet. But definitely not happening. Doc was the only guy for her.

Her smile disappeared. Not getting a clue as to his whereabouts sucked. Fi punched the doorbell a second time. 'C'mon, Vel, open up.'

At last the door swung wide, Velimai behind it. She signed something, too fast for Fi to catch.

'Slow down, I don't understand.'

D-O-C-D-O-C-D-O-

'Doc? You know where Doc is?' Fi almost grabbed Velimai's hands, remembering at the last minute about the wysper's super-scratchy skin.

Yes. Velimai pointed upstairs. *First room,* she signed slowly.

Fi took off, not waiting for more info. Damian ran with her and together they skidded to a stop on the marble floor outside the room Velimai had indicated. Fi opened the door and went into the guest room. A sleek, black leopard sprawled on the bed.

'Doc!' Fi ran to his side and wrapped him in a hug.

His big head came up, his golden eyes blinking in her direction. He pushed his head against her arm and exhaled through his nose, blowing warm air over her skin.

'I'm happy to see you, too.' She kissed his head.

He made a whuffing sound, then dropped his head to the bed again.

Fi sat up, finally noticing that Velimai had come into the room as well. Fi looked at her. 'He feels hot. Really hot. Is something wrong?'

Velimai pointed to her arm, then to Doc.

Fi checked his front leg. A long, scabby gash ran the length of it. Fi turned back to Velimai. 'What happened?'

The wysper shrugged, put down the towel she held, and picked up an e-tablet and stylus. She scribbled a note, then held it up for Fi to see. *Arrived in leopard form. No idea what happened. Fever. Smells of brimstone.*

Fi's insides went cold and she could feel herself wavering between corporeal and spirit forms. She knew two creatures that carried that stink. Neither was good news. 'Is he going to be okay?'

Should be, Velimai signed. She wrote a second message. *He needs to rest/heal enough to shift human again. Then he'll explain.*

Fi nodded, stroking Doc's silky fur. 'Okay,' she said softly, lying down beside the big purring beast. 'But I'm staying with him until then.'

Chapter Twenty

Chrysabelle couldn't help but stare at Mal the way the tourists stared at her. He walked toward her, in all his dark and beautiful glory, lit by the blazing Louisiana morning sky. It was like something she'd dreamed, not that she was prepared to admit that to him. She could barely admit it to herself. A few of the women set up to tell fortunes paused from laying out their cards to gawk as he strolled past their tables. Chrysabelle wanted to tell them to mind their own business.

Instead, she bent her head and sipped the tall cup of chicory coffee Mortalis had picked up at a nearby café. She had no place to feel that way about Mal. No place. She glanced at the fae, who, because of the amount of iron fencing surrounding Jackson Square's abundantly green park, stood a little farther away nursing his own cup of java.

'Started to wonder if you were going to show,' Mortalis said as Mal approached.

'I had a little incident,' Mal answered, closing the gap between them. He looked to his left at the soaring façade of the St Louis Cathedral. 'We had to meet on this side of the square?'

'Can you feel it?' Chrysabelle asked, tipping her face in the direction of the magnificent church.

He nodded. 'Like ants on my skin.'

'I know the feeling.' Mortalis nodded toward the wrought-iron fence. 'That thing makes me feel like I'm chewing tinfoil.' He lifted a finger from his cup to point toward the street that bordered the river. 'Tell me about this incident while we walk.'

As the three of them started around the square, Mal spoke. 'Couple of fae on patrol. Smokesingers, maybe. They took the bribe like you said they would.'

'Describe them.' Mortalis lifted a hand to greet a street performer, a man dressed head to foot in silver clothing and matching face paint and moving like an old-time robot.

'Short gray horns, silvery skin' – Mal pointed back at the man Mortalis had just waved to – 'not that silvery, but close. And lavender eyes.'

Mortalis nodded. 'Those were definitely smokesingers. Cousin to the shadeux, but they don't really get dangerous until they go through their first burning. If the ones you saw still had gray horns and not black, they hadn't. They might not have even been a real patrol. Just juvies shaking you down in the name of the law.' He frowned. 'You shouldn't have anything else to worry about so long as we're together.'

'I don't plan on going off on my own again.' Mal turned to Chrysabelle. 'You okay?'

She tossed her empty cup into a trashcan. 'A little tired, but good. Thanks.' She gave him a quick smile, trying to hide the pain arcing along her spine. The smile *was* real. He hadn't had to come on this trip and probably shouldn't have, considering the city's policy on vampires, but she was glad to have him. She wasn't a hundred percent, but having him at her side meant that didn't matter. Mal could push her buttons like nobody's business, but he always put her safety first. Even if that meant solutions she didn't agree with.

Mal growled at a man who pointed his camera in her direction, causing the human to stumble into a display of T-shirts. Fortunately, the SUV was just ahead of them now. Amery got out as they approached and opened the doors. 'I see you made it,' he said to Mal.

Mal said nothing, just climbed in after Chrysabelle and resumed his original seat. When they were all in, Amery steered into traffic and started across town.

'Where are we going?' Chrysabelle asked.

'Garden District,' Mortalis answered. 'That's where most of the fae live now. The Vieux Carré is home to a few of us, but there's still a lot of iron there.'

'Vieux Carré,' Chrysabelle repeated, practicing her French. 'That means "old square," right? Do the fae speak French, or is that a holdover from the original settlers?'

'Fae were among the original settlers.' Mortalis caught her eye in the visor mirror, pulled down against the sun. 'Those of us born here speak a kind of pidgin. A mix of French, English, and fae. Our own version of Creole.'

So Mortalis had been born here. Interesting. 'Why did the fae come to New Orleans?'

'It wasn't just to New Orleans, but to much of the southern United States. Mostly they came to escape the vampire nobility in Europe who were intent on wiping them out.'

The scenery around them changed from office buildings and hotels to small shops, which then gave way to massive live oaks standing guard alongside block after block of palatial homes. Strands of plastic beads dangled from the higher branches and streetlamps, an odd contrast to the leaded glass, white columns, and stately front porches facing the street. 'Why are there beads on the trees?'

'Leftovers from years of Mardi Gras. St Charles is one of the main parade routes.'

She went back to studying the houses. 'These homes are breathtaking.'

Mal snorted softly. 'You don't exactly live in a tent.'

'No, but these homes have character. Charm. There's more to them than just their size.'

'Charisma spells,' Amery interjected.

'That's a little strange, wanting someone to like your house that much,' Mal said.

'It's more than that,' Amery continued. 'The spell prevents vandalism by creating in the viewer a desire to protect. In this neighborhood, even small things like littering have been virtually wiped out.'

'Leave it to the fae,' Mal said, shaking his head.

Mortalis shot a smile back at Chrysabelle. 'We always have been the brains of the othernatural realm.'

Amery turned down a side street off of St Charles and drove another block or two, then turned again and parked. 'We're here.'

'Which house?' Chrysabelle asked.

'This one.' He jerked a thumb toward the house on the driver's side.

For a house painted entirely in shades of gray and black, the ornate Victorian should have seemed dull, but there was something both welcoming and serious about it. As if you'd better have business when you stepped onto its front porch, but so long as you did, come on in.

Mal leaned across to look out her window. 'A high-ranking fae lives in a house with this much ironwork?'

Amery shook his head. 'It's not iron – it's painted aluminum. Maintains the historical integrity without the nasty itch.' He pointed to a few houses across the street. 'They're almost all aluminum these days.'

Mortalis shifted to look at Mal and Chrysabelle. 'The chances that Hugo will invite you in, Mal, are nil. He's one of the elektos. Giving a vampire access to his home isn't even up for debate. You might as well stay in the car.'

'Absolutely not,' Chrysabelle said. 'He comes. This Hugo might be one of your leaders, but he's not mine and he's got something that belongs to me. Besides, Mal might be the only thing that keeps me from killing this idiot outright.' Her body tensed as her anger grew, sending a quick jolt of pain down her spine. 'If Hugo won't let him in, I'll burn his house down.'

'Chrysabelle . . . ' Mortalis tipped his head as if he were dealing with an unreasonable child.

'Don't, Mortalis. You have no place to speak. Mal comes.' She opened her door and got out, tired of waiting, tired of discussing, ready to *do*. She slid her sacrès on over her long coat, happy to have their slight weight back on her body.

Except for Amery, the others got out behind her. She stood in front of the chest-high gate, studying the house. A curtain in one of the upstairs windows swayed as though it had been dropped back into place. Being watched was no surprise. Nor was whoever had been at the window feeling no need to hide their inspection. Clearly, she and her group were to understand that they were no longer on their home turf. What Hugo failed to comprehend was that she hadn't been on her home turf in a long time. Every day was filled with lessons in adaptation, and if this Hugo thought he was going to have some sort of advantage because this was his city, his house, his rules ... he was wrong.

Mortalis pushed a button concealed in one of the flowers decorating the elaborate metal fence surrounding the property. A buzzer sounded and he pushed through the gate.

She followed with Mal behind her. They waited on the porch while Mortalis rang the bell. The leaded glass on the double doors was mottled in such a way that only shapes were visible through it. The one coming toward them wore black.

The door opened and a doughy butler, who looked very human, addressed them. 'Good afternoon.' He stepped aside, holding the door wide. 'Do come in. Mr Loudreux is waiting.'

Mal glanced at Chrysabelle. She understood that the butler wasn't the home owner, so his invitation meant nothing to Mal. She stayed put, squaring her shoulders in preparation for the anticipated battle. 'We need a more personal invitation. From Hugo himself.'

The butler lowered his hairy brows and squinted at her. His gaze moved to Mal, where it stopped, and his brows resumed their normal height. 'Ah, yes, I suppose you would.' He frowned and shook his head at Mal. 'I should call the guardian, but what good would that do? Mr Loudreux is not going to be happy about this.'

'I don't care if he cries like a little girl. Go get him,' Mal said. 'We need an invite.'

'Hmph.' The butler shut the door as he turned on his heels. His penguin shape disappeared back into the foyer.

Mortalis sighed and stared at the blue painted porch ceiling. 'This isn't going to happen. I'm telling you.'

'So noted.' She gently pushed him aside to stand in front of the door. A minute or two later, two shapes came toward them, the penguin and a tall, slim figure.

Mr Loudreux opened the door this time. He stood a head taller than any in their party, his slim build, narrow face, and freckles giving him away as a cypher. Nothing about his expression read as kindness. 'I understand you expect me to grant a vampire entrance into my home.'

Chrysabelle lifted her chin. 'I do.'

'No. If the rest of you want to come in, you may, but I suggest you do so quickly, as my patience tends to be nonexistent.'

She stepped forward, putting herself in his personal space and halfway into his house. 'And I understand you wanted to see me before returning my property. Seeing me includes those in my company. If that doesn't meet with your approval, then give me back *my* ring and we're gone.'

He smiled. 'I accepted the ring for safekeeping. The circumstances for its return were not discussed.'

Meaning Mortalis had handed it over quickly and without properly wording the details of the agreement. She knew how fae could be. Everything was open to interpretation. She narrowed her eyes and lowered her voice, moving quickly to slip one of her wrist blades into her hand. 'Then you'll understand if I use whatever means necessary to recover it.'

His mouth opened and he looked down to where her bone blade pressed against the ivory silk vest covering his belly.

'Try me,' she whispered.

His mouth snapped closed and he shuddered. 'You may all enter.'

With a sharp snap of her wrist, the blade retracted. He stepped back, anger flashing in his eyes. Apparently, he wasn't used to being dealt with in such a manner. She sailed past him into the house. Too bad for him. She was done playing games with beings who felt superior because of the power they wielded. Come tonight at midnight, the balance between those with power and those without was going to shift in a big way.

The butler scurried past her to open a pair of French doors and direct them into the parlor. Mortalis and Mal joined her, with Hugo bringing up the rear. He nodded to the butler, who closed the doors.

From a dim corner of the room, the darkness moved and a petite female shadeux fae emerged. Her charcoal leather pants and half vest, only slightly darker than the rest of her exposed skin, showed off a defined midsection and well-muscled arms that sported a row of barbs. Her black hair was braided down the center of her skull, leaving visible her pointed ears and a slender set of horns that jutted from her forehead, then arched back and around to follow the curve of her jawbone. The needle-fine ends were tipped in silver. She wore a sword strapped to her back, and blades at her wrists and thighs. She could have been Mortalis's twin. Her presence explained Loudreux's boldness. Chrysabelle had never known a cypher to be particularly daring without heavy backup.

The bodyguard's gaze danced over the group, stopping on the other shadeux fae. Still, her face showed zero emotion. 'Mortalis.'

His face hardened with displeasure. 'What the hell are you doing here?'

'I'm Mr Loudreux's personal security detail.' She tipped her head to one side. 'Is that any way to greet your sister?'

Lola gasped. A baby? 'Are you sure of what you're saying? My daughter had a child?'

The chief nodded. 'Yes. The levels return to normal within three to four weeks of a woman giving birth, so it was recent.' He glanced at Creek and John, then back at her. 'I know you have questions, but that's all the information I have. The PCPD is moving forward with every available asset to locate your daughter's last known residence. If this child is out there, we'll find it.'

'If?' she asked. Of course the child was out there. Newborns didn't just disappear.

The chief sighed. 'We can't be sure the child is . . . alive.'

Lola rubbed her aching brow. The weight of responsibility pressed hard. She had to keep her sanity. Keep her city from crumbling along with her. 'I understand. I want to know everything as soon as you do.'

'You have my word.' He nodded a goodbye and was gone.

She pushed a forkful of eggs across the plate without really seeing them. 'A child. Can you imagine? What else could happen?'

Creek made a strangled noise. She looked up. He broke eye contact the second she made it, suddenly fixated on his coffee.

'What do you know?'

'Nothing.' He crammed half of a guava pastelito into his mouth.

She glared at him. 'Lie to me again and your next meal will be served on a cold metal tray.'

He chewed, finally looking up. A sip of coffee, a swallow, and he spoke. 'You really want to know? Even if it will cause you more pain? Even if it might not be true?'

'Either way, yes.' Any iota of information he could give her that would help her find this child – her grandchild – she would take. No matter how awful or heartbreaking it was.

Creek shot a quick look at John, then came back to her. 'We – meaning myself, Mal, and Chrysabelle – were told by another person that he'd seen your daughter with a baby and the man believed to have fathered the child in Little Havana.'

She shrugged. 'If you think it bothers me that my daughter lived in such a desperate part of town, it does, but not so much. She is Cuban American, after all.' Despite how Julia had taken her father's side in the divorce, she was still Lola's daughter. Nothing Julia did could ever erase that.

Creek nodded. 'I live there, too. That's not the point. The man she was with—'

'The baby's father.'

'The man we suspect fathered the child. He's ... Look, there's no easy way to say this. He's a vampire. And not just an ordinary one. He's the only one any of us has ever known who can daywalk.'

Her body went hot, then cold, then numb. A vampire. Her grandchild was half monster. 'How is it even possible?'

'I'm not really sure. Apparently he wasn't turned in the usual way—'

She smacked her hand down on the tabletop, making the silverware jump. 'I meant, how is it possible that a vampire got my daughter pregnant!'

Creek shrugged one shoulder. 'I really don't know. It shouldn't be possible, but Preacher's not your usual vampire.'

'You know where this vampire lives?'

'Yes.'

She shoved her chair back, threw her napkin down on her plate, and stood. 'Take John and go there. Get my grandchild and bring it back to me. Maybe there's some way to cure the child of ... '

'Being a vampire?' Creek snorted. 'It's not a disease.'

More like a plague. 'Whatever it is, it might be reversible. Bring the child to me at city hall as soon as you can.' She left them at the table as she went out to the waiting car. She was clueless as to what to do with a half-vampire child, but she damn sure didn't want a vampire to have it. This child, regardless of who had fathered it, carried some of her blood in its veins. She'd failed Julia. She would not make the same mistakes twice.

The sweet-sick smell of charred flesh reached Aliza before she had her airboat docked. It was almost enough to make her puke up the blood of the two homeless men she'd drained. Almost. A small flock of turkey vultures sat preening on the peak of the metal roof. Dread wormed through her belly, but she shoved it aside. There were plenty of good reasons for those birds. This was the Glades, after all. Stuff was always showing up dead.

She hopped out of the boat and bounded up the stairs, her old bones no longer a concern with her new vampire strength. The wooden door was open, leaving just the screen door between her and the inside. Through it, she could see into the living room.

A pair of female legs lay sprawled on the floor, hidden from the knees up by the kitchen wall. The dragonfly tattoo on the left ankle caused a sob to choke her.

With a howl, she ran into the house, almost tripping over her own feet with the speed. She threw herself down on the floor beside Evie. Pain wracked Aliza's body in waves. Pain so strong it shook her bones and dimmed her vision. Her only child lay lifeless before her, eyes staring up at the ceiling, a softball-sized hole burned into her chest.

She scooped Evie into her arms. Her body had already begun to stiffen. Aliza buried her head against Evie's neck and cried loud, hard tears. Life was damn unfair. She'd just gotten her daughter back from her stone prison. Now someone had murdered her in cold blood.

Rocking back and forth, Aliza wept until her tears dried up and the sobs wracking her body faded away. She eased Evie's body back to the floor and stared at her without really seeing much but her beautiful face. At last, Aliza reached out and closed Evie's eyes.

The hole in her chest had been made by magic. The kind of magic only a witch could produce. Aliza looked toward the side of her house. Beyond that wall sat the houses of her coven members. One of them had done this. There was no other explanation. She got up to take an inventory of the house, see what had been so valuable that it had cost Evie her life.

The demon was gone. She picked up a shard of the shattered aquarium. So that was it. Someone had stolen the demon to get the power that came with owning the creature. But how? Aliza's and Evie's blood had formed the spell that held the creature. The only way that spell could be broken was if Aliza and Evie were both dead. Aliza slammed her fist into the floor. She *was* dead. She was a damn vampire. With Evie gone, too, the spell on the demon was broken.

Why would someone kill Evie if not to have the demon for themselves? Had one of her coven seen her go into town? Wasn't like she made a secret of it. Too hard to hide an airboat anyway. Maybe someone had followed her, seen her go into the church, then watched the vampire take her body out and figured with her gone, her house was easy pickings. Aliza glanced back at her dead daughter, and a new sob wracked her chest.

The old metal TV tray lay to one side, blackened and burned.

Evie had tried to stop them. And gotten killed for it. 'Oh, Evie child. I'm gonna find who did this and I'm going to make them pay.'

Aliza headed for the door and noticed for the first time the gouges in the kitchen's linoleum. She bent down to run her fingers over one. Beside it were dried brown spots she instantly knew were blood. She licked her finger, then rubbed it on one spot and brought it to her mouth. Animal blood. It had the same earthy tang as the dog's.

Her newly keen sense of sight picked out a few small black hairs a little farther away. She gathered as many as she could and sniffed them. Why would a big cat be in her house? Because that big cat was actually a varcolai out for revenge. And the only black-furred varcolai she could think of who knew where she lived and had a reason to want either of them dead was the one she'd had under her smoke spell.

Doc. The same low-down, dirty dealer who'd sold her poor Evie the drugs that had turned her into stone for all those years. Wasn't that enough? Did he have to kill her, too?

Maybe the demon had ended that miserable leopard. But she knew better. There wasn't enough blood on the floor for her to believe there'd been a killing blow.

She stood up and stared out the door, a thousand things going through her head. She had to bury her daughter, but as soon as Evie was laid to rest proper, Aliza was going to hunt down that leopard and skin him alive. If she could get the smoke spell working again, finding him would be a snap.

Then she'd go back to that vampire who thought he'd killed her and show him just how wrong he was. Come hell or deep water, that vampire child was going to be hers.

Chapter Twenty-one

Doc stretched, trying to shake the sleep holding on to him. He opened his eyes, blinking a few times to clear the fog. Fi sat at the end of the bed, leaning against the footboard. Her eyes were closed, her mouth slightly open. She flickered like an old-fashioned movie. He smiled. His girl. Safe. That was good. Damn good.

He shifted into his human form, then propped his head on his hand and studied her. Letting her sleep was the right thing to do. She'd probably been up to all hours after he'd seen her at the church. He wasn't sure how she'd even found him there, but his girl was resourceful. And braver than he'd ever imagined. His smile faded, remembering the night they'd had there. And the rest of his. It was over now. With Aliza and Evie both dead, that chapter of his life was closed. Permanently.

He nudged Fi with his foot. She could snooze later. 'Hey, sleepyhead,' he said softly.

'Hmm?' She opened her eyes and the flickering stopped. 'Hey, yourself. You're awake. And human. How do you feel?'

'Not bad, considering.' Pretty crappy, actually. He stuck out his arm, twisting it side to side to look at the spot where the Castus had snagged him. 'Just a little scratch now. Burned like a mother, though.' And still did, but not nearly like it had.

'You're lucky it wasn't deeper.' She scooted toward him and kissed his mouth. 'I was so worried.'

'I know.' He shook his head. 'I'm sorry. What happened after I left you at the church?'

'Preacher tried to kill me, but I went ghosty and ditched him, then I went looking for you but you were long gone. I figured since you said *witch* that you were either under some kind of spell or headed to Aliza's or both.'

'Both.'

'It was that smoke we went through, wasn't it?' She bit her lip.

'Probably. Not sure.'

'Well, I am.' She sighed. 'You think Aliza's really dead?'

He nodded. 'Yeah, I know so. And so is her daughter Evie.'

Fi's eyes rounded. 'How do you know?'

He flopped back onto the pillows. 'About Evie? She tried to kill me with a bolt of heavy-duty fire magic. I grabbed a tray and reflected the fire right back at her. Blew a hole in her chest I could've put my fist through.'

Fi's face crinkled up. 'Gross. Why'd she try to kill you?'

'She's the one who had me under the spell. Forced me to bring the vampire baby to her. Then planned to kill me because she could.'

'So who gave you that scratch?'

'Castus. Apparently Evie and Aliza had the thing contained with some heavy black blood magic. Demon wasn't exactly happy about it. When Evie died, the thing broke free, which is how I know Aliza's dead, too. If she'd still been alive, I'm sure the spell would have held. Aliza's not dumb. She'd know to put that kind of fail-safe in place with a monster like that.' He scrubbed a hand over his face, wishing he could erase the images in his head. 'Worst part is, the demon got the kid. Scooped that thing up like a twelve-year-old girl with a brand-new kitten.'

'That sucks, but do you think it matters? I don't mean to be insensitive, but it's a vampire baby. Isn't it kind of with its family now?'

'I can only imagine what a creature like that would do with another creature like that. Maybe Mal or Chrysabelle will know.' He sat up a little. 'They back yet?'

'No. But I hope they hurry.' She bent her knees under her chin. 'We had some excitement of our own last night, right after you disappeared.'

'Yeah?'

'A vampire showed up and nabbed Saraphina, the new comarré. According to Damian, she was happy to go with the vampire and never wanted to escape in the first place. Dumb comarré sliced Damian's shoulder open.'

He sat up completely. 'How did the vampire know where to find her? Did you see Tatiana?'

'Don't know and no. But we're sure she must have had her hands in it somehow.'

He swung his legs over the side of the bed. 'I need to talk to Damian now. If a vampire can just walk onto this property, how are we going to protect ourselves against the Castus that's now running loose?'

Worry crinkled her brow. 'And tonight is Halloween.'

He grabbed a robe from a nearby chair. 'Don't remind me.'

*

Chrysabelle closed her mouth before it became obvious that she was staring. Mortalis had a sister. Now that Chrysabelle saw them together, the resemblance was uncanny. She bent her head to adjust the strap of one sacre, using the moment to slant her eyes at Mortalis. The barbs on his forearms were fully extended, a sure sign of his displeasure. Seeing his sister here had been a surprise for him, too, apparently.

'A word with you outside, Blu,' Mortalis said.

'Not while I'm on duty. I have nothing to say to you anyway.' She looked at her employer. 'My apologies, Mr Loudreux.'

He nodded and she moved to stand behind the chair he'd taken.

Mortalis's mouth settled into a thin, hard line. Clearly, this wasn't over.

'Please, sit.' Mr Loudreux indicated the chairs and sofa across from him, then glanced toward the butler. 'Fellows, give us some light, will you? And offer our guests some refreshment.'

The butler stiffened. 'Right away, sir.' As he left, he flipped a switch that illuminated a beautiful crystal chandelier above them. It glowed half-heartedly, like the available electricity wasn't quite up to the task. Still, it *was* electricity. Mr Loudreux wanted them to know he had means, in case the house, butler, and private bodyguard didn't do it. The overkill worked her nerves.

Mal took a seat on the sofa, leaving room for Chrysabelle beside him. She took it. Mortalis settled into the chair as though he might spring back up at any moment.

Fellows came in bearing a large silver tray with a china tea set and all the accoutrements. He took it to the side table and began fixing a cup of tea for Loudreux.

'Extra sugar, sir?' Fellows asked.

Loudreux nodded. 'As usual. And for you, comarré?'

She'd had enough of the pretend hospitality. 'I came for my ring, not tea. You've seen me. Now give me my ring.'

Loudreux laughed. 'My, you're a direct one, aren't you?'

'Get her the ring,' Mal said.

Loudreux sniffed. 'I see our Southern charm is wasted on you.' He took the tea Fellows brought him, sipped it, then put it on the side table. 'Fine, business it is.'

At last.

'Sklar, the current guardian of our fair city, is worthless. Unfortunately, he's also the son of the elektos Prime.'

Mortalis exhaled. 'Sklar's a smokesinger. That explains the band of juvies Mal ran into today.'

'Let me guess.' Loudreux addressed Mal. 'They let you go for a bribe.'

Mal leaned back. 'Yes.'

Loudreux shook his head, disgust bracketing his mouth. 'That's been the way of it since that slack-wit took over. He's a disgrace to this city. A hollow threat. He lets more vampires in than he keeps out. Meanwhile the elektos have their hands tied because none of us dare speak against the Prime's son.' Loudreux cursed in faeish.

Chrysabelle held her palms up. 'Fae politics mean nothing to me. Why are you telling me all this?'

Mal put his arm across the sofa back. 'He wants you – us – to get rid of this problem for him.' He gave Loudreux a bitter look. 'Then you'll get the ring back.'

Loudreux smiled. 'It would be a great boon to New Orleans to have a proper guardian in place.'

Chrysabelle's hands ached from clenching her fists. Her back ached because it just did. 'Mal is right, then?'

Loudreux nodded and sipped his tea.

Mortalis shook his head at the cypher. 'Taking bribes bothers you but assassinations are fine? So long as the greater good is served?'

'Now, you just wait a minute,' Loudreux barked. 'I never called for anyone's assassination. How you go about fixing this problem is your business, not mine.'

'As long as you don't get your hands dirty.' Mortalis stood. 'Nothing's changed, has it?'

Loudreux pounded his fist against the arm of his chair. 'Plenty has changed. You think this city stood still waiting for your return? No. Life here goes on, with or without your family.' He twisted in his chair to reach up and pat Blu's arm. 'Don't you mind that statement, sugar. Wasn't meant for you at all.'

The barbs on Mortalis's forearms flexed in and out. Chrysabelle tried to refocus the situation. 'I'm not killing anyone for you.'

Loudreux shrugged. 'Your vamp friend brought that up, not me. You can remove the guardian any way you like. As far as replacements go, there are a few people on my shortlist, but they may take a little convincing. That's the second part of your *assignment*.'

She had to talk her way through this or she was going to blow up. 'Why do the fae even need a haven city? Most vampires can't stand the taste of fae blood. It's not like you're getting picked off by nobility in this part of the world. I can see the lure of being able to daywalk, but are vampires really that much a threat to your way of life here?'

With thinly disguised contempt in his eyes, Loudreux tilted forward. '*Chérie*, the haven city isn't to protect the fae, it's to protect the rest of you. Some of the kin contained in these city limits make your shadeux friend here seem about as dangerous as a bunch of daffodils. We don't even like to speak their names lest they hear us and think we're calling them, so you don't worry about the why, just the doing.'

Maybe she should just run her sacre through this cypher's gut and be done with him. But then she wouldn't get the ring, and her chances of finding her brother would disappear. 'Where do I find the current guardian and the possible replacements?'

'So you accept?' Loudreux looked surprised.

She scowled at him. 'What choice did you give me?'

'You could always abandon the ring.'

The comment snapped one of her few remaining threads of control. She leaped over the table that separated them, coming down inches from Loudreux. His cup and saucer rattled on the table beside him. Blu whipped out a knife and poised to throw it, but Chrysabelle ignored her, leaning down and confronting the wide-eyed cypher as face-to-face as a person could get. 'That ring is mine. You have no claim to it. None. In fact, the only ones who seem to have any real claim to it besides me are the Kubai Mata. Would you like me to tell them where their ring is? Because I'm sure they'd find a way to get it back.'

'You wouldn't,' Loudreux breathed.

'Not yet, I wouldn't. But I'd like to point out that you should be very glad I'm not willing to abandon that ring, because if I was, I'd have no reason to keep you alive.'

Loudreux closed his mouth and swallowed. Without taking his eyes off her, he lifted a hand and snapped his fingers. 'Fellows, that envelope from my desk.'

Chrysabelle straightened as the butler left. She kept her eyes on Loudreux while Fellows was gone, enjoying the way the cypher's discomfort grew with every passing second.

Finally, Fellows returned. 'Your envelope, sir.'

Loudreux took it and held it out by the end toward Chrysabelle. 'All the information you need is in there.'

Chapter Twenty-two

Svetla met Tatiana and Daci at the front door of Grigor's estate. Tonight she wore crimson silk. The color made her already pale skin chalky, washing her out in a way that made Tatiana smile. Svetla didn't return the expression. 'The council is waiting, as they have been for the last eighteen hours.'

With Daci at her elbow, Tatiana entered and steeled her mind against any potential invasion from Svetla or Grigor. Daci would be doing the same. No one in this house was to be trusted. She shrugged out of her fur and handed it off to a servant, but kept her gloves on and her metal prosthesis covered. Being here meant she was missing Samhain in Paradise City. A night in which she could have gathered residual power in bundles. A night in which she could have at last been victorious against the comarré. But no, she was here at the council's whim. If things did not go her way, she would break from the nobility and their rules and do as she damn well pleased. 'Hello to you, too, Svetla. I'm not sure which is paler, the snow covering the ground or your skin. Perhaps you should feed.'

Svetla sniffed. 'Why am I not surprised a gypsy fails to understand the beauty of porcelain skin?'

Tatiana let the gypsy comment roll off her and turned to Daci. 'Svetla is the Elder of the House of Rasputin. She was the *second* female Elder to ever be appointed.'

Having already been briefed with this information, Daci smiled at Svetla as though she were about to speak to someone with a head wound. 'It must be difficult for you.'

'What must be?' Svetla asked.

'The constant comparison,' Daci answered. 'Being in the shadow of someone like Tatiana. What a high bar to reach.'

Svetla scowled, gave Daci a dismissive glare, then turned and strode off down the hall. Tatiana followed, giving Daci a wink. What a treasure this one was turning out to be. Tatiana had never had a sister in her human life, only brothers who'd treated her like a servant. Impulsively, she reached out and gave Daci's hand a squeeze.

Daci responded by mocking Svetla's hip-swaying walk, making Tatiana cough to cover up a sudden laugh. She smiled. A rare, genuine smile. She couldn't recall the last time she'd felt this way. Her hand found the locket around her neck. Yes, she could. It had been many, many years ago.

They rounded the corner, turning down the hall that led to the council meeting room. Svetla stopped them before the doors. 'I'll go in and see if they're ready for you.'

Pompous git. 'They're ready.' Tatiana pushed past and swung into the room. The Dominus were all there, seated as before with their Elders behind them. She made a shallow curtsy. The pressure of Grigor's mental probing tested her walls. What arrogance. 'My lords, I apologize for my late arrival, but I understand you were made aware of my situation.'

Svetla rushed in behind Daci. 'I'm sorry, my lords. She barged in before I could announce her. And her *guest*.' Svetla cut her eyes at Daci.

Lord Syler raised his hand. 'It's all right. We were expecting her, after all.' He gestured to an empty chair at the table. 'Please be seated, Tatiana. Your guest will have to wait outside. At least until our matter is taken care of.'

'Of course. My guest, Daciana Bracey, is an upstanding member of the House of Tepes. If I ascend to Dominus, she will become Elder.' Tatiana turned, nodding to Daci to indicate that it was all right to wait outside. She bent her head in response and left. Tatiana took her seat, pleased that the council's attitude seemed more . . . mellow toward her. It wasn't a word she'd ever thought to associate with this group of musty old males, but whatever had brought the change about, she liked it. Perhaps this was a good omen that she was about to achieve the position she'd been striving for.

'Already appointing an Elder?' Lord Zephrim snorted loudly. 'As always, you assume too much.'

She gave him a full-on stare that had reduced lesser vampires to bumbling fools. Of course, in Zephrim's case, he already had the fool part down. 'I've only assumed that the council is ready to give me an answer. If that's not the case, why else have you called me here with such urgency?'

Svetla took her seat behind Lord Grigor as he spoke. 'You assume correctly. The ancient one was located. He told us to bring you back, then summon him so he might announce his decision.'

At last. Tatiana's joy threatened to bubble over into something very unbecoming. She looked down for a moment to compose herself.

Grigor laughed softly, an unpleasant sound that grated on her nerves. 'You should be worried. The ancient one seemed more agitated than usual.'

She held still for a few long seconds. Was this not going to turn out the way she thought? If the ancient one was upset with her ... She'd had no communication with him in some time. And she still didn't have the ring or the comarré. Her joy evaporated and she lifted her head, resolved to whatever might happen. 'I'm sure the ancient one only wishes, like I do, to be done with this endless waiting. As I have said before, I will abide by whatever they decide. May the ancient ones be served.'

The others recited the words in unison. 'May the ancient ones be served.'

Lord Timotheius raised his wineglass toward Grigor. 'As we are still in your house, the privilege to call them falls upon you.'

He nodded stiffly. 'Of course. It is my honor.'

Tatiana pursed her mouth against a laugh. An honor that made him tremble.

Grigor stood, outstretched his arms, his palms up. With a deep sigh and a slow blink, he spoke. 'Castus Sanguis, hear your children. Come to us and grace us with thy presence.'

Unlike the last time Grigor had called the ancient ones, Tatiana wasn't disappointed. A great flash of light and the sharp piercing sourness of brimstone and unwashed flesh shattered the air at the room's far end. Smoke billowed up around the towering Samael, his body clad from the waist down in a skirt of shadows shifting with faces and limbs. From the waist up, his skin was a shiny, dark red, like dried meat.

'My children,' he greeted them. His eyes went to Tatiana. Was that a spark of pleasure? Could he be pleased to see her? With no small hope, she allowed herself a fraction of a smile.

Grigor bowed his head. 'My lord, as you know, the House of Tepes is in need of a new Dominus.' He pointed his hand at Tatiana. 'This one comes to take the position. We await your approval.'

The Castus's mouth pulled back in a mutilated grin. 'Granted.'

And just like that, she was Dominus. Her smile went smug, but she didn't care what the other Dominus thought. She was one of them now. Their peer. They could no longer command her about like an underling. She nodded with as much humility as she could muster, despite the unrelenting surge welling up inside her. 'Thank you, Ancient One. I will not disappoint you.'

'No, you will not.' The Castus's voice spilled from his gullet like shards of rock tumbling down a metal grate. He turned his attention to the others again. 'Now, I have a matter of my own that needs attending.'

The lords murmured in obeisance. 'Of course, Ancient One. Anything. Yes, my lord.'

Parrots, the lot of them. She lifted her voice above the others, determined to show them immediately how different her reign as Dominus would be. 'What is it you desire, my liege?'

Samael cast his gaze upon her, the sparkle in his eyes undeniably amused. 'The witch who is responsible for Ivan's death. I want her dead. Then burn her house and the houses of her coven to the ground.'

Tatiana stood and made a small curtsy. 'Consider it done, my lord. What else would you like?'

He threw his head back and laughed, shattering the carafes of blood and vodka on the table and giving them all a glimpse of the dagger teeth that surrounded his black maw. 'My daughter, you please me. As such, you may expect a visit from me later.'

Her smile faltered. That was not the result she'd intended. She played it off with a shake of her head and lowered eyes. 'You honor me and my new Elder, Daciana.' Daci must be listening to this from her bench outside the doors.

His gaze razored across the other Dominus while one talon-tipped finger pointed at Tatiana. 'Mind your sister. She and her' – he paused, a slight wicked grin bending his mouth – '*family* are to be protected. Any harm befalls them and my anger will be assuaged with your ashes.'

Another brilliant burst of fire and flame and Samael vanished. The faces of the other Dominus were pricelessly stunned, a mix of open mouths and incredulous gazes. Tatiana lifted her chin and snapped her fingers to get their attention. 'Have the driver bring my car around. I'll be taking the Dominus's jet. I expect it to be fueled. Svetla, be a dear and fetch my fur, will you?'

The council and their Elders sat staring.

With nary a trace of humanity upon her face, Tatiana bellowed, 'Now!'

At last, the old men jumped to their feet to do her bidding. Grigor sent Svetla scurrying out. Smiling, Tatiana went to collect Daci and return home. Well, Tatiana would be returning home in the plane she arrived on to await the Castus. Daci would be taking the Dominus's supersonic jet straight back to Paradise City to capture Chrysabelle and bring her back for real.

The reign of the House of Tepes had finally begun.

Velimai answered the door at Chrysabelle's, her eyes shifting to Havoc with a question. Creek appreciated that she had let them onto the property without knowing more, until he saw Doc and the comar behind her, both with weapons aimed in their direction. Fi peeked around from the entrance into the living room.

'This is John Havoc, wolf varcolai. He's the head of security for the mayor. He's cool. Havoc, Velimai here basically runs the house. She's a—'

'Wysper.' Havoc signed something.

Velimai returned a few new signs, then Havoc responded, to which she laughed her soundless laugh. She glanced back at the two men and nodded. Creek made a mental note to ask Havoc what he'd said later. Doc sheathed the dagger in his hand and stepped aside. 'What's up?'

They entered and Creek made a quick intro as Velimai shut the door. 'Havoc, this is Doc. He's the leopard-shifter I was telling you about.'

Havoc stuck his hand out. 'Good to meet you. Creek speaks highly of you.'

'Does he?' Doc shook Havoc's hand, but his gaze stayed a long moment on Creek before returning to Havoc. Doc tipped his head toward the comar. 'Damian is Tatiana's former comar.'

Havoc pushed his shades onto his head. 'Tatiana's the vampire after Chrysabelle, right?'

'That's the one.' Creek jerked his head at Damian. 'Where's the comarré who was with you in the guesthouse?'

Damian snorted. 'Long story.'

'For another time,' Doc added. 'Let's just say she had other plans than hanging out here. What brings you two here?'

'First of all, another of Dominic's comarré has turned up dead.'

'That explains the cops at Seven,' Fi said, coming to stand beside Doc. 'What's second?'

'The mayor knows Julia had a baby right before she was murdered. She also knows the baby isn't fully human. She wants the kid brought to her.' Creek sighed. 'I'm not going to rip the kid out of the father's hands, but I figure we should at least check and see if this vampire is taking care of the baby or what.'

'Or what,' Doc answered. 'Preacher doesn't have the baby anymore.'

'How do you know?'

Fi crossed her arms. Her jaw tensed and for a split second, she flickered transparent. To Creek, it looked like her throat was torn out, but the image disappeared as quickly as it had come. He knew Mal had killed her. Maybe that was how he'd done it. Poor kid.

Doc slung his big arm over Fi's shoulders. 'Because under a spell controlled by the witch's daughter, I took the baby from Preacher and delivered it to her. But don't bother thinking you're going to rescue the kid. There was a fight and Evie got killed by her own magic. The Castus got loose and grabbed the baby. Before it could finish me off, it disappeared.'

'Castus?' Havoc asked.

'Remember the thing that attacked me right after I found Julia's body?' Creek nodded. 'It's that.'

Havoc swore under his breath.

'You can say that again,' Damian added. 'If the witches had it contained in the first place, they must be pretty knowledge-able. It takes strong blood magic to call one of the ancient ones. More blood to hold it.'

It was Doc's turn to swear. 'They had Mal's blood. I can't imagine blood more powerful than his.' He pulled Fi a little closer. 'This city's going to get seriously weird come midnight, and we have no idea if Mal and Chrysabelle will be back before then. Best thing we can do now is prepare for tonight.'

'Good idea.' Creek turned to Havoc. 'You've got to convince

the mayor that all Halloween-related activities need to be canceled citywide. No parade, no trick-or-treating, no parties, nothing. I don't care if she has to make up a bomb threat. She's got to keep people in their homes.'

Havoc shook his head. 'That's a tall order. I'll do what I can. What do you want me to tell her about her grandchild?'

'Tell her the truth. The child is gone, beyond our reach. There's no point in keeping anything from her.' Creek pointed to Doc. 'You feel secure here?'

'Not after the hit we took last night, but it's better than Mal's.'

Creek would find out more about that later. 'What about Seven?'

Doc's eyes narrowed. 'What about it?'

'It's probably the most secure place you could be considering what could go down tonight.'

'Not a chance in hell I'm going there or that Dominic's going to let us in.'

Damian nodded. 'Fi and I went to see him earlier and he refused us. I say we stay here. We're armed and we're formidable enough in our own right. As long as we stay inside, we're fine.'

'You're sure?'

Doc glanced at the others around him. 'Positive.'

'All right, then.'

'What about you?' Fi asked.

Creek planted his feet. 'I'm staying here with you. If Tatiana's still in the city, you can believe she's going to take advantage of tonight.' Creek glanced at the front door. 'She'll be back.'

Chapter Twenty-three

A mery parked them on a side street in the business district. Mal waited while Chrysabelle scanned the information Loudreux had given her one more time. Mortalis sat in the seat in front of Mal, staring straight ahead. Since they'd left Loudreux's, the fae had practically shimmered with anger but had yet to say a word. Sooner or later, it would come out and when it did, Mal knew from experience it wasn't going to be pretty. *Maybe he'll kill you.*

'I don't know how I'm going to do this.' Chrysabelle folded the paper and tucked it back inside the envelope. Frustration tensed her pretty face. 'What reason would this guardian have for stepping aside? He's apparently living a pretty high life. I can't offer him anything better. And I'm not killing him. I'm not a murderer.' Her hands balled into fists, the signum glinting. 'I just want my ring back.'

'I'm sorry,' Mortalis muttered. 'If I had any idea that Hugo was going to do this—'

'Enough, Mortalis,' Chrysabelle interrupted him. 'What's done is done. Loudreux's machinations are solely his responsibility.'

Mal rested his hand over hers. 'I need to speak to you alone.'

'You have an idea?'

He flicked his gaze to the front seats, then back to her. 'Alone.'

'All right. Let's take a walk down this alley.' She looked at Mortalis. 'We'll be back shortly.'

He grunted a reply.

Mal got out, held the door for her, then shut it behind her. She winced as she got out, the tightening of her body so subtle that if he had blinked, he would have missed it. She was hurting, but if she wasn't going to acknowledge it, neither was he. They walked to the middle of the alley in silence. She checked both sides, then turned to him, her gaze dancing across his face as though she'd never seen him before.

'What?'

She smiled. 'It's strange to see you with sun on your face. Good strange.'

'Likewise.' He reached up and ran his fingers over a sleek blond strand hanging past her cheek. Artificial light lit her signum up, but daylight gave her an almost otherworldly glow. He understood why people looked at her. It was hard not to stare with a gaping mouth and a dumbstruck tongue. Her eyes really did match the sky's ethereal blue. He swallowed and opened his fingers, letting the hair loose. 'You shine like . . . the sun itself.' Damn, he was an idiot with words around her. *No, just an idiot.*

'If you're trying to sweet-talk me, you might want to save it for when we get home.' But her smile didn't disappear. And now the faintest hint of pink colored her cheeks. Was she blushing? This woman? At least she hadn't slapped his hand away. *Or staked you.*

'So.' She blinked and looked back at the car. 'What's your

idea, because I know you must have something cooking in that head of yours. Don't say you'll kill him either. That's not an option we're taking.'

He shoved his hands into the pockets of his jeans to keep from touching her more. 'I can persuade him to give up the position.'

'Persuade? As in use your power?' She shook her head. 'I know you can do that with varcolai, but that doesn't mean you can do it with fae. Their magic is completely different. You try that and fail and no bribe is going to protect you.'

'I can do it. I've done it already. With the smokesingers that stopped me on my way to meet you. There's just one thing.'

'Always a catch, isn't there?' Her eyes narrowed a little. 'What is it?'

'Persuading a fae to tell me his name is one thing, persuading one into giving up a position of power is utterly different. It will take a lot of work and leave me drained afterward. I'll need to feed.' Why he felt like he needed to justify his request boggled him. He was a vampire, she was a comarré. It was no secret to either of them how this worked. There was, of course, the complication of him not being able to drink from her vein and the extracurricular contact that necessitated. The hot, mouth-to-mouth extracurricular contact. Which she'd denied him earlier. He blew out a breath to keep a growl from leaving his throat. *Drain her.*

'Blood is easy.' If she was thinking about the kiss that would come after, he couldn't read it in her eyes. 'How are you – we – going to explain your weakness to Mortalis after seeing this guardian? He'll know something's up.'

'Will it matter if we succeed?' His entire body tightened knowing that she was so willing to give her blood to him again.

The voices whined with fear and excitement. They loved her blood but hated the way it calmed them. 'I'm not worried about Mortalis. If he finds out what I can do, so be it, but Amery . . . ' Mal shook his head. 'I don't know him, don't trust him. I don't even like you knowing.'

She scowled. 'You don't trust me?'

'I trust you implicitly. I don't like burdening you with information about what I can and can't do. I don't like the possibility that someone could use it against you someday.'

She rolled her eyes. 'It's not a burden, and I can take care of myself.' She turned toward the SUV. 'We should get a hotel room. I can drain blood there and we can ditch Amery. Maybe Mortalis, too. I can tell him I want to make the first attempt alone with you to guard me, that I want him out of it so if something goes wrong, none of the blame falls back on him.'

Mal checked the sun's position. 'We're not going to make it back to Paradise City in time for Samhain.'

'We might, but it doesn't look good. I hope Doc and Creek can keep everything under control.' She exhaled hard. 'This is so much more than I can handle.'

'No, it's not. You're doing great.'

She glanced back at him and smiled weakly, her signum sparkling in the sun. 'Don't read too much into this, but it helps that you're here.'

He held his hands up in mock surrender. 'I won't read anything more into that than face value. Wouldn't want to assume you like me or anything.' But she did. *Right now.*

She laughed. 'Good, glad that's all clear.' Her laughter faded and she went serious. 'What do you think is up with Mortalis and his sister?'

Mal lifted his brows and shrugged. 'Bad blood, that much is

certain. Whatever his family's history in this town, it isn't good. At least not where it concerns him.'

'He seems wound pretty tightly since we left Loudreux's.'

Mal nodded. 'He'll be all right.' He hoped. Having the fae blow a gasket was only going to complicate an already tangled situation.

Chrysabelle's fingers landed lightly on his arm. Beneath the sleeve of his coat, the names writhed at her touch. 'Let's go get that hotel room and get you fed, shall we? The sooner we wrap this up, the sooner we can get home to clean up the next mess.'

At the thought of tasting her, his fangs jutted down, grazing the inside of his lower lip. He swallowed the saliva pooling under his tongue and nodded. 'After you.'

He followed her back to the car, his mind on the one thing neither of them had mentioned. The kiss that followed her giving him blood. Did that mean she was going to deny him again? He hoped to hell not.

Aliza washed the last of the earth from her hands. It swirled down the drain of her kitchen sink. She turned the water off and stared out the window into the never-ending swamp surrounding her house. The house Evie had died in.

Burying Evie in the coven's plot hadn't been easy, but her coven had been there to help and to say their words of respect. A few had cast protection spells over the grave, and all had vowed to help Aliza get revenge. They'd taken the news of her turning better than she'd expected. Didn't mean she trusted any of them not to do something wily, but at least there hadn't been any sudden uprising against her. Vampire or not, she was still the leader of the coven, still the superior force and talent. More superior now that her new situation had amped up her powers.

She dried her hands and went to her private altar room to recast the spell that would give her sight through the varcolai's eyes. She'd find out where he was, track him down, and kill him. That alone would take the edge off her grief. Maybe. The hole in her heart caused by Evie's death seemed bigger, not smaller. Like nothing could fill it.

Revenge was a good start, though.

She closed the hidden door behind her and kneeled before the wood slab that served as her altar. The spell's ingredients were still out, but they'd been moved. Used. The silver bowl holding them was blacker than she'd left it.

She inhaled, using her new, stronger senses to test the air. The scent of Evie's shampoo lingered, along with the scent of blood, most likely Evie's from using the spell, but below that was something darker. A scent that stung Aliza's nostrils like ammonia. Silver. Not only had Evie been in here and used the spell, but she'd added silver to it to make it stronger. Aliza's gut turned over. For Evie to find out about the room was one thing – secret spaces weren't so unusual, all witches had them – but to add silver? It would have pushed the magic to a new level. Evie's control over the varcolai would have been powerful strong. He would have felt her upon him like a hand pressing him forward.

And he would have fought it, fought whatever Evie compelled him to do. He would have gotten mad. An angry varcolai was dangerous enough, but Doc had history with her girl. Bad history.

Aliza sat back on her heels. What had Evie seen? What had she made the varcolai do? Why had she brought him here? How had she not seen the danger? She'd gotten herself killed because of it. Anger welled up in Aliza's churning innards. Anger at herself for not closing out the spell after she'd used it the first time. Recasting it would have been a simple enough task.

But how was she to have known Evie would find it and open it for her own purposes? That she would change it up in such a way that she'd end up losing her life?

With a strangled sob, Aliza grabbed the lighter and lit the wick on the oil lamp, her purpose for opening the spell renewed. The varcolai had to die. This whole mess had to be tidied up and put behind her, for Evie's sake and the sake of Aliza's new life. Being a vampire made her powerful, but it made her vulnerable, too. Her blood held double the power it had when she was just a witch. No telling what schemes some of the shadier members of her coven might be thinking up just to get a sample of it.

A revenge killing, something swift and decisive and merciless, would set a good tone for this new era of her life. Show her coven and the rest of the world that she was not to be trifled with.

She ground the proper amount of ingredients in the mortar, dumped them into the bowl, and set it over the flame. The fire crackled and hissed. Then she pricked her finger and added a drop of blood. Time to see just how powerful her vampire blood was. If things went the way she thought, she should be unstoppable. Combine that with the coming Samhain and getting her revenge should be a snap. Getting the vampire child even easier.

Smoke coiled out of the bowl, flattening almost instantly into a hazy screen. Already she could tell the spell was responding faster. 'Let me see through his eyes,' she whispered.

The fanned-out smoke rippled once, then went shimmery like the surface of the glades in the early morning sun. Aliza leaned in and the smoke bent to meet her, enveloping her face like a mask.

She blinked hard at the smoke in her eyes and coughed. 'You okay?'

Aliza whipped around to see who'd spoken, but new images filled the tiny altar room. Images of the ghost girl and some fae and a man covered with the same gold markings as the woman who'd come to rescue Doc with the anathema vampire.

Aliza was in.

Chapter Twenty-four

A brutal jab of intrusion sucked the breath out of Doc. How the hell? Both witches were dead.

'You okay?' Fi scooted closer to him on the couch.

'No.' Someone was in his head again. Someone powerful. They weren't making any demands yet, but they were there, filling his mind with their presence. Evie was dead, so it wasn't her. That must mean Preacher hadn't really killed Aliza, dammit. He closed his eyes to keep her from seeing more than she already had.

'What's up?' Creek asked. He clicked off the news they'd been watching.

Doc shook his head, unwilling to say anything to tip Aliza off that he knew.

'Something's wrong. Is the fever back?' Fi grabbed his arm. 'Do you have a headache?'

'You could say that.' He put a finger to his lips, then used that finger to very slowly spell out the word *witch* in the air. Finished, he pointed to his head. He made scribbling motions, indicating he wanted a pen.

'What's going on?' Damian asked.

'I'll explain in a minute,' Fi answered him. She tugged on Doc's arm. 'Let's get you to the couch.'

He nodded and let her lead him. Footsteps came and went around him, and a moment later, an e-tablet and a stylus were shoved into his hands. Eyes still closed, he jotted a quick note and hoped it was legible. *Aliza's not dead. Using the spell to control me again. Can't talk. Don't say anything you don't want her to know.*

'Sounds good,' Fi said.

Doc held out the e-tablet and made a wiping motion. Fi's hands brushed his and the e-tablet moved under the pressure of her erasing the screen. He placed it on his knees and wrote some more. *Put me in a room away from you. Lock me in. See if you can find a way to break this spell. Maybe the KM knows. Or Vel.*

Fi's hand cupped his cheek. 'Okay,' she whispered.

He knew she wouldn't be happy leaving him, but what else could they do?

Her arm wound around his waist. 'Let's go.' Eyes still closed, he tried to follow the path they took, using his memory of the house's layout, but he wasn't that familiar with Chrysabelle's place. They went down some stairs. He hadn't realized she had a lower level. Basements were impossible in this part of New Florida without some kind of magic because of the water table. Her mother had been Dominic's lover. Maybe he'd installed the lower level for her? Seven went deeper into the earth than should have been possible, too.

Fi brought him to a stop. 'Here.' Her hands found his face again, this time pulling him down and planting a soft kiss on his mouth. 'We're going to work.'

He nodded. Her hands fell away and her footsteps faded. A

door shut and a key was turned. He opened his eyes. Perfect. A wine cellar. Besides the racks of old bottles, the room held a small pub table and two tall chairs. He climbed into one, prepared to wait it out.

He didn't have to wait long. The compulsion to leave grew, the urging in his head like someone poking at him. 'No can do, Aliza.'

A dull roar, a very unhappy sound, echoed in his brain.

He smiled, his suspicions confirmed that it was the old witch. His head might hurt, but winding her up was at least entertaining. He pushed the other chair out and kicked his feet up. 'I'm not going anywhere, so you might as well get out of my head.'

Get up.

'No.' Was this what it was like for Mal with all those voices screaming in his brain? Man, sucked to be him.

Now. Get up and leave the house.

'Locked in, you dumb biddy.'

More howling. His feet jerked off the chair and hit the floor. His body followed, yanking him upright. He took a few unwilling steps forward, lurching like the monster in the old Frankenstein movies.

He struggled against the urge to head for the door, forcibly sitting back down. Again, she yanked him up, this time getting him halfway across the room before he grabbed hold of a wine rack and looped his arm through one of the brackets. 'You just don't get it, Aliza. Your daughter tried this and look how she ended up. You really want me at your house? What's the matter – death wishes run in the family?'

That earned him a hard, angry pain in his head. It dropped him to his knees, his bones jarring on the inlaid stone floor. He went to all fours, splaying his fingers on the cool stone. He had to find a way to ... What had he just been thinking? *Get out. Go to Aliza's.* No, something about finding a way to numb something. Urges. Yeah, that was it. A way to numb the urges taking over his brain.

He lifted his head. *The door. Go to the door.* Staring, unfocused, he fought to regain his own thoughts. He could see only part of the door through the wine racks.

Wine.

Break the door down. Get free. Now.

Wine. He got one hand around the neck of the closest bottle and tugged it free. A red. Probably a really pricey one that he wouldn't even appreciate. The glass was as cool as the stone floor. He concentrated on the way it felt, how smooth the glass was, the weight of the bottle, the script on the label, anything and everything to fill his head with thoughts that belonged to him.

Bottle in hand, he grabbed hold of the wine rack and pulled himself to his feet. *The door.* He stumbled, half dragging himself back to the table, where a small wooden box sat in the center. He hoped what he thought was in there actually was.

He plunked the bottle down and flipped the box open. Success. A corkscrew.

Aliza yowled, realizing what he planned to do. *Drop it.* His hand opened. The bottle fell, splattering red wine and glass fragments in a jagged circle. His head turned toward the door, thoughts of the bottle disappearing.

Then his gaze latched on to another bottle. A big one. A magnum of champagne. He could work with that if he went fast. With Aliza moving his feet toward the door, he snagged the bottle as he slogged past, popping out a claw to rip through the wire cage securing the cork. *Stop. Door.* His fingers slipped off the bottle's neck, almost dropping it. This needed to go faster.

And there was only one way he knew how to do that. It wasn't going to help the mess in his head either.

With a deep breath, he half shifted to bring his leopard teeth out.

Immediately, Aliza's compulsion spell doubled in strength. He stared at the wire basket in his hand. What had he been doing? Think. Think.

Going to the door, breaking it down, and getting to Aliza's as fast as you can.

He set the bottle down on the table but kept his hand on it. That didn't seem like what he really wanted to do. *Yes, it is.* No, it wasn't.

The bottle. That was it. While the thought was stuck in his brain, he clamped his teeth down on the cork, then twisted and pulled the bottle away at the same time. It uncorked with enough power to knock out the two teeth he'd dug into the cork. He ignored the pain as blood and champagne filled his mouth. He spit the teeth and blood out, then tipped the bottle back and chugged it.

Near the end of the bottle, the bubbles began muting the yowling enough for him to drain the bottle and grab two more. He had enough control to pop the next cork the old-fashioned way. His jaw throbbed where he'd lost the teeth, but the pain was good. It and the alcohol were helping him maintain his own head. He found a spot on the floor where he could put his back to the wall but still see the door. Shifting fully human, he sat and lifted the bottle to his mouth.

By the time he was halfway through bottle number three, Aliza's spell was a distant ringing in his ears. He leaned onto the floor, bent his arm beneath his head for a pillow, and closed his eyes to wait out whatever fix Fi could come up with.

Door, Aliza whispered.

Doc just laughed, the sound like tiny bubbles bouncing off the walls.

Chrysabelle handed the bellman a tip as he left. The hotel room hadn't just been for Mal and a place to ditch the fae. She was desperate for a few moments alone to center herself against the throbbing in her back. Time in the car hadn't helped, but the stunt she'd pulled at Loudreux's had really caused the ache to flare up.

'Nice.' Amery ogled the living room of the penthouse suite Chrysabelle had just booked them into at the Westin Hotel at the edge of the French Quarter.

'It should be for what it's costing her,' Mal answered the fae.

'It's all right,' Chrysabelle said. Mal was so defensive about her money. Maybe it bothered him that he didn't have any to spend himself. He'd tried to return the bribe money she'd given him. She'd refused, telling him to hang on to it in case another situation arose. 'The security of the top floor is worth the price.'

Mortalis went to the bank of windows, checking them for what she wasn't sure.

'Crazy, though,' Amery continued. 'That a four-thousand-square-foot hotel room has only one bedroom.'

Chrysabelle glanced at Mal, gave him a subtle roll of her eyes, then turned to the fae. 'Amery, could you go out and get me something to eat? New Orleans is famous for its food, right?'

His eyes lit up. 'Oh yeah, the food here is awesome. Jambalaya, crawfish étouffée, gumbo, grillades and grits, po'-boys—'

'Whoa.' She held her hands up. 'Whatever you think. It all

sounds fine.' She reached into her inside pocket and fished out a few large bills. 'Here. Get a lot of food. Comarré have large appetites.'

He took the money. 'Do you want—'

'Yes. I want everything.' She smiled to soften her sharp tone, made worse by her back. 'I'm not picky as long as it's good, so don't skimp.'

'Yes, ma'am.' He started toward the door, then paused, looking back at Mortalis. 'Sir?'

'Do as she asked,' Mortalis answered without turning away from the window. His gaze seemed to be focused on something far below.

'Okay.' Amery nodded and left.

With another quick glance at Mal, Chrysabelle went to stand beside Mortalis. Not close enough to be within his personal space – that wasn't something she was willing to challenge, considering his mood – but close enough to be noticed. 'Something down there I should know about?'

He pulled his gaze up to stare out over the river. 'No.'

She studied him for a moment. 'You want to talk about it?'

'No.'

Pretty much what she'd figured. 'Can you use your mirror to return to Paradise City and let the others know we won't make it back by tonight? I would appreciate it. I'm sure they're wondering.'

He planted his arm against the glass, flattening the barbs against his skin, still not looking at her. 'They'll be fine. They know how to handle themselves.'

Her try at being gentle was over. Pain had sapped her patience. She let some of her frustration edge her voice. 'How can they? They don't know what's coming any more than we do. But, hey, if you're satisfied that they're going to be all right, then what do I need to worry for?'

'I don't have a mirror with me.'

Mal settled onto one of the sofas. His brows lifted as if to say *what now*?

She stepped into Mortalis's space then, trying to jar him just enough so that he'd take her seriously. 'I find it hard to believe you didn't leave yourself a quick out.'

Finally, he turned. His eyes held a distant thunder that caused the scars on her back to itch. Angry didn't begin to describe whatever was going on with him. 'I'm responsible for you while you're here. I don't need more blood on my hands.'

She wanted to ask what blood was already there and where it had come from, but refrained. At the moment, she wasn't sure she cared. 'I won't move until you get back.'

'I won't let her,' Mal added.

Mortalis peered at both of them as if calculating the risk. 'I don't believe either of you.'

Chrysabelle held up her wrist, turning it so he could see the veins, fat and ready to be drained. 'Mal needs to feed. I need to drain. We're *not* going anywhere.' She dropped her hand and walked to the bar. 'You can believe what you want, but that's the truth.' She took down a large goblet from the bar and set it on the coffee table in front of Mal. 'I'll fill that after I take a shower.' She gave Mortalis one quick look. 'Do what you want.'

Not a word was spoken as she left. Inside the massive marble bathroom, she shut the door and eased her side against it to listen. The suite was well soundproofed. Only the low rumble of male voices came through, nothing intelligible.

With a sigh, she cranked on the shower's hot water, stripped out of her clothes, and then bent, wrapping her hair in a towel to keep it dry. She stepped under the pulsating stream, letting it beat against her scars. The heat helped the pain. Reaching back, she turned the temperature up a little more, then braced herself against the marble.

Steam coated the glass door and wall. She shut her eyes and tried to empty her head of the chaos to find a quiet, pain-free place. The deep, concentrated breathing taught to all comarré helped some, but didn't remove the pain altogether. She tried not to think about what that meant for getting the new signum inlaid.

'Chrysabelle?'

She jolted upright, the movement sending a fresh burst of pain zipping along her spine. 'Mal?' She rubbed a little spot in the steamed-up glass. The door was open a crack but he was still on the other side of it.

'Didn't mean to scare you.'

'You didn't.'

'Your heartbeat says otherwise.'

She frowned. Lying to a vampire who could hear your pulse was like trying to beat a lie detector. 'Just startled me is all.'

The door opened a little farther. 'I wanted to let you know Mortalis will be back in an hour.'

So he *had* gone to deliver her message after all. Good. 'Thanks. I'll be right out.' Or Mal could get in. She had no doubts his big hands on her back could work miracles. Maybe she could blindfold him. Or just grow up and let him see her naked.

'Take your time.' The door shut, leaving her more alone than she'd wanted to be when they'd first gotten here.

Water beaded off the peephole she'd made, trickling down the glass and leaving lines behind. Why had he said *take your time*? Did he know she was in pain? Maybe she should just tell him. But then she ran the risk of him handling her like glass, something she despised. She turned the water off, got out, and slipped into one of the lush robes the hotel provided, then shook her hair free.

Water ran down the small of her back, the subtle sensation like fingers trailing over her skin. She stared at the door he'd just been on the other side of. His blood ran in her veins. For that reason alone, she should want nothing to do with him. Instead, being near him made her body ache and her heart beat faster, just like the scars marking her skin. Pain and pleasure. Two sides, one coin.

She reached for the doorknob, knowing that she balanced on the thin edge of recklessness. Knowing that Mal was everything necessary to push her over that edge. Not caring that this wasn't the time or the place.

Holy mother. What was she about to do? She glanced at herself in the mirror, but the steam-covered glass reflected a hazy image.

'Not the time or place,' she whispered. That wasn't too much to remember, was it? She hoped not, especially when it came time for him to kiss her after he fed. His mouth on hers. A shiver ran through her, a remnant of the memory of the last kiss they'd shared.

Remembering *that* wasn't going to help at all.

Chapter Twenty-five

Fi ran into the living room, glad the rest of them were still there. 'Doc needs help.'

'I gathered that,' Creek answered. 'What's going on?'

'Aliza's got ahold of him again.'

Velimai signed something.

Fi nodded. 'Preacher said he killed her, but he must not have. Now she's worked up that spell that lets her into Doc's brain. She can see whatever he sees – that's why he wouldn't open his eyes. We've got to stop her. She'll do everything she can to get Doc to her house so she can kill him. If she can't do that, she'll get him to tell her where he is, then she'll come *here* and kill him and maybe us, too.'

Creek shook his head. 'Not going to happen.'

'The only way to break a spell created with blood magic is for the witch who cast it to break it. Voluntarily or otherwise,' Damian said.

Fi looked at Damian. 'I know comarré study all kinds of things, but how do you know so much about witches?'

'Not long after Tatiana became my patron, I realized she was pretty interested in the dark arts. Her library is filled with books on the subject.' He shrugged. 'I had a lot of time to read.'

'So if the witch dies, that would be the *otherwise* part?'

He nodded. Fi turned to Creek. 'You know how to get to her house.'

Creek got up from his seat near the window. 'I know exactly where she lives, but I don't like leaving you and Velimai here alone.'

A small noise from the foyer made Creek look past Fi. She turned to see what had pulled his attention. Mortalis stood on the landing. He tucked something round and shiny into one of the many pockets in his leather gear.

Fi's mouth opened in surprise. 'I thought you were in New Orleans with Mal and Chrysabelle.'

He nodded. 'I am. Was. They still are and I'm going back as soon as I let you know we're probably not going to make it back in time for whatever happens tonight. You need to stay in this house and be on constant alert.'

'No can do,' Creek said. 'The witch Aliza has got her hooks in Doc's head. She's got some spell on him, trying to make him come to her house so she can kill him. That or she'll find him and kill him here.'

'Where is he now?' Mortalis asked.

'Locked in the wine cellar,' Fi answered.

Creek walked up to join her and Mortalis at the front of the living room. He jerked his chin at the fae. 'Now that you're here, you can come with me to Aliza's, that way Damian can stay at the house. We need to get in quick and strike fast.'

'No, I can't stay. Chrysabelle's waiting for me to get back so she can do what needs to be done and return home herself.'

Fi crossed her arms. 'Mal's with her, right?'

'Yes, but she's not going to be happy waiting on me.'

'Where exactly are they waiting?' she asked.

'In a suite at the Westin.'

The edge of Fi's mouth curled up. 'Yeah, that must be killing the both of them. Look, Doc needs your help.'

Damian joined them. 'I can go with Creek, and the fae can leave. So long as Fi stays inside, Velimai can protect everyone from Tatiana.'

Velimai signed something to Mortalis. He signed a reply and she shook her head, clearly upset. Fi only made out the words *no* and *you* and the spelling of Doc's name, but understood Velimai was pushing for Mortalis to help.

His last signs were sharp and short. The barbs on his arms extended a little, then snapped against his skin like he was making an effort to stay calm. 'I'll stay for an hour. That's as long as I told Mal I'd be gone. No more.'

'Thank you,' Fi said. Then she stepped into Damian's personal space. 'You have to kill Aliza because there's no way she'll break that spell voluntarily. Can you do that? Kill a woman?'

He leaned down a little, wickedness sparking in his impossibly blue eyes. 'How do you know I haven't already?'

Fi stepped back and nodded to Creek. 'He's as full of himself as Chrysabelle is. He'll do.' She exhaled, feeling the tension of the last few hours like a knot being tied over her body. Time to go ghost and let her body rest. 'Be quick, but be safe. Doc and I are counting on you.'

Lola's office door burst open, causing her to lose the thread of the statement she'd been dictating to her secretary. Something had to be said about the possibility that Paradise City had a serial killer on the loose now that a third body had been found. 'John, you're back sooner than I expected.' He was alone. No Creek, no child. She nodded at her secretary. 'That's all for now, Valerie. We'll finish up later.'

'No problem, ma'am.' The woman left, shutting the door behind her.

Lola dropped the smile. 'What's going on? Where's the child?'

John frowned. 'The child is gone. Taken by . . . they're called the ancient ones. They're like the fathers of all the vampires. Really bad news. Anyway, one of them got the baby. Look, you're not going to like this, but you've got to cancel all the—'

She stood. 'Go after this ancient one. Get the child back.'

His jaw popped to one side, then slid back into place. 'You don't understand, it doesn't work that way with these beings. Nothing about them is human. They're demons. Fallen angels. You can't just go after them.'

She crossed herself as she walked around to the front of her desk, the horror of his words settling over her like a blanket of ice. 'A demon has my grandchild.'

'Your grandchild *is* half demon.'

Her mouth opened in disbelief. 'How dare you say that.' A hot-cold flash of anger sliced through her heart. She slapped him across the face, then gasped at what she'd done. She clutched her hand to her heart. '*Ay Dios mio*, I am so sorry.' She went back to her desk and leaned against it, trying not to cry or scream or break something. Her world wasn't just crumbling, it was disintegrating into strange pieces she no longer recognized. She glanced back at John. He hadn't moved. His dark sunglasses still sat on his face, the only change the red handprint rising on his cheek.

She dropped her gaze. 'You think I'm a fool, don't you? A sad, human fool who doesn't have a clue as to what's really going on in this world.'

'I don't think that.' But the words came too fast and without conviction.

She laughed. 'Am I just supposed to give in? Float along with the tide, accepting whatever comes my way?' She straightened, turning to look at him again. 'Or should I fight? Is there even any way to fight this?' Her arms wrapped around her rib cage and she shook her head. 'I'm lost.'

'You're not lost. You have me. And Creek. And we both have networks of support in place. I have an entire pack of varcolai ready to respond, should I need them.'

She stared, seeing him like she'd never seen him before. 'So what do I do, then?'

'About the child?'

'About any of it.'

He came toward her, tapping one of the chairs in front of her desk as he took the other one. She sat. He pushed his sunglasses up onto his head. His eyes were an almost silvery blue they were so pale. How she'd never noticed the inhuman gleam in them before, she didn't know. Or maybe that was part of what the covenant had done. Or undone. It was all so maddening. 'First of all, you have to cancel every Halloween-themed celebration going on in the city tonight that you can. The parade, trick-or-treating, everything. Call it a terrorist threat, a homeland security issue, poisoned candy, whatever you have to do, make it happen.'

'Why?'

'Because Samhain, Halloween, is a night of power for othernaturals. No one really knows what will happen tonight with the covenant broken, but the thinking is, tonight will be the final melding of the two worlds. Magic is going to run wild. Keeping people inside—'

'You mean humans.'

'Humans, yes, but tonight will affect all races. Keeping them inside is the safest thing.'

She cradled her forehead in her hand. 'This is not going to make me popular.'

'This isn't about being popular. It's about saving lives and protecting the city you swore to serve.'

She slanted her eyes at him from behind her hand and let the sarcasm drip from her words. 'Thank you for that reminder.' She dropped her hand to the arm of the chair. 'I'll go with terrorist threat. I'll set a curfew and get the chief to run patrols. Maybe they'll catch whoever's killing these comarré girls, too. You know there's been a third victim? Three in three days.' Her city was being destroyed from the inside out.

John shook his head. 'That's not good. But you're right, maybe the patrols will turn something up.'

'What about the child?'

He shrugged. 'I really don't know. The Castus, the ancient ones, they're nothing I've ever dealt with before. Creek and his crew have. Probably best to let them handle it.' He paused, looking into her eyes more deeply. 'They don't want the ancient ones having that baby any more than you do.'

She stood, her head in a thousand different places with all the work ahead of her. 'Get someone in here to take your place, then get back with them. I want you to make sure that's the case.'

Chapter Twenty-six

The second the bathroom door began to open, Mal flashed
back to the sofa, feet up on the coffee table, eyes closed.
Liar. He listened as Chrysabelle's soft footfalls grew closer on
the thick carpet. Her perfume, stronger now that she was freshly
out of a hot shower, wafted over him in warm, silky waves. His
already thin control narrowed further. Not joining her in that
shower had been test enough, but her words about not the time
or place, whether knowingly for him or not, had stirred what
little sense he had left. Their relationship, such as it was, held
together by his willingness not to cause her trouble. *Or drain
her. Weakling.* Getting into the shower with her would definitely
qualify as trouble and probably earn him a few bruises. Plus, he
had his suspicions about her physical well-being.

The cushion beside him sank down. He opened his eyes. She
sat inches away. Wearing nothing but a robe. Son of a priest,
didn't she have any idea what she did to him? He might be a
vampire, but he was also still a man. *A dead one.* He shifted
away from her a little. 'You really didn't have to get out so
soon.'

She shrugged. 'It's okay.'

Was it? Her pulse had risen and stayed that way since they'd gotten on the plane to come here. It had still been elevated when he'd met up with her again in Jackson Square. She'd been on edge. Maybe it was just the task ahead of them, but maybe it wasn't. He'd seen her wince, and his gut said she was hurting and trying to hide it. He decided to take a risk. 'The heat helps, doesn't it?'

'Yes, but not— What? I felt grimy from traveling. That's all.'

In this case, he hated being right. 'You're a bad liar.'

'No, I'm not. You're just hard to lie to.' She picked up the empty glass she'd set on the coffee table earlier and turned it in her hands. 'I'm fine.'

'You're in pain. I'm sorry.' He was responsible for that pain, something not even the voices needed to remind him about. 'Why don't you have a shot of whiskey? It might help.'

She set the glass back down. 'I can't, you know that. I have to stick to comarré rules, at least a little while longer.' She pushed the sleeve of her robe up, exposing a glinting length of flesh. Her right hand curled, her fingers flicking open the hidden blade of the ring she wore for just this purpose.

'Wait.' *No! Blood. Now.*

Her brows lifted. 'You don't want to feed, that's fine, but I need to drain anyway or I'll get sick.'

'No, I want the blood. But I can't stand seeing you in pain.'

'I said I'm fine. Leave it.'

He couldn't. Not with her. He cracked his knuckles, flexing his fingers. Her gaze went to his hands, and the look in her eyes told him what to do next. 'Turn around.'

'Why?' Suspicion replaced interest in her eyes.

'Relax.' He made a circular motion with one finger. *Around you?*

'I can't.' She twisted a little, still trying to watch him.

He put his hands on her waist and turned her the rest of the way around so that her back was to him. 'I'm aware of that. Which is why I'm doing this.' He moved her hair over her shoulder, reluctant to let the silky length out of his hands. Someday, he wanted to brush it for her. Like that would ever happen.

He started on her shoulders, pressing his thumbs into the pads of muscle on the slope of her neck. Her ragged inhale stopped him. 'Too much?'

'No.' Her head dipped forward, giving him more room to work.

He began again with the same pressure, making small circles into her skin. This time, he stopped on his own.

Her head came up slightly. 'What's wrong?'

'Robe's too thick.' Without asking, he slipped his fingers into the neck of the fabric and tugged it down gently, exposing her shoulders and upper back.

The scars shone more brightly than her signum, each one like a dagger to his own flesh. She pulled the robe tighter but made no effort to re-cover herself. His hands returned to her body. At first contact, she inhaled again, flinching a little.

She laughed softly. 'I should have fed you first.'

He rubbed his hands together to warm them up. 'Cold hands, warm heart. Or no heart, in my case.'

'Don't say that.' The kindness in her voice drove the scar daggers another inch deeper.

'No talking. Just relax.'

'You can't stop me from thinking it.' But her head dropped

back down as his thumbs traveled the sides of her spine, covering the white, pebbled marks where her signum had once been. He wanted to kiss them. Instead, he kneaded and massaged as best he could, trying to coax away the pain clinging to her. Where she wasn't scarred, her skin was warm satin.

Her soft sighs and gentle moans told him his efforts were working. Her grip on her robe loosened, dropping the folds of fabric until the small of her back was exposed. He ignored the desires of his flesh and focused on the soothing of hers, but if he was honest, this was as much for him as it was for her. Yes, he wanted to take her pain away, but he'd been desperate to touch her since the first night she'd walked into his life and nearly killed him. *She should have.*

She was warm with the life he'd never have again, but touching her made it seem like his future could somehow be different. At least if she was in it. *She won't be.*

He shoved the voices away and went back to work. His fingers stroked each muscle until she leaned into his touch. He went a little harder and she rewarded him with a sigh. 'That feels amazing.'

'How's the pain?'

She was quiet for a moment. 'It was gone about five minutes ago, but I didn't want you to stop.'

'I won't until you tell me to.'

'You can. If you want. You must be tired, too, what with not having daysleep and all.'

'And if I don't want to stop?'

She didn't answer, but her body stiffened, undoing what he'd been working so hard at. Damn it, he'd pushed too much.

'I . . . I need to feed you. But a couple more minutes wouldn't hurt.'

He splayed his fingers over her back, using lighter strokes this time, tracing the remaining signum as he worked his way up toward her neck again. Maybe he hadn't pushed too hard after all. Maybe . . . He bent forward and brushed a kiss across one of the worst scars.

She sucked in a deep breath. And leaned into him a little more.

He added a second kiss, letting his mouth linger on her skin.

'Mal,' she whispered. 'We shouldn't.'

'I know,' he whispered back, placing a third kiss on the sun signum on the back of her neck. He rested his head against the golden mark, content just to be with her in that moment. Her beating heart filled his ears, the rush of her blood throbbing into his skin with a siren's call. His fangs descended and the beast within him reared its head, erasing the traces of his human face. *Bite her. You're so close. Do it. Drain her.*

Unable to help himself, he pressed his face into the crook of her neck and opened his mouth. *Yessssssss . . .*

Her hand crept up to cradle the back of his head, her fingers threading through his hair, and she turned, somehow exposing more of herself to him. The touch almost undid him. 'I want it, too.'

Her words were so soft only his ears could have heard them. They couldn't be real. Something inside him broke. He pulled away. *Fool.* 'Don't say that.'

She twisted to look at him, then quickly looked away. 'You're right. I didn't mean it.'

He grabbed her arm. 'Yes, you did. And I understand, but feeling that way and saying it to me are two very different things.' He let her go, realizing that he was trembling and that she could feel it. 'I have a bloody hard time controlling myself around you as it is.'

She tugged her robe back up and secured it. 'I know. I shouldn't have said it. Heat of the moment. Too much blood in my system. Won't happen again.'

He stared at her, knowing he should keep his mouth closed but unable to. 'The moment or the words?'

Pushing her sleeve up, she exposed her wrist. The next second she had the blade on her ring flicked out and was holding her arm over the glass. A sharp jab and blood flowed into the glass.

The dark, seductive aroma set him on fire, but he held still, waiting for her response. She didn't say a word. 'You're not answering me?'

Without taking her gaze from what she was doing, she shook her head noncommittally. 'I don't know.' She sighed. 'Maybe. Probably.'

'To which one?'

She bent her arm, pressing her thumb over the puncture mark, and stood. 'You'd better drink that while it's warm.' Then she walked away, leaving him unanswered.

He picked up the glass, the heat of her blood warming his hand immediately and making his jaw ache. As soon as he drank this, he'd get his answer, because there was still one kiss left.

Chapter Twenty-seven

Tatiana had sent Octavian to another part of the house while she waited alone in the living room. There was no need for him to witness whatever was about to happen, no need for him to be in harm's way. Now that she was Dominus, the need to protect her small family had become a priority, regardless of how loyal Daci truly was. So far, she had done nothing to lose Tatiana's trust, but her actions in Paradise City would go a long way toward cementing her place in Tatiana's inner circle. She actually hoped Daci did well, and not just because Tatiana desperately wanted to close the comarré chapter of her life.

The hard truth was, Tatiana liked Daci. Maybe she wasn't cut from exactly the same cloth, but they were very similar spirits. Letting someone in was dangerous, but then, she'd let Octavian in and up until a few weeks ago, he'd been a servant. Now he was her most trusted ally.

Her fingers worried the scrollwork on the chair's carved arm. Had power made her soft? No, not soft. She was still capable of carrying out whatever had to be done. But power had shown her that she needed a few good people around her. Trusting Daci was a risk, but not such a great one. Tatiana had been removing obstacles from her path since her formative human years. She lifted her metal hand, flipping her wrist out and transforming her fingers into blades, then back to fingers as she flicked them in toward her body. Removing obstacles now required less effort, but greater cunning.

Perhaps being Dominus would change her further. Mellow her. She laughed at the thought. If five centuries hadn't mellowed her, nothing would.

The vile stench of brimstone and rotting flesh suffused the room, and the lamps grew dim as though something swallowed the light. She tucked her hands into her lap to keep from further digging her fingers into the chair's arms. The Castus had arrived.

With great reverence for the creature who had just made her Dominus, she eased from her seat and kneeled without making eye contact. 'My lord.' From her position near the floor, she could just see the crusted edges of his hooves.

His gnarled, raw-skinned hand appeared before her face.

She kissed his ring, careful not to touch his flesh.

'Arise, my child.'

She got to her feet, at last making eye contact briefly before looking down again. His penetrating gaze unsettled her. 'Thank you, my lord, for your trust in me and for making me Dominus. I am humbled.'

'My child.' One curled nail tucked beneath her chin and lifted her head, forcing her to meet his eyes. 'I saw promise in you the day you were turned.' He dropped his hand and began to pace, the shadows covering him from the waist down shifting with his movement like a funeral shroud. 'The ring . . . ' He shook his head. 'The ring is gone. Destroyed perhaps. I cannot sense its presence on this plane any longer.' He reached the fireplace and turned. 'For that, we will punish the comarré whore who stole it, but for now, I have a greater mission for you.'

A greater mission? Trying to obtain the ring had almost cost her her life and had left her with a metal hand. 'Yes, my lord.'

He smiled, a hideous stretching of skin that displayed an inhuman number of teeth. 'Always willing. This is why I chose you.'

Had there been another who hadn't been willing? They must not have lasted long. She tried to smile back, but in the face of his frightening glory, it was difficult to pretend even for her.

'Do you have someone around you whom you trust?'

Did he mean Daci or Octavian or both? If she said yes and either of them betrayed her, it could mean her death. No, it *would* mean her death. The Castus would not tolerate the betrayal. 'Yes, my lord.'

'Good, because for this mission, you may need the help.' The shadows around him shifted. He raised a hand toward the door. The locks clicked shut. Then the shadows rose to cover him, completely blocking him from her view with a blackness that became an abyss in the middle of the room. Things moved within the abyss, dark, horrible things that stared back at her with red glinting eyes and open mouths.

The abyss closed. The shadows returned then drifted away. The Castus stood before her, a shadow-wrapped bundle in his arms. He held the bundle out to her. The shadows melted away.

His arms cradled a baby.

'Is . . . that a gift?' Newborn blood was supposedly delicious, but she'd been a mother once. That was a line even she wouldn't cross.

'No, not a gift. This child is your mission. I want you to raise it for me.' He held the child out to her.

She took it reluctantly, and as she did, the child blinked and opened its mouth to cry.

Tiny pearl drop fangs gleamed between its lips.

Her own mouth opened in utter shock. 'A vampire child? How is this possible?'

'It's only half vampire. The other half is human. Until now, it wasn't possible.'

She cradled the little vampling. How long had it been since the precious weight of a baby had filled her arms? A barrage of Sofia images clouded her brain and turned her eyes liquid. A baby. Of all things for the Castus to present her with, this was not one she would have ever guessed. 'I'm again humbled by your faith in me.'

'You had a child, did you not?'

'Yes . . . ' There was so much more to say and yet none of it did she wish to share with the Castus.

'Then raising this one should not be so difficult.'

'What's its name?'

'Name?' He blinked. 'Pick one. I do not care.'

No point in asking the sex of the child, then. 'I will take the very best care of this charge.'

'I know. Because if you do not, I will kill you.' Smoke billowed up around him, increasing the stench of sulfur to almost unbearable levels. The Castus was gone.

The baby began to cry.

*

Lola stood behind the podium in the main foyer of city hall, the hastily gathered press waiting expectantly before her. She knew they thought they were here because of the three murdered women. They were going to be disappointed.

John Havoc's brother, Luke, stood a few feet to her side. John had assured her he was a capable addition to her security team. Across from him was Chief Vernadetto, who'd been briefed on the way over but was only just grasping the reality of what was happening.

She took a breath and greeted the audience. 'Thank you for coming today. My statement will be brief and only a few questions will be taken.' She glanced down at her notes, happy for the short respite from the glaring television camera lights. This announcement wouldn't make her popular, but it might keep her city from dissolving into an irreparable nightmare. She hoped eventually the people would understand. She'd done her best to arrive at a compromise between what Creek wanted and what she thought would keep the citizens from rising up against her.

Maybe it wouldn't be as bad as she thought. She brought her head up and forced herself to look confident and mayoral. 'A recent and credible threat against our city has made it necessary for all of tonight's Halloween activities to be canceled and a curfew put in place.'

Murmurs of dissent rose from the press core. One person shouted out, 'Miserable kids equal miserable parents, and parents vote.' Another: 'What kind of threat? Is this because of the serial killer?' That comment brought more noise from the crowd.

She held her hands up, asking for peace to continue. She hated that they'd leaped right to the serial killer conclusion. That would only raise more panic. 'Trick-or-treating will be allowed from five p.m. to six-thirty p.m. Curfew begins at seven p.m. sharp. Any unauthorized persons out after that time will be considered dangerous and treated accordingly. Arrests will be made. Please understand that the Paradise City Police Department is handling this situation with all seriousness, and the safety of our citizens is their first priority. Help them do their job by staying inside. Thank you.'

A reporter from the *PC Pace* stuck his mike toward her. 'Mayor White, is this threat because there's a serial killer loose in Paradise City?'

She paused before leaning toward the microphone. 'I cannot reveal anything that might damage the ongoing investigation, but I will say that this threat is of a homeland security nature.'

'Terrorism?' another reporter asked.

'We're not labeling the threat in any way at this time.' She glanced at the chief. He nodded, having already agreed to back her decisions. She closed her remarks. 'Thank you for your time.' With a cacophony of questions still raining down, she clicked off her lapel mike and stepped away from the podium.

Luke immediately moved between her and the crowd. 'Your car's waiting.'

'Thank you.' Luke and John could have been twins. Maybe they were. He went ahead of her, checking the exit before he let her out. The car idled at the sidewalk.

A group of kids, all in Halloween costumes, came charging around the corner. Luke put his hand out, holding her back.

'They're just kids,' she scolded him.

A straggler in an odd little costume trailed behind the rest. He veered toward them with a horrible laugh and a mouthful of teeth that looked surprisingly real. His tongue wagged out, eyes shimmering yellow.

Yellow? Before she could say anything, Luke pushed her toward the car. 'Get inside.'

She stumbled, her hand making contact with the handle as the little beastie leaped toward Luke. He caught it by the throat. Its tail whipped out and opened a bloody line across his cheek. The next second, faster than she could follow, he had a dagger rammed up the creature's sternum and was dropping it to the sidewalk.

It melted into a gooey, yellow-green puddle.

She took a step toward Luke. 'That wasn't a kid.'

'It might have been to start with, but by the time it got to us, it wasn't anymore.' He stared at her, shaking his head slightly. 'You should have canceled trick-or-treating, too.'

Creek had said cancel everything, but he didn't understand what it took to run a city, to keep your constituents happy. 'I didn't think anything would happen until after dark.'

He glanced at the mess at his feet, then back at her. 'Now you know better.' He stepped over the puddle and opened the car door. 'Get in – you're safer in there. We're going straight to John and Creek, let them know what happened. You do know where they are, don't you?'

'Yes.' Not exactly.

'Great. I just need to talk to maintenance, tell them not to let any of this get on their skin.'

She wanted to ask why but that could wait until later. 'What was that thing? I mean, besides a formerly human child turned monster.'

'Goblin.' He shot a sideways look into the car's interior.

She got in. The second he shut the door and headed back inside, she dialed her secretary. The office phones must be rattling the walls after that press conference.

Valerie picked up on the third ring. 'Mayor's office.'

'Val, it's me. I need you to check the tax records, get me the address for Maris Lapointe.'

'The cosmetics mogul? She lived out on Mephisto somewhere, I think. At least I thought I read that in the papers once.' Lola heard keys clicking. 'Here it is . . . yep, Mephisto. Number six.'

'Thanks. Phones going nuts?'

'You have no idea. Did you really cancel Halloween?'

'Be happy it wasn't Christmas.'

'Holy stones, you've got some big ones.'

Lola laughed, despite the situation. 'They're about to get even bigger. I need to issue an addendum to the press conference. Ready?'

'Go.'

'Due to further threats, all Halloween activities, including trick-or-treating, have now been canceled. The mayor's office thanks the citizens of Paradise City for helping to keep us all safe by their cooperation.'

'Yikes.'

'Indeed. One more thing – as soon as you get that sent out, go home. And stay inside.'

A moment of heavy silence passed over the phone line. 'This isn't just a terrorist threat, is it? There's a reason all these strange things have been happening, isn't there?'

'Yes. But, please, just go home and be safe, okay?'

'Will do. You too.'

She hung up. Lola leaned back and stared out into the city that was slipping away from her. What would happen if the other side took over? If the othernaturals won? Would they kill off the humans? Turn them into slaves? What kind of life would they have?

The door opened, startling her. Luke slid into the seat and rapped the glass partition, letting the driver know he could go. She pressed the intercom as the car moved slowly into traffic. 'Mephisto Island, number six.'

Luke took his sunglasses off. 'You okay?'

She stared at him. He had the same blue eyes as John. She was suddenly struck by the gut-wrenching thought that she was trapped in a car with a man who could become a wolf at will and who had just been attacked by a goblin. Whatever that was. She took a few breaths and tried to remain calm.

Luke eyed her strangely. 'I'm here to protect you, you know.'

Apparently, she wasn't doing so well on the remaining-calm part. 'You read minds, too?'

'No, but I can hear heartbeats and yours just went into overdrive.'

'I'm fine.' She pointed to his cheek, ready to talk about anything else. 'You should clean that.'

He reached up and touched the cut, then looked at the blood on his fingers like he'd forgotten about being sliced. 'You have a tissue?'

She reached into a compartment on the car's side panel that also housed the television and bar and pulled out the med kit. 'Here.'

He rummaged through it, found an antibiotic wipe, and dabbed at his skin. With the blood gone, she could see the cut was, too. 'Wow, you guys really heal fast.'

He balled up the wipe and stuck it into his pocket. 'The trick-or-treating needs to be stopped.'

'Already called my secretary and issued a statement to that effect.'

He nodded and turned to look out the window.

She moved a little farther to her side, wishing she were somewhere else. Wishing she'd never heard of the covenant or comarrés or vampires or any other kind of strange creature. Paradise City. Now there was a brutal stab of irony if she'd ever heard it. Maybe they'd have to change the name again. Not back to Miami, but something different. Something more descriptive.

Like Hell Town.

Chapter Twenty-eight

Chrysabelle walked through the suite with no real direction or purpose other than putting some distance between Mal and herself so she could think. Breathe. Make sense of what had just happened.

He could have bitten her. She'd almost begged him to. What was wrong with her? Did she have a death wish? It's not like he could have stopped himself. No, not a death wish. Something darker. She wanted his mark on her. With a shudder, she slumped down onto the bench of the piano occupying the suite's grand foyer. Her fingers trailed over the keys. The way Mal's fingers had trailed over her.

No, not like that at all. His hands had moved with purpose and the most delicious pressure and she was falling into a hole there was no getting out of.

She rested her head on the piano's top then her arms on the keys, the discordant sound echoing in the marble-lined room.

'I don't recognize that tune.'

She jumped at Mal's voice, not from surprise, but from the way it shot heat through her already sweltering body.

'That's the second time I've startled you.' He dipped his head. 'I apologize. I know how you dislike that.' He walked toward her.

She stood, pushing the bench back. 'Amery should be here soon.'

The announcement didn't stop him from moving in her direction. 'He won't be able to get in. I had the front desk change the key code.' His eyes went silver. 'I didn't want us to be disturbed. I know you like your privacy when it comes to matters of blood.' His gaze seemed fixed on her mouth.

Only the bench was between them now. 'Yes, I do.' She retreated, hitting the keys again. The softly discordant notes mirrored her chaotic thoughts. 'You're going to kiss me now, aren't you?'

He reached down and shoved the bench out of the way. It screeched across the floor. 'Yes.'

And then she was in his arms, his body warm with the power of her blood and hard with years of muscle. His mouth descended toward hers, but their last exchange had unleashed something in her that would not be tempered. She met him halfway, taking what he offered, then coaxing him to give more.

He responded as she'd suspected he would. With enthusiasm. His arms went around her, one hand cupping her backside, lifting her and setting her down on the piano. A new dissonance erupted from the keys, but it sounded like a ballad to her ears.

He breathed with her, his body as close to mortal as it could be in those few minutes when her blood restored him. She could hear his heart thudding, feel it against her chest. Her hands found their way to his shoulders, the column of his neck, into his hair. She wanted to touch him the way her comarré life had never allowed her to touch a man.

But more than that, she wanted this. Whatever this thing was between them, she wanted to at least have a chance to figure it out. The time for denying it was over. Almost. One last trip to the Aurelian and her ties to all things comarré would be severed.

The snick of a keycard in the lock broke them apart. Mal was uncommonly flushed. Chrysabelle's chest rose and fell with exertion and adrenaline. The tattoo of her pulse must be deafening him.

'Damn it,' Mal growled.

A knock came after the handle was tried and no entrance granted. 'Hello?' Amery called out. 'My key's not working.'

She patted Mal's chest. 'It's okay.' She extricated herself from his arms and adjusted her robe as she went to let Amery in, the smile on her face impossible to remove. 'It's not like we can't do that again.'

'Slim Jim.' Creek waved a greeting to the man. He was in his usual spot, out on his front porch, with a hound at his feet, a cheroot in his mouth, and an assault rifle across his lap.

He slung the gun up to his shoulder as he stood. 'Hullo, Thomas. Good to see ya, son. Who you brung with you?'

'This is Damian. He's a comar, like Chrysabelle.'

Slim Jim's eyes lit up at her name. 'Yep. Know jess who you're talking about. Pretty sparkly thing, ain't she.' He tugged at the brim of his Gators cap. 'You're just as sparkly, son. You kin to her?'

Damian sneaked a look at Creek before answering. 'In a way, I guess we are.'

'Well, then, any kin of hers is all right with me.' He chomped down on the cheroot and inhaled, making the tip glow cherry red. 'Y'all need a boat, I take it?'

'Yes, sir,' Creek answered. 'Headed out to do some business with the coven.'

'Shady lot, those witches. But they pay their tab with me, so what do I care?' He motioned toward the dock. 'Last one on the end is fueled up and got keys in it.'

Creek peeled off a few bills. 'Same as usual?'

'Yep.' Slim Jim took the money, counted it, and tucked it into the front pocket of his overalls.

Creek and Damian started for the boat, but then Creek stopped. 'Any chance you have one of those nice-looking guns to rent, too? In case of gators.'

Slim Jim smiled his missing-tooth smile. 'Now, son, much as I tend to look the other way about things, you know you can't possess a gun with your record.'

At least Slim Jim hadn't called him a convict. But then Slim Jim probably would've killed Creek's father, too, if he'd shown up and seen what Creek had seen. Slim Jim believed in biblical justice, Southern style.

Creek hooked his thumb toward Damian. 'No, but he can.'

Slim Jim narrowed his gaze a little and patted the Bushmaster over his shoulder. 'You know how to work one of these?'

Damian inhaled and, Creek imagined, took a guess. 'Just aim and squeeze the trigger, right?'

The old man smiled. 'Close enough. You can borrow the rifle on me, but the box of ammo's gonna cost you.'

Creek peeled off another bill and handed it over.

Slim Jim added it to the rest. 'Be right back.'

When the door to the cabin closed, Creek turned to Damian. 'You don't have a clue what to do with that, do you?'

Damian tapped the strap of the sacre sheath running across his chest. 'This is all I need.'

'That and the other blades you've got hidden on you, right?' Creek shook his head. 'We have no idea what we're going to find out there. The last time I came for a visit, I almost died.'

Slim Jim came back out carrying a second Bushmaster and a box of ammo. 'Here you go. You boys be careful now.'

They were on the airboat and headed for Aliza's five minutes later. Damian seemed content to watch the scenery. 'You know this area well?'

'The Glades?' Creek nodded. 'I'm half Seminole. Spent a lot of time out here as a kid with my grandparents. My mother lives out here with my grandmother now, my sister, too, when she's not at college. But we grew up in Little Havana. My father moved us there.'

Damian took his eyes off the water to stare at Creek. 'What record was that man referring to?'

'My criminal record.'

Damian's mouth thinned.

'I came home one night, found my mother beaten unconscious and my father about to do worse to my sister. So I killed him.'

Damian was quiet a few more seconds. His gaze went back to the water. 'Seems like the logical thing to do.'

Creek raised an eyebrow Damian didn't see. 'Jury didn't think so.'

'Human courts rarely understand the justice required in the real world.'

The comar got more interesting by the minute. 'Agreed. That mean you're okay with whatever's about to go down?'

'Killing the witch will save Doc's life, correct?'

'That's the way I see it.'

'Then yes.'

More silence passed between them until Creek decided to do some fishing. 'How well do you know Chrysabelle?'

'We're from the same house, the Primoris Domus, but what I know about her comes from her reputation, not from really knowing her personally.'

'Meaning?'

'She holds the record for highest price ever paid for blood rights. She was always held up to us as the example of a perfect comarré. Most comarré get their first signum around ten years old and complete the first set by age twelve. The second set is typically completed in the thirteenth year. No more than that are required, but there are seven sets in all. By fifteen, the year she got her patron, Chrysabelle had the first four sets completed and had started on the fifth.' He shook his head and exhaled. 'You have any idea how much pain that equals?'

'I've got a lot of ink, I can imagine. How many sets do you have?'

'I just completed the last signum of the sixth set last year.'

'So you have more than Chrysabelle now.'

He laughed. 'No, she completed the seventh set her twenty-second year. I think if there were more, she'd get them.' He shook his head. 'That's just who she is. Who she's always been. I had a few classes with her, spoke to her a few times, but she wasn't the social sort. Never had many friends. Of course, she had her patron at fifteen. After that, she moved out of the Primoris Domus, coming back only for classes and to recover from the signum.'

'You ever think she had no friends because no one made the effort?'

Damian nodded. 'I see what you're saying. Maybe. She was

always sort of this ideal. When she ran . . . no one expected that. Even with what her aunt had done claiming libertas.'

'Mother.'

Damian twisted around. 'What's that?'

'Maris was her mother, not her aunt.'

His face went blank, his mouth opening slightly. 'How did she find that out?'

'Maris told her as she lay dying in Chrysabelle's arms.'

'That's . . . ' Damian disappeared into thought, coming back a few minutes later. 'I can't imagine finding out who your parents are.'

'Didn't you ever think about it?'

'Sure, I guess. It's not like we can do anything about finding out, though, so I never wasted much time on it.'

Creek dropped the subject. Damian seemed content with that as they traveled in silence the rest of the way. At last the grouping of coven houses appeared. Except there was an extra building. 'That's a new one.'

'New what?' Damian asked.

'House.' Creek pointed to the sleek steel and glass structure sitting adjacent to Aliza's. How the hell had they put up a house that fast? It sure looked brand-new. He turned the motor off and let the boat glide forward on the remaining momentum. Any element of surprise they could gain would be a good thing. Damian seemed to get that.

'I'll go in first,' Creek whispered. They were twenty feet from the dock now. No sign of the old witch, but her boat was parked in its usual spot beneath the house. 'You stay outside, but be ready.'

Damian nodded.

Creek would have much rather had Mortalis by his side, but

he got that the fae wanted to protect Chrysabelle. Couldn't fault him for that.

An angry shriek rang out across the glades. A cormorant perched on Aliza's dock took off. The sound was high and loud, and two seconds after it started, the windows in Aliza's house shattered, shards falling like glitter into the water below.

Damian glanced at Creek, his eyes wide and voice low. 'I didn't know witches could do that.'

'They can't.' Creek unholstered his crossbow. 'We need a plan. Here's what I'm thinking . . . '

Chapter Twenty-nine

Fi hung close behind Big John, as she'd started mentally referring to the wolf varcolai, and together they went to answer the front door. He swore it was just his brother and the mayor of Paradise City, so Velimai had given the okay to the guard shack and opened the house gate, but Fi kept a tight grip on her appropriated chef's knife anyway. Better safe than sorry. Plus, she was kind of in a stabby mood with Doc being under Aliza's spell and all. Of course, if things really went south, she was going ghost and heading downstairs until she hit the wine cellar. Possessed Doc was still safer than most of the crazies running around this town lately.

John opened the door. 'Luke, everything all right?'

'No.' A varcolai who looked like John's twin ushered the mayor into the house, pulling the door out of John's hand to shut it. 'It's already started.'

The mayor looked like, well, like she'd seen a ghost. Except there was no way she knew Fi was one, did she? Fi slid the chef's knife into a drawer of some fancy table in the foyer. 'You're the mayor, huh?'

'Yes,' the mayor said with a little half smile, like she was happy to be occupied with something besides being a stranger in someone's home. A home Fi was starting to feel pretty possessive about considering it wasn't hers. Chrysabelle would probably freak if she knew all these people were here, traipsing in and out of her secured estate like it was Grand Central Station. The mayor held out her hand. 'And you are?'

'Fiona.' She shook the mayor's hand. 'Sorry about your daughter.'

'Thank you, very kind of you.'

'My parents lost a child.' Fi knew she shouldn't do what she was about to do, but she was angry about Doc, angry about Mal not being here, angry about Mortalis ditching them the minute John had arrived.

The mayor tipped her head. 'I'm sorry for them, and you. A brother?'

'No, not a brother.' Fi paused, a true student of dramatic effect. 'It was me. Courtesy of Mal.' She sliced her finger across her throat and made a cutting sound. 'You met him, right?' She flickered once on purpose, just to see the mayor's eyes round, then turned without waiting for an answer and walked into the living room where she took her usual seat. Doc wouldn't have liked what she'd just done. Just knowing that made her feel guilty, but not enough to apologize.

She grabbed a magazine and used it as a cover to watch as John, Luke, and the mayor came in and took seats.

'Where're Creek and the others?' Luke asked. He sat in the chair next to Fi. He smelled like fall, smoky and outdoorsy.

'Creek and Damian went after a witch who lives in the Glades. She's got Doc – ' She looked at Luke. 'He's a leopard varcolai – under some kind of possession spell. Until they get her to break the spell, he's locked up in the wine cellar to keep him safe.' The mayor listened intently, a sort of blankness filling her eyes. Fi continued. 'Mal and Chrysabelle are in New Orleans taking care of some business. They'll be back when they're through. Which won't be tonight.'

Velimai glided in just then, giving the mayor a new reason to tense up. Fi had to admit, the mayor looked a lot better in person than she did in 3-D. Not that holo-vision made her look bad; she just seemed prettier and younger in person. But also sad. Which was to be expected considering her daughter's murder.

The mayor watched Velimai settle onto the sofa opposite where she and John sat. She cleared her throat and inched forward, her knees aimed at the fae woman. 'I'm sorry, I don't mean to be forward, but I know what vampires and comarrés and varcolai are now, but I am not familiar with your kind. May I be so bold as to ask what you are?'

Velimai signed a response. John began to translate, causing her to sign more as he spoke. 'Her name is Velimai. She's a wysper fae and, she wants you to know, a very dangerous woman.'

At that Velimai laughed, the sound coming out as soft puffs of breath.

'Is she deaf?' the mayor asked.

'No,' Fi answered. 'Just mute. But not entirely. Wyspers have a scream that can kill vampires.'

That perked up the mayor's ears. 'Really? How useful.' She smiled and settled back into the sofa a little more. 'Pleased to make your acquaintance, Velimai. You can call me Lola.'

Luke leaned his elbows on his knees. 'Now that we're all assembled, you need to know the change in the city has already begun. A goblin tried to attack the mayor. I'm sure it started out as a costumed trick-or-treater.'

John narrowed his eyes. 'I thought you canceled all Halloween events.'

'I did,' the mayor said, her fingers knotting together. 'But these children were already out. The stores downtown give free candy to any child in a costume.' She turned to John. 'I think it's best we stay here, at least until Creek gets back. The city is going to be locked down, and with the patrols going on, it might be best to stay out of their way. Hunker down, settle in, and ride out the storm.' She quickly glanced at Fi and Velimai. 'That is, if it's all right with you? I don't know who's in charge with Chrysabelle not being here.'

Fi looked at Velimai. She signed that it was okay with her. Fi signed back that Chrysabelle probably wouldn't like it. With a smile, Velimai nodded but slowly spelled out it would do the mayor well to owe Chrysabelle a favor. Crafty wysper. 'Sure,' Fi said. 'You and the wolfies can stay.' She hopped off her chair. 'I'm going to check on Doc. Rest of you might as well make yourselves at home. Vel, maybe you could see what's available for dinner? Mayor—'

'Lola, please,' the mayor corrected her.

'Lola, if you're handy in the kitchen, feel free to jump in.' Maybe putting the mayor to work peeling potatoes wasn't the most appropriate thing, but the woman looked like she might implode with nothing to do, and Fi was still feeling guilty about showing off her murdered side.

Lola nodded and stood, taking off her jacket. 'We're in this for the long haul and I'd be happy to help. Is there a computer I could use first? I'd like to check some e-mails I sent out earlier.'

'Sure, there's an e-tablet in the kitchen. Velimai can show you.' Fi shot her a quick smile, then headed for Doc. The freakin' mayor. Too bad she couldn't tell him without Aliza finding out. Well, she'd tell him if Creek got him free. *When.* Fi couldn't accept any other outcome.

Just because he didn't eat didn't mean Mal didn't derive great pleasure from watching Chrysabelle chow down on the food Amery had brought back. She'd changed out of the robe and back into her clothes, which was a good thing, because Amery's curiosity about her signum had meant wandering eyes over the vee of skin exposed at her chest. Those wandering eyes had raised serious amounts of jealousy in Mal. Jealousy he almost felt okay with. Even now, sitting beside her at the table, the oddest sensation of happiness filled him. Happiness. In him. With her. *Sap. Fool. Idiot.* He shook his head and sighed.

She wiped her mouth with a paper napkin and swallowed. 'Something wrong?'

'Not a thing.' *Except you still want to drain her. And you're not worthy of her.*

'Good,' Mortalis said as he walked in from the other room. 'Because we need to get moving.'

Mal didn't have to check a watch to know the fae had been gone longer than an hour. 'What's wrong at home?'

Mortalis shook his head like he didn't want to discuss it. So not the answer Mal was looking for. He motioned for Chrysabelle to keep eating. She scooped more dirty rice onto her plate and grabbed another piece of fried catfish.

Mal leaned back in his chair. 'We're not going anywhere until you tell us what you found out at home.'

Mortalis cracked his neck, rolling his head from side to side.

'Aliza's taken over Doc with some kind of possession spell, but Creek and Damian have gone out to the Glades to deal with her. They have Doc secured in the wine cellar at Chrysabelle's so no harm will come to him. I'm sure it will be fine.'

'It better be, if you didn't stay to help.'

'Mal.' Chrysabelle put her hand on his, her touch drawing every bit of his attention. 'Mortalis's priorities lie here with us. Creek can take care of things, especially with Damian. He's had the same training I have. He knows how to handle himself.' She grabbed her glass of sweet tea, downed the rest of it, and stood. 'Let's go. I'm ready as soon as I grab my coat and sacres. Mortalis, you're driving. Amery stays here. No argument. This is my neck on the line. We're playing it my way.'

Mal wanted to smile but didn't. When Chrysabelle got forceful with someone else besides him, it was rather entertaining to watch. Mortalis hesitated, maybe thinking about arguing. Whatever he decided, it wasn't that. 'Fine.'

Twenty minutes later, they were parked half a block away from the home of the current guardian, again in the Garden District, but this house wasn't quite so grand. Very nice, but not the in-your-face grandness of Loudreux's. A light rain had begun to fall, graying out the last of the sun's afternoon rays.

'Mortalis, Mal and I are doing this alone,' Chrysabelle said, her hand on the door handle. 'I think you going in might only complicate things more.'

Surprisingly, Mortalis nodded from the driver's seat. 'I don't like it, but I agree. Especially if you kill him.'

She sighed loudly. 'No one's killing anyone. Not me, not Mal, so stop saying that.'

'Chrysabelle, you don't—'

'Enough, Mortalis. I don't want to hear it. Mal, let's go.' She jumped out of the car.

'Right behind you.' Mal joined her on the sidewalk.

Together they went through the gate and walked up to the front door. 'As planned,' she whispered.

'As planned,' he answered.

She rang the bell. Seconds ticked by, then they heard footsteps. The door opened and a smokesinger fae, this one with horns as black as soot, greeted them. He gave Chrysabelle a quick once-over, but his gaze lingered on Mal, his eyes narrowing. 'What the hell are you doing on my porch?'

Chrysabelle stepped into his line of sight. 'You're Sklar? The city's guardian?'

'Yes. Who are you?'

She smiled in the same charming, blinding way Mal had only seen once before. 'We need your help.'

The smile had zero effect. 'You need to get off my porch.' He still stared at Mal. 'If you think I don't know what you are, you're wrong. Coming to my house was not a smart move—'

'The way I see it,' Mal began, 'is that I paid to be here, so here I am.' He pulled a small amount of power into his voice, holding the eye contact. 'Since you agree with me, you're going to invite me in.'

Sklar blinked and shook his head. 'What are you—'

Mal pulled more power. 'Invite us in.'

Only a brief hesitation this time. Sklar backed away from the door, opening it wider as he did. 'Please, come in.'

Chrysabelle squeezed Mal's hand, then went inside. Mal followed quickly. 'Shut the door, Sklar.'

The fae did as he was told.

'Is there anyone else home?' Chrysabelle asked.

'No,' Sklar answered. 'Who are you again?'

'We're friends,' Mal told him, keeping his power of persuasion smooth and even. With a fae like this, a slight hitch could mean losing him. From what Mortalis had said about smokesingers, an angry one was not something either of them wanted to contend with. 'Let's sit down and discuss this.'

'Yes, let's.' Sklar led the way into a sitting room. He pointed to a massive sofa in front of an equally massive fireplace. 'Make yourselves comfortable.'

Mal sat as Sklar did, making sure they were across from each other and he was able to make eye contact.

Chrysabelle stayed at the entrance to the room as they'd discussed. In case anything went wrong, she'd be able to get out in time. Hopefully.

'Where would you live if not in New Orleans, Sklar?' Knowing and using the fae's name made the persuasion more personal and a little easier for Mal to control. Focusing like this also meant the voices took a backseat.

The fae's lavender eyes went dreamy. 'Brazil. The beaches, the music, Carnivale . . . Mardi Gras is close, but not the same.'

Mal wished he could look at Chrysabelle and see if she was as surprised as he was. But it made sense. Rio de Janeiro had been a fae haven since the Redeemer statue had been erected, making it virtually impossible for vampires to inhabit the city under its holy watch. 'You want to move to Brazil. You want to *retire* from the very stressful life of guardian of New Orleans and spend the rest of your days on the white, sandy beaches of Brazil, soaking in the sun, listening to the samba beats, dancing in the Carnivale. This is your dream and you've decided to make it happen.'

Sklar nodded. 'Yes, it is my dream.'

'New Orleans is dirty and crime-ridden and has no beach.

You don't like the music here and Mardi Gras is mobbed with tourists. Besides, Brazil has no vampires.'

'Not a single bloodsucking undead.' Sklar was a million miles away in Rio by now.

Mal ignored the comment, unwilling to lose his concentration for something so petty. 'Ten minutes after we leave, you're going to the elektos to resign. You have no memories of us being here. You've been alone all day, thinking about this decision. Nothing will dissuade you.'

'I will go and resign. I have no memory of you being here because I've been alone all day thinking about this decision. Nothing will dissuade me.' Sklar's pupils were blown wide, his gaze dreamy and lost.

Without breaking eye contact, Mal lifted his hand and pointed toward the door.

'Going,' Chrysabelle said, getting out of Sklar's sight line in case the persuasion wore off before they got out. Having a face to remember would be a very bad thing, especially if that face was Chrysabelle's.

'Brazil.' With that as his final word, Mal got up, still keeping his gaze fixed on Sklar. The room spun like Mal had been drinking, but he knew it was the drain on his power. Even Chrysabelle's blood couldn't fully restore him unless he took it from the vein, something he couldn't do without killing her. Something he hadn't done to anyone since he'd killed Fi.

He kept hold of the couch, working his way toward the door. He stumbled out of the room, his body somewhere between drunk and exhausted. With so little control left, the whine of the voices drilled through his brain. Blood hunger welled up in him so quickly he almost retched. He sagged against the wall in the hallway.

Chrysabelle waited there. Heart beating seductively, her scent wrapping him, inviting him ... *Bite her. Blood. Now.* She grabbed his arm, swung it over her shoulders, and started hauling him toward the door. Neither of them said a word, understanding that doing so might break the glamour holding Sklar still for the requisite ten minutes.

Mal leaned into her, her perfume like a drug, her glow like a beacon. He wanted her so bad his bones ached. He buried his nose in her hair and inhaled. *Blood blood blood.* The swarming, crying, cajoling mess in his head got louder. The fight to maintain control got harder.

A few steps later, they hit the front door and got out. He staggered, almost falling. Chrysabelle hoisted him up, maneuvering him down the stairs and out the gate. He inhaled her scent again. 'You smell like summer. And blood.' He groaned at the way his body tightened with need just at the speaking of the word.

She laughed softly. 'You sound a little wasted. Pretty drained after using all that power, huh?'

'Mmm-hmm. Let's go back to the hotel room and be alone.'

Beneath her signum, a faint pink colored her cheeks. 'Save your energy and stop talking.'

'I need to feed,' he muttered into her hair. *Then bite.*

'I know. That's why we tucked a bottle of blood in your inside pocket before we left, remember?'

He patted the outside of his coat, finding the hidden bottle. He reached for it, but she grabbed his hand.

'Not now. In the car. Drinking blood on the street is a great way to out yourself as a vampire. We're almost there.'

A minute later, she shoved him through the passenger door. He slumped back into the seat, feeling the daysleep coma dragging him down. He wanted to give in to it, but they had so much left to do. *Blood*, the voices screamed. Reminded, he reached into his coat and pulled out the water bottle she'd filled for him. With enormous effort, he unscrewed the cap and drank it down. The blood was only slightly warm and already starting to clot, but it tasted like mother's milk to him.

Chrysabelle got in and shut the door. 'Mission accomplished. Now to find a replacement.'

'Is he dead?' Mortalis asked.

'No, I told you no killing. He's going to resign.'

'You actually got him to resign. How the hell did you get Sklar to do that? What reassurance do you have that he'll actually do it?' Mortalis whipped around in his seat, twisting to see Mal behind him. The look in his eyes said he knew but didn't believe it.

Mal raised his bottle of blood in salute, his energy already returning. 'Might be better if we don't answer those questions.'

The muscles in Mortalis's cheeks twitched and several long seconds ticked by. 'What you did is not supposed to be possible.'

'You're assuming you know what he did,' Chrysabelle said.

'Don't patronize me,' Mortalis spat. 'I've known Sklar for years. He's not about to up and resign. Not him. He knows the consequences.'

Mal drained the last of the blood. 'He's going to resign now.'

Mortalis cursed in a language Mal didn't understand and sagged into the driver's seat. He stayed silent for about half a minute. 'Have you ever persuaded me?'

'No,' Mal answered. 'I haven't.'

'But you would, wouldn't you?'

'If it meant protecting Chrysabelle? Hell yes. Without thinking about it.'

Mortalis shook his head. 'You know if this ever comes out, the elektos will put a price on your head.'

Mal tossed the empty bottle into the back. 'Then make sure it doesn't come out.'

'Great, sounds like a deal,' Chrysabelle said. 'Now, if you two are done, can we get on to finding a replacement?'

Mortalis glanced at them in the rearview mirror. 'Read me the address. The sooner we get out of here, the better our chances are of actually getting out.'

Chapter Thirty

Fists clenched, Aliza screamed again. Her frustration with the shifter made her want to kill him even more. He'd drunk so much, he was a useless lump on the floor, but even if she could get him up, that damn ghost girl had locked him into the wine cellar. Aliza refused to let him out of the spell, though. The minute he came to, the second that door was unlocked, she'd shove every ounce of power she could muster into the spell and force him to come to her. Samhain was on its way. If she had to wait for the boost of power midnight would bring, so be it. Doc would be dead before the sun rose.

The creak of the wood steps leading up from her dock roused her attention. The spell's smoke clung to her, but she shook it off without breaking the link and got up. If one of her coven members was dropping by to see how she was holding up in her time of loss, she would thank them by drinking their blood. The hunger in her hadn't gone away yet, but maybe that was part of being a vampire. Who knew? Wasn't like there was a manual.

She stepped out of her altar room, locked the door, and went to see what was going on. Cautiously, she hung by the door of her room and used her new hearing to investigate. Over the sounds of the house and the outdoors, two heartbeats filled her ears, their rhythms overlapping like music. She'd never realized what a nice sound a beating heart made. A quick inhale brought her sour and sweet scents. The sour almost burned her nose, but the sweet was like warm honeyed sunshine, so good she inhaled again, putting up with the sour just to smell it a second time. Without knowing how, she got that both smells came from blood. One very drinkable. One very deadly.

Her screen door opened slowly, the sound almost disappearing into the breezes sighing around the house. The sweet, perfumey scent got stronger. Subtle footsteps followed, crossing the linoleum of her kitchen. A coven member wouldn't enter unannounced. Whoever was out there was no friend. She glanced around for something to use as a weapon, then almost laughed. What was she thinking? Her magic was unequaled now. She raised her hands, calling fire to the ready, and slipped out to surprise whoever had just broken into her house.

'Hello?' a male voice rang out from the kitchen. 'Is Evie here?'

The question stopped Aliza in her tracks and she dropped her hands, fire forgotten. She peeked into the kitchen. A beautiful human male stood there, glowing as if sunshine leaked out his pores. Gold markings covered him, like the girl who had come with the vampire Malkolm. The vampire whose blood had held so much power. She raised one hand, prepared to strike. 'What are you doing here?'

'Hi.' Blue eyes deep and inviting, he smiled as he spoke. Her knees almost buckled. 'Are you Evie?'

'No, Evie's my daughter. Was. She died.'

His face fell and she wanted to say something to make that smile come back. 'I'm so sorry for your loss.' He backed toward the door.

She came toward him a few more steps. 'What do you want Evie for?'

His hand hit the latch on the screen door. 'It's not important.'

She was fully into the kitchen now, the smell of him making it impossible to hide her fangs. 'Tell me.'

'A woman in the crystal shop on Bayonet said Evie might be able to help me with a spell. I shouldn't have just walked in, but the screen door was unlocked. I'm sorry for bothering you. I'll just let myself out.'

'No, wait.' Aliza took a few steps forward, breathing in his deliciousness. The sour scent was still there. 'You're one of those comarré, aren't you?'

He smiled again. 'Yes, ma'am. I'm a comar. That's what they call the males.' His gaze traveled to her mouth. 'I didn't know Evie's mother was a vampire.'

She rolled her lips together and pushed her dreads out of her face. 'Kinda just happened. Been a witch all my life, though. What kind of spell do you need help with? Maybe I can do something for you.' In exchange for some of his blood, of course. Or all of it. Maybe she'd put a holding spell on him and keep him as a pet.

'Do you think so? That would be wonderful.' He hooked his thumbs into the neck of the long white shirt he wore and tugged it over his head.

Aliza's jaw unhinged a few inches. She might be a vampire, but she was still a woman, and the half-naked man standing in her kitchen not only smelled delicious, but he also had a body to go with it. His sculpted chest and arms were covered with more of the same gold marks. Her fingers itched to touch him. To grab hold and keep him still while she sank her fangs into him.

'I have these signum all over me.' His smile was gone again. 'I'd like some kind of spell that would let me hide them when I want to.'

'I should look at them closer.' She shot to his side. He didn't flinch at the sudden movement, surprising her.

'Now,' he said, the angelic look on his face going hard. He sank to the floor, and another figure rolled into view outside the screen door. The Mohawked human who had been with Malkolm. The half-breed Evie had sent the demon after.

He held a crossbow pointed at her. 'Shouldn't have spelled the varcolai, witch.'

'Kill me and he'll never be free,' she bluffed. She wasn't sure what would happen if she died with the spell's connection still open. Maybe nothing. Not that she was going to die. She was a vampire and they lived forever. She whipped her hands up and threw two bolts of blue flame at him and the pretty decoy comar.

She turned to run as they leaped out of the way. If she could make it to her boat – A sharp whistling sound drowned out the sizzle of flames. Pain punched into her back and shoved her forward onto her hands and knees. She looked down to see the end of a bolt poking out of her chest.

She opened her mouth to scream.

And drifted to the floor in pieces of ash.

'Tatiana? *Tatiana.*'

'Hmm? What?' She looked up, slightly dazed. The library doors were cracked open and Octavian leaned through.

'Are you crying? I thought I heard . . . ' His gaze locked onto the wrapped bundle snuggled against her body. 'What is that in your arms?'

Tatiana had no idea how long she'd sat holding the baby. She'd checked and found it to be a little girl. After that, memories of Sofia and Malkolm had swept her into the past. She reached a hand to her cheek. Her fingers came away wet. She wiped the tears away. 'A baby.'

He came in and shut the doors behind him. 'I see that. Where did you get it?'

'The Castus. He wants me to raise it – her – for him.'

'Why on earth would the ancient ones want a child?'

Tatiana smoothed the blanket away from the little one's face. 'She's half vampire.' *And all mine.*

'A vampire child.' He said the words with awe and wonder as he sank to his knees before her. 'How is that possible?'

She shook her head. 'No idea. But here she is.' Tatiana lifted her head. 'We're her family now. You and me and Daci, provided she returns from New Florida. We have to protect this child, train her, take care of her. Do you know how many would like to get their hands on her?' She held the child tighter. 'Nothing bad can happen to her. Nothing.'

He nodded. 'Of course. You know I'm here for you, to help with whatever you need. For you and Daci both. And the baby.'

She stroked a finger down the baby's peach-skin cheek. 'Do you know she has a heartbeat? She's half-human, half-vampire. There's no telling what power she might have. What abilities she might wield.'

'Or what she might eat.' Octavian stared thoughtfully. 'Blood? Milk?'

'I have no idea. Can you get a wet nurse from among the

kine?' Speaking of blood . . . 'Where's the comarré we brought back?'

'I put her in the cell we held Daciana in. She seems genuinely happy to be back among the nobility, but I'm not taking any chances.'

'Good. Send Kosmina to get some blood from her for the child and then see about that wet nurse, would you?'

'With pleasure.' He leaned forward and kissed her. 'You look radiant with that child in your arms. Motherhood suits you.'

She smiled, staring down into the perfect little face staring back at her. 'It always did.' But this time, no one would take her child away from her. Not the comarré whore. Not her fool ex-husband. Just like the lioness protected her cubs, so, too, would Tatiana rip to shreds anyone foolish enough to attempt to separate this little one from her. Killing Chrysabelle and Malkolm would be a perfect way to announce that.

She lifted her locket to her lips, kissed it, then kissed the baby's head. Fate had given her a second chance.

'What's her name?' Octavian asked.

'There is so much about her I don't know, but one thing is for certain. She is a very special child. A new race of vampires has been born in her.' Tatiana nodded as the name came to her. 'I will call her Lilith.'

Chapter Thirty-one

Chrysabelle gave Mortalis the address of the first name on Loudreux's list.

He stared at her hard. 'Read that again, please.'

She did, repeating what she'd just said a little slower than the first time. 'Don't you know where it is?'

Jaw locked, his mouth bent unpleasantly. He broke eye contact before speaking. 'I know where it is.' With a soft curse and a mutter of 'Unbelievable,' he moved the car back into the street.

She shrugged it off. Mortalis's attitude since they'd arrived in New Orleans hadn't been one that invited questions. Beside her, Mal dayslept, his seat cranked back, his head lolled toward her, but otherwise he was stone-still. Despite the extra blood she'd provided him, the combination of a messed-up sleep schedule and using such a concentrated force of persuasion had wiped him out. Whoever she approached to take over as guardian, she would have to convince them to do so without Mal's help.

Hopefully, whoever it was had a price. Most people did, didn't they? And hopefully she could meet that price. Getting the ring back and finding her brother was worth emptying her mother's bank accounts if necessary. Not only did Chrysabelle feel certain her mother would understand, but also that it was exactly what Maris would want her to do. The words in her journal had been pretty clear on that, so clear that Chrysabelle swore she could hear her mother's voice urging her on. Not that she needed it. Just knowing she had a brother out there somewhere drove her.

Chrysabelle reached out to touch Mal's hand, then stopped, not wanting to disturb him. When this was over, when she'd gotten the ring and gone back to the Aurelian and found out who her brother was, she would be able to stop caring about who she'd been and focus on who she wanted to be. A woman unencumbered by rules and restraints. A woman capable of being in a relationship. She liked Creek, but her feelings for Mal were more than just female curiosity. He was a good man. She smiled. A good vampire? Whatever he was, whatever this thing was between them, it deserved a chance.

Together, maybe they could work on lessening his curse by getting some of those voices out of his head. The Aurelian had said one good deed would erase one of his names. That meant years of effort, but they had the time. Especially if he kept kissing her like that. A comarré with a powerful patron could live indefinitely. She shivered with wicked pleasure. Already she felt stronger from the last kiss.

The car slowed. She looked up from studying Mal's chiseled face. 'We're here?'

'Yes.' Mortalis parked the SUV.

She started to unfold the paper Loudreux had given her, although she'd read it a dozen times already.

'You're here to see a fae named Augustine,' Mortalis said.

She nodded, reading the name even as he spoke it. 'You know him? Any suggestions for approaching him?'

'Besides don't?' Mortalis shook his head. 'He won't take the job.'

'How can you be so certain?'

'I tried to get him to do it years ago. He's a stubborn, lazy *bala'stro*.'

Fae was one language she'd never studied, but the meaning was clear. 'I still have to try.' She paused, watching Mortalis stare down the house she was about to go to. 'How do you know this Augustine?'

Mortalis ripped the keys out of the ignition. 'We share a father.'

Before Chrysabelle could ask any more questions, he got out and shut the door behind him. A half brother, then. How much more family did Mortalis have here? Had Loudreux known? He must have. And he must be using Mortalis to some end. Otherwise, why put him through this? Chrysabelle envied Mortalis having brothers and sisters, but Mortalis didn't seem that interested in his siblings, not in any way that made sense to her. He walked around to the passenger's side and leaned against the car, waiting.

She hated to wake Mal, but with Mortalis's reaction to being here, having some backup might be a good thing. Besides, if things went badly and she didn't wake him, she'd never hear the end of it. She nudged him, wondering if his few minutes of daysleep had done him any good. He came awake instantly, eyes silver, face all hard angles and sharp bones. He shook himself, blinking his human face into place.

'We stopped.' He twisted to look out his window. 'This the next guardian's house?'

'Yes. A fae named Augustine. Who is also Mortalis's half brother. Mortalis says he won't take the job, but I still want to talk to him. Can't hurt.' Unless Augustine and Mortalis got into a fight.

'He related to everyone in this town?'

'Seems that way, doesn't it?'

'What else did he say about him?'

'That Augustine is lazy and stubborn. And he called him a *bala'stro*.'

Mal snorted and raised his eyebrows. 'Such a dirty word out of such a pretty mouth.'

The hint of silver in his gaze made her warm. 'What does it mean? No, don't tell me. Let's just get this over with.'

A few minutes later, she stood before an impressive set of double doors, their curved insets of leaded glass gleaming even in the gray light of the fading, rainy day. 'Judging by the size of this house, my money isn't going to be much of an incentive.'

Behind her, Mortalis huffed out a breath. 'It's not his house.'

'Good,' Mal said. 'Maybe money will work.'

'Not likely,' Mortalis shot back.

'Enough,' she hissed as she knocked. 'Let me do this, okay?'

They both went silent. A figure came down the entrance hall toward them, at last opening the door.

'Hello there, darling.' The old woman smiled, leaning on a crystal-topped cane. She wore a peacock-colored silk caftan covered in a blinding array of crystals that threw sparks of light onto her sleek silver-white bob. Something about her seemed familiar, but there was no way Chrysabelle had met her before. Those amber eyes would have been hard to forget. 'How can I help you young people? Collecting for something?'

'No, ma'am.' Chrysabelle smiled at being called young.

However old the woman in front of her, Chrysabelle was still older, no matter what she looked like. 'I was hoping to have a word with Augustine?'

'May I tell him who's calling?'

'Certainly. I'm Chrysabelle Lapointe. He doesn't know me, but I have something I need to discuss with him.'

She leaned forward a bit and lowered her voice. 'You're not with child, are you, love?'

'Typical,' Mortalis muttered.

Chrysabelle reared back. 'What? No.' What kind of character was Augustine?

The woman held out her hand, the gnarls of age slightly disguised by a gumdrop-sized amethyst surrounded by diamonds. 'Nice to meet you, *chérie*. I'm Olivia Goodwin, but if you behave, y'all can call me Livie.'

'Olivia Goodwin? The movie actress?' No wonder she looked so familiar. Comarré were limited in what they were allowed to watch, but her late patron, Algernon, had glommed on to anything even remotely vampire related. Olivia had played a vampire queen in a series of movies that Algernon had watched repeatedly, enough so that Chrysabelle could quote a few of Olivia's more famous lines.

Olivia smiled and gave her a little wink. 'That's right, but that's the past, darling. I like to live in the present.'

'Liar.' The teasing voice came from farther down the hall behind Olivia. 'You love being recognized and you know it.' The body that belonged to that voice strode into view, long and leanly muscled, and except for his skin being a lighter shade of gray, a close copy of Mortalis. The genes in that family must be ironclad.

'Augie.' Olivia tsked. 'You're a wicked boy.'

He bent and kissed her snowy-white head. 'That must be why you keep me.' Then his gray-green eyes turned to Chrysabelle and the men with her. The mirth in his gaze vanished when he saw Mortalis. 'I'm not interested in whatever you're selling.'

Olivia swatted his leg with her cane. 'That's not polite at all.' Then she pointed the cane at Chrysabelle. 'You children come into the parlor and have your discussion. Augie, act proper or I'll boot you out on your blessed pointy ears.'

He put his arm around her. 'Livie, I adore you, but that's Mortalis out there. You remember what happened last time he and I talked.' She nodded. 'And see beside him? That's a vampire.'

She squinted past Chrysabelle. 'Hmm. So I see.' She ducked under his arm and started back down the hall. 'Better get the bourbon.'

Creek wasn't halfway out of Chrysabelle's borrowed car when Doc and Fi ran out the front door to greet him. Well, Fi ran. Doc sauntered, showing no signs of what he'd been through. In fact, the lopsided grin on his face looked like it belonged on someone who'd had a few shots too many.

Creek shut the car door and a second later, Fi collided into him with a hug. 'Thank you, thank you.'

'You're welcome.' He glanced at Damian as he came around the side of the car. 'Thank the comar – he played bait.'

'Yes,' Damian said. 'And got scorched for it.' He pulled at the burned sleeve of his shirt, revealing a patch of blistering skin.

'Oh no!' Fi went to him and took his hand. 'Let's get you inside and fix that up.' She pulled him toward the house, leaving Doc and Creek on the driveway.

Doc stuck his hand out. 'Thanks, man. You did me a solid. I don't forget that kinda stuff.'

Creek shook his hand, then started walking with the shifter back to the house. 'You been celebrating? You smell like a still.'

'Hey,' Doc laughed, 'that's Chrysabelle's best bubbly you're talking about. I drank myself into a coma to keep Aliza's urges from taking over.' He shrugged. 'Probably going to have a headache tomorrow, but it worked, so I'm cool.' He stopped before Creek's hand reached the knob. 'Speaking of the old witch, what happened?'

'She was a vampire.'

Doc's mouth dropped open. 'You kidding me? Guess Preacher didn't do such a hot job of killing her after all. Wow, wonder how that went down.'

'Don't know, but she's ash now. I set fire to the house, too, just to be sure.'

'That explains why you smell like smoke.'

Creek eyed Doc, looking him up and down. 'You feel all right? Other than the alcohol?'

'Yeah, I feel fine. Why you looking at me like you're expecting to see a third eye?'

'Aliza said if we killed her, you'd never be free. I figured she was lying, but also figured I'd better ask.'

Doc rapped his knuckles against his head. 'Just me up there.'

'Good to hear. What's happening inside?'

'Dinner, in case you can't smell that.' Doc grabbed the door handle and went in.

Creek followed, inhaling the best thing he'd smelled in a long time. 'What's cooking?' he asked, heading into the kitchen.

The mayor turned around from a steaming pot at the stove, a spoon in one hand. *'Arroz con pollo.'*

'I didn't expect to see you here.' He leaned against the fridge, giving a nod to Velimai, who glided through the space with fae efficiency.

'I was attacked by a goblin – previously a costumed child – as we were leaving the press briefing where I canceled all Halloween activities.' Lola turned back to the pot. 'Coming here seemed like the right thing to do.'

'You okay?'

She shrugged and stirred. 'My daughter is dead. As are two more girls. My city is being overrun by God only knows what, not to mention finding out vampires, varcolai, and fae have been living among us for who knows how long . . . ' She sighed. 'No, I'm not okay. But I'm dealing.' She set the spoon down and faced him again. 'What are *you* exactly?'

'Just a man.'

She crossed her arms. 'Lie to me again and I swear to the Virgin Mary, I will punch you.'

Not that that presented such a threat, but it probably was time to tell her. 'I'm Kubai Mata.'

'And that is?'

'The KM is an ancient organization designed to be activated at times like this. Our main goal is to protect and preserve human civilization against othernatural intrusion.'

'So you're not human?'

'No, I'm human. I'm just . . . enhanced. And totally here to help you. And by *you*, I mean the city.' And that was all he was going to say about that. 'Any news from any other parts of the state or country?'

'I put out word on the mayor's loop and sent an e-mail to the governor. Heard back from a few who think I'm crazy and a few who thanked me for putting the pieces together. Those are the ones who've canceled events in their cities. The rest ... who knows. I can't do more than warn them.' She stared at the floor. 'Should probably check in with Chief Vernadetto, see what's going on.'

'After dinner.' He looked at the clock on the oven. 'It's only seven, there's time.'

She shook her head. 'Then why do I feel like this might be my last meal?'

Chapter Thirty-two

Mal took a chair outside the more intimate circle of Chrysabelle, Augustine, and Mortalis. When Olivia returned with a bottle of bourbon, he got up and took the bottle from her. 'Let me help.'

'*Merci.*' She looked him over with what could only be described as a sinful gaze. 'Take that bourbon to the bar.'

'Yes, ma'am.' He stifled a grin. He hadn't been inspected that thoroughly since the time on the freighter when Chrysabelle had been blood drunk and high as a cloud.

Olivia followed him, hoisting herself into one of the high chairs in front of the mahogany bar top. 'I like mine neat.'

He set the bottle down, then surveyed the bottles already on the shelves. 'You want me to pour this bourbon that's already open?'

'*Cher*,' she said, her bright amber eyes as sharp as jewels. 'If I wanted that bourbon, I wouldn't have brought out the reserve. That rotgut is for visitors I don't like.'

Smiling now, he opened the new bottle and poured a few fingers' worth into one of the crystal glasses stacked near the sink. 'Here you are.'

She let the glass sit on the bar. 'I don't like to drink alone. Actually, I don't mind it, but it's more fun to drink with someone. Pour yourself a glass, vampire. I'm waiting.'

'How do you know I can even drink bourbon? Maybe I only drink blood.'

'Oh, shut your mouth. You vampires drink like fish.' She hurried him along with a wave of her hand. '*Allons*, I'm thirsty.'

He poured a glass for himself. 'And you know this how?' He clinked his tumbler against hers, then lifted it. 'Cheers.'

She raised hers, then took a taste. 'Had a vampire lover right after I moved back here.'

Mal choked on the liquid, swallowing the smoky-sweet alcohol just in time to keep from spewing it all over her.

'Don't look so surprised.' She sipped her bourbon. 'If you weren't so enamored of that one over there' – she nodded toward Chrysabelle – 'I might take a go at you.'

'How do you know I'm enamored of her?' The old woman was a live one, that much was certain. No wonder Augustine lived here. Maybe he was paying his rent horizontally. Didn't seem like Olivia would be against such a thing.

'I know a lot of things. Like you live under a darkness.'

Darkness didn't begin to describe it, although the voices were just a low hum at the moment. 'How ... '

She tapped a frosted nail near one eye. 'You think this color comes from human bloodlines? My mother was a quarter fae. Haerbinger, if my *grand-mère* was to be believed. We Goodwin women have always had a touch of the sight.' She twisted in her seat to look at Augustine. 'Just like I know he's going to say no to whatever your friend is offering.'

'Guardianship,' Mal offered.

She turned back around. 'Of the city? Never happen.

Mortalis tried once before. Augie isn't made for that kind of work.' She smiled, sipped her bourbon. 'Plus he's watching over me.'

'Is that why he lives here?'

'I like the company. Plus I'm a poor, defenseless old woman.' Her smile turned wistful. 'I need him.'

Mal swirled the liquid in his glass. 'I better see how it's going.' He'd been half listening to the conversation and could tell it wasn't going in Chrysabelle's direction. 'If you'll excuse me.'

Olivia nodded, now engrossed in the other conversation herself, if the faraway look on her face was an indication.

He sat beside Chrysabelle, who didn't pause to acknowledge him.

'I understand this job is a big responsibility, but I'm offering you enough money that you could have a house like this of your very own.'

Augustine leaned forward. 'I don't want a house like this of my very own. The space I have here is plenty.'

'You live in the attic,' Mortalis said. 'Like a squirrel.'

Augustine scowled. 'This conversation has come to an end.'

'Please.' Chrysabelle shifted to the edge of the sofa cushion. 'You could just take the job for a week, then resign. I don't care.'

Sitting back, Augustine raised one brow, then looked at his brother. 'You should really educate your friends better.'

Chrysabelle shot Mortalis a glance. 'What does he mean?'

'I tried to tell you this earlier but you stopped me. The guardian is a lifetime position.'

'Until someone resigns.' She glanced at Mal. 'Just like Sklar will have done by now.'

'Then he's already dead.' Mortalis shook his head. 'A guardian either dies in the job or chooses *fin'denablo.*'

'The final honor,' Augustine translated. 'Any fae who resigns from the position of guardian is basically asking to be killed. Mortalis is right – as much as it pains me to speak those words. If Sklar resigned, he's already been dispatched. The elektos take those kinds of pronouncements very seriously.'

'Loudreux said he was the Prime's son. Surely that carries some weight . . . ' The color drained from Chrysabelle's face and she went very still, very silent.

Augustine shook his head. 'The Prime may have killed Sklar himself to save face.'

She inhaled a ragged breath and dropped her head, closing her eyes for a moment. 'Holy mother,' she whispered. 'I hate this.'

Mal covered her hand with his. Her skin was like ice. 'I'll kill Loudreux if you want.'

'Blu might have something to say about that.' Augustine gave a little smirk. His gaze went to Mortalis. 'Is she even talking to you? Considering the company you're keeping.'

'No,' Chrysabelle answered Mal, pulling her hand out from under his. 'No killing. There's already been enough of that.' A little spark came back to her eyes, and she finally made eye contact with him. 'But Loudreux has just made my enemies list. I will not be used as a pawn.' She turned away to speak to Mortalis. 'I apologize for not listening to you. My stubbornness gets in my way sometimes.'

For the first time since they'd arrived in New Orleans, Mal saw a hint of softness in Mortalis's eyes. 'You didn't know,' the fae said. 'I'm sorry Loudreux took advantage of you. It's what he does. But that's no excuse. I should have tried harder to explain things to you.'

Augustine nodded. 'Yes, you should have.' He turned to Chrysabelle. 'So you see why I have no desire to take the job.'

She nodded. 'Yes, of course. I'm sorry to have bothered you.'

'It's okay,' he said, his face suddenly lighting up. 'Listen, you ever need anything in New Orleans? Call me. Any enemy of Loudreux is a friend of mine. Be happy just to take you out and show you what a great city this really is.'

Mal eyed the fae with a look that unfortunately couldn't kill.

'Hear, hear,' Olivia said, raising her glass to Chrysabelle but winking at Mal. 'Of course, that goes for your boyfriend, too.'

'My wha— Oh, you mean Mal,' Chrysabelle said.

At least she hadn't corrected Olivia. Mal smiled at the old woman for her indelicate way of letting Augustine know that Chrysabelle was spoken for. Sort of. Chrysabelle stood. 'Thank you.' Her thumb worried the hidden blade ring on her right hand. 'Mortalis, we're through unless—'

He was out of his chair as well. 'No, we're through.'

'Typical,' Augustine said.

Mortalis didn't respond to his brother, only screwed his face into an angry glower and headed for the door. 'I'll be in the car.'

Shaking his head, Augustine got up and joined Olivia at the bar. He took a glass down and set it on the counter, then grabbed the bourbon. 'Where to next?'

'We have another name on the list.'

'Who?' He poured himself a double shot, then topped Olivia's glass.

'Someone named Daw, I believe.' Chrysabelle looked at Mal, then slanted her eyes toward the door. She was ready to go, ready to get this over with.

Mal nodded. 'It was a great pleasure to meet you, Olivia. Thank you for your hospitality.'

'You're welcome anytime, *cher*,' she said.

'He won't do it,' Augustine stated, hoisting his drink.

'What?' Chrysabelle asked.

'Daw. He won't take the job.' Augustine swallowed a finger's worth of bourbon and set the glass back down. 'I can give you the name of someone who will, though.'

'Why hasn't he already stepped up, then?'

'And go against the Prime's son? No one's that foolish. But with Sklar gone, it's anyone's game.' He smiled. 'Anyone but mine.'

'His name?' Chrysabelle didn't smile back, a sure sign that she was reaching the end of her patience with this day. *Or with you.*

Augustine rummaged around behind the bar and came up with a pen and paper. 'His name is Khell.' He scribbled some lines down, then held the paper out. 'And here's where you can find him – La Belle et la Bête.'

Chrysabelle took the paper. 'Beauty and the Beast?'

'Your French is *très bien*.' Olivia smiled at her. Augustine raised an appreciative brow.

'Mal's is better.' Chrysabelle tucked the note into her pocket. 'What kind of place are you sending us to?'

Augustine acted like he hadn't heard her comment about Mal. 'It's the oldest othernatural bar in the Vieux Carré. Goes without saying vampires aren't welcome.' He spared a half-second look in Mal's direction. 'Khell's a mutt, but he's got enough wysper in him to be effective.'

'Thank you,' Chrysabelle said. 'Olivia, nice to meet you.'

'You too, darling.' Olivia grinned, but her gaze skipped to Mal. 'Y'all come back now, ya hear?'

Chrysabelle didn't speak again until they were outside and halfway down the sidewalk. 'Loudreux is going to get his for making me kill Sklar.'

Mal nodded, unsure what to say since his offer to kill the cypher had gone flat. 'You didn't really kill him.'

'But I'm responsible for his death.'

'Technically, I'm the one who persuaded him.' *Killed him.*

'And you did it because of me.' She stopped and wheeled to face him. 'It is what it is, don't try to sugarcoat it.'

'Wouldn't dream of it.'

She stuck her finger into his chest. 'But when this is done, when I've found my brother and my comarré life is truly behind me, Loudreux's day of reckoning is going to come. So help me, holy mother.'

Mal nodded again and got the car door for her, an inordinate sense of pride rising up in him. Loudreux was in deep. Without the restraints of the comarré mores, there was no telling what kind of vengeance Chrysabelle might wreak. The side of his mouth curved up as he rounded the car to his side.

He'd never wanted to kiss her so badly in his life.

Doc leaned on the bathroom counter and stared at himself in the mirror. Dinner had knocked the last of the alcohol out of his system, so there was no way to pass off what had happened as a hallucination.

He pushed off the counter and stalked to the other side of the space. Ridiculous how big the bathroom was, but folks on Mephisto lived large. He reached the shower wall and turned again, faced with his own reflection.

Maybe it had been a hallucination. Maybe it was one of those things that would wear off over time. Maybe it would kill him. Or Fi. At that gut punch of a thought, blue flame burst off his skin, shooting toward the ceiling.

He tried to calm himself and forced his breathing to slow.

The flame wrapped his body, cool as a breeze, then sputtered into nothing.

Fire had never been a varcolai trait. Never. This had come from Aliza somehow. Maybe she hadn't been lying about never getting rid of her. She must be laughing from the grave. All those years she'd kept him shackled with the curse of being unable to fully shift, and now he was prone to spontaneous combustion.

It had happened right after a sharp jolt had woken him in the wine cellar. Even through the champagne haze, he'd immediately known Aliza was gone from his head. Or so he'd thought. He'd leaped to his feet and let out a whoop. A split second later, he'd been covered in cool, blue flames.

If Aliza had planned this as a punishment so that he'd have to live the rest of his life with a reminder of how Evie had died, she'd done a great job. If she hadn't planned it and it was just a freak side effect of her being killed while linked to him through a spell, then his life was destined to spiral downward until it stopped at the gates of Hell.

Time to see just how bad this was. He grabbed a tissue, stuck his hand out, and thought angry, horrible thoughts until the flames burst out of him again. He dropped the tissue into the fire on his palm. It went up in a puff of smoke.

His gut knotted. He'd been hoping the flames would be as cool and harmless to everything else as they were to him. Definitely not the case.

How was he supposed to live like this? How was he supposed to make love to Fi if every time his emotions went nuts, he flared up like a Molotov cocktail? She'd be toast.

Literally.

He sank down against one of the tile walls, leaned his head

back, and closed his eyes. The cool ceramic felt good. Maybe the fire would go away on its own over time. Aliza had just been killed. Maybe there was some kind of expiration date on the spell. If he could hide it long enough, there might not be a reason to after a while.

'Doc? You in there?' Fi's voice came from the other side of the door. 'Everything okay?'

'Yeah, baby,' he answered. 'Just getting an early start on my hangover.'

'You want some aspirin or something?'

He could picture her leaning against the door, her pretty brown hair tucked behind her ear, her eyes filled with worry. Over him. 'It's all good. Be out in a minute.'

'Okay. The others just put the TV on to see the news, and Creek thinks we should set up a watch system for the rest of the night.'

'Good idea. Happy to help.'

She didn't answer right away, but he could hear her breathing, the muted pulse of her heartbeat. Even without varcolai senses, he'd have known she was still there. It wasn't her nature to give up so easily.

'Something wrong, Fi?'

'No,' she said, a little softer than before. Her voice sounded like that when she was smiling. 'I'm just glad you're all better and this whole mess with the witches and the curses is behind us.'

Frustration made him rap his head against the tile behind him. Flames shivered over his skin. He stilled himself, forced his anger to cool. The flames vanished. 'Yeah, baby. Me too.'

And just like that, the lie began.

Chapter Thirty-three

Chrysabelle wasn't surprised that the outside of La Belle et la Bête didn't live up to the fairy tale it had been named after. The building was gray. Or brown. It was hard to tell from the faded bits of paint not yet worn off by time and weather. Both its first and second floors sported three sets of louvered double doors, split across in the middle with a simple balcony.

All the doors were shut and not a sound emanated from the space. Not a single tourist walking by took one look at the building, and stranger still, none spared a glance at the vampire, fae, and comarré standing on the sidewalk in front of it.

'It's like they don't even see us,' she said. Not even her words turned heads.

'They don't. Not exactly,' Mortalis answered. 'Diffusion spell. Keeps the mortals out and the patrons from being gawked at.'

Mal crossed his arms. 'Is that why it sounds empty?'

Mortalis nodded. 'I can assure you it's not.' He took a deep breath.

'Not looking forward to this, are you?' Mal asked.

'No.' Mortalis turned toward Chrysabelle. 'Keep your wits about you and you'll be fine.'

'It's not me I'm worried about, it's Mal.' She probably should have insisted he go back to the hotel, but considering he'd honored his word about not causing drama, she couldn't find enough reason to keep him away. Nor did she really want to.

Mortalis shrugged. 'It's not like vampires don't ever wander in here. The general consensus seems to be if they mind their own business, they're left alone. However, if word has gotten out about Sklar and the city's lack of guardianship, that could change the mood. Just be careful.'

'Done. Let's go.' She held her hand out. 'Lead the way. This is your turf.'

'Not in years,' Mortalis muttered, but he pushed through the right-hand set of doors anyway.

As soon as Chrysabelle stepped over the threshold, the sounds she'd expected to hear outside – the chatter, the clink of glasses, the music and laughter – all hit her in a rush. The spell that sealed in the noise was a good one. Inside, the place was as charming as its exterior. Up on a dais in the front of the room, a jazz quartet played behind a singer belting out tunes that must have been very popular, judging by the patrons clapping along. A few gazes skimmed her, but most were directed at Mal. Vampires might be allowed in here, but they were certainly not ignored.

Mortalis and Mal broke away as planned while she went up to the bar. The scales flanking the bartender's neck and the shape of his teeth gave him away as a varcolai of some kind. She leaned her arm on the bar top, instantly wishing she hadn't

when the sleeve of her silk tunic stuck to the tacky surface.
Hiding her revulsion, she smiled at the bartender the way she'd
smiled at Creek's friend Slim Jim. Comarré charm was a powerful tool in its own right.

The bartender smiled back and headed in her direction, leaning in close to be heard. 'Heya. We don't get many comarré in
here. You traveling with tall, dark, and fangy over there?' He
nodded toward Mal.

'Not exactly.' She licked her bottom lip. The man smelled
like cleanser and gin. Or maybe that *was* the gin. 'He's traveling with *me*.'

The bartender's brows shot up. 'Z'at right? Well, now, I like
a woman in charge.'

'I bet you do.' She ran a finger down his arm. His skin was
the mottled green-brown of a reptile. What kind of varcolai was
he? 'You think you could help me find someone?'

The flash of red-green fire in his slit-pupil eyes almost made
her jerk in surprise. He spread his arms out wide and grinned,
showing off a pair of long, rounded canines. 'You've found him,
baby. What do you need?'

Not this. With a shudder, she realized what kind of animal he
was. Time to pull way back. She straightened a little, unstick-
ing her sleeve from the bar. 'I need to talk to a fae named Khell.
I was told I could find him here.'

The bartender hid his disappointment poorly. 'What do you
want with him?'

'Business proposition. Can't say more than that.' She reached
under the wrist sheath on her left arm and snagged the slick
plastic bill she'd stashed there earlier, then slid it across the bar
to him. Five hundred was enough to make anyone talk.

He glanced at the money before covering it with his hand, but his smile didn't return. 'Back corner table behind the spiral stairs. Green jacket.' He moved to walk away, then stopped. 'You cause trouble, I'll take you out personally, understand?'

'Perfectly.' She understood he'd lose, so long as she could get her sacre into his gullet before he went full gator on her. With a roll of her eyes, she turned and gave a short, quick nod to Mal and Mortalis, then headed back to the table the bartender had indicated.

Weaving through the crowd proved interesting, if only for the vast array of fae in the place. There were more types than she could identify. That alone made her a little nervous. Not knowing one's opponent and what they were capable of could be a fatal error in battle, which meant this had to go well.

She checked behind her. Mal and Mortalis were there. The plan was for her and Mortalis to approach Khell and explain the situation. If he was as eager for the guardianship as Augustine claimed, this shouldn't take long.

He was exactly where the bartender said he'd be, but he wasn't alone. A plump redhead sat with him, swinging her foot to the music and drinking a bottled beer. She looked up as Chrysabelle approached, her demeanor becoming less friendly the closer Chrysabelle got.

Chrysabelle tried a smile, but the woman glared. Chrysabelle almost laughed. If this woman thought she was interested in the guy next to her for anything remotely romantic ... she was sadly mistaken. The fae beside her wasn't exactly male-model material, despite his smoky wysper coloring. More young professor than guardian-to-be, but looks could be deceiving, especially in fae.

'Khell?' she asked, resting her hands on the back of the table's one empty chair.

He looked up, gray eyes curious behind a pair of black-rimmed glasses. 'Sure 'nuff. What can I do for you?'

'I have a business matter I'd like to discuss with you, if I could have a minute of your time?'

'Sure, sit down.' He pushed the empty chair back with his foot.

She slanted her eyes at his female companion. 'Privately.'

He nudged the woman with his elbow. 'Go get us another round, Norma.'

Norma kissed him hard on the mouth, leaving a smudge of lipstick behind, then got up and sauntered past Chrysabelle. The heat radiating off her almost made Chrysabelle back away.

Instead, she sat. 'Norma's some kind of fire fae, I take it?'

Khell wiped the lipstick off his face. 'Ignus fae. Harmless to anything sentient, hell on everything else.' He laughed. 'Literally.'

'So she can't burn me?'

'No, but she could scorch the clothes off your body.' He bunched his mouth to one side like he was thinking about what that might look like. Men didn't change much, no matter what their species. 'You have me at a disadvantage. I have no idea who you are, other than comarré.'

'I'm sorry. I'm Chrysabelle Lapointe. And yes, I'm comarré.' At least for a little while longer. 'Augustine sent me. He thought you might be interested in what I have to offer.'

'Augie, huh? Didn't know he knew any comarré, but then again, with Augie, nothing really surprises me.' Khell nodded absently, like he was thinking. 'So what's this deal?'

She watched him closely as she spoke the next word. 'Guardianship.'

He swallowed, his eyes rounding a little. He rolled the

edge of his damp cocktail napkin back and forth. 'What about it?'

'I was told you might be interested in the position.'

Was he trembling?

'I might be. Except it's not available.'

'Yes, it is.'

He leaned in, keeping his head down. 'I don't know what game you're playing, but if you're trying to get me to challenge Sklar, you can get the hell out of here.'

'No challenge. Sklar's gone.'

Now he sat back, his mouth open. He snapped it shut and looked around before coming back to her. 'If he'd been killed, word would be out. A fight like that? People would be talking.'

'No fight. He resigned.' Just saying the words washed anger and guilt through her.

'Yeah, I'm sure he did.' Khell sipped his beer. 'When did this resignation supposedly take place?'

'A few hours ago. No one knows yet. You want the position, it's yours. All you have to do is come back to Loudreux's with me and tell him and the rest of the elektos you accept.'

'And I should believe you why?'

He wanted to believe, she could see it in the way he couldn't stop fussing with the label on his beer and the nerves that kept him from sitting still.

'Just a moment.' She turned around, found Mortalis in the crowd, and tipped her head ever so slightly toward the table. A few seconds later, he was standing beside her. 'This is Mortalis. He can vouch for what I'm telling you.'

'I know who he is.' Khell knocked back the rest of his beer and stood. 'Did Sklar really resign?'

Mortalis nodded. 'He did.'

Khell's brows rose and he let out a low whistle. 'No kidding. How the hell'd you manage that?'

'I didn't,' Mortalis answered, hooking his thumb toward her. 'She did. She's very persuasive.'

Chrysabelle flashed her most charming smile while leaning her elbows on the table so that her sleeves fell back to reveal her wrist blades.

Khell swore under his breath, looking at Chrysabelle with new respect in his eyes.

She straightened. 'And now all you have to do is announce your intent to the elektos.' Then Loudreux's demands would at last be satisfied.

'I know the drill,' Khell said, nodding slowly. 'Get the elektos together. I'm ready to accept.'

Tatiana bounced Lilith on her shoulder, but still the crying didn't stop. 'Octavian!' she yelled again. No point in being quiet since quiet wasn't helping the child calm down. Where the hell was he? She'd heard him come in. Or thought she had. She opened her mouth to yell again.

'I'm here,' he called back from somewhere in the depths of the house. A few minutes later, he strode into the guest room Tatiana had converted into a makeshift nursery while her staff stripped the library adjoining the master suite and turned it into a proper space for a vampire princess.

Octavian dragged a timid female kine from the city along with him. 'This is Oana. She gave birth a few days ago, but the baby was stillborn. She can nurse the child.'

'Her family has been paid?'

'Yes.'

Tatiana circled the girl, Lilith's screams almost drowning out her own thoughts. 'She's clean? Healthy?'

'Yes. Kosmina vouches for her, but I also had the kine doctor look her over. That's what took so long.'

'Oana, you understand this child is the most precious thing you will ever lay your kine hands on? If you cause harm to come to her in any way—'

Oana shook her head so vigorously a few loose brown curls escaped the clip holding them back. 'Never, my lady. It is my honor to help.'

Good choice of words. Tatiana held Lilith out to Oana. 'Feed her.'

Oana took her with a shallow curtsy. 'Yes, my lady.' She went to the nearest chair, unbuttoned her blouse, and put Lilith to her breast. The crying stopped almost immediately. A second later, Oana cried out.

Tatiana whirled toward the girl, maternal instinct raging through her. 'What's wrong?'

Oana colored. 'Nothing, my lady. I was not prepared for her bite. Everything is fine, I assure you.'

'Blood and milk?' Octavian said softly. 'What a curious creature your daughter is, Tatiana.'

She smiled at his words. *Her daughter.* 'Isn't she, though?' She watched Oana for a moment, pangs of longing niggling at her, but there was nothing she could do about it. She was no longer capable of nursing an infant. She turned away, unable to bear it anymore. 'The kine comes from a good family?'

He nodded. 'As I said, Kosmina vouches for her. How's she working out, by the way?'

'Very well. She's an apt replacement for you.' She glanced back at Oana and Lilith one more time, then took Octavian by the arm and moved him into the hall. 'Daciana should be in Paradise City by now. I didn't have much time to talk to her before she left, but she's got the same portfolio of information I gave to Laurent.' Tatiana let go of him and paced a few steps away, wringing her hands. 'I have little hope for her success.'

Crossing his arms, he leaned against a demilune sideboard. 'Give her a chance. She might surprise you.'

Tatiana turned. 'You know something? Or are you speculating?'

He shrugged and dropped his arms. One finger traced the swirl of inlaid maple on the table's top. 'She's ambitious, like you. And she wants to please you desperately. If I had to guess, I'd say she wants to repay you for freeing her from Laurent.'

'She could have killed him at any time.'

He pushed off the table and came to stand beside her, his hands landing on her waist. 'But you paved that path for her. Gave her a support system.' He kissed her nose. 'And a way to cover the death.'

She pushed at him, but there was no force behind the move. Octavian's sweetness was one of her secret pleasures. Still, she couldn't bring herself to smile with Daci on her mind. 'She might die in Paradise City.'

'She knows that.' His gaze grew serious. 'She went willingly.' He tipped his head, narrowing his eyes a bit. 'Are you worried about her? That's so unlike you.'

She pursed her mouth. 'I would worry about you, if you were the one in her place.'

He laughed softly. 'Yes, but you're mad for me and cannot live without me.'

'How fast the lowly have risen,' she teased. It was sad how right he was. Octavian was unlike any of her past loves. Sweet, affectionate, able to anticipate her every need and blessed with common sense, something that might have kept a few of her late paramours alive. And she had no fear that he, unlike some of them, wanted to take her power for himself. He was content to bask in her glow.

He shook her gently. 'Tell me why you worry about Daciana.'

She lifted one shoulder and looked back toward the room where Lilith was. 'As my power grows, so does my need to trust those around me. And now with Lilith, I must have a secure inner circle. Daciana has been an upstanding member of the House of Tepes for almost four hundred years. She is as good as any to stand with me.'

'There are several nobles in Tepes who fit that description, so why her?'

She pushed away with real force this time, loosening his hands from her waist. 'You ask too many questions.'

His eyes silvered. 'We have a child to protect now, Tatiana. If you do not share what you're thinking with me, how can I help you do what must be done?'

He was right. She flexed and relaxed her metal hand, watching the way the light glinted off it, the way her reflection distorted in the curves of the knuckles. She was Dominus now. A lifetime position. There was nothing the council could do to take the position from her, so hiding her hand was no longer necessary. She looked up at him. 'Daciana feels like . . . a sister. I never had one.'

More questions filled his eyes, but she didn't see the one thing she'd dreaded. Pity. Instead, he smiled. 'Good. You've been alone too long. And you're an excellent judge of character. If you feel that way about her, I'm sure she's worthy of it.'

He closed the space between them with a few steps. 'If you're worried for her safety, I can go to Paradise City and help her.'

'No.' Tatiana shook her head and tried to smile, but revealing such an intimate thing as how she felt about Daci made her skin seem too tight. She hated being vulnerable. 'Daci wants to do this on her own. To prove herself. Whatever happens, happens. I will accept that.'

He held his hands up. 'As you wish.'

'Besides,' she continued, clearing her throat and the weakness that threatened like a storm cloud. 'I need you here. Someone has to goad those kine into finishing the nursery.'

'Say no more.' He kissed her cheek. 'I'll make it my first priority.'

The door to the room opened and Oana stood there, cradling a sleeping infant in her arms. 'My lady, your daughter is fed.'

Tatiana took Lilith from her, kissing the baby's head. She smelled like honeyed copper. Her dark lashes fringed over her shell-pink cheeks with such angelic sweetness, Tatiana almost forgot there was vampire blood in either of their veins. 'You may keep this room as your own until the nursery is done, then you'll move in there to take care of her.'

'Very good, my lady.' Oana curtsied and went back inside, closing the door.

Lilith's innocence worked on Tatiana, thinning the wall she'd erected around herself. Without looking at Octavian, she confessed one last thought. 'If Daci does not come back, I will not take it well.'

'She will come back,' he whispered, slipping his arms around her from behind. 'And she will come back triumphant.'

'I hate not being able to contact her. I can't even send a messenger because I have no idea where to send it. Council policy about the use of electronics is outdated. Mortals know we exist. Why do we continue to hide?'

He separated from her as she began to walk toward her suite, keeping pace. 'You're Dominus now. You may do as you like.'

She nodded. 'If I weren't so distracted by Lilith, I would have remembered that.'

He smiled. 'You've only just been made Dominus. It'll take a while for that to sink in.'

'I want a phone. And a computer. But they must be secure. In fact, find the company that makes these things and buy it. With access to Ivan's accounts, I have more money than I could spend if I live another thousand years.' The more she thought about it, the more she liked it. 'I'm going to remove the council's restrictions on electronic communication for all of the House of Tepes. Starting immediately.'

'Would you like me to draft an announcement?'

'Yes. It's time to join the modern world.' She laughed. 'How else will we take it over?'

Chapter Thirty-four

Creek's front pocket started to vibrate just as Velimai flew into the room where the group was gathered watching the news from around the world. Her hands were moving too fast for him to even try to guess what she was saying. He got up and went down the hall to answer his phone. He didn't need to check the screen to know it was Argent.

'Creek,' he answered.

'Where the hell are you?' Argent replied.

'I'm with the mayor.'

'And where is that?'

'At the comarré's.'

The sector chief went quiet for a second. 'Are you any closer to recovering the item?'

'Maybe.'

'That's not an answer.'

'Because I don't have a better one to give you.' Something was going on in the other room. The best he could make out was that the pressure sensors had lit up a warning for the rear of the property.

'If you're not any closer to the item and the mayor is protected, you need to be in the city. We have reports of a lesser demon running through the streets. Get over there and kill it.'

'I don't know if I should—'

'Of course you should. It's your job.'

'I was going to say I don't know if I should leave the mayor.'

'The comarré can protect her. Now go. That's an order, not a request. The demon's location has been forwarded to your phone.'

The line went dead before Creek could explain Chrysabelle wasn't here. Maybe it was better Argent didn't know. The less Creek was on the hook for her and her plans for the ring, the better. The KM were not going to be happy when he had to tell them she'd melted it down and stitched it into her skin.

As he shoved the phone back into his pocket, the doorbell rang. Maybe it was whoever had set off the pressure sensors. Or maybe Mal and Chrysabelle were back.

He walked toward the living room and rounded the corner. John, Luke, and Doc made an impenetrable wall in front of the open door. Fi and the mayor were behind them, and through the legs of the shifters, he could see Damian's white trousers and Velimai's silky gray pants.

'You can't cross the threshold, so don't even try,' Damian snarled.

Creek came up beside Doc. A petite blonde vampire stood in the open door. 'Hear me out,' she said.

'Who are you?' Creek asked. She had the scent of nobility about her.

'She's Daciana,' Damian answered. 'House of Tepes. Wife to Laurent, the vampire who kidnapped Saraphina, the comarré who was with me.'

'What do you want?' Creek asked her.

'To die, I'm guessing,' Fi said. Velimai nodded in agreement.

'Please,' Daciana said. 'I seek asylum.'

Fi snickered. 'More like you should be in one.'

'Are you working for Tatiana?' Damian asked.

Fear washed over Daciana's face. 'No, you must believe me. My husband was, but he didn't do as she asked and she killed him. I barely escaped with my life. I had nowhere else to turn.'

'There are a thousand places in the world you could have disappeared to.' Damian's hand inched toward his sacre. 'Why here?'

'To help. I have information.' Daciana swallowed and looked behind her like she thought someone might be there. 'Tatiana is . . . horrible. She needs to be stopped.'

One of the Havoc boys snorted.

'Hey,' Creek said to get their attention. The group turned to look at him. 'This isn't my house, so I'm not making the decision, but I can tell you Chrysabelle wouldn't let her in. Now I have KM business to attend to in the city. Demon on the loose.'

The mayor paled but said nothing. Creek brushed past Daciana, who stared with big, pleading eyes. Like that was going to change his mind. Behind him, the group called out a few questions. 'Gotta go. Duty calls,' he answered back.

He climbed onto his Harley, cranked the engine, and notched the kickstand back. This was what he'd been trained for, what the KM had gotten his prison sentence commuted for. Part of him was looking forward to the fight. Another part of him hoped he won and won fast, because if this demon was anything like the Castus he'd fought earlier, it wasn't going to be any kind of fun.

The gate opened and he roared through, startling a cloud of

blackbirds sitting in the trees. He motored off Mephisto Island and went straight toward the coordinates Argent had sent. The streets were deserted, as they should be. He hit the city hall block and pulled over to check the address again. Gargoyles swooped overhead, but they didn't seem to be causing any trouble.

The screen showed he was within blocks of the demon. He unholstered his crossbow and rested it between the handlebars, notching it into a fitting he'd machined to mount the weapon should he need it while driving. The wind shifted and sulfur scraped his nostrils with the rotten egg stench of demon. He was close all right.

Heading the bike back out, he took the next turn. Two blocks away, the demon's back came into view. Being this near to such a foul monster made the brands on Creek's body throb like some kind of demon-detection device. The blue-black creature stood nearly four stories, its tail smashing out car and shop windows as it swished back and forth. Something dark flew overhead, but Creek didn't look up. He had no time for gargoyles. The demon peered into buildings, periodically punching its fist through a wall or window and digging in up to its shoulder. Probably looking for a mortal snack, Creek guessed.

Fortunately, most of the buildings were vacant. It was almost nine. The workers had been gone for hours. The whole business district was empty, the streetlights casting shadows on nothing. Creek raised his crossbow toward the beast. This angle wasn't going to work. He needed to be higher up. Heart level. He studied the buildings available to him, trying to determine which one would give him the best access.

Suddenly the creature reared its head back and unleashed a horrible roar. Creek parked the bike and yanked the crossbow free as he jumped off and ducked into the nearest doorway. The parking garage across the street would make a great bunker and give him the height he needed.

The demon seemed occupied with something. What exactly, Creek couldn't tell, but he used the distraction for cover and ran to the parking garage. He found the stairs and went three stories up, coming out on the street side. Tucking himself behind a concrete pylon, he leveled his bow. The stench threatened to bring up the mayor's *arroz con pollo*. The demon stood at a slight angle, hunched over something. There was no way for Creek to hit it properly. He'd have to wait until the demon moved.

Through the bow's sight, his field of vision was a small circle of blue-black flesh. Then he heard a woman's voice. An angry woman's voice.

'Eat me and I will haunt you for the rest of your unnatural life.'

The demon laughed.

Ducking and running, Creek got a couple pylons ahead of the beast, fixed his position, and took another look. From the new vantage point, he could see more of the creature's front and the woman he held captive in his car-sized hands. She wore some kind of wig of black feathers. So much for the mayor canceling all Halloween events and setting a curfew.

'Go ahead and try, demon,' the woman taunted. 'I'll tear you apart from the inside.'

Not only was she bad at following directions, but she was crazy, too. Great. Creek lifted the bow and took aim. The demon snarled and lifted the woman toward his mouth. Creek released the first bolt.

It thunked home in the demon's eye. Yowling, the creature dropped one hand from the woman to claw at its face, lifting its head and giving Creek perfect access to its heart. He planted the second bolt dead on target.

Hissing like a wet cat, the thing released the woman. She hit the ground hard and didn't move. The demon went down next, taking off the corner of the First Florida Federal Bank. As it writhed on the ground, Creek ran for the stairs. Any second now, the demon would probably go up in flames. He had to get the woman out of danger, if she weren't already dead.

He burst out of the parking garage, his crossbow already tucked away, and ran toward her. Keeping watch on the convulsing demon, he scooped her up and made tracks down the side street and out of the path of demon shrapnel.

Just past the crosswalk, the demon blew. Chunks of burning flesh and ribbons of acid-hot blood launched into the air. Creek pulled up beneath an awning, shielding the woman with his body, and hunkered down to ride out the downpour.

When the last piece fell – a toe by the looks of it – Creek unhinged and stood, at last taking a good look at the woman he'd rescued.

Her head lolled back over his arm. The feather wig stayed put. He walked out from beneath the shadow of the awning and into the light of the streetlamp. She wasn't wearing a costume. The feathers were her hair. An icy memory swept through him, a snippet of a fairy tale his grandmother used to tell him when he was a little boy about a woman whose sorrow turned her into a raven, gave her the power to gather souls because she had none. That story had always fascinated and terrified him.

He snorted at his own foolishness. Samhain approached and its magic had started to affect him. He shook it off and chalked up the feather hair to the night's power. That's all it was.

Anything was possible tonight. He kneeled with the woman in his arms, setting her gently on the sidewalk so he could feel for a pulse. There was none.

Sitting back on his heels, he sighed. Not the way he'd wanted this to go. 'Sorry,' he muttered. What a beauty she'd been. Seminole maybe, with that pretty olive skin. Around her neck, she wore a tiny beaked skull on a silver chain. Her vest of textured black leather exposed a few inches of taut belly above her low slung dark jeans. Maybe she had ID in her pocket. He leaned forward to check.

The woman's body seemed to move.

He jerked back, then exhaled. She wasn't dead after all. He reached to check her pulse again and her body exploded into a cloud of cawing, squawking ravens. He fell back on his hands, then shifted to whip out his halm.

Feathers floated down like black snow, and the birds swarmed into a column in the middle of the street. Then somehow, as he watched, the woman who'd died in his arms walked out of the column and the ravens were gone.

The little boy who'd trembled at his grandmother's story urged him to run, but Creek wasn't eight anymore. He shoved to his feet, his halm at the ready.

She stepped onto the sidewalk but didn't come any closer. 'Thank you.'

'For what?'

Her eyes were as black as her hair. As black as a raven's wing. She laughed, a dark, cawing sound that wasn't as unpleasant as he'd expected. 'You saved me.'

He couldn't take his eyes off her. Probably the wisest decision anyway, considering what she'd just done. 'I don't think so. I'm pretty sure you were dead.'

She tipped her head, peering at him. 'I didn't mean from the demon. I meant from the swamp witch.'

'I don't follow.'

She tipped her head to the other side. 'You set me free when you burned down her house.' She blinked slowly. 'What is your name?'

'Creek.'

'I am Yahla.'

But he'd known that since he was eight.

Tucking her hands beneath her thighs, Chrysabelle forced herself to be still in the small sitting room on the second floor of Loudreux's house. She leaned back against the sofa, tried to relax. It had taken the other members of the elektos half an hour to arrive after being summoned; now Khell's swearing in dragged on in the office below. It *had* to come to an end soon. She checked a small crystal clock on the coffee table. Only nine minutes had passed since Khell and the elektos had entered the office and locked the door behind them, but each tick of the second hand stretched like an hour, and since she was unfamiliar with the ceremony, she had no way of judging how soon it would end.

Mortalis stood beside Mal with his back to the sitting room door. She glanced at him, then sighed. Mal raised a brow at her, his lanky form braced against the wall. The threat of a smile played at the corners of his mouth. She exhaled a short, quick breath out her nose and returned her attention to the clock.

So glad her impatience amused Mal. He had to understand how desperately she wanted that ring in her hands and to return home. It would be midnight in a little under three hours. She wasn't sure what that meant for Paradise City, but if the magic had been leaking through before sunset, things could only be getting worse.

Mal closed his eyes and tipped his head back. 'Watching that clock isn't going to make it go faster.'

'I know,' she said, tapping her fingers on the sofa's arm. 'Can't you hear anything?'

'In a fae house?' Mortalis asked. 'They have spells in place for that.'

Mal looked at her. 'Are you impatient to be home? Or are you anxious about getting the ring back?'

Her fingers stilled. 'Why? You think Loudreux is going to try something else?' If he didn't give the ring back after all this ...

'No,' Mal said. 'He wouldn't dare. I'll make sure of that.'

'I'll make sure of it,' Mortalis corrected. 'Being fae doesn't mean I'm on his side.'

'You've proven that,' she told him. After all, he knew that Mal's persuasion worked on fae and hadn't said anything.

Voices filled the foyer below. 'They're done,' she whispered. 'At last.'

Mal stayed where he was. 'I'm sure Loudreux will be up to get us soon.'

Mortalis snorted. 'You mean Fellows will be. Loudreux doesn't do any of his own work if he can help it.' He cracked the door and peered out, then shut it again. 'Almost gone. Shouldn't be long now.'

She stood, too antsy to sit any longer, and paced to one of the side windows. She moved the lace curtain out of the way. The lights were on in the first floor of the house next door. A mortal family sat around their dining room table, laughing and talking and eating their dessert. Her stomach growled, but her hunger wasn't for food. She turned away, the desire to know such a life almost too painful to bear, the need to find her brother redoubled. 'How much longer will it take him to retrieve the ring?'

'Not long.' Mortalis gave her a curious look. 'We're going home immediately?'

'Of course.'

'I'll call Amery, tell him to check out.'

She shook her head. 'He can stay if he wants. Tonight is paid for.'

Mortalis cracked a thin smile. 'He'd probably eat that up.'

'He's a good kid. Eager.'

'Yes, he is. You need him, he'd probably come work for you.'

She scrunched her brow. 'I thought he worked for Loudreux.'

Mortalis shook his head. 'He's my cousin. I hired him for this trip.'

'Good to know you have at least one family member who's still on speaking terms with you.' He scowled, but she ignored it. 'I don't know what I'd need him for, but I'll file the info.'

'Security,' Mal said.

'I can protect myself.' How many times in her life was she destined to repeat that sentence to him? Would he ever get it?

'I know, but you shouldn't be your own first line of defense. You said you hated always being on guard, always waiting for the next attack. You need bodies on the ground, not just cameras and sensors.'

Mortalis nodded. 'He's got a point.'

'I'll think about it. Right now I've got two comarré living in my guesthouse, a driver in the quarters above the detached garage, and Velimai in the main house. I'm not a hotel. That house is big, but it still has its limits.' She crossed her arms. 'Not to mention I'd rather live alone. But that's not going to happen any time soon thanks to Tatiana.'

Someone knocked on the door. Mortalis moved enough to open it. As predicted, Fellows stood there, nose in the air. 'Master Loudreux will see you downstairs now.'

When they entered the parlor, Loudreux stood waiting, Blu at his side. He held his hand out. On his palm sat the ring of sorrows. Chrysabelle hesitated, expecting one last trick, but he only lifted his palm a little higher. Maybe Loudreux had no idea what the ring was capable of. Or maybe he didn't care now that he'd gotten what he wanted. Either way, she wasn't risking him changing his mind. She marched over and snatched it, then turned away without saying a word to him. She caught Mal's gaze. 'Let's go.'

'No "thank you," Miss Lapointe?' Loudreux drawled.

She spun to face him, taking a few steps back to get up close and personal. Blu bristled but made no move. Chrysabelle leaned in. 'You should be thanking *me*, Loudreux.'

He arched a thready brow. 'You're right. You did an excellent job resolving my problem.'

It would have been really nice to have fangs to bare at him. 'No, you half-wit. For letting you live.'

Loudreux choked on his next breath. Blu whipped out a blade, but Chrysabelle pulled back, one hand raised, the other fisted around the ring. 'Still your blade, fae. I have too much to do to start something now.'

With that, she sailed out of the house.

Chapter Thirty-five

'**M**y vote is totally no.' Fi didn't need to think it over. No way a vampire was getting into the house. No. Way. She kinda hoped the vamp tried something while John was outside watching her. He seemed like the sort of guy who wouldn't hesitate to take off a vampire's head if the need arose.

Doc nodded, his hands clenching and unclenching like he was agitated about something. Or about to reach for the switchblade in his belt. 'I say we stake her. Over and done.'

'Except,' Damian said. 'She might have information we could use.'

Everyone looked at him. He held up his hands. 'I'm not saying let her into the house, but maybe we could put her in the guesthouse.'

'How do you know you can trust her?' the mayor asked.

'You can't.' Damian worked his jaw to one side. 'She's a vampire. None of them can be trusted.'

'I wouldn't say none, bro.' Doc glanced at Fi, but even without reading the look in his eyes, she knew what he was thinking.

'I'd trust Mal with my life. I have. Doesn't mean I like everything he does, but he's as tight as you get.'

'Yeah,' Fi added. 'I know him better than anyone and I'd vouch for him, too.'

'Does that mean you're for keeping the woman?' Luke asked her.

'No ... I don't know.' Fi hadn't even entertained the thought that the vampiress might be telling the truth. 'You think she's for real?'

Velimai slapped the table in the center of the living room. *No,* she signed. *No, no, no.* Her hands flew again. Luke translated. 'She says anyone who worked for Tatiana is up to no good.'

Damian stood and tapped a finger against his chest. 'I worked for Tatiana. I didn't have a choice. Maybe Daciana didn't either.'

Velimai shrugged one shoulder and signed, *Sorry.*

Doc leaned back. 'But you're a comar and she's a vampire. There's a big difference.' He crossed his arms over his chest. 'You sound a little too much on her side.'

Damian tipped his head back, anger lining his face. 'I am *not* on her side.'

'Actually, I think he's got a point,' Luke said, sliding to the edge of his seat and leaning his arms on his knees. 'We don't know the real circumstances. And she could have info. We should treat her like a prisoner of war until she proves otherwise. She wants asylum? Let her earn it.'

'What does that mean?' the mayor asked before Fi had a chance to.

'Let Damian, Doc, John, and myself have a chat with her outside. See if she gives us anything, then we'll go from there.'

Doc stood. 'It's gonna have to be damn good to change my mind, but I'm willing to hear her out.'

Fi jumped up beside him. 'I'm coming, too. Tatiana killed me after Chrysabelle's blood made me fully corporeal again, so if anyone has a say in this, I feel like I do.'

'Fine with me,' Damian said as the group moved toward the door.

Doc smiled and grabbed her hand, giving it a squeeze before quickly letting it go. 'Maybe we should turn Daciana over to Dominic and let him work her over.'

Fi raised her brows at him. She was surprised he'd suggest giving Dominic anything after the vampire had almost killed him, but maybe Doc was softening up. She snorted. Doc? Softening up? Yeah, that was going to happen.

Outside on the front landing, Big John had Daciana under Damian's sacre and had shifted into his half-wolf form for more power. His ice-blue eyes almost glowed under the security lights, but his gaze stayed focused on the vampire as the rest of them exited and shut the door. 'What's the decision?'

'That's up to her,' Doc said.

'I want to stay, please,' Daciana said, glancing from the sword aimed at her to the men gathered in front of her. She didn't look at Fi. Didn't she think Fi had any say? One more reason not to like her.

Luke nodded. 'Vampire, what information can you share with us that will convince us you're telling the truth?'

Daciana's eyes filled with hope and pleading. 'What do you want to know? I'll tell you anything.'

Doc snorted. 'Just start talking.'

She opened her mouth, shaking her head slightly as if

searching for what to tell them first. 'She's just been made Dominus.'

'That was inevitable,' Damian said.

'She lost her hand in some big fight and has had it replaced with a metal one that she can transform into any shape.'

'That's not news,' Fi said. 'Chrysabelle's the one who lopped Tatiana's hand off in the first place.'

'And I saw the metal hand in person.' Doc rolled his shoulders like he was trying to shrug the memory off.

Daciana drew herself up a little taller, although she still wasn't an inch over Fi. 'If you release me, and she finds out I've told you any of this, she'll kill me.' She swallowed and wrung her hands together. 'In front of the council, the Castus told Tatiana he was coming to visit her alone after she was made Dominus. Then he told the rest of the council that she and her family were to be protected.' Daciana shook her head. 'I don't know what he meant exactly, but Tatiana doesn't have any family. Unless he meant the rest of the House of Tepes.'

'The baby,' Doc muttered. 'That's what he meant.'

'You don't know that,' Fi said.

He turned toward her like his head was on a swivel. 'You think a demon can raise a child? He's more likely to eat it. No, my gut tells me he's given it to her. Dammit.' He bent his head. Fi could have sworn she saw a flicker of blue flame dance across his fingers. She reached to grab his hand, but he balled both hands into fists. He exhaled and lifted his head, his eyes the fierce green-gold of his half-form. 'Put the vampire in the guesthouse.'

'The soulless woman,' Creek whispered.

Yahla nodded, her smile kind but forceful. 'You know me.' It was neither question nor statement, but a mind reading.

He swallowed. 'You're not real.'

'Aren't I?' She spread her arms, the shadows clinging to her like wings.

'You died.'

She dropped her arms, clasping her hands before her with an unearned innocence. 'And now I am reborn. I have no soul, I cannot cease to exist.'

He backed up one step in preparation to leave. 'Samhain approaches. The covenant is broken. Nothing can be trusted tonight.'

'Meaning me, but those things have nothing to do with me. I have always been. Always. Until the witch caught me in her spell and confined me in her house.'

'Why would she do that?'

Yahla laughed, lifting her head and revealing the pale line of her neck. 'Why did the witch do anything?'

'Power.'

She nodded approvingly.

Something exploded in the distance. He glanced toward the sound, convinced she'd be gone when he looked back. She wasn't. His pocket vibrated again, no doubt Argent texting him the location of the next demon to take out. 'I have to go. I have work to do.'

'Yes, you are Kubai Mata. You protect the city. And now I protect you.'

How she knew that about him, he couldn't guess. 'I don't need protecting.'

'It matters not what you need. You freed me.'

'If this is one of those things where you have to save my life for us to be even, I'm good. Really.' Everything he remembered from his grandmother's stories told him Yahla, if this really was her, which he still couldn't believe, was prone to harsh moods and fits of anger. She wasn't exactly known for her rational thinking, either.

She laughed again, the sound like a songbird's trilling. 'The city is besieged.' She walked to the corner and stared toward the demon's carcass. 'There are more than just this one to deal with.' She stared back at him, the lamplight outlining her ethereal beauty with its solar glow. 'I will help you.'

The tales swirled in his head. 'How do I know you won't turn on me?'

'You freed me. I cannot hurt you. I would not.' She held out her hand to him. 'Come.'

He took a step forward but shook his head, remembering. 'I won't touch you.' He shuddered, because he had touched her already. She must have been dead when he'd picked her up or he would be, too.

With a smile, she dropped her hand. 'Your grandmother taught you well.' She ran her hand through her hair and plucked out three feathers. She pinched them between her thumb and forefinger and offered them, her arm outstretched from her body and the strange, shadowy wing visible again. 'Take these to her. She will make you a charm to wear to keep you safe from me.'

He hesitated for a moment, then came close enough to take the feathers by their pointed tips. She held very still until he'd stepped back again.

'When you have your charm, I will see you again. Soon.' She did the slow blinking thing, then spun apart into a cloud of ravens. They rose, silent except for the rasping of their wings against the air, and disappeared into the blackness of the night sky.

He stared after them for a moment longer than he should have, finally tucking the feathers into a hidden pocket on his chest holster. He had demons to kill and mortals to protect, no time to think about the mythical, dangerous woman who'd just pledged her allegiance to him.

Or why he wished she'd stayed.

Chapter Thirty-six

'Straight to Seven, please, Jerem.'

Mal had barely gotten into the car. He stared at Chrysabelle in disbelief. 'Just to drop off Mortalis and tell Dominic we've returned his plane, right?'

'I can find my own way,' the fae offered, but Mal wanted her answer.

She looked out the window, her face reflected in the glass. She was avoiding him, not taking in the scenic drive from the airport. 'No.'

'You need to rest. To prepare. You haven't even fully recovered from losing the signum.' His back teeth ground together in anger. 'This is not the time to get them redone.'

'I'm completely recovered.'

'Then why are you still in pain?' *Because of your presence.*

'No drama, remember?'

It infuriated him that she'd yet to make eye contact. In his mind, that confirmed that she knew she was wrong. 'Don't confuse my concern for you with drama. Ever.' Still she stayed turned away from him.

'Jerem,' he called out. 'Take us to Mephisto Island.'

She laughed softly, finally turning his way. 'My driver knows better than to listen to anyone but me.' The laughter died away. 'I can't afford to wait any longer to get the signum put back in. It will take me long enough to recover from that as it is.'

He slid closer. 'What's the rush? You have plenty of time.'

'The ring is back on the mortal plane. Detectable. That means I'm a target again.'

'She's right about that,' Mortalis said.

Chrysabelle continued. 'Plus, we have proof the Castus has been here in Paradise City. He attacked Creek, for crying out loud. What's to stop him from showing up at my house? Or Tatiana? Or both of them?' She sighed and shook her head. 'I don't have time. Not until this is done.'

'At least take a day to recover from this trip. I know it wore on you.' *Or you did.*

'I'm fine.' She looked away again. 'I'd rather have you with me than not, Mal. Please don't make this any more difficult than it already is.'

He slid back, the weighted feeling of defeat pressing him into the sedan's soft leather seats. *You should be used to it.* Raging at her would do no good, except to reinforce her stubborn desire to have her own way. He put his knuckles to his mouth and stared out the window. How could he love a woman this mad? *Because you're mad, too.* Because he *did* love her. He knew that. She was a drug in his veins, not just because of her blood but her very being. Having her near stroked the tiny threads of humanity in him at the same time that her closeness aroused the dreaded blackness taking the place of his soul.

He was lost to her, brain, body, and beast.

And now, because of her hardheadedness, she might be lost

to him. He turned, mesmerized for a moment by the shimmering glow that always surrounded her. He couldn't imagine his life without that light. 'Has a comarré ever died from getting signum?'

She snorted softly, facing him. 'Asking those kinds of questions isn't going to make me—'

'I'm not trying to make you do anything. I'm past that. I'm just trying to prepare myself for every possibility.'

The mirth left her face. 'It's happened. Not common, but it's happened.'

Not the answer he'd wanted. Not at all. 'Those comarré who didn't make it, were they in perfect health to begin with?'

Tension settled into fine lines around her eyes. 'All comarré who receive signum are in perfect health.'

Except you. But he didn't have to say it, because it hung in the air between them like smoke.

Mortalis shifted and Mal realized that for the first time, the fae seemed uncomfortable with the conversation. Mal couldn't recall Mortalis ever looking so miserable.

Mal shrugged. 'So what do you think your chances are, then? Seventy-five percent? Fifty?'

'Stop it,' she whispered, her voice quieted by the rasp of anger. 'I know what you're doing and it's not going to work.'

He went back to staring out his window. He'd said enough. She had plenty to think about until they got to Seven. But when they finally arrived, her mind-set seemed no different.

Mortalis sprang from the car before Jerem could open the door. Chrysabelle followed him, but Mal got out on his side.

Without further words, Mortalis led them into the club and down into the labyrinth beneath it. Minutes slipped away and with each one, Mal wondered how many more Chrysabelle had.

What if she really did die getting the signum? It pained him to think of his miserable existence without her in it. He bent his head for a moment, wishing he could pray, wishing he could stop her, but the chances of either one happening without one of them getting hurt was nil.

Mortalis stopped in front of Atticus's door and drew the runes to open it. When it did, he stepped aside. 'If you want me to stay for any reason, I will. Otherwise, I'm going to your house to check on things, then home to Nyssa.'

'Sounds good,' Chrysabelle said. 'I'll be *fine*.' She shot Mal a pointed look with the last word.

'Very well. We'll talk again soon, I'm sure.' He nodded at Mal and went back the way they'd come.

Chrysabelle started to enter the corridor to Atticus's apartment, but Mal put his hand on her arm. 'Wait.' He tapped his ear as if listening for something.

'What?' she asked, but he shook his head and put a finger to his lips. She furrowed her brow and looked down both sides of the long hall, then shrugged.

When the sound of Mortalis's footsteps had disappeared, Mal drew her to him, his hands on her arms. 'I know I can't keep you from this path and I'm done trying, but if anything were to happen to you . . . ' He paused, knowing what he wanted to say but not knowing how to say it. 'I can't lose you.'

'You won't.' She half smiled as if to appease him. He knew she didn't get what he was trying to say.

'Chrysabelle, I . . . that is . . . ' Son of a priest, he could kill a man without blinking, but finding the words to speak to her was somehow harder? *Pitiful*. 'You don't understand. What I'm trying to say is—'

'Don't. Don't say it. Not another word.' The smile flattened and her hands came up like a shield. 'Stop trying to keep me from getting—'

He pulled her in and kissed her soundly, fully aware it might be for the last time. When he let her go, she sucked in a deep breath. 'Not trying to stop you.' He shook his head. 'Not anymore. Just figured I might not get another chance to say what I need to.'

'You will.' Her chin wobbled once. Out of anger or another emotion, he couldn't guess. Maybe she did understand what he was trying to tell her after all. If only he knew for sure. Or could gauge what she was thinking.

'I'm glad you're so sure.'

She hauled back and punched him in the chest.

'What the hell was that for?'

'Bad timing.' With that, she spun around and marched toward Atticus's door.

Half an hour to midnight and Creek had killed more demons, goblins, rabid fringe vampires, and a whole bunch of other unnamed nasties, including a giant centipede, than he could keep track of. Despite the mayor's assurances to the police that he was one of the good guys, a few of the officers he'd encountered hadn't trusted him until he'd rescued them. He'd rescued varcolai along with them, too, all men sent out on patrol to do the same thing he was doing, trying to keep the city from being overrun. When they'd let him, he'd given the police a quick lesson in bringing most creatures down with a shot through the heart, throat, or eye, then either removing the head or putting a stake through the heart. At least the varcolai had serviceable blades. The police, on the other hand, were going to need some new weapons more appropriate than guns for this kind of fighting.

A thin sheen of sweat, blood, and guts covered him. Fortunately, only a little of the blood was his. Other than some scratches, a cut above his left eye, and a gash on his right bicep, he was in good shape. His clothes, on the other hand ... he would have to burn them when he got home because there was no washing machine on earth equipped to get this kind of stench out.

He leaned back on his bike and wiped his face with his forearm. He was tired, but it was a good tired, like after a hard workout. Which could sort of describe what he'd just been through. Except it wasn't over.

As if on cue, his phone started vibrating. With a hard sigh, he dug it out of his pocket. Not a text this time, but a call. From Argent, because, who else?

'Creek,' he answered.

'How's it going?' Argent asked.

'KM three hundred, bad guys zip.'

'I do not understand.'

Creek rolled his eyes skyward. The gargoyles were still flying. 'It's going fine. I've killed more creatures than I can name. You know some of these demons breathe fire?' He also wanted to ask if they were related, but knew better. Just like he knew to keep the news about Yahla to himself. He didn't need his boss thinking he'd been hallucinating. Or worse, been affected by the magic.

'Yes, we are aware. I'm calling because our source in Corvinestri has checked in with disturbing news. Tatiana was in Paradise City recently. She apparently came in the guise of another vampiress, who she kept prisoner in her home while traveling with the vampiress's husband. He was successful in capturing and returning with a comarré, but that comarré was not Chrysabelle, obviously. The husband then committed suicide or was killed because of this error. Most likely Tatiana killed him and covered it up. She's also been made Dominus, so her power has increased.'

'Great. Just what she needs – more resources.'

'It's good and bad. Yes, it gives her more resources, but it also eats into her time. As Dominus, she can't just flit off on a whim. She has a house to run. That's not the worst of it, though, or the main reason I'm calling.'

How much worse could it be? 'Lay it on me.'

'Tatiana has somehow come into possession of a half-vampire, half-human child.'

Creek closed his eyes and dropped his head. 'Hell. Worse is right.'

'When this crisis is past, you are to recruit the comarré and the anathema vampire and send them to Corvinestri to retrieve the child. Once they return with it, the Kubai Mata will take charge of the child. It is imperative. We believe this child is the key in turning the swelling tide of vampire power.'

'Just like that, go get the kid and bring it back? How exactly do you think I'm going to get them to do that? Tatiana wants to kill both of them. I don't think they're going to waltz in and grab this child just because I say *please*.'

'Tell the comarré she will do it, or her life will be forfeit in exchange for the ring she has yet to return to us.'

A chill washed over him. 'If she doesn't go after the child, you're going to kill her?'

'No,' Argent corrected him. 'You are.'

Chapter Thirty-seven

He loved her. Chrysabelle knew that was what Mal had wanted to tell her. The very idea both elated her and made her want to shove her sacre through him. Not anywhere fatal, just someplace it would leave a mark. Why would he want to tell her such a thing like that at a time like this? She was about to have molten gold stitched into her flesh in a ritual that required her to be as calm and centered as possible. And he loved her. Holy mother, it was hard not to punch him. Or kiss him again.

If that wasn't what he'd meant to tell her ... She'd just not think about that now. Or anything else. Instead she knocked on Atticus's door. Thankfully, he answered without making her wait too long.

'Good evening, Chrysabelle. And you've brought Malkolm with you.' His soft smile faltered. 'You want him present?'

'No. Yes. Maybe. Is that a problem?' Making him watch would be a great punishment. Especially if she squeezed his hands until she broke every bone in them.

'It's unorthodox to say the least, but as we are not under the

strictest of circumstances, I believe an exception can be made.'
He stepped to the side. 'Come in. You have the gold?'

'Yes.' She fished the ring from her interior pocket as she
entered, Mal following her. She dropped the circle into Atticus's
upturned palm.

'Oh,' he breathed. 'There is power in this gold. Deep power.'
He turned it in his fingers. 'Neither black nor white, but in the
wrong hands . . . '

'I know. It's the ring of sorrows.'

His brows rose a little. 'And you feel comfortable using
this?'

'The melting will most likely destroy the power, won't it?'

'Very possible, yes.'

She smiled weakly. 'Good enough. Besides, I have no
choice.'

'There's always a choice,' Mal growled.

'The vampire is right. You do not have to do this.'

'Yes, I do. And if either of you tries to convince me
otherwise, it's not going to be fun to be around me for a long
time.'

'Center yourself, comarré, or this will not go well. Your anger
has no place here.' Atticus shut the door, putting them in complete darkness.

'My apologies. Could we have some lights?' She hadn't
meant to upset him. That wasn't something you wanted to do to
the man who was about to tattoo you with burning metal.

'Ah, yes, of course.' He called for the lights, then gestured for
them to follow him. 'Come, let us prepare.'

The room he led them into wasn't the one they'd been in
before, but she recognized it immediately. Her back twinged
in pain at the metallic scents of blood and gold, the same

familiar aromas that filled the signumist's room at the Primoris Domus. This space was a perfect replica right down to the long red leather padded table and red silk-draped walls patterned with the seven sets of signum, the five female sets on the left, the five male sets on the right, the two shared sets on the head wall. A shiver of déjà vu ran through her body, and her instinct was to run, but this was not Corvinestri. She was not back at the Primoris Domus, no longer under Rennata's thumb.

Fingers squeezed hers and she jerked, coming out of the memories. Mal dropped her hand. 'Whatever you need, I'm here,' he said quietly. 'Don't be upset by anything I said.'

She nodded, not trusting her voice.

Atticus stood before his melting pot. The base glowed orange, proof that like most signumists, he kept the fire burning constantly. He held the ring over it. 'You're sure you want to use this ring?'

'Positive.'

He dropped it into the pot and began to lay out his things on a stainless-steel tray.

Mal leaned over. 'Why so much red in here? Why not white like everything else?'

She ran her tongue over her teeth, not really wanting to tell him but knowing the truth was best. 'It is our ritual color. And it hides the blood.'

For a moment he seemed to pale, but it was probably a trick of the dim room. She squeezed his hand as he'd just done hers, then spoke to Atticus. 'You have a place I can prepare?'

'Yes, through the door behind the men's fourth set. Everything you need is in there.'

'I'll go change.' She turned to Mal and pointed at a tufted

hassock. 'Put that at the head of the long table. You can sit there while Atticus does his work. Be back in a few minutes.'

Mal nodded, looking as unsettled as she'd ever seen him. Well, he'd wanted to come. Now he was about to get what he'd asked for. Maybe he'd learn not to be so stubborn. She pushed the red silk drape aside and slid back the pocket door she found.

This room, too, was exactly what she'd expected. Even the red silk robes hanging beside the shower were the same. Atticus had to be the real deal. No one else but a true signumist would be able to replicate these things. She hoped that meant he'd be able to supply her with a gold pipette like the one she'd need to draw the portal to the Aurelian, since her mother's had been destroyed in the boat fire.

She turned on the shower to warm the water, then hung her leather coat and slipped out of her tunic, pants, and underthings. As much as she wanted to linger in the water, she rinsed quickly, got out, and dried off.

In a carved wooden box on the dressing table, she found more of what she expected. With the supplied hairpins, she wrapped her braid around her head and secured it out of Atticus's way. From the vial of attar of roses, she dabbed a small drop of the oil beneath her nose. It was supposed to mask the odor of blood and burned flesh, and she guessed it did for some. For her, it was just another step in the ceremony.

Lastly, she took the bundle of white feathers from the box. Comarré were taught these were feathers from an angel's wing, but she was no longer sure what was truth and what was legend. Still, she carried out the ritual of brushing her body down with it.

Then she went to the small kneeling bench to offer up a

prayer. She bent her head. *Holy mother, give me peace and comfort and strength to accept these signum. And give Malkolm peace and comfort and strength, too. And the understanding that I must do this.* Praying for a vampire. She was definitely not comarré material anymore. *Guide Atticus's hands. Let them see what his eyes cannot. Let me bear this pain with grace.*

At last, she rose and donned one of the red robes, then made her way back out to the room where Atticus and Mal waited. 'I'm ready.'

'So am I. Let's begin.' Atticus held his hand toward the table. Mal sat at the end like she'd asked.

She walked to the side of the table. 'Mal, close your eyes until I'm in place, please.'

Without hesitation, he shut them.

She dropped her robe and positioned herself on the table facedown, moving the red silk drape to cover her lower half. 'You can open them now.'

He did, looking directly into hers since they were now eye to eye. Shards of silver played in his gaze. She reached her hands out and offered him a tiny smile. 'I've done this many times before. There's nothing to be worried about.'

'I'm not worried.' He took her hands. 'Squeeze as hard as you need to.'

'I will. Feel free to pull away if it gets to be too much.'

He gazed a little more deeply into her eyes, his as earnestly silver as a newly minted coin. 'Never.'

Atticus laid his hands on her back. 'I'm going to sand down these scars now.'

'Okay,' she whispered. In truth, that part scared her a little. She had no idea what to expect.

A moment passed and nothing happened.

'Are you going to begin your breathing?' he asked.

'Yes, of course.' The pain would start immediately, then. She lowered her head into the concave space in the table, closed her eyes, and recalled the breathing techniques comarré were taught from their very earliest days. She focused on the rhythmic inhale and exhale, the depths of her breath, the way it moved through her body. She imagined pure light cocooning her, protecting her from what was to come, the way the light would absorb the pain and transform it into something beautiful. The practice quickly swept her into a meditative state. This was nothing new. Her body understood what to expect, her mind knew how to shelter her from it.

Vaguely, she was aware of him placing some sort of nozzle against her back. A soft hum filled the space. Then the pain came. Her mind worked quickly to compartmentalize the scouring heat of what Atticus was doing to her, shutting her into a safer, brighter place in her head. One where a welcome fog bathed her in control and acceptance.

Time lost significance until the hum stopped. The sudden silence seemed louder than the sanding machine had been. Blood scent weighted the air.

Atticus touched her right shoulder. 'I'm going to clean the area now.'

She answered with a small nod, then raised her head to look at Malkolm. His eyes were still silver, and there was a tension around them that hadn't been there before. She suddenly realized his hands were shaking in hers.

'It's okay,' she whispered.

He swallowed, nodded shortly, but said nothing.

Atticus wiped her back down with a warm damp cloth, and she rested her face into the table again. The tang of molten gold took over as the blood scent faded. The next pain she felt would be the signumist's needle.

She concentrated on her breathing again. Atticus wheeled his tray closer. He smoothed his hands along her spine where her scars had been. 'The skin is perfect. We may proceed.'

She gave him another small nod and took a deep cleansing breath. The comarré chosen for breeding liked to talk about how the pain of receiving signum was nothing compared to birthing. She firmly believed those comarré lied. She'd not been in this position in fifteen years, but the memory of that white-hot metal sinking into her skin was as sharp as the needle's tip.

Without meaning to, she tensed.

Atticus pressed his hand to her shoulder. 'Relax, comarré. Breathe. You have taken the needle many times in your life, yes?'

'Yes,' she whispered, her voice muted by the fabric draping the table.

'Pain fuels the journey of life.'

She almost smiled. Every signumist she'd ever known used that quote. 'I am ready.'

His rolling stool creaked as he sat. 'And so I begin.'

Having taken the first watch, Doc paced back and forth in front of the guesthouse. Nothing about the decision to keep the vampire here felt good, but he couldn't deny her information had sounded right on. When Creek returned, Doc would ask him what he could find out through the KM to verify Daciana's intel. He stroked the sides of his goatee.

If she wasn't telling the truth, Doc might try to use his new fire power on her. Vampires hated fire. He snorted softly. Maybe his new power wasn't such a curse after all.

He spun at the almost noiseless footsteps padding up behind him.

'Hey.' Fi held out a can of cola. 'I thought you might be thirsty.'

He took it. 'Thanks.' Condensation wet his hand from the ice-cold can. He popped the top and took a sip. 'You're not supposed to be outside.'

She shrugged. 'Yeah, but if there's trouble, I can get ghosty and that's about as safe as you can get.'

'True.' He wanted to hug her up against him, but until he had really good control of the fire, that wasn't happening. He took a few steps back and leaned against one of the columns framing the front porch.

'You all right?' Her expression told him she knew something was up. She usually did. How, he wasn't sure, but Fi had a way of knowing when something in his world was off.

'I'm cool.'

Her mouth bunched to one side the way it often did when she was less than happy with him. He hated that look. He drank his soda to keep from having to say anything else.

The front gate started to swing open. He put the soda down. 'Who is that?'

She planted her hands on her hips. 'If you hadn't distracted me with your *lies*, I would have told you. It's Mortalis.'

'That means Mal and Chrysabelle are back, too.'

'Suppose so.' She arched a brow. Damn, she was getting worked up.

He cupped her elbow and led her away from the house, keeping his voice low. 'Look, there is something going on, but I don't want to talk about it here. Too many ears, you dig? When we're alone, okay?'

She softened instantly. 'But you're okay?'

'Right as rain, baby. Straight as steel.' He crossed a finger over his heart.

'Okay. But we will talk about it later, then.'

Of that, he had no doubt.

Mortalis parked and got out, but there was no one else in the car with him. He gave Doc and Fi a short nod in greeting.

Doc nodded back. 'How was New Orleans?'

'Hellish, as expected. How are things here?'

Doc jerked his thumb toward the building behind him. 'We have a vampire in the guesthouse.'

Mortalis's eyes widened as he walked over. 'You need me to kill it?'

'No, we're holding her as a prisoner of war, seeing what info she can provide us with. She claims to want asylum from Tatiana.'

The fae shook his head. 'Chrysabelle's not going to like it, no matter what the reason.'

'How come she and Mal aren't with you?'

'Went straight to Seven. Where's Creek?'

'Still out.' Doc glanced at the main house. 'How long before Chrysabelle gets home?'

'Maybe two hours. Why?'

'Her house is full of people. I know that's not her favorite thing.'

Mortalis shook his head. 'And she's not going to be in any kind of shape to have people around. Who's in there?'

'Luke and John Havoc, the mayor, Fi, Velimai, and Damian. The mayor's driver is in her car.'

Mortalis rubbed at one of his horns, his gaze on the ground for a moment. At last he looked up again. 'Obviously, Velimai will stay. It might not be the safest thing to send the mayor home at this time, but with both the Havoc boys, she should be all right.' He paced a few steps to one side, his head down like he was thinking. 'We can't put the comar back in the guesthouse with a vampire in there, but I don't like the idea of leaving that vampire in there to begin with.' He lifted his head. 'You have secure places on the freighter, right?'

Doc knew he meant the kind of places where they'd once locked Mal up, back when he'd strictly been on animal blood and the beast within him would occasionally rise up and try to get some of the human variety. 'What are you suggesting?'

'Take the vampire there. Lock her up. Then she's out of Chrysabelle's hair and the comar can move back to the guest-house. I'll help you. No vampire is dumb enough to try something with a shadeux watching her.'

Doc looked at Fi. 'What do you think?'

The corner of her mouth lifted as she shrugged. 'Mal will hate that, but for Chrysabelle's sake, I think he'll be okay with it. Who's going to guard the vampire? Make sure she doesn't get out? Because if she does and she really is working for Tatiana, having her loose in Mal's home is a really bad idea.'

'True,' Doc said. 'So how about we take Damian with us? Let him stand guard? Then Chrysabelle won't even have to deal with him being in her guesthouse.'

Mortalis nodded. 'Good plan. After that, the three of us will go track down Creek, let him know what's going on and that the mayor's on her own. No need for him to come back here and disturb Chrysabelle either.'

'Just one thing,' Fi said. 'What car are we going to fit all of us into?'

'Easy,' Doc said. 'We'll take the vampire with us in Mal's

sedan back to the freighter, and Mortalis can follow behind in Dominic's car.' He looked at the fae. 'That is whose wheels those are, right?'

'Yes,' Mortalis answered. 'If he didn't have more vehicles than he needed, I'd worry about getting it back.'

'Hold on.' Fi threw her hands up. 'I am not riding in the car with that vampire chick.'

Doc gave her a wink. 'Don't worry. She'll be in the trunk.'

Chapter Thirty-eight

Mal was sure at least one bone in his right hand was broken. Did it matter? No, not in the slightest. Chrysabelle could break every single one if she needed to. *She should.* He still wasn't letting go.

If he'd had breath to hold, he would have as Atticus lowered the needle toward her back. Her grip tightened, as if she could sense it. Maybe she could. The needle's tip glowed red hot. The heat had to register, even with the breath work she was doing.

The needle pierced her skin with a sizzle. Mal tensed, expecting her to cry out or flinch, but she did neither. Not even a sudden inhale. Her strength amazed him.

Blood welled from where Atticus worked, his blind eyes seemingly focused on her back as his hand moved over her skin. The scent of blood mixed with the gold's metallic tang and the occasional wisp of smoke. The beast, confused by the muddle, rumbled softly in Mal's head but remained controllable.

Another bone in Mal's hand fractured, but his pain was nothing compared to hers. It couldn't be.

'First one finished.' Atticus spoke in such a small voice that Mal wondered if he was even meant to hear it.

The new signum sparked to life as if lit from within, then the glow faded, melting away into the subtle light that always surrounded her. 'Is that normal?' Mal asked. He kept his voice low, too.

'What?' Atticus asked, his head coming up.

'The glow.'

'Yes.' With a look that cut off any more talking, Atticus bent his head and went back to work.

A sharp sizzle and a trailing column of vapor rose off his needle. Mal's jaw ached from clenching it. 'How can she stand this? No human should be able to. It's not possible.'

'I should not have allowed this. You're breaking my concentration.' With a sharp exhale, Atticus lifted the needle and leaned back. 'You assume the comarré is human.'

'I know she is. I've met her mother.'

Atticus's eyebrows lifted, but he didn't ask for more details. 'Yes, well, you haven't met her father. You won't either. I can't imagine you'd last long in his presence.'

Mal squinted. 'Who *is* her father?'

'Not who. *What.*'

'You're going to drop that bomb and then walk away from it?' Chrysabelle would want to know this when she came out of whatever pain-numbing trance she was in.

Atticus shrugged. 'I only know rumors. Guesses. Nothing concrete.' He bent like he was going back to work.

'What do you know?' Mal's temper shaded the edges of his vision red. The beast rumbled louder.

'All I will say is' – he paused as if searching for the words – 'gold is not the only reason her blood tastes so divine.' With that, he shut Mal out, bending over Chrysabelle and applying the needle with greater concentration.

Mal thought on the signumist's words, but shearing part of his attention away from Chrysabelle made little sense. There would be time for thinking later. Maybe she'd know what Atticus had meant.

The signumist continued down the length of her spine and back up the other side, implanting the signum and announcing each one as it was finished. Blood rose from the welted skin and trailed down her sides like ribbons. How she stood it, Mal had no idea. Halfway through the first side, he'd begun to shake with emotions he couldn't name. He wanted to take her place. To hurt Rennata for making Chrysabelle go through this again. *To kill.* To shove Atticus away from her. *To maim.* To rage against the injustice of life. To cradle her in his arms and make the pain go away.

If Chrysabelle sensed any of it, she made no indication, but watching her go through this was more intense than he'd imagined. His hands had long since gone numb. Even the voices in his head had quieted. At least it went quickly.

Finally, Atticus lifted his needle. 'Finished.'

The last signum lit up as the others had. This time the glow spread, brighter and stronger than before. The other new signum began to glow as well. Then the existing signum came to life. She moaned softly.

'Are you sure she's supposed to glow like that?'

Atticus stood, flexing his hands. 'You're a vampire. All comarré glow to you.'

'Not that brightly. Each one of her signum look like the sun is shining through it.'

Atticus stopped moving his tray out of the way. 'That can't be.'

'It is. I'm watching it happen right now.'

Chrysabelle moaned again, louder this time.

'Something's wrong.' Atticus frowned.

Mal jumped up. 'What do you mean something's wrong? Fix it. Now.'

'I can't. What's done is done.'

'Not good enough.' If not for Chrysabelle's hands gripping his, he would have leaped across the table and clamped them around the signumist's neck. 'What's happening to her?'

Atticus shook his head, his eyes darting from side to side as if seeking answers. 'The power in the ring could have survived the melting, or . . . '

'Or what?'

'Her blood could somehow be tainted.'

A sharp chill dug into Mal's gut. 'Tainted how?' But he already knew the answer.

'When her original signum were stripped, was she hospitalized? An infusion of normal human blood could cause problems.'

'No. No human blood.' Just vampire. Once again, he was the reason she suffered. *Of course.*

'Maybe it's the power in the ring, then.'

Chrysabelle's hands spread wide, releasing Mal's. She lifted her head and opened her mouth like she was struggling to breathe, but her eyes stayed closed. 'So . . . hot . . . '

'Hold her down,' Atticus said. 'She shouldn't move so soon after having this done. The flesh needs to seal. I have to clean her off at least.' He hurried to the side counter.

Hands aching, Mal latched on to her upper arms and kneeled down so he could talk softly to her. 'Hang on, Chrysabelle. It's going to be okay. I know it hurts. Breathe.' *You can kill me later,* he wanted to say. *She probably will.* He bent farther so his head touched hers. 'I'm right here. I'm not going to leave you.' But she'd leave him. Just as soon as she realized what he'd done. *She should.*

Atticus came back with a bowl of steaming water scented with some kind of herb and a cloth. He began to mop the blood from her. She moaned and lifted her head again. Her eyes fluttered open. The summer blue of her irises was shot through with flecks of gold, making her eyes glow almost as much as her body. 'Am I dying?'

A shudder ran through him. The voices rejoiced. He shook his head. 'No, you're not. Don't say that. Don't think that.'

'You're not dying, comarré.' Atticus squeezed the cloth over the bowl. The water ran scarlet. 'You're having a reaction to the ring's power. I'm sure this will pass when it settles into your body.'

She shivered as if cold and reached her hands out. Mal took them in his, but there was no strength in her grip. 'I'm glad you're here.'

He couldn't answer. Instead, he nodded. Then a hard tremor racked her body. She cried out. Her body tensed, the outline of her muscles stark beneath her glowing skin. A second later, the glow was gone and she lay limp on the table.

'Is she . . . ' Atticus shook his head.

'No,' Mal answered, relief flooding him. 'I can hear her heart beating.' *Too bad.*

'She will need much rest.' Atticus emptied the bowl into the sink. 'Days of it.'

Then, as if nothing had happened, she lifted her head. 'Holy mother,' Chrysabelle breathed out. 'I'd forgotten how much that hurts.' She leaned up gingerly on her elbows, gathering the fabric around her front and looking over her shoulder. Her eyes were their usual blue, not a fleck of gold to be seen. 'Am I sealed? Can I get dressed?'

Atticus's mouth came open, but he said nothing.

Mal stared at her. 'You just told me you were dying, now you're ready to go home?'

'What? I never said that.' Her eyes were heavy-lidded and on the verge of closing. 'I've been tranced out since Atticus said he was ready.'

'No,' Atticus corrected her. 'You haven't been.'

Afraid she'd realize she'd had a reaction based on the presence of his blood, Mal changed the subject. 'I can explain to her on the way home. Is she really ready to get dressed?'

'This is most unusual,' Atticus muttered. 'She may dress. Right now she feels little pain because the sealant in the washing water contains a variety of natural anesthetics, but when that wears off, the pain will return. It will be intense. She'll probably fall asleep soon, but you should get her to wherever she's going to convalesce, and quickly.' He picked up a small red pouch off his tray and handed it to Mal. 'She'll want this when she's ready.'

He had a feeling he knew what was in that pouch, but he tucked it into a pocket without looking at it then grabbed the robe she'd discarded and held it out to her, closing his eyes. 'Get this on and let's get you home.' And somehow, during the car ride to her house, he'd figure out a way to explain that more than just gold had gotten under her skin.

'H-how long are you going to leave me here?' Daciana asked.

Fi hovered a few feet off the ground in her ghost form. Being corporeal made her feel vulnerable around the bloodsucker, especially after her experience with Tatiana. 'You're a vampire, you can't be afraid of the dark.'

'Just get in,' Doc said. 'You're lucky we haven't ashed you yet. Once we find out if what you told us is true, we'll come get you. If it's not true, then you're in serious trouble.' He pointed toward the shipping container's interior.

Damian had his sacre out and resting on his shoulder. 'I'll be out here the whole time, too.'

'To keep me safe?' Daciana asked.

He shook his head. 'To make sure you don't try to escape.'

Fi had never seen a vampire cry. Daciana looked like she was about to change that. 'Oh, get in already. We have things to do.'

Slowly, Daciana walked into the container. She stood in the center, her hands folded primly in front of her, eyes round and slightly weepy. 'Please don't take long.'

Doc and Damian shut the doors, then locked them and linked a thick length of chain through and padlocked that. Damian tucked his sacre back into its sheath. 'See you when you get back.'

Doc tugged on the padlock. 'You going to be all right here?'

The comar tipped his head toward the cooler of food Velimai had insisted he take. 'I'll be fine. I couldn't eat all that in a week.'

'We won't be gone that long,' Doc said. 'As soon as we find Creek and get some confirmation, we'll be back. After that, Fi and I will be here until Mal and Chrysabelle make the final decision as to what to do with her.'

'I'm good till whenever.'

'All right, bro. See you later.'

Fi waved. 'Bye, Damian. Back soon.'

He returned her wave and sat down on the cooler, his back to the container's doors, his body silhouetted by the LED lamp at his feet.

Fi floated alongside Doc as they headed back to the main deck and the car where Mortalis waited. 'So spill.'

'Spill what?'

She moved in front of him, blocking his path through the corridor. 'Don't act like you don't know. What's going on? You told me something was up and that you'd tell me when we were alone. Well, we're alone now.'

He sighed and rolled his head around like he needed a massage. Tough. She wasn't laying a finger on him until he came clean. 'Creek killed Aliza to break the hold her spell had on me.'

'I know that part.'

'I don't know if it's because Preacher turned her into a vampire – and you know he's not exactly a normal vampire to begin with – or because her power is just that strong, or even if it's because the spell had to be broken some other way, but I think some of her power attached itself to me.'

That sounded bad. She tried hard not to let the image of her torn and bloody body show, but it was tricky when she got scared or worried or tired. 'What is that supposed to mean? Attached itself how? What kind of power?'

He held his hand out. Nothing happened. 'It's not working. That's the problem. I can't control it.'

'Control what?'

With a snarl, he punched his fist into the metal wall, making her jump. His eyes flickered green-gold, the pupils slitting down to razor-thin slices.

Flames burst off his hands and forearms.

'That,' he said, splaying his fingers. The blue fire danced over his skin, mesmerizing her. Then she blinked and looked at him. His eyes, no longer leopard, held fear and anger.

'It's okay,' she said. 'Actually, it's better than okay. It's cool! You have a new power. What other varcolai can wield fire?'

The flames had begun to die but sprang to life again. 'It's not cool,' he growled, shaking his hand to kill the fire. 'I can't control it. When my emotions peak, the fire just shows up.'

'Does it hurt?'

'Not me.' He exhaled. 'But the fire is very real.' The last wisp of blue disappeared off his fingers. He leaned against the wall he'd just punched and stared up at the ceiling. 'I'm afraid to touch you, Fi.'

She drifted close enough to cup his face in her transparent hands and brush her mouth over his. 'When I'm like this, nothing can hurt me.'

'But when you're not? When we're in bed together?' He shook his head and took a few steps away from her down the corridor. 'That can't happen. Until this is fixed.'

Her heart sank. She loved being curled up in bed with him. It was a safe place for her. Or had been. Worse, she had no real way to comfort him. And she hated that. 'Who can fix it? Aliza and Evie are dead. Not that they'd help anyway.'

'Maybe it'll play out.' He glanced at his hands. 'That's what I'm hoping.'

'And if it doesn't? We have to talk to someone. Find somebody to help.'

'There might not be anybody to help.' He raised his head and met her gaze. 'We just have to accept that.'

'What are you saying?' She charged forward until only inches separated them. 'Are you breaking up with me?'

'Fi, you can't look at it like that. This is for your own good.

And my sanity. If I ever did anything to hurt you . . . ' He turned away.

She went corporeal and dropped to the floor with a soft thud. As soon as her feet touched, she kicked him in the shin. 'You are *not* breaking up with me over this. Do you understand me? Hell no.' She shoved past him and headed for the car. 'I'll tell you when we're broken up, and it's not now. Men. Unbelievable. Like a little fire is reason to break up. Seriously, I can't even believe—'

'Fi.'

She stopped her march and looked back at him, hands on her hips. 'What?'

He smiled and tiny flames wobbled on the tips of his ears. 'I love you.'

'You better believe you love me. Now let's grab some weapons and go find Creek so we can start working on the real problem.'

He caught up to her in a few strides. 'The fire?'

'Yeah, I'm concerned it's making you stupid.' She shot him a sideways look. 'We're going to figure this thing out, and then you're going to ask me to marry you because I'm tired of waiting.'

His mouth opened, but he had sense enough not to say anything.

'Keep walking, kitty cat.'

Chapter Thirty-nine

Tatiana bounced Lilith on her knee while across the room Octavian went over some ledgers at the desk. It was shocking how quickly they'd become the happy little family. She watched him for a moment, his head bent, his concentration fixed on the pages of numbers that represented everything now under her control as Dominus.

He was a good man. Becoming a vampire had yet to change him. Maybe it wouldn't. Maybe he would stay the way he was, without the harsh cynical edge that so many of her kind developed. Only the years would tell that.

He looked up, caught her watching him, and smiled. She smiled back. Did she love him? She might. It was hard to tell if the emotion was true or born out of the buoyant joy Lilith brought her. Either way, she liked having him as part of this new stage of her life, even if it scared her a little to have people close to her that she cared about. But being Dominus meant she needed that sacred inner circle more than ever. And now with Lilith to protect . . .

She kissed the sweet child in her arms, burying her face in

the baby's sweet-smelling skin. It wouldn't take long for the other houses to find out about Lilith, to speculate where the child had come from, what her powers were, what she meant for them and their future.

So many would want to hurt her. To possess her for their own. Use her in a way that would benefit them. The Castus had chosen wisely by bringing Lilith to Tatiana. They knew her past, understood that she would not allow another child to be taken from her.

A knock sounded at the door. 'Come,' Tatiana called.

One of the servants entered, bowing. 'My lady, Lord Edwin, Elder of the House of Bathory, is here to see you. Would you like to receive him here?'

Tatiana glanced at Octavian. His gaze came to rest on Lilith. 'There's no point in hiding her.' He closed the ledger and stood. 'They will all know soon enough. And Lord Syler is an ally.'

'He's as close to one as we have.' The Dominus of the House of Bathory and the Dominus of the House of Tepes had traditionally sided together, but she was not Ivan and had no clear idea of how Syler felt about her in the position of Dominus. Perhaps that was what she was about to learn. She nodded to the servant as Octavian moved to sit at her side. 'Show Lord Edwin in.'

'Very good, my lady.' The servant exited, returning some minutes later with Lord Edwin.

He dipped his head in greeting and Tatiana responded in kind. His gaze skimmed the bundle in her arms but didn't falter. 'I bring greetings from the House of Bathory, Dominus Tatiana.'

The sound of her new title gave her no small thrill. 'Thank you. Please, sit.' She gestured to the chair across from her. 'Would you care for wine or brandy or blood?'

He sat where she indicated. 'No, thank you, I'm fine.' His gaze drifted again to Lilith, but he covered by brushing an invisible piece of lint off his trousers. 'If you are amenable to it, Lord Syler would like to host a ball in your honor. There has not been a new Dominus in the House of Tepes for almost four hundred years, as you well know.'

'I do know.' She smiled. The alliance was alive and well, then. 'That is very kind of you, and I am happy to accept your gracious offer.' It was the responsibility of one of the houses to host the ball and a relief that Syler had reached out and made the offer. She'd doubted any of the other houses would.

Alliance firm in her mind, she decided to take the next step. 'It will be a wonderful opportunity to introduce all the families to my daughter, Lilith.' She turned slightly so Edwin could see Lilith's face.

The expression on his was almost unnamable. Curiosity seemed the strongest. 'Forgive me, I didn't know you had a daughter. Congratulations.'

Whatever she said now, whatever information she gave him, would color what was said about Lilith and the opinions that were formed. She chose her words carefully. 'The Castus have chosen me to be Lilith's mother. They believe I am the best suited to raise her and teach her our ways. She is the *first* vampire child.'

Edwin nodded, his mouth opening slightly as if he'd almost spoken, then thought better of what he wanted to say. 'So . . . Lilith is not your blood child?'

'Of course not. How could she be?' Idiot. 'But she is now a child of my heart.'

A shimmer of understanding sparked in Edwin's eyes. 'Well, whoever turned her did it quite young. Astonishing, really.'

'No,' Octavian corrected him. 'Lilith wasn't turned. She was born vampire.'

Shaking his head, Edwin leaned back. 'I confess, I don't understand. How is that possible?'

Octavian looked to Tatiana, giving her the reins of the conversation. Lilith cooed and grabbed hold of Tatiana's finger, causing Tatiana to smile. She kept her eyes on her daughter's. 'Lilith is a mystery of sorts, but all anyone needs to know is that she is a daughter of the House of Tepes, and with her, a new age of vampires has begun.' She raised her head to peer into Edwin's eyes and make sure nothing she said was mistaken. 'Anyone who tries to harm her will bring upon themselves the full rage of the ancient ones.'

Edwin nodded. 'I understand. I will be sure to let Lord Syler know.'

Lilith pulled Tatiana's finger into her mouth, her tiny fangs trying and failing to pierce her mother's metal hand. Her face crumpled and a wail bellowed out of her. Cracks shot through the porcelain lamp on the side table.

Tatiana stood, causing Edwin and Octavian to rise also. 'If you'll excuse us, my daughter is hungry. I look forward to the ball. I'm sure Lord Syler will send more details when things are settled. Unless there is anything else he wishes to speak to me about before that.' Like a firmer alliance with the mother and guardian of the only vampire child ever known to exist. She flicked her gaze to Octavian and then the door, indicating she was ready to leave. 'I'll send a servant to see you out.'

Doc was glad to drive. It was a good distraction from his thoughts, something to focus on besides the weird power he'd inherited. He glanced in the rearview mirror. Fi was sprawled out on the backseat, catching a few z's. He'd thought about trying to make her stay with Damian, but after her speech in the freighter, he knew better than to even start that conversation.

'Where do you think Creek's going to be?' Doc asked Mortalis, beside him in the passenger's seat.

He had the window partially rolled down. The tangy smell of smoke occasionally drifted in. 'Wherever the action is.'

'Looks like it's already been here.' They'd passed burned-out cars, some still ablaze, buildings that looked like they'd had bites taken out of them, giant puddles of foul ooze, even a couple of bodies – none of which had looked human.

'You hear that?' Mortalis asked.

Doc powered his window down. Sounds of distant fighting. He pulled the car over on the next block and parked. 'On foot from here.'

Mortalis nodded. 'Agreed.'

'Fi, up and at 'em.' Doc reached back and gave her a shake.

'I'm up.' She yawned and ran a hand through her hair.

He snagged the short sword he'd brought from Mal's collection on the freighter, then the three of them got out and headed toward the noise. A flash of light brightened the night sky. Doc broke into a run, Mortalis and Fi behind him. They turned the corner and found Creek crouched behind a Dumpster, facing down a two-headed serpent coiled overhead in one of the few remaining power lines. Sparks showered over the creature's skin and down onto the ground, making it hard to get near. The electricity seemed to feed it. As if in confirmation, a third head popped up.

'Need some help?' Doc skidded to a stop at Creek's side.

'Love some.' Creek leveled his crossbow at the thing and sent a bolt into its body. The serpent howled, its voice high and oddly feminine.

'We need to take the heads off,' Mortalis said. Out of nowhere, he brandished a short curved blade. 'We need to get it on the ground for that.'

'I can bring it down,' Fi said.

'Like hell you will.' Doc shot her an angry look. 'Get behind us.'

Creek shook his head. 'This isn't a game, Fi.'

She flipped them off. 'Nothing can touch me in my ghost form. Just get ready to kill it.' Without waiting for them to respond, she darted out from behind the Dumpster and toward the serpent. Doc grabbed her arm, but his hand closed around nothing. When she was ghost, there was nothing to grab.

'Hey, slimy,' she yelled. She levitated a discarded bottle and chucked it at the creature. The bottle shattered against the light pole. All three heads swiveled in her direction.

'I do not like this,' Doc whispered. He was fighting the fire within hard, trying to breathe and stay calm enough to keep from combusting.

'She'll be fine as long as she doesn't go corporeal,' Mortalis answered. 'She's a little crazy, that one.' But there was admiration in his voice.

'It's working,' Creek said.

The serpent slithered down the pole, its heads dancing closer and closer to Fi. Every so often, she took a step back, turning as she moved so that the creature's back was to them.

Creek pulled a knife from his boot. 'I'll take the head on the right. Doc, you take the middle, Mortalis, the left. On three.'

'Got it,' Doc answered.

'On three,' Mortalis repeated.

'One,' Creek said.

Fi threw something else at the serpent, and the front half of the creature hit the asphalt.

'Two,' Creek said.

She took another step back. 'Come and get me, you disgusting worm.'

It disengaged from the light pole completely.

'Three!' Creek yelled.

They sprang forward, each man attacking his assigned head. A few sparks still snapped from the transformer, biting into the flashing blades. Metal found flesh and sinew. Blood spewed into the air, drenching them, but the battle was over almost as soon as it had started. The headless serpent twitched on the corner of Alafaya and Vine, its blood pooling in the street and trailing into the storm drain.

'Yay,' Fi cried, clapping as she came toward them. 'That was awesome.'

'Yeah, awesome.' The sticky ooze covering Doc made him itch. He hated being dirty. He tried to breathe. One freak-out and he'd go up like a Fourth of July finale.

Creek turned to Doc and Mortalis. 'Thanks for the help.'

Fi stopped at Doc's side and wrinkled her nose. 'You guys look really gross. You don't smell so hot either. You get in Mal's car like that and he'll make you wish that snake thing had eaten you.'

'You think I like this?' Doc asked. Heat built in his hands. He looked down to make sure there were no flames. There weren't. Yet.

Mortalis frowned. 'And I thought Nothos guts were bad. This stuff feels like acid.'

'We need to wash it off before it does any permanent damage.' Creek pointed halfway down the block to a fire hydrant. 'There.'

'How are you going to open that without a wrench?' Fi asked.

Creek hoisted his crossbow, took aim, and fired. The bolt sheared off the main nut on the hydrant, sending a plume of water into the air. 'Like that. Let's get cleaned up. Here, Fi, hold this.' He gingerly held out a small black rectangle.

Doc was under the spray before she got corporeal to take the phone. Water had never felt so good. He scrubbed at himself as best he could. Creek and Mortalis joined him to do the same.

'Hey!' Fi yelled. She waved at them.

'What?' Doc asked, the rush of the hydrant's geyser filling his ears.

She held up the phone. The screen was lit up. 'Creek's got a call.' She glanced at the screen. 'Somebody named Argent. You want me to answer it?'

'No.' Creek darted out of the water and snatched the phone from her fingers. He swiped a finger across the screen. 'Creek here.' He listened for a moment, then nodded. 'Will do.' He hung up and turned back to Doc and Mortalis.

'Something up?' Mortalis asked as he stepped out of the spray.

Doc came out behind him to hear better.

Creek nodded. 'Police need some help down in Little Havana. They think they have the comarré killer.'

Chapter Forty

A screaming wall of pain jerked Chrysabelle out of a deep, dreamless sleep. She woke up gasping for air, belly-down on her bed, arms and legs tangled in sweat-damp sheets. The trip to the signumist came back to her in a hard rush of memory and throbbing, fiery pain.

A hand touched her shoulder and she yelped, shrinking away from it. The move shot fresh heat through her back. The new signum there burned like brands.

The hand disappeared. Mal's silver eyes came into focus, his face somehow suddenly inches from hers. 'It's okay. You're home. Stay still and rest.'

She stared into his eyes, the cool of her pillow a comfort. She lifted her hand and touched his cheek. 'Home?'

He nodded. 'Do you want anything? Velimai is here.'

The wysper appeared behind him, peering over his shoulder with concern-filled eyes. *If I can do anything,* she signed, *just tell me.*

'No,' Chrysabelle whispered. The pain made her eyes water. 'How long ... home?'

'A quarter hour, maybe a few minutes more,' Mal answered. 'But you've been asleep since we got into the car.'

'The city? Samhain . . . the covenant . . . ' The effort of words drained her.

'Don't worry about any of that. Just rest and recover. Try to go back to sleep.'

She tried to shake her head but only succeeded in turning it farther into the pillow. 'I need to . . . ' Even breathing made her body ache. 'The Aurelian.'

'Soon enough,' Mal said. He patted a small red pouch on the nightstand. 'For when you're ready, but for now, you need to sleep and heal.'

She closed her eyes, meaning to say something else about how she couldn't wait, didn't want to wait, needed to find her brother, but the depths of sleep consumed her, pulling her blissfully under once again.

Octavian paced the sitting area of the master bedroom. 'Word will spread now. Every house will know of Lilith's existence as surely as they know you are Dominus.'

Tatiana tore herself away from listening to Lilith's soft coos as she fed from the wet nurse in the next room. The nursery wasn't completed, but Tatiana wanted Lilith close, so she'd set up the wet nurse in her dressing room. 'You seem worried.' She sprawled back against the nest of pillows on the bed. 'Don't be. The Castus made it clear to the other Dominus that I and my family are to be protected at all costs. None would dare cross us knowing how firmly the ancient ones are on our side. One look at Lilith and they will see where his favor lies.'

'That's what worries me,' Octavian said. 'There will be jealousy unlike anything the families have ever seen.'

She smiled, his concern touching. 'Sweetheart, don't you think I've given this much thought?' She slid off the bed and came to his side, taking his hand. 'This is exactly the position I – *we* – want to be in. The other houses must align with us or they will be of little consequence in the new age.'

He smiled back at her. 'You're so sure of yourself, so confident.' He feathered kisses across her forehead. 'So fearless.' His lips brushed hers and she welcomed him in, flattery one of her greatest aphrodisiacs. 'I am so proud to be at your side.' Hands splayed on her hips, he pulled her closer. 'I cannot wait to see you at that ball. You will leave the men bitter with want and the women wondering how you are everything they are not.'

She tipped her head back as his mouth trailed kisses down her neck. 'If you're trying to get me into bed, it's working.'

He laughed against her skin, his fangs grazing the curve of her shoulder. 'I adore you, Tatiana. Do you know that?'

'You've made that delightfully clear.' She nipped at his chin, drunk on affection and the rare air of happiness. 'I feel the same way about you.'

His expression grew more serious, but the silver in his eyes didn't fade. 'That you could feel that way toward me when I was little more than your servant a short while ago ... ' He turned away from her.

'Don't,' she whispered, clinging to him. 'The past is just that. We'll talk of it no more.'

Head bent, his gaze came at her sideways. 'Tell me of the future, then. Tell me of your plans.' The curve of his mouth broadened into a grin. 'I love hearing you talk about your ideas and desires for the vampire nation.'

She flew to the door and locked it, then was back at his side, tugging him toward the bed. She could almost understand how

Daciana had married Laurent. With a man like Octavian, such a commitment didn't seem so hard to accept. Maybe they should marry. For Lilith's sake. And to show the rest of the families just how strong their bond was. Her legs hit the side of the bed. 'I want to take over the world.'

He tumbled down on top of her, shoving the pillows out of the way. His fingers worked the buttons of her silk blouse. His mouth followed them down. 'How will you do it?'

'I will start with . . . Oh, that's the spot.' A shiver of pleasure trilled down her spine and joined with the places his hands caressed. 'I will . . . I . . . '

'Will I be at your side?' He breathed the words over her bare flesh, raising an army of goosebumps across her thighs, exposed by the skirt he'd shoved up to her hips.

'Yes,' she whispered. 'Always.' Because she was almost sure she loved him.

His tongue raked across her stomach. 'I am afraid,' he said softly.

The chill returned, but for a whole new reason. She struggled to her elbows and stared down at him. 'Afraid of what?'

He rested his head on her taut belly. 'That I love you far more than is wise.' His thumb drew a small, delicious circle near her navel. 'You will be the queen of the vampire nation. Then you will find another and break my heart.'

She laughed softly so as not to wound him further. 'You worry for nothing. You'll see.' She lay back down and threaded her fingers into his hair, guiding him back to where he'd been when he'd stopped. 'At the ball, you'll see.' She would announce their union. That would stun the families, wouldn't it? She did love to make a scene.

Soft kisses teased her flesh. 'Until the ball, then.'
She could have sworn she felt him smile against her skin.

Doc stomped the brakes and brought the car to a stop behind
Creek's motorcycle. Keeping up with the KM had been an
effort. Mal's beaten sedan wasn't exactly as limber as the bike,
and dodging some of the things currently roaming Paradise
City's streets was no small feat.

Creek waited for them on the sidewalk as they got out, but
the second the first door opened, he was off down the street
toward the cop cars they'd followed here. The cops jumped out,
guns drawn as Doc, Mortalis, and Fi, still in her ghost form,
hustled to catch up to Creek. 'A woman called in, said she heard
the sounds of a struggle out her window, looked out and saw a
blonde girl with gold marks on her being dragged into this alley.'

He cocked his crossbow. 'You three stay here, let me suss it
out.'

'You sure you don't want more help than those two cops?'
Doc asked.

'They've been briefed. One cop is varcolai.'

Doc nodded and took a better look at the cop, recognizing
him as a member of the pride. 'Shout if you need us.'

Creek ducked into the alley. Doc inhaled, testing the air for
scents. Blood. In spades. And the faint hint of vampire. But
between the two was the familiar musky scent of feline shifter.
Had to be the cop. Suddenly, a deep guttural snarl broke through
the other sounds of the city.

'Doc.' Urgency laced Creek's voice like a poison. 'Now.'

With Fi at his side, Doc spun around the corner, unprepared
for the scene before him. A large feline varcolai in half-form
crouched over the torn body of one of Dominic's comarré. If she

wasn't dead, she would be in another heartbeat or two. Blood dripped from his clawed fingers and pooled beneath the girl like a morbid blanket, unfurling slowly toward the street. The varcolai stood, stepping back carefully to avoid the puddle.

The cops had their guns raised, but they were out of their league. 'Guns aren't going to do much good,' Doc said.

'Copy that. Besides, we need to take him in alive,' Creek answered. His crossbow stayed up on his shoulder. 'You know this cat?'

'Maybe. Definitely leopard, but it's a little dark to really make out—'

One of the cops flipped on a handheld spotlight, bringing the killer into clear view. The varcolai cop muttered a curse.

Doc swore, too. 'What the hell?' He stepped forward, a little past Creek and enough to block the KM's shot. 'Sinjin?'

The man snarled again, showing a small chip in his left fang and confirming Doc's identification. How could he forget the varcolai who'd cast him out of the pride?

Sinjin shook his head as if telling Doc not to say another word. Doc snorted in derision and took another step forward. 'You think I'm going to stand by and let you murder these girls? Like hell.'

With a quick shake, Sinjin shed all signs of his leopard half and took on his full human form. 'Siding with the mortals, Maddoc?' He shook his head. 'Don't you see what's happening? The vampires grow stronger every day. We have to seize whatever opportunity we can, and tonight we're seizing a big one.'

'There's no *we*, Sinjin. You kicked me out of the pride years ago, remember?' Heat coursed through Doc's bones. 'And I don't consider killing humans an opportunity.'

'I didn't kill this girl. I found her here. The victim of a vampire.'

'Her blood is on your hands, and I bet when the police search you, they'll find the container of vampire ashes you've been planting beneath their nails.'

Sinjin's mouth bent in a cruel sneer. 'You're weak. You always have been.' His eyes reflected the cop's light with a green-gold glow Doc knew must be shining in his eyes, too. The heat in his body got more intense. 'That's why I'm the pride leader.'

'I never wanted that job, no matter how much you thought I did. Time to give yourself up. This game is over.' And time for Doc to calm down.

Hands fisted at his side, Sinjin stretched his neck and growled the low, threatening call that meant one thing. Challenge.

This wasn't the time or place to answer that call. Not with the fire in his system just begging for a way out. Doc turned and walked back toward Creek. 'Cops have any tranquilizer darts? That's what I'd use—'

Creek's mouth opened but Fi's yell hit Doc's ears first. 'Behind you,' she wailed.

Doc twisted in time to catch Sinjin's charge full in the chest. It took him to the pavement hard enough to knock the breath out of him and dent the asphalt. He was vaguely aware of Fi telling Creek to shoot and Creek saying he couldn't get a clean shot.

Sinjin raised his hand, claws out. Doc rolled as the hand came down, throwing Sinjin off. Doc flipped to his feet and caught Sinjin as he did the same, then shoved him back into the alley wall. The sounds of bones and bricks cracking filled the air.

'I'm going to kill you like I should have done instead of kicking you out,' Sinjin snarled.

Doc ducked a punch, then threw one of his own, planting his fist in Sinjin's gut. 'I doubt that.'

Sinjin backhanded him. Doc tasted blood, staggered a step. Sinjin came after him, latching on and taking him to the ground again. 'When I'm done with you,' Sinjin whispered, 'I'm going to end that freak girlfriend of yours, too.'

Doc's vision went blue. Flame blue. With a roar like a house on fire, he exploded into burning rage. Flickering blue light washed the alley. Sinjin's eyes rounded and he tried to let go of Doc, but it was too late. All Doc knew was that keeping Fi safe meant taking Sinjin out. The fire consumed Sinjin, swallowing him in a flood of searing flame. He howled in pain and anger, finally stumbling free to bat at himself. He collapsed a moment later, a charred version of the powerful varcolai he'd been just a few short minutes ago.

Doc's chest heaved as the fire dancing over him snuffed out. An odd silence took over the alley. He turned slowly as he realized that his secret was not a secret anymore.

Mortalis had stayed at the mouth of the alley, one arm wrapped around Fi's shoulders. Doc had no idea how the fae was keeping her from freaking out, but he was grateful. Creek shook his head. 'You said you were okay.'

He shrugged, too spent to give energy to excuses. 'I lied.'

The varcolai cop stepped forward. Doc couldn't recall the pride member's name. Fear and disbelief etched lines around his eyes. Eyes that held the same green-gold glow Doc's did. He pointed a finger at Doc. 'The pride leader challenged you and you killed him.'

Doc shook his head. Hell no, this was *not* the right time for that business. 'It means *nothing*. What I did was done in self-defense. Let it go.'

The cop jutted his chin forward. 'Can't. Pride law. Makes you the new pride leader.'

Double hell to the no. 'I decline. Find someone else.'

Fi finally broke away from Mortalis and ran to Doc's side, her hands all over him, checking him for injuries. 'Are you okay? Are you hurt?'

The cop brought his gun up and aimed it at Fi. 'Miss, you need to keep your hands to yourself and step away from the pride leader.'

She slanted her eyes at him. 'Look, five oh, I don't know who you think you are or who you think my fiancé is, but I'll put my hands on him anytime I want to.'

'Yeah,' Doc said. 'It's cool. She's with me.'

The cop shook his head and kept the gun raised. 'Your wife's going to have something to say about that.'

Fi and Doc turned at the same time. 'Wife?' they said in unison. Doc held his hands up. 'Look, I know pride law says the new pride leader takes all spoils, but Sinjin wasn't married.'

'Yes, he was,' the cop answered. 'As of two months ago. And as of five minutes ago, so are you.'

Chapter Forty-one

Chrysabelle opened her eyes and blinked, already wincing in anticipation of the pain in her back. But it was oddly absent. Maybe because she was so still. She lifted her head slowly, waiting with every inch for the sharp sear that would cause her to cry out or fold back against the bed.

It never came. Not even when she grabbed the side of the mattress and pulled herself to the edge of the bed. Her back was achy and tight and just this side of hot, but somehow not awash in the pain she'd experienced after every visit to the signumist.

She lay flat again and reached behind her to feel what she could of her back. The skin was very warm and almost hard. That was nothing unusual. The signum took days to soften beneath the skin. But what was strange was the lack of scabbing. The raised welts caused by the signum weren't there. Her skin was as flat and smooth as though nothing had been done.

A panicked shock ran through her. The trip to the signumist hadn't been a dream, had it? Turning her face to the other side, she glimpsed the small red pouch on her nightstand. No, not a dream. That had to have come from Atticus.

Dawn's pale light glowed beneath the edges of the drapes, giving her enough light to realize that she was alone. Mal must have succumbed to daysleep by now, which was good. He needed it. Maybe Velimai was sleeping, too. Knowing the wysper, she was probably making coffee or polishing Chrysabelle's sacres. Either way, there might not be a better opportunity to do what she had to.

Chrysabelle eased from beneath the covers, giving her head time to adjust to being upright again. Even as she straightened carefully, she felt no pain. There should be. The lack of it caused a prickly feeling in the back of her brain, but she ignored it. She had work ahead of her. Hard work.

Nude except for a pair of white boy shorts, she slipped into the satin robe laid out for her on a nearby chair, tucked the red pouch into the pocket, then quietly locked the door. She could not be disturbed.

Once inside the bathroom, she locked that door, too, then cranked on the shower and let it run. Neither Mal nor Velimai would believe she was taking a shower this early in her recovery, but it would buy her a little time, and a little time was all she needed.

The robe wasn't the proper ceremonial dress, but that didn't matter. This would be her last trip to the Aurelian. Her final act as a comarré.

She twisted her hair up with a pair of gold and diamond sticks that had been Maris's, then kneeled on the white marble floor. The robe spilled over her knees, the fabric not nearly as fine as the gown she should be wearing. She pushed the satin off her shoulders to bare her new signum.

She took the red leather pouch from her pocket and opened it, peering inside. She smiled. Atticus had been as thoughtful as she'd suspected he would be. She withdrew the scrap of paper that held the portal signum. He'd known she'd need them for what she was about to do. Resting the pouch across her lap, she closed her eyes, bowed her head, and chanted softly the calming mantra known to all comarré. There wasn't enough time to prepare the way she would have liked, but it would be enough. She hoped.

At last she raised her chin and opened her eyes. From the pouch, she removed the gold pipette, its small end tapered to a needle-thin point.

With a deep breath and a final thought to the holy mother, she lifted the pipette, the pointed end facing her. She inhaled, already dreading this new pain. It would all be over soon. Everything she had endured would finally be worthwhile. She wrapped her left hand over her right and plunged the pipette into her chest.

Hot, stabbing pain sucked the air from her lungs, but she held still, allowing only the slightest tremor to shake her. Index finger over the pipette's open end, she slid it from her chest. Blood trickled from the wound and trailed over the curve of her breast.

She picked up the chanting again, using its persuasive rhythm to stay focused on the task and not the pain. *Lux sancta matris intus me fulget. Lux sancta matris intus me fulget . . .* Using the pipette like a fountain pen and her blood for ink, she traced a perfect circle on the marble. At the top of the circle, she drew the phoebus, the sun symbol that was every comarré's first signum. It made her smile to think that the brother she would soon find also had that mark.

Circle completed, she leaned forward and continued with the pipette, this time copying the signum from the paper into the circle's interior. She whispered the name of each one as she fin-ished.

With the last one done, she set the pipette aside and stood, pulling her robe back over her body. She lifted her arms, hold-ing her palms up over the circle. Within it, the signum she'd traced began to expand. Atticus's signum were working. Blood filled in the blank spaces within the circle, expanding until a solid pool of red shimmered before her.

The blood rippled like water and a flash of golden light gleamed across the surface. The gateway to the Aurelian was open. There was no turning back now. Not that she wanted to.

With a final calming breath, Chrysabelle stepped into the portal.

Blood, the voices whispered. It took Mal a second to realize that the scent of blood wasn't in his dream. It was real. And strong enough to wake him from daysleep. The next second, his mind went to Chrysabelle. Something was wrong. She hadn't been bleeding at all by the time he'd gotten her into bed, a task Velimai couldn't do because her sandpaper-like skin would have only injured Chrysabelle further.

He leaped off the fold-out couch in the small interior room that otherwise served as a hurricane shelter, blinking as he stumbled into the hall and a bright shaft of sun. Before his skin could crisp, he hugged the wall, staying in the shadows until he made it upstairs. After he'd gotten her into the house, he'd closed all the curtains on this floor so that nothing would disturb her ability to rest and recover. It was also the reason he'd yet to explain his suspicions about what had happened at the signumist's. There'd be plenty of time for that when she was healed.

He went to open her door quietly, but the knob wouldn't turn. He had no idea what went into recovering from such a procedure. Maybe Velimai was in there, washing Chrysabelle's back. That might explain the smell of fresh blood. Or if Velimai had accidently touched her. He tipped his head toward the door and listened. Running water. Maybe that was exactly what was—

Velimai appeared at the end of the hall. She held her hands up as if asking what was wrong.

Hell. 'A lot if you're not in there. Door's locked.'

Her eyes widened and she sped to where he was. She made shoving motions with her hands like she wanted to push the door in.

'Knock it down? Don't you have a key?'

Yes and no, she signed. She thrust her hands at the door a second time as if telling him to hurry.

He didn't need to be told twice. He grabbed the door handle again and wrenched it, tearing the metal free from the wood. Velimai pushed past him. Her elbow brushed the top of his hand, leaving a line of raw skin behind. Ignoring the already closing wound, he followed.

The room was empty, the bed disheveled. Blood scent hung humid in the air. The door to the bathroom – the location of the running water – was shut. 'If she's taking a shower—'

With the coldest expression, Velimai held up a hand, shook her head, and pointed back to the bed.

Mal scanned it again. 'What?'

Night something, Velimai signed.

'Night? Night what?' His gaze caught on the nightstand. Nothing out of place, nothing missing. He went deadly still. Nothing missing but the red leather pouch Atticus had given her.

He'd seen that pouch before. He knew what it contained. 'Son of a priest,' he whispered. 'She's trying to open the portal.'

He flashed past Velimai. Chrysabelle was way too weak to attempt something like this now. Stubborn, stubborn woman. His fist hit the door. 'Chrysabelle, I know you're in there and I know what you're doing. Let me in or I swear to Hades, I will knock this door down.'

No answer, just the shush of the water.

Velimai motioned for him to break in. He heaved his shoulder into the door, cracking the door frame and flinging it wide.

Nothing in the bathroom, except for the gold pipette and circle of blood on the floor. *Blood blood blood . . .* Chrysabelle was already gone. Mal slumped to his knees beside the puddle. The beast within him strained its bonds at so much blood, but the weight of helplessness pressed Mal into a dark place where ignoring the voices became a very easy thing. He slammed his fist onto the marble tile, leaving a small crack. The rage building in him tested his power of control. It was the kind of rage that fed the beast. 'We're too late.'

Velimai pointed at the circle, then at Mal, then back at the circle.

'No. I'm not going after her. Creek and I did that last time and almost got her killed. The Aurelian is not a patient woman. She'll punish Chrysabelle if that happens again, and I won't be the reason for that.' A shimmer of gold rippled over the blood. The portal was definitely open. 'We'll just have to wait for her to return.'

If she returns.

He closed his eyes. She would. She had to. Because if she didn't, he would let the beast free. There was no reason not to if she was gone.

Chapter Forty-two

Chrysabelle went to her knees the moment her feet hit stone. She kept her head bowed, her mind filling in the details of the room based on what she'd seen the last time. Books and scrolls overflowing the shelves lining the walls, and before her, a massive table, also piled high with more scrolls, charts, and star maps. Seated behind it, the tall, slender Persian she'd come to see.

The Aurelian.

A chair scraped the stone floor. 'You are a determined soul, aren't you, comarré?'

Chrysabelle lifted her head. 'Yes, my lady.'

The Aurelian gestured for her to rise. 'You don't belong here, not anymore. You've been disavowed by your house.' She laughed, a not altogether pleasant sound. 'At least you didn't bring the vampire and the Kubai Mata with you this time.'

As she got to her feet, Chrysabelle wanted to remind the Aurelian that she hadn't actually brought them with her the last time. They'd come after her by accident, according to their side of the story. But she kept her mouth shut and let the Aurelian guide the conversation.

'What do you want, comarré? What has driven you to return to me?' Her eyes narrowed with suspicion. 'You should not even be fully healed from Rennata's efforts.'

Rennata's *efforts*? Is that what the Aurelian called having two strips of flesh cut from her body? 'I have always been a fast healer.' The Persian had once invited Chrysabelle to call her by her name, Nadira. Doing so now could either soften the Aurelian or anger her. Chrysabelle decided to take the chance. 'I am here, Nadira, because I am desperate for an answer to a question, and as every comarré knows, you are all-wise and all-knowing. The key to the past and the future lies with you.' It was almost word for word what she'd been taught about the Aurelian in school, but it was also flattering and that worked with certain types of women.

Nadira's smile extended into her coal-black eyes. 'That is so.' Her fingers traced the hilt of the massive sword resting across the front of the table. 'But first you will answer some for me. Where did you find a skilled signumist willing to work on you?'

'Who said he was willing?' Atticus had been kind to her. She would do nothing to cause him harm. If that meant protecting him with a lie, so be it.

Nadira crossed her arms. 'Where did you acquire the sacred gold?'

'For the right price, anything can be had.'

Nadira's smile vanished. 'You try me. You expect answers but give me none?'

'My lady, I simply seek to protect those whose part in this is inconsequential.'

Nadira went still for a long moment. 'I will accept that. What is it you wish to know?'

A shiver of excitement shook Chrysabelle. At last. 'I come seeking my brother's name.'

'You ask a question I can't answer.'

The shiver of excitement turned into a tremor of anger. 'Are you saying there is something you *don't* know?'

Nadira's gaze darkened. 'I'm saying you've been disavowed by your house. That information belongs to the Primoris Domus. A house you can no longer claim.'

'Last time you told me I would know him by his signum. You have to give me more than that, please. That means nothing to me.'

'You've wasted your energy, comarré.' She walked back behind the desk and sat. 'Return to your home. Forget the way here, because I will not allow a third visit.'

Chrysabelle began to seethe. This woman would stand on propriety now? 'Do you know what I have endured to return here?' Chrysabelle thrust her arm out, pointing to the shelves behind the Aurelian. 'The books behind you are marked Primoris Domus. Get the right one down and read his name to me.'

Nadira burst to her feet. 'How dare you speak to me that way. Get out. Now.'

'Not until I have his name. That information is nothing to you, and Rennata never needs to know. Give it to me and I will leave, never to return.'

The Aurelian planted her fists on the table. 'You should not even know you have a brother.'

'But I do.' Chrysabelle wished she'd taken the time to change into something besides her robe. Something she could fight in. Something she could fight *better* in. 'Can you tell me anything about him? Anything at all? Is he even alive?'

'He lives.'

'Then you do know about him.' Chrysabelle began to

tremble, from rage or some other emotion, she couldn't tell. 'His name. *Please*.'

'No.'

Then she would get the name herself. Fueled by anger and the reckless knowledge that Rennata had already renounced her, Chrysabelle leaped forward, vaulting onto Nadira's desk and reaching for the Primoris Domus register.

With a cry, Nadira swung her massive sword up. The metal flashed in the glow of the candelabras lighting the room.

The tip caught Chrysabelle beneath the rib cage. Heat and pain followed the sword's path into her body. She staggered a step to the side, her hand inches from the book. She lowered her gaze. Blood spilled down the sword's blade and wicked through the robe's thin fabric.

Nadira's face held no remorse.

Time slowed. Chrysabelle took hold of the blade and yanked it out, slicing her palms and fingers open but feeling little. Water pooled in her mouth as the edges of her vision tunneled in. Each breath became a struggle, her lungs taking in less air with each inhale. The sword had penetrated deeper than she'd guessed.

The Aurelian mouthed a name, but the ringing in Chrysabelle's ears deafened her. That name ... She fell backward, hitting the stone floor hard enough that bones cracked. But there was no more room in her body for pain.

Just darkness.

And death.

Velimai slapped Mal hard across the back of the head. She signed something, her fingers blurring, then pointed to the portal again before opening her mouth and tapping a finger against her throat.

He jumped to his feet. 'Go ahead and threaten me. I'm not going. What part of *I'm not willing to endanger Chrysabelle* don't you understand?'

With a frustrated grunt, Velimai went to the bathroom counter, yanked open a drawer, and took out a makeup pencil. She started scrawling on the wall to wall mirror. *She's already disavowed. No worse trouble. Plus the portal is open for you to come back through.* She underlined *come back* then stabbed the pencil against the glass for punctuation.

Mal stared at the words, trying to avoid seeing the image of his true face reflected behind them.

What if something happens? she added. *C could be in trouble.*

'And if she isn't? And my arrival makes that crazy Aurelian even crazier?'

Take the chance, Velimai wrote. She caught his gaze in the mirror and mouthed the words again. *Take the chance.*

He turned away from the mirror and back at the portal. 'Guard this with your life. If Chrysabelle has to go back through the Primoris Domus, Rennata will kill her this time.'

The wysper nodded solemnly, sketching a cross over her heart. She pointed at the shimmering puddle once again.

Mal nodded. 'I get it. I'm going.' He stepped into the portal.

And found himself standing in the Aurelian's chambers.

Chrysabelle lay sprawled like a rag doll in front of the enormous table. Her eyes stared unblinking at the ceiling. Blood drenched the stomach of her robe. Not a heartbeat or an inhale. The chains that held the beast snapped. 'What have you done to her?' he roared.

The Aurelian sat behind the table, cleaning blood off her

mammoth sword. She flinched and clutched her sword a little tighter. 'Get out. Or I'll kill you, too.'

The blackness of the beast crept over him, the names unfurling to cover his skin and drown the shreds of humanity that otherwise kept him sane. He fought to retain his sanity long enough to deal with the Aurelian. 'All she wanted was her brother's name. Was that such a trespass you killed her?'

The Aurelian stood, hefting her weapon. 'Get out, demon spawn.'

'Answer me.' A chorus of voices filled the room as the souls trapped inside him came to life as the beast.

Fear trickled into her eyes. 'She attacked me.'

'So you didn't tell her.' The darkness spread almost faster than he could control it now, winding around his bones and seeping into his muscles like a fever. 'Then you will tell me.' He flashed to her, pinning her against the bookshelves behind her and rendering her sword useless. 'What is her brother's name?'

'Go back to hell where you belong.'

He backhanded her. She slumped to the floor. The beast tore at his resolve. Time was running out to get Chrysabelle back before he turned completely. He scooped Chrysabelle's limp body into his arms and turned. The portal was on the floor behind him. He kissed her forehead and stepped through, his next step landing on the bathroom's marble tile.

Upon seeing Chrysabelle, Velimai went almost transparent, her mouth opening and a soft keening wail slipping out.

The beast reared back in pain at the sound. 'Wysper,' Mal ground out. 'Control yourself. I did not do this.'

He strode to the bed and eased Chrysabelle's body onto it with the last shreds of humanity he had left. He stared down at her, the beast clawing at his insides for escape. Rage poured hot through his veins, building the beast up. He shook his head.

Chrysabelle was dead. There was nothing left for him. No reason to keep the beast leashed. No reason to care whether he was cursed or not.

Sorrow freeing every desperate urge within him, he turned his head toward the French doors that led to her balcony. The curtains drawn over them darkened the room almost completely, but the pervasive light of day leaked under the bottom edge.

With one leap, he could be through the glass and into the sun. It was the wisest choice. For himself and for humanity, because he knew in his long-dead heart that the only other way to assuage the pain of her loss was to return to the darkness and blood that had once shrouded his world.

Death or the beast. Those were his options.

On the other side of the bed, Velimai trembled like a wind-whipped tree, tears streaming down her face, mouth open in silent pain. The one person who'd cared for Mal was gone. No one would mourn his passing.

He dragged himself toward the doors. The beast fought each step. He grasped a handful of fabric. The beast roared, snapping at the last of his resolve. The thrum of the voices reached a high-pitched whine of desperation and persuasion. He yanked the curtain back.

Sunlight seared his skin. At the pain, the beast broke free and hurled him back into the room's shadows. He lay staring at the ceiling, wishing like never before that he could end it all. 'Velimai,' he whispered, sorrow giving him the strength to use his own voice one last time. 'Open your mouth and kill me.'

The fae sobbed. Not for him, he was sure, but for Chrysabelle. Still, he took the sound as a yes and braced himself.

A soul-deep gasp shattered the room's silence, penetrating the chaos in his head. He turned. That wasn't the sound he'd been expecting.

Chrysabelle arced off the bed, her eyes open, chest heaving. Her signum were lit up like they were on fire, like they had been at the signumist's.

The beast stumbled in confusion. Mal got to his knees, control returning to him in waves.

She shook like she was freezing. Gold sparks filled her eyes. 'I was dead,' she whispered. She glanced down at her stomach, one hand coasting over the bloodstain on her robe. She stopped suddenly and held her hands out in front of her. 'My signum. What's happening to me?'

'You can see that?' he asked. He pushed to his feet and went to her side. He wanted to gather her into his arms and crush her against him, but he held back.

She nodded, still trembling. 'I feel . . . strange.'

'It happened when Atticus finished. Your whole body lit up like that.'

'The ring of sorrows.' She shook her head, pulling her robe aside to look at her legs. 'The power is in me. It must have reacted with your blood. And Samhain.'

'You're alive.' He sat on the bed. Every muscle that had ached with grief now tensed in relief. 'That's all that matters.'

Her mouth turned down and she looked toward the bathroom. 'Is the portal still open?'

Velimai, tears long gone, stepped into Chrysabelle's line of sight and shook her head.

'It's not open, or you don't want me to return?' She swung her legs off the side of the bed opposite Mal and got up, wobbling slightly. She grabbed the headboard. 'Doesn't matter, I'm going back. Get me my sacre. She knows my brother's name, and this time she's going to say it so I can hear it or—'

'No.' Mal stood. 'She *killed* you. Do you understand? You're not going back. Ever. It's over. We'll find another way.'

Velimai nodded. Chrysabelle, her tremors worse now, looked like she wanted to argue, but her eyes rolled back in her head and she slumped to her knees. Mal was beside her a half second later and had her in his arms. He put her back in bed. Stubborn, stubborn woman. But alive and he planned to keep her that way.

She stayed unconscious, but her heartbeat never faded, her breathing never faltered. He pulled up a chair next to the bed and settled in. Doc and Fi stopped by, tried to tell him something about a vampire being kept on the freighter with the comar then something else about Doc being the new pride leader. Creek came with news of Samhain night. Then Mortalis to get an update for Dominic. He waved them all away, refusing to listen or talk. Nothing mattered until Chrysabelle was awake again. And no way was he leaving her side again until she was truly recovered from everything that had happened.

Hours slipped by. Velimai checked in on them from time to time, even bringing him a glass of blood once.

The edge of light beneath the curtains brightened, then warmed to gold, finally darkening to purple before vanishing completely. Still she slept, sometimes moaning softly, sometimes thrashing like someone was attacking her. There was little he could do but sit and watch. And hope.

When she quieted, he leaned over and brushed a strand of hair from her face. Eyes tightly closed, she turned her face into the pillow and uttered a single word.

'Damian.'

Glossary

Anathema: a noble vampire who has been cast out of noble society for some reason.

Aurelian: the comarré historian.

Castus Sanguis: the fallen angels from which the othernatural races descended.

Comarré/comar: a human hybrid species especially bred to serve the blood needs of the noble vampire race.

Dominus: the ruling head of a noble vampire family.

Elder: the second in command to a Dominus.

Fae: a race of othernatural beings descended from fallen angels and nature.

Fringe vampires: a race of lesser vampires descended from the cursed Judas Iscariot.

Kine: a vampire term for humans, archaic.

Libertas: the ritual in which a comarré can fight for their independence. Ends in death of comarré or patron.

Navitas: the ritual in which a vampire can be resired by another, to change family lines or turn fringe noble.

Noble vampires: a powerful race of vampires descended from fallen angels.

Nothos: hellhounds.

Patron: a noble vampire who purchases a comarré's blood rights.

Remnant: a hybrid of different species of fae and/or varcolai.

Sacre: the ceremonial sword of the comarré.

Signum: the inlaid gold tattoos or marks put into comarré skin to purify their blood.

Vampling: a newly turned or young vampire.

Varcolai: a race of shifters descended from fallen angels and animals.

Acknowledgments

It's hard to keep this section short because I am so fortunate to have so much support. I'm always afraid I'm going to forget someone. If I have, please know that at some point too late to make the appropriate changes to this acknowledgment, I woke up in a cold sweat with your name at the forefront of my memory.

To begin with, I want to thank my Creator for the gifts He's given me.

Without question, I must thank my agent, Elaine. She's everything I ever wanted in an agent and more. I feel blessed to call her friend. Big thanks to the whole TKA family.

Thanks to the entire publishing team at Orbit: my tremendous editor, Devi; her able assistant, Jennifer; Lauren, the high priestess of awesome covers; the amazing publicity guys, Alex and Jack, who go above and beyond; Siri, the production editor; the copy editors; and Mike, the best sales guy in the business.

Thanks to Rocki and Louisa, whose support really surpasses that word. They're more than friends. They're The Best. They make the hard days bearable and the good days great.

More thanks go to the rest of my 'crew,' who give me feedback, support me, encourage me, and remind me I'm not in this alone: my parents, Matt, Jax, Laura, Leigh, Carrie, Carolyn, Briana, Denise, the Critwits, the Fictionistas, STAR, and the gang at Romance Divas.

Lastly, big thanks to my husband. In the book of my life, you're the spine. Without you, I'd fall apart.

extras

about the author

Kristen Painter's writing résumé boasts multiple Golden Heart nominations and advance praise from a handful of bestselling authors, including Gena Showalter and Roxanne St Claire. Having lived in New York and now in Florida, Kristen has a wealth of fascinating experiences from which to flavor her stories, including time spent working in fashion for Christian Dior and as a maître d' for Wolfgang Puck. Her website is at kristenpainter.com and on twitter at @Kristen_Painter.

Find out more about Kristen Painter and other Orbit authors by registering for the free monthly newsletter at www.orbitbooks.net

if you enjoyed
BAD BLOOD

look out for

TEMPEST RISING

by

Nicole Peeler

Chapter One

I eyeballed the freezer, trying to decide what to cook for dinner that night. Such a decision was no mean feat, since a visiting stranger might assume that Martha Stewart not only lived with us but was preparing for the apocalypse. Frozen lasagnas, casseroles, pot pies, and the like filled our icebox nearly to the brim. Finally deciding on fish chowder, I took out some haddock and mussels. After a brief, internal struggle, I grabbed some salmon to make extra soup to – you guessed it – freeze. Yeah, the stockpiling was more than a little OCD, but it made me feel better. It also meant that when I actually had something to do for the entire evening, I could leave my dad by himself without feeling too guilty about it.

My dad wasn't an invalid – not exactly. But he had a bad heart and needed help taking care of things, especially with my mother gone. So I took up the slack, which I was happy to do. It's not like I had much else on my plate, what with being the village pariah and all.

It's amazing how being a pariah gives you ample amounts of free time.

After putting in the laundry and cleaning the downstairs

bathroom, I went upstairs to take a shower. I would have loved to walk around all day with the sea salt on my skin, but not even in Rockabill was Eau de Brine an acceptable perfume. Like many twentysomethings, I'd woken up early that day to go exercise. Unlike most twentysomethings, however, my morning exercise took the form of an hour or so long swim in the freezing ocean. And in one of America's deadliest whirlpools. Which is why I am so careful to keep the swimming on the DL. It might be a great cardio workout, but it probably would get me burned at the stake. This is New England, after all.

As I got dressed in my work clothes – khaki chinos and a long-sleeved, pink polo-style shirt with *Read It and Weep* embroidered in navy blue over the breast pocket – I heard my father emerge from his bedroom and clomp down the stairs. His job in the morning was to make the coffee, so I took a moment to apply a little mascara, blush, and some lip gloss, before brushing out my damp black hair. I kept it cut in a much longer – and admittedly more unkempt – version of Cleopatra's style because I liked to hide my dark eyes under my long bangs. Most recently, my nemesis, Stuart Gray, had referred to them as 'demon eyes.' They're not as Marilyn Manson as that, thank you very much, but even I had to admit to difficulty determining where my pupil ended and my iris began.

I went back downstairs to join my dad in the kitchen, and I felt that pang in my heart that I get sometimes when I'm struck by how he's changed. He'd been a fisherman, but he'd had to retire about ten years ago, on disability, when his heart condition worsened. Once a handsome, confident, and brawny man whose presence filled any space he entered, his long illness and my mother's disappearance had diminished him in every possible way. He looked so small and gray in his faded old bathrobe, his hands trembling from the anti-arrhythmics he takes for his screwed-up heart, that it took every ounce of self-control I had not to make him sit down and rest. Even if his body didn't agree, he still felt himself to be the man he had been, and I knew I already walked a thin line between caring for him and treading on his dignity. So I put on my widest smile and bustled into the kitchen, as if we were a father and daughter in some sitcom set in the 1950s.

'Good morning, Daddy!' I beamed.

'Morning, honey. Want some coffee?' He asked me that question every morning, even though the answer had been yes since I was fifteen.

'Sure, thanks. Did you sleep all right?'

'Oh, yes. And you? How was your morning?' My dad never asked me directly about the swimming. It's a question that lay under the auspices of the 'don't ask, don't tell' policy that ruled our household. For example, he didn't ask me about my swimming, I didn't ask him about my mother. He didn't ask me about Jason, I didn't ask him about my mother. He didn't ask me whether or not I was happy in Rockabill, I didn't ask him about my mother . . .

'Oh, I slept fine, Dad. Thanks.' Of course I hadn't, really, as I only needed about four hours of sleep a night. But that's another thing we never talked about.

He asked me about my plans for the day, while I made us a breakfast of scrambled eggs on whole wheat toast. I told him that I'd be working till six, then I'd go to the grocery store on the way home. So, as usual for a Monday, I'd take the car to work. We performed pretty much the exact same routine every week, but it was nice of him to act like it was possible I might have new and exciting plans. On Mondays, I didn't have to worry about him eating lunch, as Trevor McKinley picked him up to go play a few hours of cheeky lunchtime poker with George Varga, Louis Finch, and Joe Covelli. They're all natives of Rockabill and friends since childhood, except for Joe, who moved here to Maine about twenty years ago to open up our local garage. That's how things were around Rockabill. For the winter, when the tourists were mostly absent, the town was populated by natives who grew up together and were more intimately acquainted with each other's dirty laundry than their own hampers. Some people enjoyed that intimacy. But when you were more usually the object of the whispers than the subject, intimacy had a tendency to feel like persecution.

We ate while we shared our local paper, *The Light House News*. But because the paper mostly functioned as a vehicle for advertising things to tourists, and the tourists were gone for the season, the pickings were scarce. Yet we went through the motions anyway. For all of our sins, no one could say that the True family wasn't good at going through the motions. After breakfast, I doled out my father's copious pills and set them next to his orange juice. He flashed me his charming smile, which was the only thing left unchanged after the ravages to his health and his heart.

'Thank you, Jane,' he said. And I knew he meant it, despite the fact that I'd set his pills down next to his orange juice every single morning for the past twelve years.

I gulped down a knot in my throat, since I knew that no small share of his worry and grief was due to me, and kissed him on the cheek. Then I bustled around clearing away breakfast, and bustled around getting my stuff together, and bustled out the door to get to work. In my experience, bustling is always a great way to keep from crying.

Tracy Gregory, the owner of Read It and Weep, was already hard at work when I walked in the front door. The Gregorys were an old fishing family from Rockabill, and Tracy was their prodigal daughter. She had left to work in Los Angeles, where she had apparently been a successful movie stylist. I say apparently because she never told us the names of any of the movies she'd worked on. She'd only moved back to Rockabill about five years ago to open Read It and Weep, which was our local bookstore, café, and all-round tourist trap. Since tourism replaced fishing as our major industry, Rockabill can just about support an all-year-round enterprise like Read It and Weep. But other things, like the nicer restaurant – rather unfortunately named The Pig Out Bar and Grill – close for the winter.

'Hey girl,' she said, gruffly, as I locked the door behind me. We didn't open for another half hour.

'Hey Tracy. Grizelda back?'

Grizelda was Tracy's girlfriend, and they'd caused quite a stir when they first appeared in Rockabill together. Not only were they lesbians, but they were as fabulously lesbionic as the inhabitants of a tiny village in Maine could ever imagine. Tracy carried herself like a rugby player, and dressed like one, too. But she had an easygoing charisma that got her through the initial gender panic triggered by her re-entry into Rockabill society.

And if Tracy made heads turn, Grizelda practically made them spin *Exorcist* style. Grizelda was not Grizelda's real name. Nor was Dusty Nethers, the name she used when she'd been a porn star. As Dusty Nethers, Grizelda had been fiery haired and as boobilicious as a *Baywatch* beauty. But in her current incarnation, as Grizelda Montague, she sported a sort of Gothic-hipster look – albeit one that was still very boobilicious. A few times a year Grizelda disappeared for weeks or a month, and upon her return home she and Tracy would complete some big project they'd been discussing, like redecorating the store or adding a sunroom onto their little house. Lord knows what she got up to on her profit-venture vacations. But whatever it was, it didn't affect her relationship with Tracy. The pair were as close as any husband and wife in Rockabill, if not closer, and seeing how much they loved each other drove home to me my own loneliness.

'Yeah, Grizzie's back. She'll be here soon. She has something for you . . . something scandalous, knowing my lady love.'

I grinned. 'Awesome. I love her gifts.'

Because of Grizzie, I had a drawer full of naughty underwear, sex toys, and dirty books. Grizzie gave such presents for *every* occasion; it didn't matter if it was your high school graduation, your fiftieth wedding anniversary, or your baby's baptism. This particular predilection meant she was a prominent figure on wedding shower guest lists from Rockabill to Eastport, but made her dangerous for children's parties. Most parents didn't appreciate an 'every day of the week' pack of thongs for their eleven-year-old daughter. Once she'd given me a gift certificate for a 'Hollywood' bikini wax and I had to Google the term. What I discovered made me way too scared to use it, so it sat in my 'dirty drawer', as I called it, as a talking point. Not that anyone ever went into my dirty drawer with me, but I talked to myself a lot, and it certainly provided amusing fodder for my own conversations.

It was also rather handy – no pun intended – to have access to one's own personal sex shop during long periods of enforced abstinence . . . such as the last eight years of my life.

'And,' Tracy responded with a rueful shake of her head, 'her gifts love you. Often quite literally.'

'That's all right, somebody has to,' I answered back, horrified at the bitter inflection that had crept into my voice.

But Tracy, bless her, just stroked a gentle hand over my hair that turned into a tiny one-armed hug, saying nothing.

'Hands off my woman!' crowed a hard-edged voice from the front door. Grizelda!

'Oh, sorry,' I apologized, backing away from Tracy.

'I meant for Tracy to get off *you*,' Grizzie said, swooping toward me to pick me up in a bodily hug, my own well-endowed chest clashing with her enormous fake bosoms. I hated being short at times like these. Even though I loved all five feet and eleven inches of Grizzie, and had more than my fair share of affection for her ta-ta-riddled hugs, I loathed being man-handled.

She set me down and grasped my hands in hers, backing away to look me over appreciatively while holding my fingers at arm's length. 'Mmm, mmm,' she said, shaking her head. 'Girl, I could sop you up with a biscuit.'

I laughed, as Tracy rolled her eyes.

'Quit sexually harassing the staff, Grizzly Bear,' was her only comment.

'I'll get back to sexually harassing you in a minute, passion flower, but right now I want to appreciate our Jane.' Grizelda winked at me with her florid violet eyes – she wore colored lenses – and I couldn't help but giggle like a school girl.

'I've brought you a little something,' she said, her voice sly.

I clapped my hands in excitement and hopped up and down in a little happy dance.

I really did love Grizzie's gifts, even if they challenged the tenuous grasp of human anatomy imparted to me by Mrs Renault in her high school biology class.

'Happy belated birthday!' she cried as she handed me a beautifully wrapped package she pulled from her enormous handbag. I admired the shiny black paper and the sumptuous red velvet ribbon tied up into a decadent bow – Grizzie did everything with style – before tearing into it with glee. After slitting open the tape holding the box closed with my thumbnail, I was soon holding in my hands the most beautiful red satin nightgown I'd ever seen. It was a deep, bloody, blue-based red, the perfect red for my skin tone. And it was, of course, the perfect length, with a slit up the side that would rise almost to my hip. Grizzie had this magic ability to always buy people clothes that fit. The top was generously cut for its small dress size, the bodice gathered into a sort of clamshell-like tailoring that I knew would cup my boobs like those hands in that famous Janet Jackson picture. The straps were slightly thicker, to give support, and crossed over the *very* low-cut back. It was absolutely gorgeous – very adult and sophisticated – and I couldn't stop stroking the deliciously watery satin.

'Grizzie,' I breathed. 'It's gorgeous ... but too much! This must have cost a fortune.'

'You are worth a fortune, little Jane. Besides, I figured you might need something nice ... since Mark's 'special deliveries' should have culminated in a date by now.'

Grizzie's words trailed off as my face fell and Tracy, behind her, made a noise like Xena, Warrior Princess, charging into battle.

Before Tracy could launch into just how many ways she

wanted to eviscerate our new letter carrier, I said, very calmly, 'I won't be going on any dates with Mark.'

'What happened?' Grizzie asked, as Tracy made another grunting declaration of war behind us.

'Well . . . ' I started, but where should I begin? Mark was new to Rockabill, a widowed employee of the U.S. Postal Service, who had recently moved to our little corner of Maine with his two young daughters. He'd kept forgetting to deliver letters and packages, necessitating second, and sometimes third, trips to our bookstore, daily. I'd thought he was sweet, but rather dumb, until Tracy had pointed out that he only forgot stuff when I was working.

So we'd flirted and flirted and flirted over the course of a month. Until, just a few days ago, he'd asked me out. I was thrilled. He was cute; he was *new*; he'd lost someone he was close to, as well. And he 'obviously' didn't judge me on my past.

You know what they say about assuming . . .

'We had a date set up, but he cancelled. I guess he asked me out before he knew about . . . everything. Then someone must have told him. He's got kids, you know.'

'So?' Grizzie growled, her smoky voice already furious.

'So, he said that he didn't think I'd be a good influence. On his girls.'

'That's fucking ridiculous,' Grizzie snarled, just as Tracy made a series of inarticulate chittering noises behind us. She was normally the sedate, equable half of her and Grizzie's partnership, but Tracy had nearly blown a gasket when I'd called her crying after Mark bailed on me. I think she would have torn off his head, but then we wouldn't have gotten our inventory anymore.

I lowered my head and shrugged. Grizzie moved forward,

having realized that Tracy already had the anger market cornered.

'I'm sorry, honey,' she said, wrapping her long arms around me. 'That's . . . such a shame.'

And it was a shame. My friends wanted me to move on, my dad wanted me to move on. Hell, except for that tiny sliver of me that was still frozen in guilt, *I* wanted to move on. But the rest of Rockabill, it seems, didn't agree.

Grizzie brushed the bangs back from my eyes, and when she saw tears glittering she intervened, Grizelda-style.

Dipping me like a tango dancer, she growled sexily, 'Baby, I'm gonna butter yo' bread . . . ' before burying her face in my exposed belly and giving me a resounding zerbert.

That did just the trick. I was laughing again, thanking my stars for about the zillionth time that they had brought Grizzie and Tracy back to Rockabill because I didn't know what I would have done without them. I gave Tracy her own hug for the present, and then took it to the back room with my stuff. I opened the box to give the red satin one last parting caress, and then closed it with a contented sigh.

It would look absolutely gorgeous in my dirty drawer.

We only had a few things to do to get the store ready for opening, which left much time for chitchat. About a half hour of intense gossip later, we had pretty much exhausted 'what happened when you were gone' as a subject of conversation and had started in on plans for the coming week, when the little bell above the door tinkled. My heart sank when I saw it was Linda Allen, self-selected female delegate for my own personal persecution squad. She wasn't quite as bad as Stuart Gray, who hated me even more than Linda did, but she did her best to keep up with him.

Speaking of the rest of Rockabill, I thought, as Linda headed toward romance.

She didn't bother to speak to me, of course. She just gave me one of her loaded looks that she could fire off like a World War II gunship. The looks always said the same things. They spoke of the fact that I was the girl whose crazy mother had shown up in the center of town out of nowhere, *naked*, in the middle of a storm. The fact that she'd *stolen* one of the most eligible Rockabill bachelors and *ruined him for life*. The fact that she'd given birth to a baby *without being married*. The fact that I insisted on being *that child* and upping the ante by being *just as weird as my mother*. That was only the tip of the vituperative iceberg that Linda hauled into my presence whenever she had the chance.

Unfortunately, Linda read nearly as compulsively as I did, so I saw her at least twice a month when she'd come in for a new stack of romance novels. She liked a very particular kind of plot: the sort where the pirate kidnaps some virgin damsel, rapes her into loving him, and then dispatches lots of seamen while she polishes his cutlass. Or where the Highland clan leader kidnaps some virginal English Rose, rapes her into loving him, and then kills entire armies of Sassenachs while she stuffs his haggis. Or where the Native American warrior kidnaps a virginal white settler, rapes her into loving him, and then kills a bunch of colonists while she whets his tomahawk. I hated to get Freudian on Linda, but her reading patterns suggested some interesting insights into why she was such a complete bitch.

Tracy had received a phone call while Linda was picking out her books, and Grizelda was sitting on a stool far behind the counter in a way that clearly said 'I'm not actually working, thanks', But Linda pointedly ignored the fact that I was free to help her, choosing, instead, to stand in front of Tracy. Tracy gave that little eye gesture where she looked at Linda, then looked at me, as if to say, 'She can help you,' but Linda insisted on being oblivious to my presence. Tracy sighed and cut her telephone conversation short. I knew that Tracy would love to tell Linda to stick her attitude where the sun don't shine, but Read It and Weep couldn't afford to lose a customer who was as good at buying books as she was at being a snarky snake face. So Tracy rang up Linda's purchases and bagged them for her as politely as one can without actually being friendly and handed the bag over to Linda.

Who, right on cue, gave me her parting shot, the look I knew was coming but was never quite able to deflect.

The look that said, *There's the freak who killed her own boyfriend.*

She was wrong, of course. I hadn't actually killed Jason. I was just the reason he was dead.